Rock And Roll Never Forgets

The Story of a Girl and a Rock Star

A Fictional Memoir

Book One of the Rock and Roll Trilogy

So you know...

All rights reserved. No part of this book shall be reproduced, stored, or transmitted by any means, without written permission from the author, except in the case of brief quotations represented in articles of review.

Rock and Roll Never Forgets is a work of fiction, (part of my 'rock and roll fantasy'). Any names, characters, places, and occurrences are purely a product of my creativity, or they're used in a fictitious manner. Any resemblance to persons, living or dead, locales, companies, businesses, or events are coincidental.

Unless otherwise noted, the song lyrics contained in the story are my words, poetry that 'sings' to me.

Previous Publications

Sweet Surrender – February 2012
Available at Amazon.com/Kindle

Rock and Roll Never Forgets cover designed by Jeff Robin Manalo
Author photo by Dawn Zattau
Divinity album cover created by Dylan Seaman

DEDICATION

*"One good thing about music, when it hits you,
you feel no pain."* Bob Marley

Music is entertainment, it's art, it's comfort, and for some it's a living. For me... it's an escape, sometimes a refuge. I love that music inspires me. It takes me places that I'm not sure the writers of the melody or lyrics ever dreamed, but it's my 'happy place' and I hope some of my journeys become a happy place for you.

I dedicate this book to all of us who let music take us away – wherever it takes us...

A friend, who read *Sweet Surrender*, told me, "Keep listening to the music and keep the books coming."

Here you go, the next/first book from the "sound-track of my life"...

Love, Barbara

ACKNOWLEDGMENTS

This one is my heart… the one that started my journey.

"Crazy legs" woke me the first time I started, followed by Andy Steven's voice in my head with a story. Every time "crazy legs" woke me the story grew. I'm not really sure when I actually began, I just know that the first time I saved it to something other than the hard drive on the PC was in October 2003… and from there it evolved and almost ten years later here it is – a finished book… I'm ready to push this baby out of the nest.

The title came when I was driving along one day and I heard Bob Seger singing, and the words 'rock and roll never forgets' stuck in my head – because they told me where the story would go…

If you've traveled even part of this journey with me then you know this is really the first book – *Sweet Surrender* was the catapult that helped me answer *'now what?'*.

My heart is full of gratitude. Thank you to my sweet husband, Gene. He's lived through many sleepless nights (and leg bouncing) as I typed (possible upside to restless legs!). Thank you for reading the pages I gave you over and over. I know you were waiting for something to blow up or explode… they did, they just had a love story instead of murder or espionage. I love you for traveling this unknown path with me.

To my encouragers, Geni, for reading the very first draft and telling me to 'go on', 'Nurse' Pink, thank you for loving Andy and Bethy and believing in my dream enough to push me forward when I told you about it. Thank you for reading and walking me through some of the 'technical stuff' in the story – helping me keep it real.

My sweet Johannes family – what a blessing you are to me. I don't say this lightly, but if someone in our lives hadn't had cancer, I wonder if our paths would have ever crossed? I'm just glad they did. Thank you to 'my JMac' and our coffee dates at Panera – the sweetest gift of your time and heart. I am so glad, happy, and thankful, that over coffee I blurted out the words; *'I wrote a book!'*. You were the accelerant that set my fire ablaze! You helped me answer *'now what?'* Thank you for believing in me enough to share your family with me, and encouraging me to do something with this little piece of my heart. Most of all, thank you for believing in me when I didn't believe in myself. Your words; *'You can't put it away again'*, helped push me along when I doubted. Lynne and Jan, thank you for navigating me through how to get from where I was to where I am! Lynne, your time, patience and love mean so much to me. You helped me remember grammar that I didn't know I forgot! Thank you for reading through this *with* me and helping me learn my way around. Thank you for sitting with me for hours and not just handing notes back with red marks on the pages, but talking to me about WHY. I'm saving all the pages we worked through together (*'Babs, this is so you!'*), they are a treasure to me!

Really, Wendy? Really? Thank you for sharing this experience with me in the middle of your biggest production... Your time in the middle of planning a wedding was priceless! I loved every challenge you gave me... really! Thank you for helping me with design questions – who knew fonts were such a big deal? Thank you for helping me *see* a Rock and Roll font!

Thank you to my readers, Judy, Jen, JMac, Dawn, and Cathy for the final read, to help find what might have slipped by. Thank you for showing me what worked and what needed a little tweak.

Recently, I read that the cover of the book is the most important thing. The story might be the greatest ever written, but if the cover doesn't grab a reader's attention, they may never pick it up. Jeff, thank you for a new friendship, and for helping me 'see' my story.

I have to thank my favorite singer for giving me a dream! You may never see these words, but thank you for keeping a song in my heart and lyrics in my head that helped me make up some of the stories in my writing, not just with *Rock and Roll*, but in the pages to follow in the next two books of the trilogy...

And lastly... Thank you to every one of you who took a chance on me by reading *Sweet Surrender*. I hope you will read this book and say, 'Wow, she's come a long way!'. And I hope you'll follow my journey through the *Rock and Roll Trilogy* and say the same thing after each book. The next dream is already alive... Thank you all for being part of my 'rock and roll fantasy'!

Preface
Norton Edwards - My Look Back

I've been writing for music publications like *Billboard* and *Rolling Stone* since the early 1970s, and love what I do. The opportunity this offers has led me to meet many intriguing people; musicians, celebrities, as well as music and movie executives over the years. Some I'm asked to interview, some I seek because of a personal interest. There's always that one story, the one personality that sticks in your mind. It's that story you just have to get. Sometimes the story goes away before the opportunity arises. Some that you think will go away, never do.

Beth Morgan was that story for me; the one I had to have, the one that never went away. She lived life in a world of fame, in a spotlight she tried to avoid but couldn't. The story took more than twenty years to get, but it's the one that always stayed in my mind. I asked, more than once, for the opportunity.

In the 1980s, Beth was everywhere; everyone wanted to know something about her. She was on the arm of one of the most famous rock and roll singers at the time. People wanted to know anything they could learn about her. She attributed that to the man in her life. There were pictures and information that we had access to, but we wanted more.

It was a very special, very exciting, thrilling time when life had her on a never-anticipated course. She was young, cute, protected, and very elusive. Who was she? What was it about *her* that made a 'Rock God' choose her as his partner?

We first met in 1982, while I was doing an article on Andy Stevens, lead singer for the rock group *Traveler*. My first thought was that she was average. She was small, not strikingly beautiful, but pretty. Her hair was short, and a reddish color. Her skin was fair and smooth with youth. She had laughing eyes, an impish grin, complete with dimples, and a shy quietness about her that made her intriguing. But there was that understated look that sparked the imagination. Her laugh lit up everything and everyone around her.

Beth and Andy Stevens were *the* hot ticket at the time. They had been together for a while when I got the chance to interview him. Beth joined us, but, Andy made a specific request before he agreed to talk to me that she would not be the focus of the interview. She wasn't ready and he wanted to make sure she was, before she participated. I respected their wishes, but I must admit the time I spent with them only made me want to know more about her.

Beth went along for a photo shoot for the spread, which only intrigued me more. There was just something about her. She was fun to watch, and it was a joy having her with us. She loved to laugh and even through the shyness, there was that spark. She was, as she has said, "just a girl." But there was something more there.

While I was working with the magazine on the layout, reviewing the pictures, choosing which would be used, Beth got in my soul and I couldn't put her away. I looked at the pictures again and again and realized that she *was* beautiful, but not in a stunning way that strikes you. I believe even she didn't know it. Her beauty was subtle, like a double take. It was a look that came out through her smile; her eyes. It was pure charisma.

Shortly after the article ran in *Rolling Stone*, I contacted her for the first time. I wanted her to share her thoughts. There was a lot going on in her life. She declined my request for reasons that will come out in her story to follow. Over the years I contacted her several more times. Always gracious, she wanted to stay out of the limelight as much as possible, and I respected that. But I also wanted to get her story.

I'd kept tabs on her through the years. She'd been in the public eye, to some extent. She tried to lay low, but it wasn't easy. She developed a passion for charity work and became very involved in the Cancer Foundation. Her fundraisers were *the* place to be. Everyone wanted to come, to be seen, to help out. She would laugh that the interest in her events was probably more in who might show up at the event than the cause itself. But that didn't matter to her because they were successful. She has spoken in public about her passion for this work, but has never acknowledged her earlier life, the life she shared with Andy Stevens.

Surprisingly, twenty years later, people still ask about Beth. They want to know her story. Where is she now? What happened to her? Due to changes taking place in her life, now was the right time. Beth sent word that she was ready to talk about "them"; her life with Andy, and her life without him. The opportunity thrilled me. She had been through so much that she was hesitant, knowing it would thrust her into that same spotlight again, but she had a story to tell. It amazed her that anyone really still cared about "that life" she led before.

When I met with her, I found a woman in her forties, a mother, a wife, a friend. She still looked the same. A few lines graced her face in a way that Andy likened to a good bottle of wine; she just got better with age. There was poise, that while present before, only made her more appealing, now. The grin was still there, more wise, thoughtful and cautious though. There was still the sparkle in her eyes, but there was a different glow about her I hadn't noticed on those occasions when I had seen her before. She finally seemed settled and peaceful.

We met several days a week for a few months. Sharing coffee, dinners, and family occasions with those she loved. I asked questions, and she talked like I was an old friend. Beth allowed me to tape those conversations. I have played them back and listened more than I needed to for this story. I found something soothing and comforting about listening to her voice as she talked about her life.

She had journals that she'd kept over the years. She shared them with me and I read them over and over. They helped tell the story, in her words. She referred to all those journal entries as the quilt she called her life. It was a glimpse into how she felt, thought, and dreamt during those times.

I met with her friends and family, as well as Andy, to get their thoughts. I met with the two of them together on several occasions. It was an experience I'll never forget. Even after all the time that had passed, there was still a great bond between them. It was love. He loved her - deeply. She loved him. They were soul mates. They finished each other's sentences, laughed, cried, joked and shared. It was truly one of the most beautiful experiences of my career.

Beth's wish for this project was simple. She wanted a story that would be a celebration of her life and loves. I used her journals, the many conversations we shared, and conversations with her family and friends to pull together pieces from everything I learned, and piece together a quilt of my own. The journals were so full of heart, warmth, and passion. I used 'pieces' of them in the story that follows.

She talked to me about how the journaling began.

> *November 8, 2001 ~ I can thank my Pops for so many gifts over the years, but one of the best gifts he ever gave me was my first journal. He had written inside the front cover; 'A place to keep your thoughts and your dreams. Dream big Baby Girl. Love Pops' I still have that journal and all the others that followed it as each one was filled. It became my passion.*

> ~ ~ ~

> *Beth's First Journal Entry, July 13, 1963 ~ Today is my 8th birthday and Pops gave me this book to write in. He said one day I could go back and read them and remember what I was doing when I was writing. It's a pretty pink book with a yellow flower on the cover.*

I will tell you that I now know what it was about her; she was just special – period. Here is the story of 'just a girl' that rock and roll never forgot…

CHAPTER ONE

September 29, 2001

Beth lay awake, alone in her thoughts, finally alone. She was on her side, looking around, not really seeing anything but the wall across the room. It was quiet except for the whir of the air conditioning.

It was late afternoon and there was no light on to illuminate the room. From the window she could see outside. The late September sky was dusky, the sun was setting below the window level, and the room was gray. She thought about how appropriate the color gray was. There was no black and white now, there was just that place in between. '*Gray,*' she thought.

She closed her eyes for a moment, allowing her mind to drift away. As it did it took her a million different places; a lifetime of places. She had so much to think about, plans to make... details. She tried to focus, to make her mind think forward, but the past kept flashing in pictures, like fast-moving frames from a slide-show.

She knew what she wanted, what she needed, she just needed a plan to make it happen. As she lay there waiting, thinking about what she needed to do, she remembered...

~ ~ ~

Beth Morgan and Kimmy Jones were best friends. They'd known each other for sixteen years. Beth was a twenty-two year old working-girl and part-time student. The two were always looking for fun, and this night they were anxious, about to see their favorite band, 'up close and personal'.

June 24, 1978 ~ Back stage passes for Traveler! Somebody pinch me!

The two young women stood at the Will-Call at the arena in Orlando waiting; giggling as they watched the crowd shuffling into the arena, excited to see their favorite band, *Traveler's Timeless Tour.* Kimmy's cousin, Mark Jones, had taken over as drummer for the band a few months earlier after a shake-up in their roster. Together, they released their first album, Timeless, in March, and were touring. He'd left tickets and back-stage passes for them.

"I can't even believe we are here!" Beth said excitedly.
"I can't believe that Mark is in the band!" Kimmy yelled.

Finally, a security guard arrived to escort them to a packed back-stage room; the area where Mark was waiting to introduce them to the band members. The whole idea of him being part of their favorite band was just thrilling. When they arrived, he greeted them with hugs and conversation as the other band members were making their way into the room. Mark introduced them to Nigel Rose, the bass guitarist, Nathan Perry, the keyboardist, and Dane Allen the guitar player. After a few minutes, Mark and Kimmy wandered off to mingle. Beth was talking and laughing with Nathan. She looked up when she saw him, and in a moment, her life was forever changed.

~ ~ ~

Andy Stevens entered the room looking like the rock star he was. He wore tight white jeans and a black leather vest with no shirt. His brown hair was long, and hung straight down his back in a ponytail. He was walking with another man, and they were deep in conversation. Beth was watching him, she heard every word that Nathan was saying, but over his shoulder she was watching, intently. She noticed everything about him; the olive skin, the golden eyes, the width of his shoulders and muscular arms, the length of his legs. 6'4" she'd read somewhere…

Suddenly, she realized that Andy was no longer talking with the other man. She looked away, embarrassed that he'd caught her staring at him.

~ ~ ~

Andy spotted her almost as soon as they entered the room. He heard the giggle, turned to look, and liked what he saw. She was nice looking, comfortable, standing there laughing with Nathan as they talked. She wore jeans that hugged her body and a *Traveler* t-shirt. As he looked, Andy noticed every curve of her body. She had a beer in her hand, and as he watched, she captivated him. He watched and caught her watching him. A twinkle in her eyes gave a glimpse into her soul, even in that brief moment.

"Roddy, who is that with Nathan?" Andy asked his manager, Roddy Beamer.

Roddy looked up, "Mark got tickets for his cousin. That's either the cousin or her friend," he said.

Andy listened as Roddy spoke, but he was watching Beth. She intrigued him, and she knew he was watching her, because she was watching him.

"Are we done?" Andy asked as they finished up whatever business they were discussing. "I want to walk over there."

"Yeah, go," Roddy replied.

~ ~ ~

His dreams never included a redhead, yet there she was, the woman of his dreams, small, petite, with short, reddish hair. He moved toward her, and as he got closer, he could see she was a mess of nerves. Extending his hand to introduce himself, he wore a devilish smile on his face. "Hey there, Andy Stevens," he told her, and took her hand.

In a soft, shaky, whisper of a voice she replied; "Beth." She looked in his eyes and they entranced her.

I saw those gorgeous brown eyes with gold flecks, like Amber gemstones, and realized where he got the nickname; 'Golden Eye.' All I could focus on was the beauty of him. I melted.

7

"Well, it's nice to meet you, Beth." The devilish smile melted into a softer grin. Andy knew she was nervous, and he enjoyed it. He was chuckling, not laughing, but her reaction amused him.

~ ~ ~

Kimmy and Mark had been across the room watching as Beth and Nathan talked. When Andy Stevens entered the room, Kimmy stopped Mark and nudged him. They glanced in the direction where Beth and Nathan were.

"She loves him," Kimmy told Mark. "I do too, but not like her," she laughed.

"Lots of young women love him," Mark laughed, but he saw what Kimmy saw and they stopped talking to take it all in. They both knew they would remember the look on Beth's face forever. It was a snapshot moment captured in time, and they continued to watch.

Mark knew enough to know what he was observing in Andy was different. In the short time he'd been with the band he'd seen Andy with hundreds of other young women. This time, he saw the same spark that Kimmy did.

Roddy Beamer watched as well. From the other side of the room he watched, and waited. How many times had he walked into a room to find those giddy girls, waiting like obedient puppies for their master, as Andy Stevens entered a room? Why would he have thought that first night with Kimmy and Beth would have been different?

But it *was* different. Andy stopped at the first sound of her laughter. It wasn't loud, just noticeable. It was a warm, infectious laugh that made you look, and then, captured your attention. He was curious to see what Andy would do with that beautiful young woman. There had been others over the years. Most of them were eye-candy that Andy had no long-term interest in. Some were around for a while, but none brought that same spark he saw that night.

"Why don't you join me over here," Andy suggested, guiding her to a nearby sofa. Beth followed, feeling as though she was drifting through a dream. Others were there but she was oblivious to everyone but Andy Stevens.

"There will be a party after the show," he said after a while. "How 'bout you and your friend join us?" he asked, gazing at her in a way that left her insides quivering.

Before Beth could respond, Kimmy and Mark made their way to where she and Andy were.

"Kimmy, this is Andy Stevens," Mark introduced them.

"Glad to meet you, I was just telling Beth about the party after the show, why don't you join us?" Andy suggested. Glancing Beth's way, he waited.

Beth said nothing. It was like she was in a trance. Finally, Kimmy said, "We would love that!"

Beth nodded and an, 'Mmm hmm' sound came from her throat and Andy smiled.

CHAPTER TWO

Around 6:30 Roddy indicated that it was time for the band to head to the stage. "Remember, come back after the show," Andy told Beth. "I'll see you then." He leaned toward her and kissed her cheek. Her hand went to the spot where his lips touched her skin, she looked up, and he was gone.

A security guard escorted Kimmy and Beth to the packed auditorium. The seats Mark reserved for them were front row, center stage. A local band was on stage as they reached their seats, like proud little peacocks. Their escort told them he'd be back after *Traveler* left the stage. Those around them saw the escort and the VIP badges and looked on in wonder as the girls danced and sang along with the band.

When the lights came back up after the opening act, there was a lot of action as the crew got everything ready for *Traveler* to take the stage. Beth and Kimmy got beers and talked and laughed about the party after the show.

"Party like a rock-star!" Kimmy laughed.
"I still can't believe it, it's so exciting!" Beth said.

As the crew finished up, the commotion on stage died down and quiet fell over the arena. The lights went out, and then there was a drumbeat. The footlights slowly came up. Excitedly they watched. They saw feet and legs moving toward the center of the stage. Suddenly, there was a loud 'BOOM!' from the drums and music filled the auditorium. The lights came up, bright, and there he was, Andy Stevens, right in front of them. They began the show with "Traveler",

10

their first hit, and a few older songs followed. The girls were on their feet, singing and dancing along with them. Finally, they played their new song, "Timeless".

Andy was glad when he spotted them so close. It not only gave them a good view of the band, it gave him a good view of them, and he watched. He loved seeing them having fun. They were out of their seats dancing and singing along to every song the band played. Beth was full of life, and he was even more intrigued. He was anxious for the show to end, eager to spend more time with her.

They played for almost an hour, and finally the lights dimmed. Andy started singing a new song. It was one Beth had never heard before. He bent down on one knee and was singing about meeting him in a 'forbidden place'.

Kimmy leaned in to Beth and whispered, "Girl, he's singing that to you!"

'He was! He was singing to me!'

> *In the light's glare*
> *I see you there*
> *What's better known is*
> *You should beware*
> *It's love in a forbidden place*
> *Let me take you there.*

Traveler received two standing ovations, and after two encores the show was over. The lights came up to prepare the stage for *Mean Street*, the headliner. Beth's mind wandered as she thought about Andy, the party, and what it would be like. It was so exciting. Their escort returned to take them back to the courtesy suite at the arena where the party would be. There was no concert the next day and the band was staying in Orlando that night, leaving out on their bus the following day. It was a packed room when they returned. There were even more people at this gathering than the pre-party.

A performance was a workout for the band and they'd gone to the arena locker rooms to shower. A short time later, Mark was the first to return. He joined Kimmy and Beth, followed by the other band members. The girls were talking with Mark and Nathan, but Beth's eye was on the door anxiously waiting for Andy to return.

*I knew when he entered the room, a warm feeling came over me,
and I saw him out of the corner of my eye. He'd changed into
jeans and a t-shirt, his hair was wet, and I was absolutely
overwhelmed just by his presence.*

"Ladies," he chuckled, as he joined them, "when the lighting was
just right I could see the two of you dancing and singing. You knew
every word, every beat!" he laughed. "How'd you like the new stuff?"

"Loved it!" Kimmy said with excitement.

"And you, Beth. What did you think?" Andy asked her.

"It was good, 'Forbidden Place' is a great love-song," she replied
nervously. The thought that he actually remembered her name left her
reeling. "I liked it, a lot," she added, and suddenly she realized that
Kimmy had wondered off. She found herself alone with Andy Stevens.

"I'm pleased." he said, his eyes fixed on hers.

He smelled like heaven; soap and musk, and Beth couldn't believe
she was there with him.

This is my once in a lifetime moment.

The minutes ticked away and finally she looked at her watch.

"You don't have to go yet do you?" Andy asked.

"No, no, I just had no idea what time it was. I can't believe it's two
in the morning already! Time flies!"

"I'm enjoying the time; enjoying the company."

"Me too," Beth said.

Around eight in the morning Kimmy and Beth got ready to leave.

"I'll have two tickets for the next show you can get to," Andy told
them.

"Atlanta!" Kimmy yelled.

Mark had Beth's car brought around, and as they said their good-
byes, Andy rushed to Beth's side and took her hand. He pulled her
close and spoke softly in her ear. She could feel his breath, warm on
her skin, and she closed her eyes.

"I'd like to call you," he whispered. Beth's surprise was clear, and
Andy liked it.

"Yeah, sure," she said, feeling certain it would never happen.

He motioned for the man she had seen him with several times during the evening. "Beth, this is Roddy Beamer, my manager, assistant, my friend." He placed his hand on Roddy's back when he referred to him as 'friend'. "Give him your number; that way I'll know where it is," he laughed.

She did, and then hurried toward the car. Andy followed and took her hand in his once more. He brought it to his lips and told her, "I've enjoyed this." He turned her hand and placed a kiss in her palm, "More than you know. I'll enjoy talking with you again, soon."

As they drove away Beth was quiet, but Kimmy noticed a big grin on her face.

"Spill!" she laughed, "what's on your mind?"

"I'm never going to wash this hand again!" Beth roared at her own words. "He asked me to give him my phone number!"

Arriving home Beth fell into bed, tired and exhausted. She fell asleep, hoping to re-dream the whole event, and slept the rest of the day on Sunday. Monday morning it was back to reality, work, school, and family, but with a special memory to keep forever.

~ ~ ~

At lunch on Monday Beth left the office to run an errand; when she returned she walked through the lobby and the receptionist greeted her, grinning from ear to ear. She pointed to a large arrangement of yellow roses on a table by the door to the offices.

"Wow, those are beautiful! Someone's gonna be happy!" Beth laughed grabbing the handle to the door.

"That would be you," Mary said, excitedly.

"For me?" She stopped, puzzled, and reached for the card, ripping it open to read, *"One for every hour I've thought of you in the last 24. Andy"* She quickly counted; twenty-four long-stemmed yellow roses. She swept the vase off the table and floated to her desk. Her smile couldn't have been any bigger; her heart couldn't have beaten harder or faster. She sat the roses down while her co-workers looked on. Grinning, she lifted the receiver and dialed Kimmy's number.

~ ~ ~

Beth and Kimmy worked together at an electronics company. They'd been friends for years, and they were inseparable, doing everything together. They met on the school steps, the first day of school in first grade, and walked in hand in hand, beginning their lives together. They were opposites in the best way, complementing each other. Kimmy was tall and thin, Beth small and petite. Kimmy was loud and confident. Beth was more subdued and quiet. But they shared a sense of humor, and a bond like Superglue.

~ ~ ~

"I know," Kimmy said excitedly when she answered the phone. "I know! Mark called me first thing this morning to find out where to send them! I'll be right there!"

Kimmy arrived, coffee in hand; "Wow, what about that," she said reading the card.

Beth replied, "My thoughts exactly!"

"Well," Kimmy thought for a moment, and parked herself on the corner of the desk, "he did stay pretty much right by your side all evening," she laughed. "You must have made some impression on him!"

Sitting quietly, holding the card in my hand; 'Yellow for remembrance...' I thought; knowing I would.

"Why me?" Beth wondered aloud.

"What's that supposed to mean?" Kimmy asked as she sipped her coffee.

"Just wondering... all those girls that were there, why me?"

Kimmy laughed, "Why not you? Maybe he likes lil' petite redheads?"

"I'm just a girl, Kimmy," Beth said. "My hair's too short, my butt's too big, and I'm a foot too short for my weight!"

"You make me laugh! You're awesome," Kimmy said again as the phone rang, bringing them back to reality.

Working in a small office Beth only had to tell her story once and within the hour everyone knew that she had met 'a nice guy' over the weekend. She decided they didn't need to know who it was. They wouldn't have believed it anyway.

Arriving home that evening Beth found a message on the answering machine from Roddy.

"Hello Beth. It's Roddy Beamer; will you please give me a call when you can. I'd like to confirm your availability," he said. He sounded formal and business-like. It was as though he was confirming a business appointment.

She dialed the number he left. When he answered and realized who it was, all formality was gone. He sounded very personable, more like an old friend than the voice on the message she'd received.

"It's nice to hear from you," he said with a smile in his voice.

"You too," she replied.

"Andy asked me to call and make sure that it was OK if he called you after the show. It'll probably be around two."

"Sure, that's fine," she said and tried not to sound as excited as she was. He really was going to call. It wasn't a dream at all.

"I'll talk to you again soon," Roddy told her.

~ ~ ~

The sound of the phone ringing woke her from a deep sleep. A quick glance at the clock said it was 2:01. She rolled over to answer it.

"Hey," he said before she spoke, "sorry it's so late, I know I woke you."

"I wasn't asleep," she lied.

"Yeah, you were, you've got that Elmer Fudd voice," he said with a laugh. "How are you?"

"I'm good. Thank you for the beautiful roses."

"I wanted you to know I was thinking of you," Andy went on.

"They're beautiful, and they smell wonderful. I have them beside my bed. I've been thinking about you too. I'm surprised to hear from you."

"I told you I wanted to call," he said.

Andy made a point to call that first time, exactly when he said he would. First, because he knew she didn't believe he would, but more so because he wanted to. He wanted to know, to explore what had begun at that party, to make sure she knew he wasn't just having fun with her. He liked her, and he wanted her to know.

He knew it surprised her, and it excited him. That night they began the 'getting to know each other' phase. That excited him, too.

They talked and talked, and he knew she was someone he wanted to spend more time with. They talked about each other, life, and family.

She told him about school, "I go on Tuesdays and Thursdays after work. I'm working on a degree in communications. I'm half-way there," she laughed, "not sure what I will do with it when I'm done, there are so many options. Hind-sight, I should have gone straight after high-school, but I wasn't sure what I wanted so I went to work instead. I got a place of my own and here I am." She laughed. "With four brothers I was ready for my independence."

"Four?"

"Uh hunh, two older, Ethan and Evan, and two younger, Michael and Mason, but I am, and I'm sure I always will be, the baby-girl," she laughed. "Don't get me wrong, I love them, I love my family, but with all those boys it got crazy sometimes! What about you?" she wondered aloud.

"Nathan, Scott and I hit the road as soon as we graduated. Actually we were out before then, but the 'real band' evolved and took off after that. Just me and my mom now, Phyllis," he said.

"You call your mom Phyllis?" she laughed.

"I do now. It started as sarcasm, and stuck," he laughed. "I remember she was getting on to me about something; I was in high school, she was really mad at me. She's a little lady, and I remember looking down at her and saying, "Oh Phyllis," and it broke the tension. We laughed and I've called her Phyllis ever since."

Later in their conversation Andy told her, "I want to know more about you, Beth. Everything," he said. "I was wondering something."

Beth asked, "What is it?"

"Beth, a nickname for Elizabeth, right?"

"Uh hunh," she laughed, trying to hide a yawn.

He asked, "Then why not Liz?"

She laughed, no longer able to hide the yawn. "My mom is the Liz in our family."

"Elizabeth Morgan," he said. Hearing him say it sounded *really* good to her.

"Elizabeth Ellen Morgan," she laughed looking at the clock, trying to hide another yawn, it was 4:33.

"I kinda don't want you to hang up, but I know you have to go to work in the morning. I'd like to call again, same time tomorrow," Andy said.

"Sure," she told him.

Like I could tell him 'no'!

16

"Sleep," he said sweetly. "I'll be thinking of you Elizabeth Ellen," he said, then added, "Bethy."

"I'll be thinking of you, too," and she heard him blow a kiss as he hung up.

~ ~ ~

Andy and Beth talked every night, a different city each time, as *Traveler*'s tour took them to Miami, Tampa, Mobile, Dallas, Little Rock, Nashville, and finally on to Atlanta. Beth spoke with Roddy often as well, making the plans for the trip. Kimmy and Beth took off work Friday to drive there.

"Something on your mind?" Kimmy asked after they'd been on the road a while.

"Nah, just anxious," Beth replied. It had been two weeks since she met him, two weeks of late night phone calls, and wondering what next.

"Anxious and nervous?"

"Yeah, I am honestly excited beyond belief..."

But Kimmy interrupted before she finished, "and scared."

"I just can't help wondering," Beth said with a nervous laugh.

CHAPTER THREE

The hotel was on Peachtree Street and they arrived just after two that afternoon. Roddy met them at the front desk. "Welcome ladies!" he said as he greeted them. He hugged them as the bell-hop grabbed their bags, hurrying to the elevator he'd held for them. The guys spent the afternoon rehearsing and going through sound checks. Kimmy and Beth dropped their bags by their room and hurried off to a lounge area, complete with a pool table that the band and crew were using as a hospitality area.

Nathan was the first to join them as they all grabbed beers. The rest of the guys trickled in, but Andy was nowhere in sight. Everyone was laughing and having a good time. About an hour passed, and Roddy came back into the room. He took Beth's hand, "Come with me," he said.

He led her down the hall and opened the door to a room, holding it open for her. When she saw him, Beth's breath caught in her throat. Andy was lying across the bed on his stomach talking on the phone.

"I gotta go, Mom."

> *July 8, 1978 ~ The sight of him left me breathless... when he hung up he came to me and folded me into his arms. I remember the feel of his arms around me. It was quiet and it seemed an eternity passed, he held me an arm's-length away and just looked at me. Finally, he kissed me. I know I touched my lips with my fingers, I wanted to feel the heat he left there...*

Roddy kissed Beth's cheek and left them.

"I couldn't wait for you to get here," Andy said. "I'm sorry I didn't get down there to meet you. I had some things to finish up here. Was the drive OK?" he asked as he led her to a sitting area with a sofa.

Beth took a seat, but Andy was still standing; he watched her as she nervously chattered on about the drive there. Finally, he took her hands in his and pulled her up from the sofa and into his arms for another hug.

"I'm so glad you're here," he said, whispering against her neck as he hugged her.

"Me too! I've been looking forward to it," Beth giggled, biting her bottom lip, nervously.

"Roddy and I decided to keep you two backstage with him this time instead of being in the audience. We thought that'd be more fun for you, something different," he told her.

~ ~ ~

The band had been through their lean years; the years when they traveled in two old Ford Econoline vans and put up their own sets. They'd moved past the times where they all slept in one double hotel room, taking turns as they traveled for who got to sleep in a bed, and who slept in sleeping bags on the floor. The vans progressed to the tour bus they traveled in now. And as the years passed they doubled in rooms. It was all a sign that they were making it now, making money. Now they could afford their own rooms. A sign of their success. *Traveler* had made it big.

~ ~ ~

They got comfortable and relaxed on the sofa, sharing more of the conversation they were getting so good at. It was part of getting to know each other. They talked about everything from movies, to religion, current affairs, and their likes and dislikes. It was special because the interest was genuine.

Roddy called around five to remind them that they had to be on the bus by six to leave for the arena.

Andy gave Beth a peck on the cheek, and she returned to her room. While they got ready Beth shared her thoughts on the time she'd spent with Andy.

"Kimmy, when he hugs me my knees go weak," she laughed. "We sat around talking. I swear we can talk about anything and he acts like what I'm saying is the most interesting thing he's ever heard."

"I think he likes you," Kimmy said excitedly, while telling Beth about the afternoon hanging out with the guys, relaxing and shooting pool.

Kimmy's insightfulness; she *knew* Beth was falling hard. She saw that first spark and watched it burn into a small flame. But she saw Andy too. His reaction to Beth was almost a mirror of her reaction to him. She knew this relationship would change all of their lives forever. She saw the beginnings of a match made in heaven, and she prayed.

At 5:50 there was a knock at the door. Beth and Kimmy followed Roddy down the hall. There was a lot of commotion as they made their way to the bus. It was older, and similar to a Greyhound, with seats in the front and a second level with sleeping bunks. Nathan grabbed the seat beside Beth. Andy sat with Roddy and pretended to pout. It was only about a ten-minute ride to the arena.

It was a sold-out show, and there was anticipation as they exited the bus at the back of the building. Kimmy and Beth were given special badges, and escorted to the Courtesy Suite while the guys went to finish getting ready. They returned with some time to relax before it was time to go to the stage. There was no party before the show this time, just some down time.

Traveler's show began at eight, and as the time approached everyone began to make the journey to the stage area. Along the corridor, security guards stood watch to make sure no one slipped in. The packed arena was wild with excitement. *Traveler* was opening for *Mean Street* again.

Kimmy and Beth perched on stools to the left of the stage with Roddy. From where they sat they were able to see everything. Roddy explained some of the behind-the-scenes things as they got ready for the show to begin. The band made their way to the stage from the other side. The music started and the girls settled in for the show.

"Hello, Hot'lanta!" Andy yelled after the first song, "Traveler".

The crowd screamed, wild with enthusiasm. The music began for the next song and Andy pointed to a group of microphones. Strutting across the stage he pointed to another set.

"Know what these are?" Again the crowd went wild. "We're recording for a live album tonight, so if you sing along, ya better make it good!" he shouted to the crowd. They responded with loud cheers, and *Traveler* began the next song.

Beth and Kimmy didn't stay on the stools long. They were up dancing, singing along and having the time of their lives. *Traveler's* success in the past months was crazy. "Forbidden Place" had been number one for two weeks and when they started to sing it the crowd went wild.

Kimmy leaned to Roddy and said, "It's different to see it from backstage!" It appeared there was a never-ending sea of people. There were flashes of light from cameras, and the light from the lighters that fans wave when they like a song.

"It looks like you're looking out at a dark, starlit sky," Beth added.

After the show, as everyone boarded the bus to return to the hotel, Andy made sure he got a seat beside Beth for the ride back. There was no after party this time, no concert again until Monday. Everyone was ready for a short break. They'd been touring since early May, going non-stop since Orlando. They were ready to unwind. It was almost midnight when they arrived back at the hotel, and the guys went to shower.

Everyone gathered in the Courtesy Suite afterward and kicked back on sofas. There were tables of food, and a bar with sodas, beer and wine. Andy settled in with a beer and a plate of cheese and fruit, and propped up his feet. There was a lot to talk about and some unwinding to do.

"Come to my room with me, Bethy," Andy whispered to her after a while.

Kimmy was having a good time with the guys. She winked and waved Beth on. His room was a suite. There was a sitting area, and the bedroom was separate. Beth walked to the window for a quick glance over the lights of the city before Andy guided her to the bed and stretched out. Lazily, he patted the place beside him. Beth joined him on the king-sized bed. She inhaled the musky smell of him on the pillow as he drew her closer. His arm around her, she rested her head on his chest, and together they watched television.

She fell asleep, and with Beth in his arms, Andy watched her, amazed that she was finally there with him, and not on the other end of the phone. She woke as he pulled the covers over them. He wrapped her in his arms and she drifted back to sleep. Later in the night, she slid away from him; sound asleep, she curled on her stomach with her left leg pulled up, her right arm cradled the pillow. She looked peaceful, and Andy watched, wanting to keep that vision in his mind forever.

Beth left him in the morning, returning to her room to get ready for the day ahead.

"Well?" Kimmy asked and laughed.

"Well, we slept together," Beth laughed. "But there was nothing more than snuggling, and sleep."

They met Andy and some of the guys for coffee and breakfast. Nathan flew home after the show the night before and would meet the guys at the next venue. Kimmy was spending the day with Mark, and the other guys were off doing their own thing. Andy asked Beth to spend the day with him, and she was anxious to do just that.

Andy wanted to romance her, make her feel special. He took her to Underground Atlanta, a city under the city, with shops and restaurants. They walked hand in hand, able to spend an enjoyable day, surprisingly unnoticed. He had a car meet them around five to return to the hotel. After a day filled with conversation, they rode back in silence. Andy took Beth's hand, gave it a squeeze, and held it in his lap.

Back at the hotel, in the elevator, he told her, "Can you meet me at seven for dinner?"

"I'd like that," she told him.

"Come to my room," he said, leaving her with a kiss on the top of her head.

While she got ready, she told Kimmy about the day. "We walked and shopped, shared a wonderful lunch and Kimmy, he held my hand. He whispered in my ear that he loved me being here with him." She sighed and added, "Girl, if I'm dreaming *do not* wake me up!"

Mark and Kimmy were going bar-hopping, and Beth went to Andy's room as planned. She took a deep breath; anticipation and excitement over being alone with him again overwhelmed her. She knocked lightly. He opened the door, and greeted her with a kiss; a quick, soft brush of his lips on hers.

"I hope you don't mind, we're not going out," he told her as she came in and took a seat on the sofa. "I'm having dinner sent up. It's just easier this way."

"No, not at all," her mind wandered.

22

He pulled a bottle of wine from the small refrigerator in the room. "I thought we'd have a glass of wine before dinner, a nice Chenin Blanc that I enjoy." He uncovered a small platter of fruit and cheeses. "Dinner will come later."

He started some music, before he joined her on the sofa. "*Bach in Woodwind,*" he told her, "Something classical, it's my favorite album for relaxing." He handed her the glass of wine, and finally, sat down beside her.

"Thank you," Beth said, nervously.

"For the wine?"

"No, for a wonderful day. I've enjoyed it."

"It's not over, Bethy," he grinned.

As they talked and enjoyed the wine his hand moved to Beth's leg, just a friendly, warm gesture.

After a while, he turned to her and said, "Bethy, I think you know that I like you." He paused and the look lingered. "A lot," he added. "I enjoy your company very much. I love talking with you. 'With' is a huge difference for me and I enjoy it. Our conversations are refreshing. I'm a person to you, not 'Andy the rock star'. You don't try to be someone you aren't to get my attention. You are real, genuine, and it's very nice. I'd like to see more of you, lots more," he said.

"I'd like that, too," she answered, as she nervously sipped the wine.

"Good." He took her wine glass and set it aside. He placed a hand gently on her neck and drew her closer. As he leaned in to kiss her, she knew this wouldn't be one of the casual 'hello kisses' she'd received so far. This one would be passionate, and she braced herself. First it was a brush of the lips, soft and gentle, and then he drew back to look at her.

It rattled her. The look was deep, intense, lingering. Leaning in again, his other hand went to her back, and he pulled her to him. He wrapped his arms around her, and it was the kiss she had dreamed of. But it wasn't a dream at all. Beth's hands slid lightly around his waist and up his back as she responded to the kiss.

There was a knock at the door, and as he let her go he whispered her name in a raspy voice; "Bethy…"

She pulled a shaky hand through her hair; he'd kissed her breath away, and she attempted to get it back. There was such passion in that kiss. The feel of his arms around her, his lips on hers, left her shaking.

Andy opened the door and let a young man in to set up for their meal. He spread a white linen table-cloth over the table and lit candles.

There was another knock, and the meal arrived. Andy looked on as Beth attempted to regain her composure, and smiled.

"Shall we?" Andy motioned to the table as the staff left the room. Beth rose on wobbly knees. He went to her, putting his arms around her, he kissed the top of her head. It was a sweet gesture.

He pulled the chair out for her and they sat down to enjoy a nice meal of Chicken Marsala, and she learned that Italian was his favorite cuisine. He opened another bottle of wine, Chianti, to go with the meal.

We savored the wonderful dinner he'd chosen, but I was feeling so much emotion that I wasn't really hungry...

Afterward they returned to the sofa. Andy slipped his arm around her shoulder and pulled her closer as soft music played. "This feels nice," he whispered in her ear, sneaking a kiss on her neck, and she shivered.

"Mmm hmm," she murmured, closing her eyes.

After a while Andy rose, took her hand, and pulled her from the sofa into his arms. Lacing his fingers with hers they moved with the music. He hummed in her ear as he nuzzled her neck. It was a tender, romantic moment. He led her to the bed, but there was no rush for anything more.

"Lay with me, I just need to feel you in my arms," he said. "I dream about this every night when we talk on the phone, Bethy, just holding you, feeling you in my arms," he said. "I want more. I want you, but for now, please just come lay with me."

Sunday morning Roddy woke them with a phone call. The guys had to get on the road and Kimmy and Beth needed to head home. Roddy had the car brought around to a private entrance at the rear of the hotel. They said their good-byes and got ready to leave. Andy walked Beth to the car.

"Be safe," he said. "I'll call this evening."

"Had a great time," Kimmy piped in. "Thanks!"

Looking at Beth he reached for her hand and held it. "It was a pleasure."

The drive home seemed long. It was the same nine hours, no different from the trip up, except that Beth's thoughts were elsewhere. Kimmy was driving and it gave Beth time to ponder.

Kimmy asked, "Need a chat?"

"No, not really, just thinking."

"And?"

"Wondering... wondering what next," Beth said with a smile.

"Take it slow. It seems that he is." Kimmy looked at her friend, "Right?"

"Yep," and that was all she needed to say.

Chapter Four

Traveler was off to the Northeast for a few dates. Andy and Beth fell into what had become their routine: nightly phone calls and conversation into the wee hours. Beth loved it, but she continually wondered. She prayed that it would never end, but he was Andy Stevens, and she was 'just a girl.' Two weeks passed and *Traveler* was heading south to South Carolina.

During one of their late-night calls, Andy asked, "Can you come to Charleston? I need to see you, Bethy. Roddy will make all the arrangements, but I'd like to fly you in for the show there. It's only one night, but it's close. Can you pull that off? I'll have him get Kimmy a ticket too, if you'd like. But I really need to see you. I've missed you."

Kimmy would have gone, if Beth asked. They talked and both agreed that Beth needed time alone with him to see what was progressing.

She flew out early on Saturday afternoon. A driver met her at the airport. He held a placard that read "Bethy". It reminded her of a scene from a movie and she loved it. She arrived at the hotel and Roddy was waiting. They dropped her bags at the front desk and left for the arena, arriving backstage just in time. The show was about to begin.

"Hello beautiful," Andy said grabbing her for a quick hug and a peck on the cheek as he made his way to the stage. Roddy dragged two stools to the side and Beth joined him. They watched as the band entered from the other side of the stage.

Traveler did nine songs and left the stage. The crowd went wild, bringing them back for one more song, and then one more after that. When it was over, the guys began filing past. Nathan stopped to hug

Beth. And then, sitting there with Roddy, she knew he was close. She felt him before she saw him, sensed his presence before he touched her. A warm sensation washed over her. He came up from behind and kissed her neck.

"Welcome to Charleston," he whispered in her ear as Roddy slipped away. He took her hand, "Come with me," he said. They slipped out a back door and into a waiting town car, not the bus with the guys. In the car Andy pulled her to him and wrapped her in his arms.

"Bethy, I've missed you," he said as he kissed her, and it was one of those passionate kisses.

"Wow," she sighed, "I've missed you, too."

He held her tighter, and pulled her on his lap and kissed again. "We're going to the hotel so I can clean up. Roddy made a late dinner reservation for us at a little local place. Being this late I think we can get in and have a nice meal without too much interference. I want to take you on a date Bethy," he said and kissed her again.

"A date?" she laughed.

"I need to woo and impress you," he laughed, and nuzzled her neck. He kissed a place behind her ear that sent a shiver up her spine and he grinned.

July 22, 1978 ~ None of that was necessary. I was already gone! He had a hold of my heart and I prayed he'd never let go...

Her bags were in Andy's room when they arrived. She freshened up a little and waited as he showered. *'A date,'* she smiled thinking about it. Andy came out in light-colored jeans, a black pull-over shirt, and smelled like heaven. The driver was still waiting when they went back out. The restaurant was close. It was small and candle-lit, and they sat at a corner table. They enjoyed 'low-country' fare, and some bold red wine. Andy held her hand as they talked and shared the evening as though they'd known each other a lifetime.

Later, the driver was there to return them to the hotel. As they rode, Andy held her hand, and sat silently, deep in thought.

"When we head out in the morning, we're flying to Los Angeles," he said, at last. "We'll be doing three shows and some TV appearances for a week. Then we're on a ten-day break; some downtime to get ready for the next leg of the tour. I'd like you to spend some of that time with me, maybe fly you to Houston for a few days. What do you think?"

With no hesitation Beth said, "I'd like that."

"Good," he said and kissed her. "Roddy will make it happen. I've told him if you want or need anything he's to take care of it. He'll be how you can reach me if you need me. Anytime. Anyplace. You only need to call him."

Back in the room, Beth went to the sofa and waited while Andy started some of his favorite 'chill music.' With each beat of her heart she knew that he could hear it. She knew what her bags being brought to his room meant. Finally, he went to her, taking her hands in his, Andy brought her to her feet. Pulling her into his embrace, his hands lightly, softly caressed wherever they touched.

"Did I say I've missed you?" he asked, kissing her neck, his breath warm on her skin.

"Mmm hmm," she murmured, barely able to breathe. The smell of him was intoxicating.

"Did I say how much?" he added as he nuzzled lower, leaving a trail of kisses from her neck down to the place where the lacy fabric of her blouse skimmed her chest. "Did I say how bad I want you, Bethy?" he whispered, looking into her eyes as he guided her to the bed.

She knew she quit breathing, anticipating what she knew came next. She knew with each touch, with each breath, that this would be the night they made love for the first time. She felt excited and nervous, iced with anxiousness and anticipation. Together they fell on the bed, his kisses sweet, tender, and romantic. Slowly he unbuttoned and pushed the lace blouse aside. He noticed that she wore no bra, and it excited him.

She lay back, watching him, waiting for what came next. His touch was exciting as he kissed and caressed. Beth drew in a breath just shy of a gasp. He lifted his head to look at her and grinned. Slowly he made his way to the jeans she wore and the exploration continued. With every touch her breath hitched. It was a slow lingering process. He was taking his time with her. Beth's hands roamed his body. As she helped him undress, she allowed her fingers to explore with a light touch. Finally, unable to wait any longer, their bodies joined together.

It was exciting, breathtaking, and beautiful. I became his. His 'Bethy', and for the second time since I met Andy Stevens, my life was forever changed.

Lying in his arms afterward, Andy whispered in her ear, "Bethy, I love that you didn't close your eyes while we made love."

"I wanted to see you, to remember this, forever," she whispered back.

He wrapped her in his arms, and they slept.

The next morning the phone woke them, their naked bodies still entwined. Andy pulled her close and wanted nothing more than to lay there holding her, he didn't want to let her go, but they needed to hurry. Beth's flight was early and she had to get to the airport. The band would be flying out a short time later to head west. They showered and continued their exploration of each other.

Andy walked with her to the car and leaned in for a kiss. "Thank you for being here with me," he whispered in her ear. He quickly changed his mind, and slid in on the seat beside her, wrapping her in his arms, he hugged her tightly.

"I'll see you in a few days," he whispered. He nuzzled her neck, kissed her again, and Beth sighed, thankful she was sitting down.

"Thank you," she said. Andy's eyes narrowed, and he flashed a devilish smile, that made them both laugh out loud.

"I'll call this evening, make sure you got home safe, and say good night," he told her as he exited the car.

~ ~ ~

Returning home Beth slipped back into whatever 'normal' was; school two nights a week, work and the late-night phone marathons she shared with Andy. They both shared whatever had been going on since they last talked. Andy told her about the concert experiences and *Traveler*'s media blitz. Beth had seen it, but it made her happy hearing about it, as Andy told her about the band's visit to *The Tonight Show*.

"It was a blast, Bethy! We met Johnny Carson and Ed McMahon; that comedian Andy Bauman, and Doc Severinsen jammed with us before we came on stage!"

She loved his excitement as he recounted the experience. Finally, realizing that he was doing all the talking, he stopped, and then whispered, "Are you asleep?"

29

"No," she laughed, "I was listening to you, enjoying your excitement."

"Bethy, I love your laugh. I know you have to work tomorrow, but I really don't want to hang up. Just hearing your voice... God, I wish you were here."

She didn't say anything, and finally he told her, "I'm counting the days."

"Me too," she said in a soft whisper.

~ ~ ~

Roddy and Beth talked almost every day about something, making plans for her time with Andy once he returned. The two of them developed a kinship that Beth loved from the beginning. He was Andy's friend and confidant, and he became the same to her.

She couldn't wait for the time away with Andy. She would be picked up after work on Friday afternoon, and return home in time for work Tuesday morning. She was beyond counting days; she had it down to hours...

When Friday finally arrived, Beth was excited, wondering how she would make it through the day. She was anxious to experience another part of Andy's life. She had everything almost packed and rushed home after work to finish. A town car arrived shortly after she did to take her to the airport. The driver took her bags and she ran to the gate where Andy was waiting.

Oh my... Can one man be more beautiful?

He wrapped her in his arms, kissing her, whispering in her ear, "I don't think I've ever been this happy to see someone. You look so good," he said as he cupped her chin in his hand, "I've missed you," he whispered. Towering over her, tilting her face up, he bent to kiss her. She noticed that he looked tired as he led her to the waiting area. He had flown straight there from Los Angeles to meet her. As they waited he handed her an envelope. She opened it to find her passport.

"Kimmy helped me get it," he explained. "I hope you don't mind."

She laughed, puzzled; "Well, I don't need that for a trip to Houston."

Andy laughed, too. "I have a surprise for you. You will need it to go to Eleuthera. We're going to the Bahamas. I called Kimmy for help surprising you. She snuck in to get bathing suits and things she thought you would need to take along," he explained.

Finally they called boarding for the flight. Andy took her hand and they walked out to the tarmac to board the plane. Three other couples joined them. It was a short flight filled with conversation, Andy filling her in on the past week and Beth telling him what she'd been doing. He told her about the cottage and the island. The plane landed, first, on the northern tip of the island and the other three couples got off. A short time later they were in the air again, and flew into a tiny airport toward the southern part of the island, in an area called Rock Sound, to begin their time in paradise.

CHAPTER FIVE

As they cleared customs, everyone seemed to know Andy. When they went out, there was an old station wagon parked, waiting for them. A man walked up and handed Andy the keys.

"Wilford, this is my Bethy."

"My pleasure, miss," the man replied.

When they got in and Andy started the car he looked at Beth to explain, "The US ships old cars over here and when I came the first time this is what was available," he laughed, explaining the red 1963 Chevy Nova station wagon.

"I call ahead and Wilford has it gassed up and ready."

> *August 3, 1978 ~ The Island was quiet because of the late hour, and it was only a short drive. The cottage was in an area of Rock Sound called Sound Point, and I saw the beautiful frame of the cottage with its gingerbread woodwork, hibiscus bushes, and palm trees swaying in the moonlight. The sky was so clear I could count the stars. Beautiful, peaceful and quaint...*

Andy pulled the car along-side the little house. Someone had opened up windows and left lights on for their arrival. They grabbed their bags and headed to the door. It was a warm night but a light breeze blew, and she heard the sound of the waves breaking softly on the beach.

Once inside there were hibiscus flowers in old glass bottles sitting around on tables. Andy found a note that said there was a bottle of rum; and a pitcher of fruit juice in the refrigerator. It was also well-stocked with food.

Beth roamed and explored as she waited for him. The cottage was small and homey. There were two bedrooms, one small and the other large. The larger room had a king-sized bed and sliding glass doors that opened out to a covered patio that faced the water. The kitchen, dining and living area were one big open room.

"I bought it a few years ago," he said about the cottage as he fixed drinks. "I could afford something in this area because it's not the touristy part of the island. It's heaven to me and I come as often as I can."

It was beautiful, very white and tropical. No dark walls and no carpet. The floors were a speckled stone with rugs here and there. The windows had sheer curtains and white plantation shutters. The furniture was wicker. There was a big overstuffed sofa with tropical print pillows. The accents were light-colored and tropical as well. Beach and seaside town-scene watercolors adorned the walls. Soft colors and a woman's touch here and there…

"My mom," he said, as though he could read her mind, and she laughed. "She came over when I bought it. I'm not so good at that decorating stuff and she enjoyed it. The paintings are local. You'll see tomorrow," he said handing her the drink. "A lady here on the island did them for me." He took a sip of his drink and pulled the band from his hair shaking it loose.

I LOVE when he does that!

"I love it here," he told her, and she could see why. They got comfy on the sofa and spent the next hour talking. When he showed her to the bedroom, there were hibiscus flowers placed on each pillow on the bed that she didn't notice on the earlier quick tour of the cottage. It was sweet and beautiful. She stepped into the bathroom to get ready for bed and when she came out Andy stood waiting. She stepped into his open arms and he lifted the nightie she had just put on over her head and she laughed.

"I've waited ten days to feel you, so you won't need this," he said. They fell into bed, on sheets that were soft and smelled of lavender. Andy wrapped her in his arms and they made love.

In the middle of the night a clawing, scratching sound sent Beth flying up, yelling, from a deep sleep. Andy took a flashlight from a drawer beside the bed and shined it on the screen to show a huge land crab clawing its way along, a true "welcome" to the islands!

Saturday morning was sunny and beautiful. Andy rose, slipped on a pair of shorts and went shirtless to the kitchen, returning with a big plastic bowl, and a grin. He opened the doors and went out. Lying in bed, Beth could smell the outside. It was sweet and salty and she got up to have a peek. A minute later, curious to see what he was doing, she went out. She rounded the corner to a very loud THUD! She found Andy standing there with a big grin on his face holding the bowl. He tipped it to show the contents. There was a coconut with a large crack. Beth followed him to the kitchen, where he finished splitting the coconut, putting the water into a pitcher, and chunked the 'meat' into a bowl. He took a bottle of rum and covered the coconut meat with the gold-colored liquid.

Beth watched intently, wondering… *'Surely to goodness that is not part of our breakfast.'*

"You'll see later," he said, and raised his eyebrows, much like Groucho Marx, and grinned when he saw the look on her face.

They ate sweet, fresh, pineapple, bananas and mangoes from the island, along with toasted Bahamian bread that Edwina left for them for breakfast. Andy told her more about Edwina, the woman who lived next door, while they ate.

"I met her when I bought the cottage and she 'adopted' me. She takes care of things here when I'm away and gets everything ready when I let her know I'm coming. She's a sweet, special lady and I love her," he said with a big, genuine, smile that touched Beth's heart. He'd already captured it, and now pieces of him kept moving in, taking up more space.

After breakfast they began a day of exploring. Beth had never even heard of Eleuthera before the trip.

"It's part of the Bahamas but not as commercial as some of the better-known islands," Andy told her. "It's long and narrow and Rock Sound is just a little south of the middle of the island."

The village was old with narrow streets lined with beautiful Bougainvillea in full color. Houses were small cottages painted pretty pastel colors, Andy's was yellow. There were no hotels and hardly any restaurants.

"Laid back and local" is how Andy described it all. They strolled hand in hand and checked out what was in walking distance. After they had been out and about for a while, they returned to the cottage for some wonderful seafood chowder that Edwina left to heat up.

"Conch chowder," he said, and added, "It's just one of her specialties."

After lunch they took the car for a quick trip around Rock Sound. At times they parked and walked. There were little churches, beautiful architecture, and everywhere they stopped chickens ran wild. It was all unique and interesting.

> *August 4, 1978 ~ Out and about, we came across a lovely old-woman making straw hats on her porch. Andy chose one for me, and the woman told him he was a lucky man to be "a'sharin' your time with such a beautiful woman, now!" Her accent was sing-songy and lovely. Later we met the artist who painted the pictures in the cottage. I picked out a small painting of a yellow hibiscus to take home. It was vibrant and beautiful, a wonderful treasure to always remember my time on the island.*

They ran into Edwina out buying fresh Bahamian bread and pineapples. Andy shared more of the history of the island with Beth as the explored.

"In the 1800s there were many pineapple plantations on the island, they are still grown in Gregory Town, an area north of here." And when they came across the markets where fishermen were hauling in their fresh catch, Andy commented, "The grouper here is the finest I've ever tasted."

They returned to the cottage, deciding to save some of the sights for the next day. As they drove Andy explained, "Most of the little eating establishments close early so they can go home and be with their families, some are actually in their homes." He spotted one that he wanted to visit, a favorite of his, and they stopped in to ask about dinner. The owner came to Andy and hugged him.

"Hello Miss Issie! This is Bethy and I want her to taste some of that good fried grouper that you always fix for me. Are you cooking it tonight?" he asked, giving her an extra squeeze.

"For you," she said. "Charmer," she said to Beth, and they shared a laugh. "Dinner is at 5:30, no later."

They returned to the cottage to relax and freshen up before dinner. Miss Issie's place was only a short walk away, and they strolled hand in hand. They enjoyed more of the conch chowder, and an incredible fried grouper dish served with pigeon peas and rice. After the meal Miss Issie appeared with a luscious lemon pie.

"I know you like this," she said. "I made it just for you." Full and happy, Andy and Beth made room for a piece of pie.

Back at the cottage after their meal, Andy dragged two lounge chairs close to the water. Sound Point is a strip of land with beach access to the west and Rock Sound to the east. He turned the lounge chairs to face the west. "I'll be right back," he said, as Beth stretched out on the chair. He was gone for just a few minutes and returned with a big, silly grin on his face. He sat down with one of the coconut halves filled with some of the coconut that he had chunked into bite size pieces.

"Taste this," he told her, and put a chunk in her mouth.

"Wow! That's potent!" The coconut had soaked in the rum all day. Beth laughed, as rum ran down her chin. Andy quickly leaned in for what she thought would be a kiss but he licked the rum off her chin instead, making them both laugh.

He pulled his chair against hers and stretched out. Taking her hand in his he told her, "Get ready for the show," and they experienced the most amazing sunset. Both the view and the company were incredible.

Wrapped in each other's arms, later, Andy's fingers gently caressed her back. Kisses were passionate and Beth's body curled closer, tighter, their bodies touched from head to toe, skin to skin. The heat in her eyes told him what she wanted. "Now," she whispered, "now Andy."

Sunday morning, Beth woke early. It was barely daylight, a breeze gently blew the curtains back, and she rose, wanting to peek outside. Naked, she pulled her nightie over her head and slid the glass door open to walk out to the patio. The sun appeared, and she experienced the smell and sounds of a light rain shower. She stood watching for a while taking it all in as a mocking-bird was singing and she could hear the waves rolling on the beach. It was warm, but a soft breeze blew.

Andy rose and joined her on the patio. Standing behind her he wrapped his arms around her. The sun, after the rain, glistened on the palm fronds like crystal beads on green satin ribbons. It was beautiful, and Beth thought it was the best way to start the day, but there was more.

She turned into him and laughed. "You're naked!"

"You're observant…" he grinned. "You might as well be naked, I can see right through that thing." He laughed, and led her back to the bed pulling her into his arms. "I love the feel of you," he whispered in her ear as he slipped the nightie she wore over her head and they made love…

The sun was fully up when they rose again. After a quick breakfast they got ready to head out for more exploring. Swimsuits were the attire for the day. They packed a bag, jumped in the car and headed north.

There is only one road, and they drove for a while. Along the way the road followed a wall lined with conch shells that paralleled the beach. They came on a man cleaning the shells, and stopped. He picked one out and handed it to Beth. It was beautiful and white on the outside and shiny and pink on the inside. He held it to her ear for a listen. She thanked him and started to hand it back and he told her, "Now it is yours!"

A little further along there was a woman selling beautiful bright-colored shirts and dresses from her porch. Andy chose a dress for Beth in shades of blue and green, a beautiful cover-up to wear with her bathing suit instead of shorts that day.

As they drove along Andy shared island information and folklore. He explained that there were caves all over the island and that people journeyed there to go spelunking. Eleuthera was also known as a great surf and dive destination, and he pointed out good spots all along the way.

I loved the gift of conversation we shared as he told me about the island.

In their travels they stopped at a place called The Glass Window. One side of the road held a calm serene beach with palm trees, beautiful white sand and the bluest-blue water. It looked like a picture on a postcard. On the other side there were rocky cliffs. They climbed to look out over deep, dark blue, almost black water hundreds of feet deep. It was such a contrast, divided only by a tiny strip of land hardly wide enough to accommodate the roadway.

They continued on to the northern part of the island. Just off the northeast coast of the island lay a small piece of land called Harbor Island, accessible only by ferry. They boarded the ferry from Whale

Point for the ten minute ride to cross the quarter-mile inlet for some beach time and exploring. Beth grew up around the ocean, she'd been going her whole life, but she had never seen anything like this beach. It was splendor at its finest. The water was the most refreshing color of turquoise blue, and the sand was *pink*.

"Beautiful, isn't it? It's from the coral," Andy explained as he pulled low lounge chairs to the water's edge and they stretched out and relaxed in the sun for a while. The warm waters of the Caribbean slapped against the ends of the chairs, tickling their toes. Later, Andy got them lobster sandwiches at a little hut on the beach.

Before leaving to catch the last ferry off the island they did a little exploring. He showed her some of the island's history. The 'birthplace of the Bahamas,' it was home to one of the oldest settlements, and at one time was the capital. Lord Dunmore was the governor at that time, and while there, they visited the Dunmore Cottage. It was crisp and white, painted with beautiful red trim. They visited The Cannons at Roundhead, a wonderful spot that gave a glimpse of the bay.

Done with the tour of Harbor Island, they boarded the ferry to return to the big island and head back to Rock Sound. Driving along they talked about the day, one Beth knew she would never forget. It was late when they arrived at the cottage. Edwina left a beautiful conch salad in the refrigerator for them. Andy said it was one of his favorite treats. It was different, tangy with lime. Later, they cleaned up and fell into bed tired from their day. In his arms, every inch of her body curled against him, touching him, giving him pleasure just by the fact that she was there, he didn't need more.

Monday morning they were both dreading the end of their time on the island, and they crammed as much into their last day as they could. They started by heading south bouncing down one-lane roads, laughing the whole way in that old station wagon. Andy stopped at a place called Ocean Hole. He led her to the edge of what Beth guessed was a lake.

They stood at the edge and Andy told her, "They call it a 'natural blue hole' and say it's bottomless and connected to the ocean. It has ebbs and flows, like the ocean's tides, but they say even Jacques Costeau has been unable to prove a connection. People swim in here, no fishing, but let me show you why I'd never dive in." He laughed as he reached in his pocket, and pulled out a muffin he'd taken from breakfast and broke small pieces off and tossed crumbs into the water. Suddenly, the water churned up and it seemed there were a million fish springing up and grabbing the crumbs, wildly splashing about.

"Oh my gosh!" Beth exclaimed, "They're like piranhas!"

They got back in the car and continued south to a secluded beach. Beth packed a picnic and they spent their last time on the island enjoying the sun.

"I'm going to hate leaving," Beth said as they headed back to the cottage.

"We will come again. It's one of my favorite places on earth. I come as often as I can."

August 7, 1978 ~ It was a beautiful time and I treasured every moment, thankful, not only for the beauty of the island, but for the opportunity to share another piece of Andy's life. It was a peaceful time, filled with the beauty of paradise, and I pondered... What comes next? But I think I don't care, in the summer of 1978, we are a couple.

CHAPTER SIX

The next weeks passed quickly, each bringing more excitement. The band had zigzagged their way across the country, and in early September Andy flew her to New Orleans for a weekend show. They had an extra evening, so it was an opportunity for them to share some time. After the show the group walked Bourbon Street listening to the local bands. In several places the bands tried to convince them to sing or play, but they declined, responding that they were there for the entertainment. Nathan did get up and play at a piano bar they visited where they were playing ragtime music, saying he couldn't contain himself.

Later, they found a sidewalk café that was still open, and the owner offered to stay open as long as they wanted. They ate gumbo, crisp, crusty, hot French bread, drank wine, and laughed until very late into the night. The next day they were tourists, complete with a horse and carriage ride through the old city.

As her relationship with Andy grew, friendships with the other guys developed as well, except with Dane. During this visit with the group Beth realized that he resented her being around. Unsure how to deal with it she talked to Andy.

"I can tell he doesn't like me being here," she said.

"I do. Just let it ride," he told her. He wanted her with him, so she went.

Two weeks later she flew to Philadelphia. The band had two shows, but no break. She flew in early on Saturday morning, and back home earlier on Monday. It was exhausting, but she was with Andy and that was all she really needed.

September 24, 1978 ~ With the band's popularity came the press and tabloids. Part of that meant my picture with Andy in print in magazines. It's odd, learning to deal with that.

Caption with a series of pictures from People magazine:

"Andy Stevens and his Bethy work hard to keep their romance under the radar, with little luck. Spotted on a stool in the wings singing along with the band last week in Philadelphia, she received a round of kisses from Traveler's lead singer between encores. Two weeks earlier they were spotted in New Orleans at a sidewalk café with the rest of the Traveler band".

Her privacy became an issue, people at work figured out who the 'nice guy' in her life was. Andy had Roddy get her home phone number changed and unlisted to try to help. If they were not together, they were on the phone. It was awesome and overwhelming all at the same time.

~ ~ ~

During one of their late-night phone calls Andy talked to Beth about his week off before Europe. "I'd like to come to Florida to spend it with you."

"Really?" She couldn't even wrap her head around what that might be like. It made her feel nervous, excited, and overwhelmed. All the attention his visit would bring, especially for her family. They hadn't been exposed to that yet. Andy talked to Beth's dad and they all agreed that if he could handle it, they could.

The weekend he wanted to come caused Beth personal conflict. It was his twenty-ninth birthday and he wanted to spend it with her, and she wanted to have that time with him more than anything. But there was something else, and she shared with him about family, the traditions involved and how important they were to her.

"In early autumn each year my Nana and Pappy make their pilgrimage to the mountains of Tennessee and they come home with bushels and bushels of apples. The next weekend is always 'Apple

Butter Weekend'. Nana and I get started real early on Saturday morning, and spend the entire day making homemade applesauce and apple butter. We've done it as long as I can remember and I love that time," she told him.

"Nana said she'd understand, but who knows how many more years we'll be able to share that special time. But I don't want you not to come," she told him. It would be another first with him, celebrating his birthday was a special event too.

Andy found no dilemma at all. "It sounds like a great time to me!" he told her. "It'll be fun! I can help peel apples!" Amusingly, Beth's thoughts went to those tabloids - wait till they got a hold of *that* story.

They talked a lot about his visit, and his excitement to meet her family. Beth laughed and reminded herself to prepare them for the chaos that would surely take place. 'Hurricane Andy' was about to hit. She just focused on enjoying every second with him. Four months had passed and she was still living the dream.

~ ~ ~

'Apple Butter Weekend' was a fun family time. They peeled, cored, diced, and sliced apples, and some were actually eaten. They put up quarts and pints of apple butter and apple sauce for the coming year. Andy set some aside to ship home, and some to send his mom. Everyone talked and laughed and told tales.

On Sunday, they all gathered for a big family dinner, like an early Thanksgiving. Nana made a warm apple butter cake for Andy's birthday that he loved. Everyone was there and made it a special birthday celebration for him. He fit right in with her family.

Early Monday morning, Andy was already in the kitchen when Beth got up. It was his birthday, and Beth was happy to spend the last day of his visit with him. He was flying out late that afternoon to New York to meet the rest of the *Traveler* guys. They had some time and space lined up before they 'crossed the pond' to rehearse, leaving from there on an early flight on Thursday.

She headed toward the glorious smell of the coffee he'd made. She saw that he'd set up his portable keyboard on the table. He was wearing the headset, his back to her, playing and softly humming. When he noticed her he removed the headset.

"Good morning, beautiful," he said.

"Mornin'. What are you up to so early?" she asked pouring a cup of coffee, carrying the pot to refill his.

"I woke with this song in my head, had to get out here to play with it." He leaned to her for a kiss, and unplugged the headset, allowing the sound only he could hear before to fill the room as he continued playing. It was a catchy melody.

"I like the tune," Beth said, as she sat across from him. He played a while longer. Suddenly, with a wicked grin on his face he added some words about a 'simple life' and then some funny, somewhat risqué lyrics about *'making sweet'* that had them both laughing.

> *It's good lovin'*
> *Don't hold out*
> *It's making sweet*
> *It's good sweet lovin,*
> *Beyond any doubt*
> *It's making sweet*
> *I'm talkin' about*

Beth went to the bedroom and returned with a wrapped box. "Roddy helped me," she said. "Happy Birthday."

He unwrapped quickly. It was a portable cassette recorder. "It's small enough that you can keep it with you, and when you get those song ideas you can record them and save it for later," she told him.

"Thank you. I love it, Bethy, a very thoughtful gift." He took it out of the box and put the batteries in, then pulled a blank tape from the box and put it in the recorder. He began playing again and sang the piece he'd been working on. He popped it out and handed it to Beth. "Hang on to this until I get back," he said and grinned.

Playing again but not looking at her he said; "Come to Houston with me for Christmas. I know its family time. I met yours, now I want you to meet my family. I want you to meet Phyllis," he paused. "She wants to meet you," he added, raising his eyes now to meet hers, his smile like a soft embrace.

He wanted her to meet his mom. She knew that his dad passed away several years earlier. She and Phyllis talked several times, and Beth was looking forward to meeting her. Andy was an only child and she knew that he was very close to his mom.

She took a big sip of coffee, savoring it, and said, "I'd like that."

"Good!" He stopped playing, reached across the table and took her hand in his, and pulled it to his lips. "Roddy and I will take care of everything."

Still holding her hand in his he rose from the chair and pulled her up. "Have you got another present for me, Bethy?" he asked with that wicked grin and led her back to the bedroom.

~ ~ ~

October 20, 1978 ~ I missed him when he left. It was special having him with me for a few days, a very different routine that I loved. Six weeks apart would be a huge test.

Traveler's success had skyrocketed during that year. It was crazy, but the band's popularity in Europe was even greater. This was their first tour out of the U.S. and they were all very excited. Andy called every day to tell her about it. His excitement was just as exciting for her. They spent hours on the phone with all the details. Being their first time overseas, this was a really big deal for them. Every one of the shows sold out; an even bigger deal.

Roddy called daily to schedule the calls because of the time difference. During that time the relationship she shared with him grew into a strong kinship. No call was ever just to set up the time for a call and buzz off. It was a conversation between friends.

As the time drew nearer for the end of their European tour, Beth grew more excited for his arrival. Even though they talked daily, the time apart gave reason to wonder about 'them'. Returning home, the band would be on hiatus for a few weeks, heading to Japan after the holidays for three more weeks to finish the tour.

School complete for the term, Beth didn't enroll for the next semester. She squeezed in extra hours at work, getting things ready for the time she was taking off. Up late every night, she was busy finishing up Christmas projects, making sure there was time for the calls with Andy.

She spent all of her spare time getting Christmas shopping, decorating, and baking finished. Packages had already been mailed to Phyllis for their holiday trip. Andy was coming to Florida first for a holiday celebration with her family before they made their way to

Houston together. Being their first Christmas together, she wanted everything perfect.

Beth loved the hectic, sometimes chaotic activity of the holidays. There was always much to do. She loved all the preparation, and made as many of her gifts as possible, putting great thought into her choices. She hoped that Andy would appreciate the gift she made for him; she wanted it personal, something special.

She planned a holiday celebration with her family, and everything was in place before Andy arrived. It was early afternoon and she'd been anxiously waiting for him. She met him at the door, his arms loaded with packages. He quickly put them under the tree, and then went to her, wrapping her in his arms.

I love that place. It feels good there, really good…

"I'm so glad I'm here with you, Bethy," he told her as he took a seat on the sofa and kicked back to relax. "What time will everyone else arrive?"

"Around six." She'd chilled a bottle of his favorite, Chenin Blanc, knowing he would want a glass. "We'll have dinner and then our celebration. I kept it small," she told him as she poured the wine.

She sat beside him and he put his arm around her shoulder, and pulled her to him. He gave a quick glance to the clock on the wall. "Good," he replied with that devilish grin she'd gotten used to seeing. Exhaustion showed in his eyes, but still that humor.

They talked a while, and finally Andy went to the tree where he'd unloaded his goods. He returned with a small package. "I'd like you to open this one before everyone arrives. It's personal to me." He handed her the box.

It intrigued her to think what would be "personal" to him.

She shook it and he laughed. Slowly, methodically she worked at the paper. "Oh! Just tear into it!" he laughed. So she ripped… Inside was a pair of gold chains, one heavier and longer than the other, both with a half of a Mizpah charm. *'The Lord watch between me and thee while we are apart one from the other.'*

"Andy, I love these," she said feeling a lump in her throat. "They are beautiful and thoughtful, and I love them," she said again, slipping hers immediately around her neck. Andy did the same.

Beth went to the tree, digging under the branches and brought a box to him. "OK," she said anxiously, "here's one for you."

Unlike Beth, Andy immediately tore into the package. He sent paper flying everywhere as he opened the box. Reaching into the package, he pulled the contents out. He shook to unfold a shirt. Saying nothing, he held it to his shoulders. It was a casual shirt in a bright, colorful, tropical print.

"It reminded me of our trip to Eleuthera," she told him.

He looked at the tag, inside, '*Hand-made by Beth*', he read. "You made this?"

"I did!" she replied as he hugged her.

'*When it comes from the hands it comes from the heart*', he finished reading the tag. "Bethy…" He pulled the t-shirt he was wearing over his head and slipped into the shirt. He acted surprised that it fit so well. "I love it," he said, hugging her.

I know that body! I knew exactly what size to make it…

He poured another glass of wine and they sat quietly, relaxing, and snuggling on the sofa. He needed some down time. Finally, it was time to get things in order for the evening's events. Andy joined her in the kitchen to help. Her family arrived just before six, with Kimmy close behind.

Andy got beautiful silk scarves for Nana, Liz, and Kimmy. They were from *Harrods* and that was a big deal to her simple family.

Liz asked, "*Harrods*, in London?"

"And Paris, yes, that *Harrods*," Andy chuckled.

He got Pops a tweed newsboy hat that came from Ireland, and Pappy got a beautiful hand carved pipe from Germany. Beth found it very special that he knew them well enough to think of personal gifts for them.

Liz and Nana gave Andy a large box to open. He dug in to find a Nine Patch quilt that they had pieced, just for him. There was a card that read '*When you sleep under a quilt, you sleep under a blanket of love*'. He was so appreciative.

It was a wonderful evening of family. Andy and Beth were leaving the next morning for Houston.

Chapter Seven

December 24, 1978 ~ This is an exciting time for me. I'm anxious to see where and how Andy spends his time off. It's another piece of him, and I'm anxious to learn them all!

They flew into a small airport on the southeast side of Houston. After the plane landed they got their bags and Andy led her to an older Chevy pick-up truck. Beth laughed, "Who woulda ever thought – Andy Stevens, rock star, in something other than a fancy sports car!"

"It's the first brand new vehicle I ever had. 1973 and I just can't think about parting with it." There was a bench seat, and when Beth got in he placed his hands on her bottom and scooted her to the middle of the seat making them both laugh. As they drove along their gift of conversation took over. Andy pointed out things along the way, sharing memories as they drove.

"I like flying into Houston and making the drive home, it gives me time to turn off all the 'other wheels' on the way."

His home was about an hour away, on the Gulf, in Galveston. It was a small house, built on stilts, overlooking the water and not at all what Beth anticipated. It was very simple, homey and comfortable. She knew of his love for Eleuthera, and then realized he just loved the water.

They dropped their bags in the living room and Andy walked to a set of double sliding glass doors that looked out to the Gulf and opened them. Close to the doors was a beautiful black lacquer grand piano, so large it seemed to fill the room. "My one indulgence," he laughed. "This is my Jaguar!"

The view was beautiful and the smell wonderful as Beth walked out to have a look. There was a cool breeze blowing and she felt Andy behind her, his arms surrounded her. "Welcome," he said as he turned her to face him, and pulled her into his arms. "We'll celebrate Christmas at Phyllis' tomorrow. Being alone with you here tonight is all I need. We'll relax this evening. I just really need to unwind."

They walked back into the room. He picked up a note on the kitchen counter and read it as he poured them a glass of wine. "My friend Tom Brown and his wife Needa look after things when I am away, they live close by. Wait till you meet their little guy, Drew. I love that kid. She left dinner for us in the fridge, and says she stocked up on whatever she thought we might need. I called ahead and told her a few things. We can heat it up when you are hungry."

"I can wait," she said as he walked to the piano and sat down. He motioned for Beth to join him. The view faced the Gulf, and in the late afternoon, the sun sparkled on the water like diamonds as he began to play. It was a beautiful melody that Beth hadn't heard before. She closed her eyes, sipped the wine, and listened as he sang about a 'new place in the world' and 'a beauty he has never known'. He was thanking someone for sharing this new place with him.

Christmas Eve 1978 ~ All I could think about was how beautiful the song was, and then, with my face in his hands, he leaned in to whisper "Merry Christmas." He handed me the sheet music, and I saw 'For My Bethy' written across the sheet in his handwriting. A song for me, about us! He called it "In My World." I cried, knowing it was a gift from his heart. We skipped dinner and snuggled under the patch quilt that Mom and Nana had given him.

In my world
It's you and me
In my world
You're all I see
You've taken me
To a new place in the world
The world I share with you

On Christmas morning, Beth woke to a ringing phone, it was 8:30. She rolled over to find Andy sitting on the edge of the bed. He was talking, and she could tell by the conversation that it was his mom. She scooted closer and kissed his bare back. He turned, reached around and caressed her back as he spoke.

"Merry Christmas, we'll see you later."

He replaced the receiver in the cradle of the phone and rolled toward her. "Hey beautiful, Merry Christmas," he said, and pulled her into his arms. She raised herself above him and stayed there a moment, looking down at him, his eyes full of desire. She lowered for a kiss and he wrapped her tight in his arms, and they made love.

They celebrated their first Christmas together with Andy's mom, and she made it special. Beth felt like she had known Phyllis forever. She was a tiny, petite woman, very unlike Andy. Her hair and skin tone resembled his dark coloring. Her warm smile and laugh mirrored Andy's. She was sixty-five and shared that she and Andy's dad had tried for a long time to have children and finally Andy came along when she was in her mid-thirties.

Her home was a very warm, comfortable, and welcoming place. As they settled in Beth walked around looking at the various stages of Andy's life displayed in pictures. She gazed at one of Andy and his dad together. The picture was a snapshot, not a portrait. There was such love in their expressions. They stood arm in arm, Andy and his dad.

'*He looks like his dad,*' Beth thought.

"Cancer," Andy said as though he knew Beth was wondering. She turned to look at him and saw sadness in his eyes. "Cigarettes." Two words and he left it at that. His pain was clear. He then added, "Three weeks before Christmas ten years ago. He was sixty-two." He said nothing more. Beth could tell it hurt him to talk about it. She wanted to say something, but nothing seemed right. It was the first time he had shared anything at all about his dad, suddenly she found that odd.

~ ~ ~

Andy was an only child from a working class family. His dad worked at the Port of Houston unloading cargo ships. It was a good job, but he worked long hours. He provided well for his family. When he was home he was a devoted father to Andy, and a good husband to Phyllis. His mom made sure Andy was kept busy and out of trouble.

She was a stay-at-home mom and taught piano in their home. Andy grew up with that love of music instilled in him. Because he and Phyllis were alone a lot of the time, they were very close.

~ ~ ~

Phyllis joined them in the living room. Andy poured wine and they exchanged gifts and shared conversation. Andy gave Phyllis a beautiful diamond bracelet.

"You shouldn't spend so much," she scolded him as he rose to latch the bracelet around her wrist. She stretched her arm out in front of her and admired it. "It is beautiful, though," she laughed.

"Enjoy it, Ma!" He laughed, and loved spoiling her.

He then handed Beth two small, numbered boxes. She opened the first one, inside she found a crystal songbird.

"I got it in Austria. I saw it and it reminded me of the night I met you. The way you were singing and 'flitting' about at the concert like a little song bird," he laughed.

She loved that bird and the thought behind it. As she opened the second, she let out a gasp. Inside was a pair of beautiful diamond teardrop earrings.

December 25, 1978 ~ They were the most beautiful earrings I had ever seen, rich and regal looking. I wondered where I would ever wear something so extravagant...

"There's more, look under the inside box." There was a worn, folded piece of paper and she unfolded it to find a telegram stating that *Traveler*'s song "Forbidden Place" had been nominated for a Grammy Award for Song of the Year, honoring the songwriter.

"How exciting!" Beth yelled.

He wrapped her in his arms. "Go to the Awards with me," he whispered in her ear.

"Yes!" she said, still not believing this was *her* life.

Afterward, the three of them went to the kitchen where Phyllis had prepared a wonderful meal. There was turkey and all the trimmings and Beth enjoyed the time with her, getting to know her as they got the dinner ready. She told Beth her side of the family was of Portuguese decent, and Andy's dad's side migrated from Wales. Another glimpse into this man... Andy sat at the table and added funny commentary, and they all laughed as Phyllis shared stories of Andy growing up - pieces of his past.

As Beth listened she heard a family dynamic that she didn't realize until sitting there as they shared their past. Most of the memories they shared were Andy and his mom. She was there for music recitals and school events. Andy's dad was a hard-working man, but it appeared he wasn't around a lot. She understood the closeness between Andy and Phyllis better. She also understood a little better why Andy hadn't talked much about his dad. She listened, not wanting to pry.

They ate in the kitchen rather than the dining room. There was nothing formal here; Beth could tell Phyllis' home was a place where the kitchen was the heart of the home, much like Nana's. After the meal they washed dishes together, still talking and sharing stories. Their first Christmas was a beautiful celebration.

They stayed with Phyllis that night. Beth slipped off to bed early to give them the opportunity to talk and catch up. Lying in bed she listened to them talk for a long time. She couldn't tell what they were saying, but the sound and tone of their shared conversation was comforting. She heard Phyllis tell Andy 'goodnight.' Shortly after that, the door opened, he slipped into bed, wrapped Beth in his arms and she fell asleep.

~ ~ ~

Beth stayed in Texas with Andy for ten days. Mark purchased a condo in Kemah, a suburb of Houston, close to the bay, and just a short trip from Andy's. He had a New Year's Eve party to show off his new place. Beth was happy to find Kimmy there when they arrived. Andy flew her in as a surprise.

At Mark's party, Beth finally met Nathan's wife, Dina. She'd heard so much about her from the conversations she shared with Nathan that she felt like she already knew her. She was an actress. Beth had seen her on TV shows and in commercials over the years. She and Nathan had recently celebrated their seventh anniversary, and they had a daughter, Megan, who was six years old and Nathan was a proud papa. He didn't fit the presumed roll of a rock star. You could tell his relationship with his family was a strong one. Dina and Megan joined him when they could, but Megan took part in many kid things that kept Dina busy. It was important to them both, with their odd-ball lifestyles, that she led as normal a life as possible.

That night Nigel Rose was with his latest girlfriend. "The 'date du jour," Andy whispered in Beth's ear and laughed. "She'll most likely be replaced with a 'different flavor' in a few weeks." This one's name was Fawn. She was exactly the type you'd imagine being with a rock star, dressed up, made up and a giggler. Anything Nigel said, she giggled. Nigel fit the rock star role. He was a partying, fun-loving guy and liked the attention he got from the ladies.

It was also at this party that Beth met Dane's wife, Candy. She was a looker. She could be described in three words – drop, dead, gorgeous, but she was not at all friendly and kept pretty much to herself throughout the evening, not really socializing with anyone. She was busy watching Dane's every move like a hawk. Her conversations that evening were only obligatory pleasantries.

At one point during the evening Dina went to where Beth sat with a glass of wine. "Noticed you drink the same as me," she said as she sat down beside Beth. She filled her in on things within the band.

"Candy's lack of trust has reason," she said in a hushed tone. "Dane likes women - a lot, but it causes a lot of stress within the band." She didn't need to add more; Beth already figured that out.

Around ten, everyone experienced one of Dane and Candy's "explosions," as Dina referred to it. They'd had words, and Candy left in dramatic fashion, slamming door and all.

Beth liked Dina's frank, open nature. As they talked Dina offered some advice; "Don't ever give up your own life, ya know," she told Beth, as she sipped her wine. "Make sure you keep your own circle of friends. Keep them close, and stay in touch with them. This is a crazy lifestyle. You never know when you may need them."

Andy spent the evening reminiscing with friends, and introducing Beth to them. The guys were excitedly talking about their upcoming journey to Japan. They had five concerts and then they would come home for the Grammys. The tour would be done. They were all looking forward to some off time, ready for a life off the road, but everyone knew that during any down time they'd be working on music for the next album. It had already begun. It would be called *Divinity*.

~ ~ ~

Dina knew of Beth before she met her. She'd heard about her laugh before she heard it, knew of her wit before she experienced it, her smile before she saw it. Nathan was so taken by Beth and the change in Andy that he shared all of it with his wife.

Dina hoped, and she prayed - Andy was a good friend and she truly hoped that he had met the woman Nathan described as, "his match." He wasn't like the other guys, more a loner and not the player like Dane. Dina loved him, and wanted him to find happiness; happiness like she and Nathan had.

Dina, Nathan and Andy had been friends since school, and she'd been through many girlfriends with him. Nathan was so excited about Beth that Dina could hardly wait to meet her. Nathan told her she was an "it girl!"

"She's got it Dina, I mean it! She's pretty, she's fun, she's full of life, and she has the best laugh. Andy melts when she's around," he told her.

She was anxious to meet this young woman she had heard so much about. And she realized when she did that Beth did have "it"… But Dina knew they'd all have different definitions of "it."

As it got closer to midnight, Andy went to Beth. The countdown began on TV as everyone watched the ball dropped on the *Dick Clark's New Year's Rockin' Eve* program… ten, nine, eight, the excitement was building. Three, two, one… Happy New Year, 1979! Andy took Beth in his arms, and kissed her.

January 1, 1979 ~ As this new day, and this New Year began, I realized I was crazy in love with this man, I'm excited, and terrified.

CHAPTER EIGHT

The Grammys were approaching fast. The closer it got the more excited Beth was, but her attire for the evening caused great stress, to the point of tears at times. Kimmy and Beth shopped every weekend, looking through lots of dresses. Over-eager sales associates showed her many dresses and the price tags on them overwhelmed her. This was all so new to her.

> *January 18, 1979 ~ What I choose is a big deal, and it has to be perfect. It's not like you shop for stuff like that every day. And it's not every day a girl gets to go to the Grammy Awards on the arm of a Rock and Roll God!*

To ease Beth's stress, Kimmy tried to make it memorable, taking her camera so they'd be able to remember the experience forever. They giggled and laughed in dressing rooms as they both tried on fancy dresses.

Andy told Beth when she found what she wanted to call Roddy to take care of the bill. They narrowed it down to three choices - two gowns and a jumpsuit. Beth couldn't decide. She went back and forth many times, and finally, left the final decision up to Kimmy. Kimmy would send her choice on to L.A. Beth had no idea what she would be wearing until she got there. It was unnerving and fun all at the same time!

Traveler began their tour of Japan in Osaka with two shows and then journeyed to Yokohama for a night. They ended the tour in

Tokyo with two sold-out shows. They were in Japan for ten days and it was a successful jaunt. The tour was done and they were heading home.

Andy flew to Florida so he and Beth could travel to Houston together. Exhausted from the time difference, concert meltdown, and little sleep, Andy spent the next few days relaxing, while Beth finished up some things at work. He suggested Beth leave her job and come on the road with him, but she wasn't ready. She liked what she was doing, and, to that point had been able to work around the time needed for their relationship.

While in Houston, the weather was beautiful and they crammed a lot into the time they were there. Andy had business to tend to, so Phyllis and Beth spent a lot of time together.

The three of them were able to carve out a fun-day. A side-trip to the Houston Zoo was great fun. Following the Zoo was a wonderful evening out at a little Cajun restaurant that Phyllis and Andy loved called *One Crazy Cajun*. It was a fun, little off the beaten path place with Cajun music, including an accordion player, and a huge dance floor. Beth looked around, and noticed pictures of Andy and the *Traveler* guys with the owner and staff of the restaurant all over the walls. The owners made a big deal over their local celebrity. People came to the table to say hello, but it wasn't like an interruption. Most were people who Andy and Phyllis knew and they were stopping by to congratulate him or just say hello.

February 12, 1979 ~ The food was wonderful but dessert was what Andy was craving. He ordered peach cobbler and said he'd "crawl over a dozen naked women to get it" - I made a mental note! The accordion player played some upbeat Cajun music and Andy pulled me to the dance floor, and I loved every second!

Before they left for L.A. there was a small get together at Andy's home with the guys and some friends, even Phyllis came. Andy sent a limo to pick her up and she loved it. Caterers were there, so all anyone had to do was eat, drink, and be merry, and there was much 'merry'. It was an evening full of excitement, and some nervousness about the award ceremonies. This was *Traveler*'s first accolade. "The real honor is just in being nominated." Andy told her.

~ ~ ~

It was beautiful in Los Angeles when they arrived, sunny and warm, even for California. Limos took them to the Beverly Hilton hotel, greeted like royalty as they arrived; Beth was in awe of all of it.

On the day of the award ceremonies, Andy treated her to a trip to a spa with Dina. She wanted to look sophisticated, but it was important that it wasn't anything too much.

In the limo on the way to there for pampering, Beth told Dina, "I've never been to a spa."

"It'll be *grand!*" Dina laughed, "They'll scrub you, pluck you, wrap you, color you, massage you, and fill you full of champagne!"

They talked, laughed, and sipped champagne while being pampered from head to toe. When they returned, Beth entered the room to find Andy was already in his tuxedo.

February 15, 1979 ~ He absolutely takes my breath away...
He is so handsome, and oh my god, I am so in love!

Beth unzipped the bag and held her breath. "I honestly have no idea what is in this bag," she laughed. "I couldn't make up my mind, so Kimmy picked it!"

Roddy had it pressed before having it sent to the room. All Beth needed to do was slip in. She was anxious as she opened the bag, and happy to find what she did. It was her favorite all along, but she wasn't sure if it was just right. Anxious for Andy's reaction, she slipped into the long black silky fabric. It felt good against her skin. Looking in the mirror for inspection, she saw Andy behind her.

"I feel like a princess," Beth sighed. Andy walked closer and put his hands on her bare shoulders. The dress was black silk, with a bandeau top and empire waist. It was very plain and simple, straight, with a flowing flare at the floor. "Simple but very elegant," the sales woman had said. There was a wrap that went with it to drape over her arms.

"Kimmy did good," he said. Still standing behind her, his hands slid down her arms. "You look like a goddess, and smell like heaven," he told her as he nuzzled her neck. He turned and went to a nearby table and returned to slip a necklace around her neck. It was the same teardrop as the earrings only bigger.

He kissed the back of her neck as he latched it and whispered in her ear, "I've been saving this since Christmas. I want you to glitter from head to toe. I want to see the sparkle in your eyes all over you." He kissed her neck again. "So beautiful…"

Beth looked in the mirror; the necklace was perfect with the dress, and she loved it. She turned into him, and knew Andy liked what he saw.

Everyone was already gathered in the lobby when Andy and Beth arrived. A limo was waiting and they all climbed in. Dina hugged Beth and whispered in her ear; "You look so beautiful!"

Dina thought about Beth telling her that Kimmy picked what she was wearing for the evening, and that she would have no idea what it was until she opened the garment bag. Dina wondered who she could ever entrust that task to, and remembered that Beth was a different spirit, another reason she stood out. Watching Beth, Dina smiled. She noticed that she'd turned from a wide-eyed ingénue into a beauty before her eyes. It wasn't a girl who slid in the limo beside Andy that night; it was a beautiful young woman. She was on the arm of the man she loved, and Dina hoped that it would stay that way forever.

The limo ride to the event was fun. Mark went solo and Nigel was with the 'date du jour'. There was champagne on ice and everyone shared a glass and a toast. When they arrived it was wild, like nothing Beth had ever experienced before. There were photographers and TV crews everywhere, as well as the fans waiting to catch a glimpse. She watched, anxiously, as celebrities from the music industry made their way into the auditorium. Andy smiled, took her hand, and squeezed it.

There were flashes of light all around them. It was crazy with paparazzi all trying to get the best photographs, and reporters and TV personalities scrambling to get a word from all the celebrities. A reporter from *BillBoard* magazine stopped Andy to talk about "Forbidden Place". He chose instead to talk about "In My World" the first single that would be released from the upcoming album.

There'd been talk and speculation from the critics, and everyone felt sure that Andy and *Traveler* would win the award that evening. As they entered the auditorium, Beth asked, "Are you nervous?"

He seemed to just be enjoying the moment, and replied, "Nah, I've got the best lookin' date in the place. Whatever happens, happens; I'm just happy for the nomination." The guys had been on TV before but this was their first time at any kind of awards ceremonies and they were having fun.

They were all seated together, Dina to Beth's left, Andy to her right, and Roddy on his right. Beth looked around excitedly. She was taking it all in, making a mental note of where she was, who, and what she could see. She wanted to remember it forever and giggled. Andy put his arm around her shoulder, and gave her a squeeze. The night was full of excitement. Finally, it was time.

Mindy McNabb, an actress, came to the stage to call out the nominees for Song of the Year. She read the list; "And the nominees are, "What a Fool Believes", Kenny Loggins and Michael McDonald, songwriters, performed by the *Doobie Brothers*, "Forbidden Place", Andy Stevens songwriter, performed by *Traveler*." Beth could hardly breathe as Andy held her hand, and they waited.

"And the Grammy goes to… "What a Fool Believes", she shouted.

Andy squeezed Beth's hand and leaned to whisper in her ear. "It's OK, really, smile," he nodded to a camera pointed toward them.

The Song of the Year was one of the last awards given. As everyone exited the auditorium, the *Traveler* entourage made their way to a waiting limo. The group was excited to attend some of the parties around town.

Andy whispered in Beth's ear, "Would you mind if we by-passed the parties?"

"No, not at all, whatever you want to do," she replied. The limo dropped them at the hotel and the others continued on to the evening's events.

When they arrived, Andy made a call for dinner, and started some music. Beth kicked off her shoes and reached to take her earrings off.

"Wait, please," Andy said as he moved closer. "Don't change yet. I want to look at you a while longer." He took her in his arms, and kissed her.

Beth snuggled against him, "Are you disappointed? About the award I mean".

He hugged tighter and shushed her, "No, uh unh, I didn't really expect to win, first nomination," he whispered. He took her hand walked with her to the sofa. They sat together and shared a glass of wine.

Finally, there was a knock at their door. Andy allowed a young man into the room. He pushed a cart in, and the room filled with wonderful smells as he set the table. When he left Andy returned to where Beth waited. He took her hand in his, leading her to the table. He poured more wine, and they shared a wonderful meal as they chatted about the evening.

When they finished, Andy rose and took Beth's hand in his. He held her in his arms and they moved together to the music playing softly in the background. "I'm so glad you were there with me." He stopped, held her at arm's length, looking at her in a way that made her melt; she looked away. He turned her back to face him. "You are so beautiful," he said in a sweet whisper.

"I'm just a girl," Beth laughed, "nothing special." Andy kissed the top of her head and pulled her close.

"Oh, but you are." With his hands on her neck, his thumbs gently caressed her cheeks. He smiled, kissed her, and once again looked into her soul, "and I'm in love with you, Bethy."

Chapter Nine

In June they went to Eleuthera for a long weekend to relax. Andy needed it, still catching up from the tour and working on the new album. Beth was just happy to join him. She knew, but didn't know if Andy would, that this was a special time in their relationship. When they arrived she was pleasantly surprised.

It was early in the afternoon and Edwina had already done her magic, opening and freshening up. Later in the evening, there was a knock on the cottage door. Edwina was there, holding a beautiful cake, fluffy with coconut. She came in and set it on the table. Andy came from the other room, and as he hugged her there was an exchanged whisper. She turned to leave and looked back with her big smile. "Bless you both" she said as she went out the door. Beth turned to Andy and he was smiling too.

"What?" Beth asked, with a laugh.

"Come here," he said. "Reach in my left pocket," and she roared with laughter. "No! I'm serious. I have something in my pocket for you!"

"I bet you do!" But he raised his arms, and she did. Beth reached in his pocket to find a felt pouch. "What is this?" she asked as she opened it and found a beautiful freshwater pearl bracelet.

"Thanks for the best year of my life," he said, and then added, "so far."

June 24, 1979 ~ Wrapping me in his arms, all I could think about was how happy I was that he remembered…

They enjoyed their time on the island, being together, sharing long walks on the beach, and lazy days relaxing in the sun. Andy kept a keyboard there and worked on music. That never stopped for him, it was a constant, he had no switch to turn it off.

~ ~ ~

In August the guys were in L.A. wrapping up the new album. Beth flew out for a long weekend and ended up staying a week. She squeezed in as much time with Andy as she could with the crazy schedule they kept while recording, but he wanted her there, so she went.

When the band got in the studio they would never leave. They had meals delivered, and there were sofas all over the place, and they would go till they just couldn't go any longer. It was 'crash and burn.' When they got up, they showered and started it all over again. Sometimes they ended up working all thru the night until they got it just right. Beth napped on the sofas, because she wouldn't leave either. She didn't want to miss anything.

There was such camaraderie between the guys, joking, and laughing. Some differences of opinion, but in the end a lot of hard work, devotion, and dedication. Andy said this album was easy; live recordings from the last tour and a few new things.

Beth spent a lot of time in the booth with Sam, the engineer. The guys nicknamed him the 'sound engine.'

> *August 20, 1979 ~ I love to watch Andy make music. Whether it's the piano, guitar, or just standing at a microphone... When he sits on that stool and sings, with his eyes closed, I can feel his passion, it's like he makes love to the microphone, and I find myself closing my eyes, feeling like he is singing only to me!*

Andy flew Kimmy in on the last two days of recording. Dina and Megan were there and it was like a huge party. The guys were wrapping up, and one more song popped up. It came with a laugh and a big collective sigh among them. It was late and they were all whipped. Everyone was in the big room where the guys played and sang while they were recording, and they were getting punchy. Andy started playing a tune on the guitar. Nathan joined in on the piano, then Nigel, and then they were all playing and everyone was singing. It was "The Letter", written by Wayne Carson Thompson, recorded in the 1960s, by *The Box Tops*.

> *Gimme a ticket for an aeroplane,*
> *Ain't got time to take a fast train.*
> *Lonely days are gone,*
> *I'm a-goin' home,*
> *'Cause my baby just a-wrote me a letter.*

It was fun and the guys in the booth loved it. Laughter could be heard on the play-back and they decided to leave it.

~ ~ ~

By mid-September the tracks for the new album, *Divinity*, were complete. The guys all decided that "The Letter" would definitely be included as the last song on the album. Andy showed Beth different versions of the album cover art. There were several smoky, hazy, looking drawings of the Greek God, Zeus. In each he held a colorful bolt of lightning, but the 'bolt' was a musical note – to represent the power of music. The drawings were beautiful, done by Dylan CeMann, who had done the artwork for their earlier albums. In addition to photographs from the last tour, each of the guys added a message to the inner album sleeve thanking producers, managers, and family. Beth saw a message to her from Andy.

> *"My Bethy… How do I say thank you for understanding this crazy life we share? I'm happy you are part of it, craziness and all. Thanks for sharing yourself, your love, and your time with me. In My World is yours and I am so glad you are in mine… All my love, Andy"*

> *September 13, 1979 ~ I keep waiting to wake up and this whole beautiful, crazy dream to end… and then I pray that it doesn't.*

~ ~ ~

They commuted between Andy's home in Houston and Beth's in Florida. Andy still suggested she leave her job, and she thought about it, but there was no financial security for her if she did. He told her he'd take care of her, but she wasn't ready for that. She went part-time at work and it worked well for her and Andy, as well as her company. She was able to work her schedule around 'them.'

The band released "In My World" and it did very well. The release of the album was still weeks away, and then promotion of the album would begin. It would be released in mid-November in time for holiday sales. The guys were doing some small appearances to get the public excited for the release.

> *October 1, 1979 ~ The guys were doing a mini concert on the TV show The Midnight Special. Kimmy and I flew out for the taping. It was soooo much fun! We got to meet The Wolfman, and had our picture taken with him. He stood between us and just as Andy snapped he gave us both a tickle poke in the ribs and we screamed!*

~ ~ ~

Beth had never been happier. She and Andy had been together a year and a half, and it was good, but she continued to feel a nagging 'something' in the back of her mind; insecurity, that kept her wondering, constantly. She always felt as though she was waiting for something to happen, never able to pin it down to anything that Andy did or said. *I'm trying to just let it go, enjoy 'the now'.* Beth thought.

"In My World" held the number one spot on the music charts for weeks. Each time it played reminded Beth of the first time Andy played it for her at Christmas. She could see herself sitting at the piano with him, and feel how special it was when she realized it was for her. *Traveler* was on the road promoting the album on radio and television.

By mid-October the guys had been on the road a couple of hectic weeks. Beth stayed home to work and share time with her family. As she and Nana got ready for 'Apple Butter Weekend' it seemed odd that Andy wouldn't be there.

They talked every night, no matter where he was. Andy liked to hear about whatever was going on in her life, and she loved to share it with him. They talked about everything; work, her family, and all about Andy's travels. Beth loved hearing about the life they were learning to share. It had been two weeks since she had seen him because of the travel, and she missed him more and more.

In early November, on a Thursday night, the phone rang. She rolled over to answer it. A quick glance at the clock said it was 1:20, earlier than usual but thinking it would be Andy she snuggled in and answered.

"Hello…" she said.

"Beth, it's Pops."

Hearing Pops' voice, she sat bolt upright in the bed. A call from him in the middle of the night couldn't be a good thing.

"It's Nana, Beth. They've taken her to the hospital… 911… ambulance…" he mumbled. She heard the emotion in his voice and felt tears well up in her eyes. "They are calling us all there," he said, his voice heavy with emotion.

November 4, 1979 ~ Hanging up, I suddenly felt so very alone.

Numbly and quickly she dressed and drove to the hospital. It took thirty minutes, and when she pulled up Pops and Pappy were sitting on the curb outside the Emergency Room waiting. The others were all inside.

"What happened?" she asked, dreading the answer as she lowered to the curb to sit down.

Pops put his arms around her and pulled her to him. "She's gone Beth."

"Gone? What? Why?" she mumbled, but there was no answer to give then.

Gone? A sob clogged my throat, but no tears came. Nana was gone. Pappy would be alone now, and my Pops was crying.

She slid an arm around Pappy, laying her head on his shoulder, he cried, too. She let the tears run down her cheeks and started making mental notes. Her family was so close. She knew this was would be very difficult.

The next hours were a blur. In a daze, she kept busy, calling family and friends and trying to comfort her family.

It was mid-afternoon when she finally arrived home, drained mentally and physically, her heart held a light spot, knowing that there would be a message from Andy wondering where she had been when he called. She needed to tell him, and talking with him would give her some peace. But the message wasn't waiting.

She checked the clock, they were in Spokane, Washington, and it would have been around noon there. Instead of dialing Roddy like normal, she dialed the hotel where she knew they were staying. She needed him. He'd shared a code word to reach him in an emergency. She always knew where he would be, but had always gone through Roddy to reach him due to his weird hours.

She dialed the hotel and asked for 'Peter Pan's' room.

"Hello?" It was a woman's sleepy voice that answered. Beth knew, right away, they misdirected her call. She apologized, but as she hung up, she heard the voice say, "Hey, Andy, wrong number."

Numb. She replaced the phone in the cradle and suddenly, sobs shook her body. The tears that did not come earlier came in a rush now. It was only a few seconds later that the phone rang. She let it go to the machine. She didn't have the strength to do anything more.

"Bethy, it's me, pick up." She heard Andy's voice. "Bethy, please, it's not what you..."

But she knew she couldn't talk to him. The bottom had finally dropped out. She picked up the phone, then hung it up, disconnecting the call and left it off the hook. She stretched across the bed and cried herself into a deep, heavy sleep of exhaustion. Sometime later Kimmy was standing in her room trying to wake her. Ethan, her oldest brother called her because they couldn't reach Beth.

She felt like a Mack truck hit her. Kimmy sat on the side of the bed, gently rubbing Beth's back, such a comforting gesture between two friends.

"Hey," she said, and then picked up the phone and called Ethan to let him know Beth was OK.

"He called me. Andy knew it was you, he called the desk and they told him someone called and asked for 'Peter Pan'. He knew it was you," she said again. "He said he tried and tried to call and finally when he couldn't reach you, he called me."

Kimmy crawled in the bed beside her and said in a soothing voice, "I'm sorry honey, so sorry. I didn't ask, I figured you would tell me, when you were ready, but maybe it's not what you think."

"Sorry? About Nana or Andy," Beth asked, sarcastically, and regretted it immediately. "I'm sorry, that wasn't called for."

"You never have to say you're sorry to me, my friend," Kimmy replied, still rubbing her back.

Beth had a sick headache. Kimmy reached to the bedside table and handed her some aspirin. She wrapped her arms around Beth and allowed her to cry out the rest of what she'd been holding back.

As she did, Kimmy told her more about the conversation she'd had with Andy. "He tried to explain to me, I told him it wasn't my business. He really wants to talk to you. He said it's all a misunderstanding, Beth. He wants to explain." She paused, and then added, "I told him about Nana."

The phone rang. Beth shook her head 'no' when Kimmy reached to answer it, but she picked it up anyway. "Hello? Andy," she said and looked at Beth. Still shaking her head 'no,' Kimmy told him, "I don't think now's a good time. She's really just not herself. It's not a good time."

He was asking her for help, but Kimmy stood firm. "No, maybe later, I have to do what Beth needs right now. I'm sorry," she told him sadly, and hung up. The phone rang again a few minutes later. This time it was Mark, he begged her to put Beth on the phone. Kimmy asked, and finally Beth agreed.

"Beth, I am sorry about Nana." He paused, "We all are. I need to…"

"No Mark, please don't, not now anyway, I have to get through this. I need to go and be with my family. Not now."

"Beth…" but she hung up before he could say any more.

"Please don't answer if it rings again. I need to get a shower and get to my Pops," Beth told Kimmy as she left the room. The water seemed to rejuvenate her.

'Maybe, just maybe, I can get through this,' she thought.

"Yes sir, I'll get her there," Kimmy was on the phone as Beth returned to the room.

"It's Pops. He wants you at the house. They're done at the Funeral Home. I'll drive." Beth felt very blessed that she was with her, that she was her friend.

The next day was like a foggy dream, nothing seemed real. It went by so fast, yet it seemed to drag on endlessly at the same time. She spent every moment possible with her family. They needed each other. People came and went. Flowers and food arrived throughout the day. Nana was well-known and loved in her community. She'd lived there her entire life, and at seventy-four she knew a great many people. There would be a wake Sunday afternoon and a funeral on Monday.

As they made preparations, answers came, too. The backache that Nana had complained about for some time, but didn't explore, wasn't just a pain that she thought came with age. She had cancer in her spine that had spread to her organs. It went undetected because she just thought the aches and pains at her age were a fact of life, and didn't seek treatment. The last week or two she thought she had a mild case of the flu and didn't do anything about that either. This surprised no one because she never complained, but it made dealing with their loss even more difficult. Everyone went through the 'what ifs'. But 'what if' had passed.

November 6, 1979 ~ Shoulda, coulda, woulda... When I arrived home each evening from being with my family the answering machine was full. Friends and co-workers called with their condolences, along with several hang-ups that I was sure were Andy, "needing to explain." I didn't talk to anyone about Andy and me, but I'm sure the fact that I didn't even mention of his name had them all wondering.

On Sunday, after the visitation, everyone gathered at Nana and Pappy's house. Their home was always what the family called 'home base.' All things important seemed to need to happen there. Beth wandered the house, seeing Nana in every inch of every room. There was a knock at the door. Her mom answered it and Beth heard her talking. It seemed a familiar voice, and then Liz went to Beth and put her arm around her, and whispered in her ear.

"There's someone here for you," she said motioning toward the door.

Beth walked into the living room to find Roddy there. She looked to Kimmy, knowing she had told him. Roddy walked to Beth, saying nothing, he hugged her.

"Let's go outside for a walk," Beth suggested.

They walked quietly for a while. Finally, Roddy took her hand and they stopped. "I'm really very sorry for your loss, Beth." Wrapping an arm around her, he squeezed her in a warm embrace.

Beth put her head on his shoulder and they started to walk again. "Thank you, Roddy." The sting of tears burned her eyes. "It won't be the same without her."

"Andy wants to come, but he didn't want to just show up without you being OK with it."

Beth didn't say anything at first, and then finally told him, "It'll make him feel better, but I don't think it's a good idea. It could get wild if he is here, the media and all."

Knowing her real fear, Roddy spoke. "Beth, it's not what you think."

"How do you know what I think?" she asked sharply.

"A sleepy sounding female voice answers the phone in Andy's room, and your suspicion is that he was with her, that's what I *think* you think." He knew she was hurting inside.

She turned to look at him. Roddy was her friend too. She'd grown to trust and love him. "Yes, that's what I think," she admitted.

"That's not how it was." Roddy said; "Will you let me explain?"

They turned back toward the house and started walking. He took her hand again. "Talk," she told him, knowing he would be honest.

"They needed to let loose. There was a party. Andy doesn't usually get into that, and you know it. It ended up in his room. The hours and their schedule, they just needed to let go. Dane had some girls there to party with. It was late and people had passed out here and there to sleep," he explained.

"The girl who answered was just there, if you had asked for him she'd have handed him the phone. She wasn't with Andy. She was with Dane, another one of his flings. She just answered a ringing phone."

Roddy's explanation wasn't like he was scolding her for over-reacting, and his words didn't come across like he was defending Andy. He was stating the facts. Beth listened, but still felt unsure, uneasy. In her mind she had already planned for this to happen. This new way of life wasn't really something she ever imagined for herself.

"I don't know Roddy," she hesitated. "I just don't know." They walked a little further, in silence. He put his arm around her shoulder again, but said nothing to push or persuade.

"I'll be home tonight," she said, finally. "I'll answer the phone." As he hugged her, she realized how much he meant to her, and she felt very thankful that he was part of her life. When they returned, Roddy went in and Beth introduced him to everyone. He expressed his sympathy, hugged Beth again, and left.

At 10:40 that night the phone rang, she expected it. Beth figured it was Andy. She stood, straight and strong and picked up the phone, believing there couldn't be tears left, but she had to fight to hold them back. Her mind wandered all evening. She tried to think and plan how the conversation would go, over and over in her mind. She felt so insecure, not believing she was really capable of handling that kind of lifestyle with him.

It wasn't Andy. It was Phyllis Stevens.

"Oh, darlin', I am so sorry about your Nana. Andy called me a while ago and told me. Is there anything I can do?"

She was so surprised to hear Phyllis's voice that emotions she wasn't prepared for overwhelmed her. The tears came in a flood.

"It means so much to me that you called." Sobbing she said, "I'm sorry."

"Oh Beth, no 'sorry', I know what happened. Andy told me. I know this is all so different for you. It's difficult. It's been that way for me as well." She began to explain, her voice motherly and soothing.

"My home is under constant watch. It's not just media, it's curious fans who have discovered his roots. A friend comes by, a strange car is in my driveway, and they think maybe it's Andy and they camp out across the street only to find one of my friends slipping out after coffee or cards. I wonder sometimes if I will ever get used to it."

She paused and Beth blew her nose. "Beth, Andy loves you. That's not easy for him," she said. "He is a loner. Listen to him before you make any kind of decisions. Let him talk to you. Let him tell you what he needs to tell you. And you tell him what *you* need to tell him."

Beth cried even harder at Phyllis' words. There was a knock at the door. "Hang on," she told Phyllis. Putting the phone down, again blowing her nose, she looked out the peephole and saw Andy. Standing there, hands in his pockets, he looked very apprehensive. Without saying a word she opened the door and went back to the phone.

"Thank you Phyllis. I can't tell you how special your call is to me - how much it means. Hang on, there is someone here you may want to speak to," Beth said and handed Andy the phone.

"Hey, I couldn't be anywhere else. I'll call you later. I love you, too." Beth heard him say, and he blew a kiss into the phone and hung up. Beth turned away, looking out the window, not knowing what to say. Andy sat on the sofa. For several minutes it was quiet.

"The funeral is tomorrow morning at ten," she said, finally.

"I know," followed by more silence. "Bethy come sit with me."

"No, I really just need some fresh air." Andy followed her out the door. They walked to the pool and he pulled two lounge chairs together. It was a cool evening. There was a bright, almost full moon. They sat in silence for a long time. Finally he turned to Beth, reached over, and took her hand.

"Bethy, I am so sorry about Nana," he started. "I know what she meant to you. I know what she came to mean to me. I'll always remember the opportunities I've had to be with all of you and the great times we shared. She was a very special lady." He thought for a minute, and then added, "It was obvious that she loved you very much."

Beth wiped her eyes, "I'm the only granddaughter, all boys but me..." she mumbled and began to sob.

He scooted closer and took her hands in his and brought them to his lips. "I'm sorrier about this misunderstanding between us. Let me talk to you, please, Bethy."

She nodded and he began, "I know this relationship is hard, this lifestyle isn't for everyone, and you have given far more than I have. You've handled this with more poise and grace than anyone could imagine. I know it's a struggle and I've forgotten along the way that I had to work at it in the beginning. I'm very sorry for that."

"I don't usually get into that whole party thing. You've been with me enough to know that. But I did this time. I was ready - mental meltdown... partying sounded good to me. It was no big deal. Some music, some rum, some women..." He paused, "Yeah, they were there, but that doesn't mean you can't trust me."

"It's me I don't trust," she said between sobs. "I don't trust me to handle this relationship. It terrifies me."

Taking her hands again, he was very quiet. Looking very deep into her eyes he finally spoke. "I'm not sure I understand what you mean." Beth could feel the hurt in his voice as he spoke.

She looked at him and tried to pull her hands free, but he held firmer. "Tell me what you mean, Bethy."

Suddenly, she was just exhausted. "No, not now, I just want to go to bed."

He let go, they rose, and walked toward the apartment. Andy closed and locked the door behind them. Beth slipped into a big t-shirt, saying nothing, she crawled into bed.

Andy came into the room with a glass of milk. He'd mixed in just a little chocolate syrup. He sat on the edge of the bed and told her, "My mom always brought me a glass of chocolate milk when I'd had a bad day and she wanted to make sure I'd sleep."

He paused a minute, in thought. "The last time she did it was the day Dad died. He'd been so sick in the end, she never left his side. I stayed pretty close to home so I was there if she needed me. Here was this incredible woman who'd just lost her husband and she wanted to make sure I slept." He sat, quietly remembering for a moment. "Drink up. It'll help."

Beth took the glass and sipped, he gently tipped up the bottom of the glass and she finished it. He pulled out his shirttail to wipe her mouth, leaving her smiling at the gesture as she snuggled into the covers.

"Where will you be?" she whispered.

"I'll be here. I won't come to your bed. I know you're troubled by all of this. But I won't leave, I'll be right here." He leaned and kissed her forehead. "Good night, Bethy."

Around four, she rolled over and looked, but the bed was empty. The apartment was dark. Beth walked to the living room and found Andy sprawled on the sofa. She pulled the loose cushions from behind him to give him more room, and lightly tossed a blanket over him. He had opened the windows and it was cool in the room.

He stirred, leaning up on his elbow. "Hey," he said, sleep heavy in his voice.

"Hey, back to you," Beth said. "You comfortable?"

"No, come here," he said as he scooted back into the sofa where the cushions had been. She walked over and sat on the edge. He eased her down, pulled the blanket over them and wrapped his arms around her. Spooning her, he said, "Now, I'm comfortable, what about you?"

"Mmm hmm," she murmured and fell back asleep.

Monday morning when she awoke it was around 7:30. She slipped off the sofa and into the kitchen to start some coffee. She needed it, and she knew Andy would want some. She walked into the closet in her room, thinking about what to wear. Her hand brushed the black evening dress from the Grammy Awards and she began to cry. She slid to the floor and hugged her knees, as tears turned into sobs. She sat like that for a while. Finally, Andy came looking, and found her there. He didn't say anything, just sat on the floor behind her, scooted close and wrapped his body around her. He sweetly kissed the top of her head as he held her.

"I never feel secure," she said finally, feeling the need to explain.

"Why?" he asked, stroking her hair.

"I'm not glamorous. I'm not a groupie. I'm surely not beautiful. I'm just a girl, Andy, just a plain'ol, simple girl."

He buried his face in her neck, and kissed lightly. "The girl I love," he said as he held her, gently rocking her in his arms.

"Why me Andy?"

He pulled her legs around, pulling her on his lap. He thought a minute, and turned her to face him. "When I walked into the room that night in Orlando, I saw those eyes and they captured me. It was like I could see your heart, and I knew it was a good heart. You crawled into my soul, became part of me. I saw the inner beauty, and regardless of what *you* think, the outside wasn't bad either," he laughed.

"We started talking," he continued, "And you mesmerized me. I felt as though you were allowing me to see what made you tick. It was like I had known you forever, and I liked it, a lot. I've enjoyed our late night phone calls more than I can tell you. You're a real person, a smart, beautiful woman. Not some giggly bimbo trying to get my attention. Those are the kind of women I meet, the ones who constantly surround me. You and I had a meaningful conversation. I think I fell in love with you at that moment. There was no one there that night but you; no one who mattered anyway."

He looked into her eyes and pulled her to him. "Let's go have that coffee," he whispered in her ear. They went to the kitchen, and the coffee was good. It seemed to pour life back into her tired body.

"I don't know how to make you more comfortable in this relationship, Bethy, except to tell you that I love you. It's you and me, my love." He reached across the table and took her hand. "We should get ready for the funeral," he said.

She looked at him, and peered into those eyes that seemed to see her soul.

"I love you," he said, and again she cried.

~ ~ ~

72

That misunderstanding helped Andy realize that he needed to gently ease her into his lifestyle. He didn't realize how hard it was for her until then. Now it was *their* life, no longer just his, and he needed to remember that. He knew it was hard, the road, the travel, the lack of privacy, the hours, the female fans, all of it. He had to help her adjust, because it was important to him. Because she was important to him.

CHAPTER TEN

The two years that followed were some of the very best and busiest times in their lives. *Traveler*'s following grew larger with each song they released. It was exciting to go from the smaller venues as the opening group, to being the main headliner. Shows were selling out all over the U.S.

Beth made some big changes during that time. Nana Morgan's family had been big in the citrus business for many years. As Nana and Pappy got older it became too much for them to manage. Pops was their only child and he and Beth's brothers had other interests. They sold the business and much of the land. Nana and Pappy led a comfortable life and set aside money for their grandchildren. After Nana's death, Pappy sold their home and moved in with Beth's parents. He made arrangements for all the grandkids to receive a part of their inheritance.

Pops helped Beth invest some of the money. They were selling the apartments where she lived as condominiums. She took part of her inheritance and purchased her unit. It was a place for her to return to when she didn't travel with Andy, so she was close to her family. They worked together to make it comfortable for Andy when he was there. It was important that it was home to him, also.

Their relationship grew stronger and Beth finally began to feel more confident, more secure. She left her job, feeling that it was time. Things were happening in the economy, her company was downsizing and after a lot of thought she resigned. It was a huge step. Giving up her source of income was scary. She knew she had Nana's money but she still worried. Pops did as well, and he told Andy so. Andy assured him that he would take care of her.

It was very different to give all of her time to Andy. It was exciting, scary, and wonderful all at the same time. When they weren't on the road they went back and forth from Andy's home in Galveston to the condo in Florida. There were also many wonderful trips to the cottage on Eleuthera. Beth was happy there...

> *June 15, 1980 ~ These times when we escape to the island are always peaceful... romantic. The beach means solitude. It's just us there, peaceful and quiet, us.*

Together, they purchased a chalet in the mountains of Colorado. They went there to ski, but being a 'Florida girl,' the cold didn't appeal to Beth as much as it did Andy. They needed places to retreat, and unlike the cottage in Eleuthera, this was *theirs* and they could share it with others. It was in an area where other celebrities resided, so it was comfortable there. They could get out and about, shop and dine, with very little interruption.

They spent many weekends combing antique stores and shopping to set up the chalet in a comfortable way that they both wanted. She wanted a homey and warm feel, but comfortable for Andy, and a play place for everyone else. It was a retreat, so they worked together to make it a fun place.

It was a gypsy lifestyle. They didn't really live any place but out of a suitcase. Beth learned that she needed five of everything, one at the condo, one in Galveston, one in her travel bag, one at the chalet, and one in Eleuthera. She'd always thought of herself as a 'homebody', a 'nester', so this new lifestyle was an adjustment, but she did it because she would have done anything to be with Andy.

Traveler outgrew their bus and purchased two custom coaches for touring. This was a big step, a measure of their success. At a show in Detroit, when rap music was first getting started, Andy was telling the audience about the buses between songs. Nathan and Mark started a beat and Andy laughed. It was "Rapper's Delight" by the *SugarHill Gang*, and Andy began singing; *"Everybody go hotel, motel, Holiday Inn..."* and the crowd went crazy singing along.

With the new coaches came more space and Beth traveled with Andy more. They now had some privacy. With the old bus there were just seats and bunks, and everyone was pretty much together all the time. Usually it was fine, but Dane made it known he didn't like Beth being there. Beth knew why. Her presence made him feel as though he didn't have the old freedom he experienced. She inhibited his freewheeling lifestyle, and he resented it. Dina came only occasionally and none of the other guys had steadies. Dane's dislike of her being with Andy made it tense at times. Beth made a point to stay out of his way, but even that caused tension between Andy and Dane. The thing was; Andy wanted Beth with him. The new coaches made it easier, so she went.

~ ~ ~

In January 1981, the band began working on their fifth album. This became a trying period. There was chaos that finally brought things to a head. Dane's free lifestyle finally caught up with him. He was using drugs and no one was happy with that. Candy left him and they went through a very nasty, very public separation, followed by an even nastier, more public divorce. It kept everyone on edge. The fighting within the group got bad. Finally, Dane left, by mutual agreement. The bad publicity with the divorce, the drugs and the masses of women Dane chose to keep made it rough. The band didn't want his lifestyle associated with their reputation. It was an unpleasant time, but everyone came through unscathed.

It took a few months and many auditions, but the guys found a guitar player named John Smith to fill Dane's place in the band. John was from another group called *Expend* that had recently disbanded. Everyone had a good laugh over his name. Sometimes they called him, 'Dear John,' but mostly, because he was so tall, they called him 'Stretch.' They got busy and the album was once again in the works.

After this, a special time of settling followed. It seemed the scenario with Dane made it feel like it was time. Both Nigel and Mark were in relationships. Nigel was in a relationship with a girl he'd met during their last bit of downtime. He and Christy rolled into the life together quickly and would be married in September.

Mark met someone who made him think about settling down as well. Anna was an accountant he met when he was working on some financial business. Mark introduced her to the group as a 'bean counter', and earned her the nickname, 'Bean'. Anna and Christy traveled with the band often, Anna more than Christy, and Beth enjoyed the female company.

It wasn't just the guys settling down though, Kimmy was too. She met a guy, Lane Parker, and their relationship blossomed quickly. Everyone knew marriage was in their future. They were a perfect match; both tall, blonde and athletic. Kimmy settled into that relationship fast, in a big way. Lane was a pharmacist and a *Traveler* fan, which made him and Kimmy being around even more fun.

~ ~ ~

September 12, 1981~ Time is flying by, but I'm enjoying every second of it. The next album, Continuing, a name they chose to let the fans know the changes in the band hadn't held them back, is in the completion stages. But this means they'll be going out on the road soon, the first time out with Stretch. They worked together to write their own material for this album. They pulled some of the original songs because of conflict with Dane, but some new exciting ones emerged. There are more ballads than the hard rock they're known for. They were anxious about that. 'Will the fans like it?' they wonder...

Beth sat in on recording sessions and wondered how they couldn't like it, they were beautiful, but they still had a rock and roll feel. Andy and Mark produced it, an anxious first for them as well. On several of the songs they recorded with the orchestra from Andy and Nathan's high school. It was a very special experience. They practiced and worked with the kids, who were so in awe. Each of them would have their name listed on the album credits and they were very excited. The kids on violins were a beautiful addition. After recording with the kids was complete, the band threw a huge pizza party at the school as a way to say 'thank you', followed by a sizable donation, a "give back" they called it, to the school's music department.

When they began touring again, Andy would fly Kimmy and Lane to join them when they could. Beth loved the times when Kimmy could be there. With four brothers, Kimmy was the sister Beth longed for but never had.

Beth was becoming more and more comfortable in her role as 'Andy's girlfriend'. Most of the time she sat with Roddy on a stool in the wings when the guys performed, and she liked it there *just fine*. She also liked being with Roddy, they'd grown into a comfortable friendship over the years and she enjoyed his company.

From her spot she could see everything that was happening. It became known as her 'perch.' There were a few times Andy dragged her on the stage to sing to her. It was a nerve-wracking experience at first, but special, and most times it just made her laugh.

CHAPTER ELEVEN

Life lived in the spotlight was never something Beth anticipated, prepared for, or welcomed. It was Andy's life and she loved him, so she learned to live with whatever the spotlight brought.

October 1, 1981 ~ I am finally getting used to seeing my picture in print, and all that goes with it. It isn't normal, but I'm adjusting the best I can. Reading the untruths they print is hard, but it seems it's part of this life. I have never done an interview, yet there were quotes; "Andy's girl Bethy says..." There will be a picture of me with a scowl and headlines that read that we've had some big blow up, or we've split. How do they get those pictures anyway? All of a sudden there's this picture. Sometimes I see one and remember where I was or what I was doing at the time, but I never remember seeing anyone around to take it. Sometimes they are just right there in our face with Andy pushing our way through a crowd.

My favorite piece appeared on the front page of a National Enquirer. I was standing in line at the grocery checkout and saw a picture of myself. It was Andy with his arm around my shoulder, as we darted out of the St. Francis Hotel in San Francisco. Inside were another picture and a short paragraph that read:

Demanding Diva ~ *"Bethy, The Diva, and Traveler's Golden Eye, Andy Stevens, seen leaving San Francisco's famed St. Francis Hotel. A hotel staff member tells us that the couple checked out after Bethy demanded Egyptian cotton sheets and towels that the hotel did not have. It is also reported that she demands fresh roses in her room every day."*

Diva? That brought a laugh from everyone who knows me. If I were that demanding it would be Calla Lilies! We did stay there, and slept on whatever sheets were on the bed. What I hate most is that they made me sound spoiled. The St. Francis contacted Roddy to apologize and let him know they'd released the staff member from their employment. Andy's life has no privacy, therefore mine doesn't either. Sometimes are harder than other times, but it's part of this lifestyle.

~ ~ ~

In early October, 1981, *Traveler's* tour schedule took them to 'the Windy City' for a week, two sold-out shows, and a meeting with Andy and famed writer, Norton Edwards, for an article for *Rolling Stone* magazine.

As Roddy made arrangements for their meeting, he relayed Andy's wishes to Norton; he wanted Beth there, but she was off-limits for the interview. The article was on Andy; Beth wasn't ready for that kind of exposure, and Andy didn't want her singled out in any way. After Norton agreed, the plan was for them to meet Tuesday at the *Billy Goat Tavern*, one of Chicago's legends, for lunch to start the process.

Norton interviewed many celebs over the years, but this was the first time Andy had agreed to an interview. Meeting at a fun place would make it easier for Beth. The *Billy Goat* is famous from the *Saturday Night Live* skits with John Belushi, Dan Ackroyd, Loraine Newman and Bill Murray. A driver dropped them at the restaurant and as soon as they were in the door, the fun started.

A big *Saturday Night Live* fan, Andy walked to the counter and ordered "Cheezborger! Cheezborger! No fries, cheeps! No Pepsi, Coke!" as Beth looked on laughing.

Andy and Norton talked for a long time; Andy was very comfortable talking about himself, his career, the band, even what he wanted to share about his relationship with Beth. She listened intently as Andy told about the early years. He told about his mom making him take piano lessons as a child, and then participating in the choir at church. But it was school that played a key role in developing his passion for music. He joined the school jazz band in junior high school, first playing the drums. It was there that he met Nathan Perry and Dina Miller, who would become Nathan's wife shortly after high school. That experience progressed into a real love of music that led to guitar. By the time he was in high school he and Nathan were in a 'garage band' playing school dances, and he loved it.

After graduation from high school in 1969, Andy and Nathan met Scott Force and they formed the band, *Traveler*. Nathan, Scott and Andy were the original band, and then Dane Allen and Nigel Rose joined. They played at bars in the Houston area in the early '70s. The response was good. They kept busy and developed a huge local following.

In 1974, they won a local bar band competition and the prize was an opportunity to record a song. They wrote a song called "Traveler", recorded it, and released it to local radio stations only. Word of mouth had the request lines as far away as Tucson requesting them. And that, as Andy said, "was that." He talked briefly about the parting of Scott Force and Dane Allen and Mark Jones and John Smith's arrival in their places. He was very positive in his words, nothing negative.

Beth joined the conversation because Andy would include her in questions, more like conversation, but she pretty much "yes'd and no'd" and let Andy do the talking.

Norton watched, curious, when she spoke, intrigued, watching her watch Andy so intently, watching him with so much love, watching her guard fall and her laughter surface. And he wanted to talk to her, but respected Andy's wishes.

The article would have pictures, so they loaded into a limo and proceeded to the photographer's studio. On the way there, conversation continued.

"I like this, it's like people just talking," Beth said. "It's not at all like the interview I anticipated."

Norton smiled and replied, "Good, that's the way I like my interviews to feel. I'm glad you're comfortable."

Andy reached over and squeezed her knee.

"You'll spend a few minutes with Teena Michaels, she's a make-up artist, just to add some 'polish' to the shine," Norton told Beth.

"Polish," Beth laughed, "I like it!"

Andy had some 'dusting' too, before he and Norton continued talking while waiting for Beth. When she finally emerged Andy smiled and let out a loud wolf-whistle.

"You look beautiful," he told her as he kissed her neck, "I don't want to mess up the artistry," he laughed.

Beth laughed, throwing her head back as she did, and Andy kissed her neck again. Her laugh was a pleasant sound, she seemed to let her shyness slip away. Norton watched and took mental notes.

The photographer chose to do some color and some black and white shots. Many snaps of the camera went off, as he took shot after shot. They changed clothes several times, and each time meant a touch up of hair and make-up. With the studio photos done, they loaded back into the limo to go to Oak Street Beach, near The Drake where they were staying.

They shared some wine and the conversation continued. Andy was very personable, comfortable, as he answered Norton's questions, but always in the corner of his eye, he watched as Beth became more at ease with the situation.

The beach was cool and breezy on that late afternoon, the sun casting off natural sepia light. Because of the time of the year, it wasn't crowded, and there was just a bit of a nip in the air.

The photographer liked this, "This will be great... windblown... not so posed," he mumbled. "More natural..." His assistant set up equipment, and once again, Teena touched up hair and make-up.

The beach at Oak Street is much like a city park, and the photographer scanned for locations to shoot. First he had Andy lean on a railing that looked out over the beach area. He wore jeans and a black t-shirt, his long brown hair blowing in the breeze. He was very comfortable in front of the camera. Norton watched Beth watching him, and was even more intrigued by her, slipping in little questions in their conversation that he didn't feel broke the agreement he'd made not to single her out.

There were several of them together at the railing. They then walked down to the beach area. Beth was wearing faded jeans and a black sweater. Walking ahead of them as Andy and Norton talked; they heard the photographer tell Beth, "Turn around."

Suddenly, he was at her side with his hand on her behind. He ran his hand slowly over the curve of her bottom as Beth stood speechless.

"Andy, the curve of this…it's fine! I have to get a shot of that." He told him, and then looked at Beth for approval.

She was too shocked to acknowledge him, and heard Andy reply, "I think that would be great," he laughed out loud. "It *is* fine!"

"Beth, walk ahead. When I say 'stop', pivot on your left foot about half a turn. Look back over your shoulder, quick. Don't smile, just turn, quick, and look back at me when I say so," he told her.

She did as he said, and when she looked back Andy and Norton laughed as the photographer snapped off pictures from different angles. Then Beth started to laugh and he took even more. Before he finished he had her lying on the sand to take a few shots. She was a damp, gritty mess, but she had fun.

After the photo shoot was complete they walked to The Drake. Andy and Norton went to wait in the lounge while Beth quickly went to shower the sand off. The rest of the *Traveler* gang joined them and they all walked to a little café on the beach. They shared a wonderful meal and conversation as Norton talked with all of them for comments for the article. The plan was for the article to run in the December issue.

The first show was Wednesday evening. During the day as the guys rehearsed and did sound checks, Dina and Beth spent the day sightseeing and shopping. Roddy called ahead to the legendary *Pump Room* and reserved the famous *'Booth One'* for them. They shared a bottle of wine and dined on Lobster Bisque and *The Pump Room Salad,* just two friends relaxing, and giggling like schoolgirls when they saw several celebrities there.

When the show began that evening, Norton joined the girls and Roddy. Beth and Dina sat on stools to the left of the stage. It was Andy's birthday, and halfway through the set Nigel began playing the birthday tune and everyone started singing.

There was a new song that Andy wrote for Beth, "In Your Eyes". Norton saw emotions all over her face when she heard the piano start. Whenever he sang it on stage he looked to find her. She knew when it started to make her way to where he could spot her. Roddy came and stood with her, as did Dina. Norton stood back and watched.

Andy started to hum the first part of the song as he walked toward Beth. With his hand extended, he motioned for her to join him. Reluctantly, she walked out. A light shined on her as Andy reached for her hand. One of the crew brought a stool and she sat while Andy belted out that song, holding her hand in his as he did.

In your eyes I see my life
In your eyes I feel love
In your eyes I know heaven,
It's what makes this life worth livin'

The lighting was just right; light from the fans' lighters could be seen throughout the crowd from their lighters. They liked the song. It was obvious, Beth loved the song.

When he finished singing, Beth stepped down from the stool and Andy brought her hand to his lips and kissed it. The cheers from the crowd were like thunder. One of the crew grabbed the stool as she started to walk off the stage. Suddenly, Mark hit a drumbeat with every step she took. She stopped, turned to look at him, questioningly. He paused, and the audience laughed. She began again. He did too. She took smaller steps, and Nathan began playing lighter notes on the keyboard. Now Beth was laughing. Andy started to move toward her so she stopped and waited for whatever came next. Suddenly, Stretch and Nigel began playing some loud notes that Beth hadn't heard before and Andy started singing about "that girl's fine behind."

That girl's fine behind
It's got me
Sssssstutterin'
As she's movin' again
A sway, a strut
But, but, but…
I love her butt…

Beth laughed and quickly exited the stage. The crowd was on their feet clapping and whistling. The guys quickly wrote a new song using the words the photographer said to Andy, and this was how they decided to debut it. Roddy met her with a hug as she exited the stage. They shared a laugh with Dina, who knew all about it. *Traveler* was hot everywhere they went.

~ ~ ~

From Chicago it was frantic, harried, but the road beckoned, and four more weeks brought them to Cedar Rapids, Minneapolis, St. Paul, Bismarck, and into Canada. It was so crazy that at times a crew member would write the name of the city on a piece of cardboard and raise it for Andy to thank the city they were in.

They were making their way east in Canada for shows in Toronto, Quebec, and Montreal for two weeks. After Canada they would have a few days to rest up and then head to Europe after the holidays. During this time Roddy was working to get everything in place for that leg of the tour.

Their pace left them all exhausted, and in much need of the scheduled down time. The drain was starting to take a toll on all of them; there was tension, some bitchy, petty squabbles, all because they were just tired. Beth decided with Christmas around the corner and with everyone on edge, she'd go home until the break. This would be her first time traveling with them out of the country, and there was much to do. Andy would head to Florida to celebrate Christmas and have a few down days and they would leave from there.

She'd been home, busy preparing, packing and planning for the very exciting time ahead. As always, when they were apart, the routine of their nightly phone conversations continued. Only Andy seemed tense and preoccupied, grouchy, and moody. Beth played it off as the fatigue of months on the road. He was tired, ready, and in need of the break. *Traveler* hadn't been on the road for this long since she'd known him. Getting away for a few days would be good for them both. Her brother Ethan and his wife Angie were about to have a baby, and she was happy to be home for the big event.

On Friday morning the phone rang. It was Roddy.

"Hey," he said. "You OK?" It sounded funny to her when he asked.

"Yeah! Why wouldn't I be?" she laughed, but the long silence on the other end said something was wrong. "Roddy?"

"I'm sorry Beth…"

"Sorry? Sorry for what?" she asked, more than puzzled. "Roddy?"

"Beth…" he said, followed by a long pause. "I don't want to tell you this."

"Roddy! What? What is it?" Panic surfaced, her mind raced trying to imagine what was going on.

"Andy left for Europe early this morning," he said.

"He left? I don't understand, he's supposed to come here. What happened?"

"I don't know all the details, Beth. I only heard that he left with someone else. Another woman..." he said with pain in his voice.

She heard his soft whisper of a voice, but those words; "another woman" rang in her head like a big bell.

"Beth?"

"Who?" she whispered in disbelief.

"I don't know. I just heard it myself. I arrived here late last night to have the guys asking me what was going on. You know I'd been in Houston, to take care of some stuff before we leave, I just got back. I haven't been able to reach him. The guys don't know much either. They said he just left, they asked around but no one knows. I don't know yet, Beth." He was mumbling.

The sentences ran together in her brain. She was struggling to breathe.

"I left a few things behind that I figured would get into Andy's bag when he came here. Can you please gather them up and get them to me if they are still there?" she said with a calm that scared her. "There can't be much."

Chapter Twelve

Beth wanted nothing more than to crawl in bed, hide from everything and everyone, but her family was gathering that evening for dinner. She plodded through the day, making herself stay busy, dressed, put her best face forward, and went to them praying, hoping... There was a new baby in the family to celebrate, and she hoped it would be the distraction she needed to get through the evening.

November 20, 1981 ~ Another woman... It rumbled through my head over and over. Who? How did this happen? What happened? My thoughts filled with questions, but no answers... my heart was heavy, full of hurt and pain like I've never felt before. Broken... I prayed prayers for the strength to function.

This all took place just as a new entertainment broadcast was ramping up. *Entertainment Tonight* was a new television show to inform the curious public of just such celebrity news events. She could see that she would probably have to deal with whatever this was publicly.

Kimmy came to Beth's parents' home later that evening, Beth called her as soon as Roddy shared the news. She gave Beth that casual hug that said, "I love you", but didn't let on that anything was wrong. Beth worked hard to keep her emotions in check. The TV wasn't on so she thought, and prayed again, that maybe she could get through the day without having to talk about something she herself had just learned.

When she was ready to leave, Kimmy hugged her and whispered in her ear. "I'll meet you at the condo."

Beth arrived to find the message light on the answering machine flashing. She ignored it. She didn't want to hear any of them. She sat at the kitchen table and focused on breathing.

Breathe in, breathe out,' I kept telling myself. It was suddenly like a normal function needed instruction on what to do to sustain life. Focusing on that allowed me to keep the other thoughts from being forefront... but they still lurked just below the surface... waiting...

Kimmy arrived and let herself in. She had a bottle of wine that she opened and poured them both a glass, but said nothing. Beth sipped and let the alcohol course through her body. She was shivering with nerves and the wine seemed to bring warmth. She was a mess. Kimmy was the best kind of friend. She asked no questions. She went to the answering machine with a pen and paper and played the messages.

"Dina, someone from *Entertainment Tonight,* a reporter from *People,* and a guy from the local TV station; I thought your number was unlisted. How do they get through? Your mom, Roddy, he will be here in the morning, two hang-ups... your brother Michael, and Mark," she said when she returned to the table.

"Please just unplug it," Beth begged her.

"No, I'll be here for a while. I'll answer it, return a call or two," Kimmy said. She walked behind Beth, leaned over her, and put her arms around her neck. It was a comforting gesture and Beth reached up and patted her hands. No words, just the embrace of two good friends. They sat in silence for a long time.

Michael called again and Kimmy talked to him. She told him to call the others and let them know Beth was OK. She then returned Dina's call. The two of them talked for a really long time, Dina expressing her own shock and dismay. She told Kimmy that Nathan called her and he was very angry at Andy, they all were. But he was more worried about Beth.

Lane called to check in, Kimmy explained what was happening and told him that she was staying there. Still, there was no conversation. Beth had nothing to say.

Kimmy crawled in bed with Beth, and they shared talk and tears, just like they had done so many times through the years, but there wasn't much sleep.

Saturday morning, they were having coffee when there was a knock at the door. Kimmy rose to answer it, letting Roddy in. He sat a suitcase down, and Beth rose, without saying anything, to take it to unpack. It was only the things she'd left behind in Canada, just a small part of what she would still need to retrieve. Beth reached for the handle, Roddy reached for her hand. With a doe-eyed gaze she looked at him. She swallowed hard and tried to blink back the tears at the rims of her eyes, anxious to escape.

> *November 21, 1981 ~ I will not cry... I won't! I repeated the words over and over in my head. I can't... if I start, they will never stop...*

"How did this happen? How could I be so blind?" she asked Roddy.

He hugged her. "Not blind Beth, no one knew. I found a message he left me after we spoke yesterday, after he was already gone." He paused as if searching for what to say next and then said, "I don't know what to say Beth, I didn't know."

"I only left last week. I just talked to him the night before." She turned to walk back to the table, suddenly feeling weak. Kimmy took the suitcase to the bedroom to allow them to talk, alone.

"He sounded stressed, tired, anxious maybe, but I certainly didn't suspect this," her voice trailed to a faint whisper.

They sat quietly for a while. Beth finished the coffee in her cup and went to the coffee pot for more. She was trembling. Roddy rose and took the pot; he poured them both a cup and then returned to the table. He sat across from her, reached over, took her hand, and held it for a long time.

Finally he spoke and his words sucked the life out of Beth's already tired body, "It's Claire." That was all he needed to say. He told her again that he didn't know. She believed him. He was her friend too.

He asked her, "What can I do? What do you need me to do Beth?"

"Can you help get my things? It seems they are everywhere, Galveston, the chalet..." she was mumbling.

"Is that what you really want?" he asked.

Beth sat there just looking at him for the longest time. Of course that was what she wanted. What was he thinking? He sadly told her that he would.

It was Claire that Andy left with. Claire Ferguson... Roddy told me that he knew it was nothing permanent, but I couldn't get past 'now' to think about that. All I could think about was that he left me behind. Three years...

Beth knew of her. She'd seen pictures of Claire in magazines when she was just a fan, when she was curious to know more about him. Andy talked about her briefly. She had been his girlfriend for a while, but that was before, way before.

Claire was from Houston, too. She was a cover girl in the early '70s and still did a lot of modeling. They met when *Traveler* played at the Grand Opening of a local car dealership. She was one of the models there to help showcase the cars. She and Andy dated for several years and then she surprised everyone, left Andy and ran off to marry a photographer.

But they were over. She and Andy were over. What happened that it started up again? When did it happen? Roddy explained that she was doing a modeling shoot in Montreal and ran into Andy in the hotel. But what after that...?

~ ~ ~

The pace of their recent schedule had taken a toll on all of them, but Andy began to feel restless and anxious. He was in a relationship that was starting to mean way too much to him and he didn't know how to handle that, or if he really wanted to.

After a show in Montreal he needed an escape. The guys had all gone in for the evening. Beth was home for a few days, and Andy was alone. He went to the hotel bar for a glass of wine. He was sitting there, thinking, pondering, wondering... He heard the bartender call "last call" and raised his glass for one more. He felt a light finger drag slowly across his back. He looked up. In the mirror behind the bar he saw Claire behind him. He turned around to speak. She was standing so close. She pulled him into her and kissed him. He responded, and knew that she was someone who could make it easy for him to stray.

He loved Beth, but he believed that she wanted more than he was ready to give. And there was Claire, beautiful, sexy and making herself very available. His restlessness led him into her arms, into her bed and the next morning, led him away with her.

He knew with Claire there would be no commitment. There would be no ties. There would be no long-term anything. He thought that was what he needed. As he boarded the plane with her he thought again of Beth. He knew it wasn't right, but he knew Roddy would handle it. Roddy handled everything. And away they went.

As soon as the plane landed in Paris Andy knew he'd made a mistake. Being with Claire was never good. It was sexual, that was the only thing that had ever been good in the two and a half years they were together before. He quickly realized that wasn't what he wanted anymore. He knew it would be volatile, they would argue, and fight, they always had.

A short time with her and he knew he'd made the biggest mistake of his life. He realized how important Beth was to him, how much he loved her, but the damage was already done, and he wasn't sure how to fix it. It caused a strained relationship within the band. The European leg of the tour was tense. No one was happy with Andy, especially Roddy. They were all being a strong front for Beth, because they loved her. He tried to talk to Dina and she told him to "figure it out." But he honestly didn't know how.

~ ~ ~

Beth went into hiding, rarely leaving her condo. Some days she barely made it out of bed. She wasn't eating and it was starting to show. Everyone worried. She didn't take phone calls, and only returned those from her closest circle. Shortly after the first of the year Andy began calling. She didn't acknowledge the calls. They went to the answering machine and were then deleted.

One evening Kimmy and Lane were there and the phone rang. Kimmy answered it. She walked into another room with the phone. Beth could hear her talking, noticed the tone as Kimmy tried to keep a sense of calm. She tried, but it was loud and clear. Beth figured out, quickly, that it was Andy. Kimmy told her he'd called her before. Finally, she returned to the room.

"He wants to talk to you," she said. "Just do it and get it over with," she continued, not covering the phone, to assure Andy could hear her. "He said he needs to explain," Kimmy continued.

January 8, 1982 ~ With a calm I didn't even know I was capable of, I took the receiver. No quiver, no shake, no yelling… "Go to hell," I told him, and hung up.

~ ~ ~

Beth had been home two long, painful months. She was miserable. She received many requests for comments on 'them', but continued to say nothing. The *Rolling Stone* article Norton Edwards did on Andy ran as scheduled. She never saw it. He tried to contact her through Roddy, to talk about what happened. But she declined that request, as well. She had no intention of wearing her heart on her sleeve for the curious world's benefit.

She spent her days trying to plan a path to move forward. She looked into school to finish her degree. With the inheritance money from Nana she could do it and still be OK. The next session would be starting in the spring and she felt like she needed a plan to get on with her life, a life without Andy.

To keep busy until she had everything in place she spent her days watching her beautiful new niece, Kira, while her sister-in-law Angie went back to work. It filled a gap, and kept her out of sight.

The bond that Beth and Roddy developed grew stronger. He was a good friend. He called often 'just to talk,' to check in on her, to make sure she was doing OK, or see if she needed anything. Dina did the same, calling almost daily.

Phyllis called early on and told Beth that she was sorry, "Andy doesn't know what he's done," she told her.

Roddy pretty much handled everything for her. She talked to him about getting out of the chalet in Colorado, but he told her to wait. "It's a good investment." Pops agreed. So she waited. Dina went out there for a few days and sent some of her personal things. Needa sent whatever was left in Galveston. Beth was moving on.

~ ~ ~

In early March, on a Monday afternoon, the phone rang. She was home alone and heard Roddy's voice on the answering machine. She picked up the receiver.

"Roddy," she said, and felt a lump in her throat.

"Hello my friend," he said sweetly. "How's my girl?"

"I'm doing good," she lied.

They chatted for a few minutes and finally, he said, "Beth, I'll be in town, tomorrow. I'd like to see you. It's been way too long."

March 8, 1982 ~I couldn't help but wonder why he'd be in town, but I happily said 'yes,' later admitting to myself how much I'd missed him. Even though we talked regularly, it really had been too long. He asked to come before, but I avoided seeing him. I was afraid it would remind me of the hurt Andy left me with. Talking to him on the phone was different. I realized that I wanted to see him. But I needed to see him even more.

"I can make reservations somewhere for dinner and pick you up," he told her, with a smile in his voice.

"No!" she replied sharply. "I'm sorry. I didn't mean to sound short. I don't want to go out. I'll fix something here, really, I'll be happy to do that."

"Or I could pick something up, or have something delivered," he offered.

"No, just come, please, just come. I love to cook and I haven't in a while. Please just come," she said again.

"OK then, I'll see you tomorrow evening, say five?"

"That's great. Roddy, I am really looking forward to the company."

That night she was happy for the first time in a long time. She let her guard down, wondering why Roddy was really coming. It was late, the phone rang and she picked it up without thinking. She hadn't done that in months, she screened all her calls.

"Hey," he said and her heart stopped beating. It was Andy.

I hadn't had to deal with the sound of his voice in my ear in a long time. I didn't know it would shake me so, stir emotions, hurt like it did.

"Yes?" she replied.

"I'm really glad you finally picked up, can we talk?" His voice sounded heavy, sad, but she couldn't let that affect her.

"I don't guess there's anything to say." There was a long pause, "You made a choice. I'm learning to live with it," her voice was a whisper. Her heart was breaking all over again. There was pain that hadn't been there for a while. It had been almost three months since he left with Claire.

Andy realized at that moment that the words '*silent*' and '*listen*' were just different combinations of the same letters. He *had* to make her *listen*.

"Beth, let me talk, please," he pleaded and waited. Knowing that she was about to hang up, he yelled, "Don't hang up! Please! Hear me out, I've tried to talk to you for weeks!" he was shouting.

There was a huge lump in her throat. "I don't know if I care what you have to say anymore." Breathing became a laboring task.

There was a pause, "Beth," he said, finally, "I'm pregnant, it's your baby." Another pause and she began to laugh. He succeeded. He had her attention.

"Talk," she said wiping tears from her eyes. She poured a glass of wine as he talked. First, he told her about the tour. It was winding down and he told her how relieved everyone was for a bit of a respite.

He sounded happy sharing the success the band was experiencing, with her. She knew no details. She hadn't turned on the television, or radio, picked up a newspaper or magazine in months. The topic of Andy and *Traveler* never came up when she spoke with anyone in her inner circle. It was like it was forbidden. They were protecting her. He excitedly told her about the reviews and sales of the album.

They fell back into that normal routine as she listened to him. Twenty minutes passed, and she realized how very much she missed him, missed *them*. She started to cry, and crying turned into sobbing.

"I miss you Bethy," he told her. That pet name that she hadn't heard in so long, it just made it easier for the tears to flow.

"I miss you too," she said, "what happened to us?"

"Not us, me, Bethy. I don't know." He was quiet a minute. "I am so terribly sorry. I know I hurt you. I've made a horrible mess of a lot of things these past few months." He paused, "Roddy quit yesterday."

"He what?" she asked, clearly shocked.

"He quit, right in the middle of a meeting with the record execs. He got up from the table, gathered his things and said he was leaving." He continued, "I sat there with my mouth hanging open. Then I exploded, yelling at him. He turned and said that he didn't know me anymore, didn't like the person I'd become and he was just tired. He walked out. Things had become strained recently. I guess he'd had enough of me." He sounded sad, not angry.

Quiet time passed, Beth was processing what he'd just said. She took a sip of the wine. "Hmm, he called earlier, said he wanted to see me. He checks in on me. I guess he wants to tell me about it. I'm having dinner with him tomorrow."

More time passed, and then she heard the temper in Andy's voice as he exploded. "I guess he wants to *see* you!"

The eruption brought Beth back to reality, with a big loud bang! The feelings she'd been holding back began to bubble to the surface. Suddenly, she remembered what she seemed to have forgotten as they'd been talking.

"Stop it!" she shouted. "Just stop!"

"You know he's in love with you!" he shouted back at her.

"I know no such thing, and what do you care anyway!" she yelled and slammed the phone down.

It rang again and she let it go to the machine. "It's me, pick up."

She did, and told him, once again; "Go to hell," and hung up.

~ ~ ~

Over the months since Andy left Beth, Roddy's priorities changed. His relationship with Andy changed as well. It became increasingly strained. The respect and friendship that they shared in the past had changed, because Andy had changed. Roddy didn't like it. He made up his mind that he would be there for Beth no matter what she needed, because he loved her.

So, Roddy was making changes, making plans. He had been there for whatever Andy needed for years. He had traveled far more miles than he wanted. As Andy's career progressed, as the band grew, Roddy knew he needed to tend to his own needs. He wanted a life of his own.

On Wednesday evening, Roddy arrived around five with two bottles of wine; one red, and one white.

"Hello my friend! I am so happy to see you!" She hugged him tightly and took both bottles, "These will work fine, red with the meal and the white with dessert," and they shared a laugh.

"It's nice to hear that laugh," Roddy said.

She wondered all day whether to tell him that she had spoken with Andy, and what he told her, or wait to see what he had to say. She decided to wait. Roddy opened the wine and Beth got the glasses, while he sat down at the table.

"Want to sit in the living room, it'd be more comfortable?" she suggested, and he picked up the bottle and the glasses and they moved to the living room.

"You look great Beth," he said as he poured. *'Too thin,'* he thought.

"Thank you, I'm finally starting to feel like myself again," she told him.

"I'm here because I wanted to tell you that I quit working with Andy." He cut right to the chase.

"Quit," she repeated, sipping the wine.

"Yeah, somehow along the way, recently, I decided that it didn't feel right working with him anymore. I think it's been a long time coming. I just don't know where his head has been lately. I'm finally at a place in my life where I am really just ready to move on. I'm ready for a change. New adventures, you know. Opportunities are available."

"I see," she said. "I have wondered the same about Andy myself these past few months." She waited a moment and added; "He called last night."

"You spoke with him?" his surprise was clear and she nodded. "So you already knew?"

"Yeah."

"Well, I wanted you to hear it from me. At least it wasn't from *ET* or something. Seems it's all over the news, everyone's talking about it already. Word travels fast, but you know that," he said sadly, as he sipped his wine.

"I haven't had the TV on in months."

"The reports are that we had this blow up, that I stormed out, and quit. Just quit. It wasn't like that at all. I've thought about it, and thought about it. I just realized that I'd had enough, and told him I was moving on. It was as simple as that, no fight, no argument, no disagreement from me. Andy yelled. I didn't."

Beth asked, "What will you do?"

"I had an offer from the record label, and I decided to take it. It's a very positive move for me, no more private management. I'll still be involved with the guys, just not Andy solely. Less travel, fewer hours… I need a personal life, ya know?"

She was curious, now, where this conversation was going.

"Beth there's something else I want to tell you, something I've wanted to share for a while. I've been waiting for the right time," he rambled. "You're so special to me."

He leaned toward her as if he wanted to assure that she heard what he was about to say, it was something important. Andy's words repeated in her head, "He's in love with you…"

"Hold that thought," she said rising from the sofa. "Let's move to the dining room and talk there, our dinner should be ready," she suggested. Beth served the meal she had prepared and Roddy poured some more wine.

"I've wanted to tell you this for a very long time," he continued once they sat down for the meal. "I feel such a bond with you," he said so sweetly.

"What is it?"

"I told you that I needed a personal life."

She braced herself, again hearing Andy's words. "Yes?"

"I've met someone." He paused, and a sense of relief washed over her.

"He's a really great guy, his name is Vince."

"Oh my!" She tried to swallow the wine.

"You don't approve," Roddy said, sadly.

She had to laugh. Roddy's face expressed displeasure in her reaction. She held up a hand, "Wait, Roddy, wait," she said and regained her composure. "I am not laughing at you. I love you, I would never hurt you. It's just that, well, I'm laughing because when I spoke to Andy last night he told me you were in love with *me*."

"He what?" Roddy asked, shocked.

"He did. Last night I told him you were coming here."

Suddenly, Roddy was laughing. "I do love you, Beth, since the very first time I met you, but I'm not *in love* with you, I'm gay. I thought you knew, and I assumed that Andy did!"

It was an enjoyable evening spent with a good friend. They finished both bottles of wine as Roddy told her about his new partner. Beth realized that she was very glad for his company. It had been a long time since anyone but family had been there and longer since she had laughed. He left close to midnight with a promise to talk to her soon. After he left, she realized how blessed she was to have his friendship.

~ ~ ~

Roddy left, happy for the time they had shared. He missed her more than he really knew. He left with a revelation as well. As he drove, he thought about the last few months. He realized that the 'new, different Andy' he had experienced recently was the man who had evolved from his loss. He was so lost without Beth that he lashed out at those closest to him. He felt tremendous sadness when it hit him.

Andy made a mistake. But he was having a harder time living with it than Roddy realized until the evening he spent with Beth. It saddened him that Andy allowed himself to get to that place, sadder for Beth because she loved him so much.

CHAPTER THIRTEEN

Beth was sleeping soundly, and at 1:33 the phone rang. She didn't answer it, she knew who it was. She let the answering machine pick up. First she heard the piano and sat up hugging her knees to her chest to listen, and then she heard Andy's voice, singing.

Been to hell and back,
So sad, so true
You're not here
Gotta get to you

He sang until the tape ran out, and then the phone rang again.
"What?" she said as she lifted the receiver.
"How'd you know it was me?" he chuckled. "Did you like the song? It came to me last night after you hung up on me."
They talked for hours.

~ ~ ~

Beth had two days to get ready. Andy was coming on Friday evening. She needed to get her head straight, to think, and know her thoughts clearly. It had been months since she had seen him, and she was more nervous than the first time they were alone. She agreed to meet with him, to talk. They had to settle things, one way or another. They needed to do it. She didn't know where the conversation would go, but she knew it was right to do it. It was time to figure out what came next, or get it over with and really move on.

She told Kimmy that Andy was coming, but no one else. She wanted her to know. She knew Kimmy would get it when no one in her family would, and she did. She needed to work it out; on her own, with Andy. It was important enough to her to find out why it broke, and to *know* if there was any chance to salvage their relationship.

Her family was always very protective of her. It would have been hard for them to move past the hurt and pain that Beth had experienced. Andy and Beth talked about it and agreed that he would come to the condo. She didn't want to have to deal with anything, or anyone else. The whole situation was enough wonder and worry for her.

March 22, 1982 ~ As I waited, I paced, and paced, and paced. I was a nervous wreck, and as I planned and prepared for his arrival, it was more emotional planning, I didn't do anything special. This wasn't a social call, it was a meeting. I slipped on jeans and a t-shirt. I wasn't going to make a big deal of his visit in any way.

When I heard the knock I took a deep breath, and tried to find some kind of composure, some kind of strength to mask the nerves that were running rampant... I went to the door and saw Andy through the peephole. I pulled a nervous hand through my hair and repeated to myself; 'Breathe Beth, breathe...' I wiped anxious, sweaty palms on my jeans and opened the door.

"Hey," she said as casually as she could. He swept in and leaned to kiss her.

Just a kiss on the cheek', he thought, but she stepped aside. He came in with a full shopping bag and Beth wondered how on earth he could get into a market and shop unnoticed. Knowing that, she appreciated the gesture.

"Thanks for letting me come," he said to her as he started to unload the bag. First he removed a bundle of Beth's favorite Calla Lilies. She took them and found a vase as he continued to unpack the groceries; wine, cheese, crackers and fruit. He made himself at home, knowing where glasses were, cork screw, whatever he needed. He took the cheese and sliced some and put it on a plate with some grapes. Beth placed some crackers around the plate and took it to the living room and placed it on the coffee table. Still they did not talk.

Andy looked over his shoulder, to get a good look at her. She had lost too much weight, and it concerned him, but he said nothing. He poured them each some of the wine. "Merlot," he said as he handed her a glass.

'Not his favorite, Chenin Blanc; Merlot, my favorite,' Beth thought.

She thanked him, thinking he looked very tired. He'd pulled his hair in that ponytail that hung down his back, and he had on jeans and a tan pullover shirt. The color of the shirt only enhanced the color of his skin and eyes, making him look so beautiful to her that her heart skipped a beat. They moved from the kitchen to the living room. Andy chose his seat in the rocking chair, a safe place. That made it easier. There was still no conversation.

He leaned forward finally, elbows on his knees, arms crossed, head bowed. He didn't look at her, choosing instead, to focus on a spot on the floor that Beth couldn't see as he said; "I'm sorry, Bethy."

She sat and looked at him, quietly for a moment, then asked; "What for?"

He looked up. "I'm not sure," his eyes met hers and she noticed again a weariness that wasn't normal for him, that spark and vibrancy were missing. "I don't know what happened. Midlife crisis?" he added with a weak chuckle and half-smile.

"I think thirty-four might be a bit young to use that one," she said.

There was a long silence again, although his eyes never left hers, and finally he asked, "You OK?"

"Yeah," she replied too quickly, followed by a long pause. "I think I finally am. Trying to settle things in my mind, it has taken some time."

He got a cracker and some cheese, but it seemed he needed something in his hands more than his stomach. "I'm sorry," he said again. "Do you hate me?"

Beth thought a minute, took a sip of the wine, and hoped that the gesture would give her the courage to go on. "Not anymore," she told him. Again his eyes and hers met.

He laughed a tired, sad laugh, looking away, focusing again on that imaginary spot on the floor. After a moment he said; "So you did."

She sat the glass down, because she could feel her hands tremble. She looked at him, and replied, as calmly as she could, "Yeah, for a while, I did." She could feel her insides begin to quiver, but she couldn't let him know. *'Be strong Beth!'* She repeated it to herself over and over in her mind.

Andy rose and walked to the window, he stood there a while looking out. Then he went to the sofa where she sat. He didn't say anything; he just sat down there, beside her.

After a while he reached for her hand, but she jerked it away, crossing her arms across her chest as if it would keep her safe. "Bethy, I'm such an ass, can you forgive me?" he asked, it was almost a whisper.

There was a long pause before she responded, "I don't know Andy, it still hurts. A lot," she added softly.

The clock on the wall ticked away the minutes. It was a soft ticking sound, there were no words spoken. And then, Andy Stevens did something she had never seen him do. He leaned back into the sofa, laid his head back, and cried.

She wasn't sure how to react. His emotion was so real that she just let him cry. She wouldn't. No matter what, she would not cry, she couldn't. She couldn't show that weakness, couldn't let her guard down, or she would fall apart. It wasn't gut-wrenching sobs, just tears, and when his tears were gone he rose, went into the bathroom and washed his face. He came back and sat down. The room was quiet for a long time. Beth got up and poured them some more wine. She thought they both needed it, she knew she did.

"Thanks," he said finally, breaking the long silence. "I apologize. I think it's been a long time coming." Beth still said nothing. She felt incredibly numb. "I screwed up, in a big way, and I don't know if we can fix it. I hope we can." He looked at her, but she didn't acknowledge his comment, He wanted to reach out to her, he wanted to touch her, but he didn't want to push her. "Say something Bethy, please. Your silence is killing me."

But she was too afraid. "I don't know what to say Andy. I'm scared, terrified," she finally said.

"Me too."

"What the hell are you afraid of?" she asked, sharply, turning so that she was facing him. The tone of her own voice surprised her. There was a long quiet pause. Finally he looked, peered into her yes.

'Oh God, those eyes,' she thought, and had to look down.

"I'm afraid you think we're done, broken, and not worth another chance. I messed up. I let a good thing slip away because it scared me. We were good, really good, Bethy. It was comfortable and that scared me, and scared led to stupid. I panicked. I ran. I screwed up." He paused, maybe to get the courage to continue.

"When I saw Claire, ran into her in the bar that night, I don't know what happened. We had a drink. We talked. I knew being with her wouldn't be a good thing, it never was. It wouldn't be permanent. It was an escape. She used me, I used her." He stopped and looked away, ashamed. And then, "She was there and it was an easy out for me in a moment of panic."

Beth took time to process what he told her. "Why did you panic? Why did you feel the need to escape?" she asked, in that whisper of a voice. "You could have talked to me, you should have. I deserved that. What did you want? Did you *want* me to be mad at you? To scream, or yell…? Or did you just want to hurt me? What did you want?"

She got up, wine glass in hand, and paced, emotions she wasn't ready for erupted from inside. Andy sat quietly, waiting, and then suddenly, in a loud, sharp voice she asked; "What the hell did you want?" When he didn't answer, she asked again, louder; "What, Andy. What?" Still, he said nothing. "What do you want *now?*" she paused, trying unsuccessfully, to hold back the tears that had already started making their way down her cheeks. "Why are you here?" she asked, yelling now.

Finally he looked up at her, his eyes full of hurt and sadness, he said, "I want you…"

Three words. Plain and simple. That was all. *'I want you.'* She heard them again in her head, and she broke. It came in a maddening flood. She laughed a sarcastic laugh and said, "You want me?"

She sat the wine glass down abruptly, sending wine spilling over the rim, then reached for the zipper on her jeans, and jerked to lower it. She ripped the t-shirt over her head, flinging it his direction. She never wore a bra, so she was bare to him. He rose, silently, picked up the shirt and walked toward her as she started to shimmy out of the jeans.

"Stop, please," he said calmly.

Beth started to sob. She said she wouldn't, but she did. It was the wine. It was the time. It was all the months of pent-up emotions that she had never really let loose. He held the shirt to her bare chest.

"Put this back on," he said, tugging her jeans back up over her hips.

She shouted, as she was striking out, hitting his chest, but he held her close as she did. "Isn't this what you want?"

"No," he said quietly, "not at all."

Her body shook with sobs. She thought that she must have finally gone totally, completely mad. Andy pulled the shirt back over her head and she shoved him away. She went to the sofa, hurt, embarrassed and a million other emotions that overwhelmed her, and curled up and cried. Andy went to the kitchen and put the food away, put the cork back in the wine bottle and came back to where she was sitting.

She was crying so hard she could barely breathe. She lay with her face in her hands, sobbing. All those months that she wouldn't cry came in a flood. Saying nothing, he sat beside her and pulled her to him. With her head on his lap she cried until she finally fell asleep.

Later, when she awoke, the room was dark; the only light was the one over the stove. Andy had eased off the sofa and was sitting on the floor softly stroking her hair.

"Hey," he whispered.

"I'm sorry," she said.

There was a horrible throb in her head from crying. She sat up. He put his hand on her leg to stop her, rose and reached to the end table and handed her two aspirin and a glass of water. He sat down beside her but said nothing. After she took the aspirin, he turned her toward him and held her, and she remembered the feel of his arms around her, and again she cried.

'How could there be tears left?' She wondered, *'but there were and they came in a flood.'*

"How did we get here?" she mumbled, and then suddenly he pulled her into him. His lips were on hers and she said no more. He kissed her again, and again, and again. He kissed her eyes, her lips, her hair; he pulled her closer to him, and wrapped her in his arms. Finally, he pulled her to her feet and they went to the bedroom. They tumbled on the bed, but only slept. Beth wrapped in Andy's arms.

They spent the weekend cooped up, locked inside and talked and talked, and talked. For three days they talked, yelled, cried, and they made love. It went on like that until they finally worked it out. There wasn't much sleep. They covered a lot of territory in that time.

It was difficult, and as much as Beth didn't want to know, Andy told her everything about Claire and the short time he was with her. He decided that he needed to come completely clean. He told her why it didn't work before and why he went back, knowing it wouldn't work again. It was hard for them both. Harder for Beth, but she needed to hear it. She experienced so many emotions. In the end it was the best thing, a cleansing; a purging of sorts.

He explained to her that he felt like she needed more than he was ready to give. "Deserved more," he said. All Beth knew was she needed to be with him.

March 26, 1982 ~ Us. Andy and me. Me and Andy. I didn't need any more than that. I had never, in all the time we had been together, talked about commitment in the way of marriage or family. I only needed commitment from his heart to mine.

First, they called Roddy. He was happy for his friends. He'd hoped all along that they would figure it out and work through their troubles. He knew they were meant to be together from the beginning of their relationship. It pleased Phyllis when they called her. As long as they were happy together, she was happy. They did not call; they went to Beth's family to tell them. They weren't as pleased. Especially Pops, he worried, and he said so. He told Andy so. Beth told him about her heart, about her soul and that with Andy was where she wanted to be, needed to be. And finally, with much hesitation, he gave them his blessing.

Their hearts came back to each other, and they were a couple again. They fell into that familiar routine, and the days turned into weeks, and the weeks turned into months. They worked together to grow stronger. It became a comfortable life together, a comfortable routine. She was happy being with Andy. That was her life.

CHAPTER FOVRTEEN

Progression… Another year and it all continued at a crazy pace. The hype by the media over Andy's indiscretion, and then his reunion with Beth had finally died down and they were settling back into their life as a couple.

There was much anticipation over the release of the new album. The song, "To Hell and Back" was released, and topped the *BillBoard* charts. The sixth album also called *To Hell and Back*, was almost complete. It would be released in March. The record label was pressuring them to tour. Roddy, working for their record company now, worked very hard with all involved to keep the guys home for a while. They'd worked so hard for so long, one album after another for several years. They needed a break.

Roddy was still very much a part of the band, no longer just with Andy. It saddened Beth that they had yet to reconcile. She knew with time they would work out their differences. She still talked to Roddy almost daily, and he was there to support all the band's needs.

They were all burned out, resistant to tour. Mostly they were just ready for a break. It seemed they were all ready to settle down. They were getting older, finding different paths, likes, wants and needs. Not that there was dissension in any way; this was a good thing.

There were changes taking place personally for the guys. Relationships that became steady, and settling. Family that brought new life into their work lives.

Nathan was ready to stay home with Dina and spend more time with Megan. She was a busy girl, involved in many activities; these were important times in her life. Time had passed much too quickly, and Nathan was afraid he would miss something good. Megan was a beautiful girl with her mother's good looks, and Nathan's tall frame. She started acting in school plays. She had good genes and everyone saw a future for her in the industry.

With each day that passed Andy and Beth grew together. They settled into the routine that was their life together, and they were enjoying it. Beth continued to adjust to the life they shared because she loved him so much. Andy tried to make it as normal as possible but with the schedules the band kept it was still a circus at times. They were happy, and that was really all Beth needed.

She began doing volunteer work for the Cancer Foundation when she was home. It was something she became passionate about, a cause that meant something to her after Nana passed away. It kept her busy, mind and time, when she chose not to travel. Dina's advice to her stayed forefront in her mind. She tried to continue a life that meant something to her and not just get lost in Andy's. She learned she needed that diversion at times, other people, and an outside force. The fact that she was Andy Stevens' girlfriend was a plus - something positive for a change. Andy and the guys did a song called "From the Heart" for the album and it would be released as the next single. They were donating all proceeds from that to the Cancer Foundation in Nana's name.

After the album was complete Andy and Beth took a bit of a respite and traveled. It was fun travel, not touring travel for a change. They spent a week at the chalet in Colorado with Kimmy and Lane in February, and did some skiing. The 'Florida girl' was getting pretty good at it. She loved it there, and it was different this time; it was a nice couple's weekend. They ate popcorn, watched movies and played poker with beer bottle caps, can pull tabs, and wine corks saved from many previous trips. It was just fun. Usually that was a very hectic, busy place. Everyone wanted to come along to play, and while there was definitely room, it just wasn't relaxing like the cottage in Eleuthera. They both loved the island. It was peaceful and they could relax, there was no pressure to make someone else comfortable. On Eleuthera it was just them and Beth liked it that way the best.

~ ~ ~

Through the years Beth was lucky enough to experience many other bands and performers, because of *Traveler*'s connections: some they toured with, some they were able to sneak in a side trip to so they could be guests. And they were able to get to see them up close and personal. *Journey, Sammy Hagar, Bryan Adams, The Rolling Stones, The Police, Van Halen, Blondie*, all of Beth's favorites. It was very exciting; all of it.

Andy surprised her with a trip to Ireland – a real vacation. They stayed at Bed and Breakfasts, toured castles as well as day trips to see the lush green rolling hills and countryside. The big surprise was a visit to see their favorite group, *Thin Lizzy*, in Dublin. Andy met Phil Lynott, the group's lead singer, in 1976 and they stayed in touch. Phil invited them and Andy made the arrangements for their trip. Phil had VIP tickets for them. It was one of the perks of their lifestyle.

~ ~ ~

These were times filled with excitement. They were spending a lot of time in Corpus Christi, a couple of hours south of Galveston, on house-hunting excursions, looking at bigger homes on the water. Andy was in the process of selling the house in Galveston and Beth would move in once they found the right place. After six years they both decided it was time, they were ready.

Exciting too, was the wedding being planned for Lane and Kimmy. He proposed on New Year's Eve as the ball dropped. There would be a Christmas wedding next year.

But even more exciting, Andy received a nomination for an Academy Award. In January of the previous year Franklin Newman the writer and director of the movie, *Time Goes By*, approached him to write a song for his latest movie. Franklin was a huge *Traveler* fan and wanted to work with Andy.

The song was the title track for the movie. But this wasn't the group, not the *Traveler* guys. It was Andy, solo. This was a first for him. He was hesitant to go it alone because of his devotion to the guys. But after hearing what Andy came up with everyone agreed, that a lone piano with just Andy was definitely the way to go. It was a beautiful song.

The movie was a box office hit, and stayed at number one for many weeks, the highest grossing movie of the year. It was a beautiful story that took a young man through the awkward stages of youth, through falling in love and then finding out he had a rare terminal illness with no form of treatment. It was a major tear-jerker, and surprising that Franklin went with no-name stars, and it was still a blockbuster.

The movie cleaned up on nominations; Best Director, Best Actor, Supporting Actor, Best Actress, Best Screenplay, Best Picture, and Andy for Best Original Song. The song went to number one on *BillBoard* the second week they started playing it and stayed there for twelve weeks.

When they notified Andy of the nomination it was exciting. There had been talk that it would be, but the verification was pure elation, satisfaction. They would be going to Los Angeles in March for the big event. With the timing of the album's release it would be a business trip as well. Andy decided he'd take two dates, Phyllis and Beth. "A beautiful woman on each arm," he said.

January 26, 1984 ~ I listen and wonder how it couldn't be the winner? Andy's style with the song, his passion, focused on the emotion of the words rather than just singing them. You can feel the messages so strongly. He wrote it while we were apart and told me that was where those feelings came from.

~ ~ ~

"I love L.A. this time of year. There is so much excitement in the air," Beth told Phyllis as they were out shopping. The three of them went out a week early and were staying at the beautiful *Hotel Bel-Air.* The shopping excursion excited Phyllis, and she wore Beth out wanting to go places she'd never experienced. They had a great time looking for their dresses for the festivities, and finally found them at a small boutique on Rodeo Drive.

They went in to browse and Phyllis would pick out a dress, step into a dressing room to try it on, and then come out to model it. She would prance in front of the big triple mirror, and giggle like a girl. The sales assistants had fun with her, too. She ended up with a beautiful deep red gown. It had long sleeves and a bateau neckline. There would be no skin showing for Phyllis.

Beth found her dress at the same shop. It was royal blue, and something she really had to dare herself to even try on. She plucked it off a rack and was admiring it.

"Try it on," Phyllis encouraged.

"Oh, I don't know," Beth hesitated, biting her bottom lip, contemplating. "I think it's a little dramatic!"

"Well you won't know for sure if you don't try it on," Phyllis said. "Go on, just try it."

The sales assistant was urging her as well. "It really is a flattering style for you, and the color is perfect."

It had only one long sleeve, cut on an angle across the front to the sleeveless side, and cut very low in the back. It was daring...

She went in the dressing room and stepped into the dress. The zipper was in the side with no sleeve and as she zipped it up the dress hugged her body. She turned and looked in the mirror, and smiled. *'Andy will like this!'*

Phyllis and the sales assistant looked at each other as she stepped out of the dressing room. "You have to get that one!" Phyllis said. The sales assistant smiled and nodded.

She walked to the triple mirror and turned, admiring. Then she looked over her shoulder and said with a giggle; "Sold!"

April 7, 1984 ~I had to consult with the sales assistant on what went under the dress. It was so fitting, I needed to make sure I didn't ruin it by choosing the wrong thing, and end up on the cover of something!

On the day of the festivities Andy treated them to a trip to the spa for the works; hair, nails, and make up. Phyllis loved being so spoiled.

Back at their room, Beth waited until Phyllis dressed so that she could see Andy's reaction to his mom. She was in a robe, ready to the point of slipping into the dress, but she wanted Phyllis to have her moment. She made a grand entrance, and Andy made a big fuss. He went to her and slipped a necklace with rubies in white gold around her neck. It went perfect with her dress.

Then, Beth slipped back into the room to dress. She wanted to surprise Andy. It took only a few minutes and when she walked out Phyllis let out a faint gasp. Andy was speechless. He walked over to where she stood and held her at arm's length. Taking her hand, he made her pirouette so he could see the back. As she turned Phyllis had her hand to her mouth and then it was Beth who was speechless.

Andy had reached in his pocket and pulled out a beautiful, emerald cut sapphire necklace. He turned Beth toward the mirror and laid it against her neck, letting it drop down her chest so she could see. It was stunning with that daring dress.

April 10, 1984 ~ I could tell my choice pleased him. I was certainly pleased by his! It was like he read my mind and knew the color and neckline of the dress, or maybe I had read his!

"Bethy, I wish we were alone," he whispered in her ear as he hooked the necklace. He then turned her to face him and rubbed his hands down her arms to bring her hands to his lips. Then she really could read his mind...

She thought he looked so handsome in a tux, she knew Phyllis thought so, too.

They arrived by limo and walked the red carpet. Someone asked 'who' Beth was wearing. Stifling the urge to say something obnoxious like; "Off the rack at J.C. Penney", Beth made sure to know the name of the designer if someone asked, and she gave a shout-out to the boutique, as well, when a reporter did ask about her dress.

Phyllis' reaction to her surroundings brought back a flood of memories for Beth. As they walked, Andy kept his hand on Beth's bare back, lightly, softly, caressing her skin every once in a while. He *liked* that dress.

He got them to their seats and settled, then excused himself to visit with some of the other attendees. He left them after a few minutes to go get ready for his performance. He was singing the nominated song, "Time Goes By" for the opening of the show. Phyllis and Beth loved the performance. It was so beautiful. He was at a white grand piano that rose up out of the floor. A hazy, smoky fog surrounded him as he played. He'd changed into jeans and a long-sleeved white shirt, his hair pulled back in a ponytail. He called the song a "simple love song" and decided that anything else would have been too stuffy. He added a solo flutist to play with him and it was even more beautiful than the original version.

You wake up one day
And it's all slipped away
The dreams you had are passing
So much to say
Gimme one more day...

Beth saw tears running down Phyllis' cheeks as he sang. She reached and squeezed her hand. She'd moved into Andy's empty seat and a seat-filler was in hers.

"That's my baby," Phyllis whispered and laughed, squeezing Beth's hand harder.

It was emotional that Andy was up there for the accolades, but also that song. It got in your heart and soul and it was hard to keep from crying.

After he finished playing, the piano descended into the floor as thunder erupted through the auditorium. A short time later, Andy returned in his tux, back to his seat. He put his arm around Beth and squeezed as Phyllis took his hand, she was so proud.

Later in the evening Nina Peters, an actress from *Time Goes By,* came out to read the nominees.

"And the Oscar goes to…" She let out a whoop, and then yelled, "Time Goes By," written, performed and produced by Andy Stevens!"

He won.

Unlike when they were at the Grammys, he won. Andy sat quietly a few seconds, taking in the moment, before he rose. Leaning to kiss both women on the cheek, he left them to return to the stage. Nina greeted Andy with a hug and the roars of applause subsided as he began to speak.

"Wow! Wow! Wow!" he laughed. "What a great feeling!"

He paused, to catch his breath. "I don't know if I can put all of this emotion into words in my time allotted! I want to thank Franklin for believing in me and including me in such a beautiful project." He raised the statue pointing in Franklin's direction.

"Nathan, man!" He laughed, "Thanks for helping me finish put the thoughts into words, and dreams into music. I need to thank the *Traveler* guys and their families for allowing me to live this dream. I would truly be nothing without them."

"Mom, thank you. You're the one who gave me the wings, and believed in my flight."

He paused, looking out to Beth and took a deep breath. "My Bethy, thank you. Your endless love was the inspiration for the song." Then he blew a kiss her direction.

The movie cleaned up, winning the award for each nomination. It was exciting. They took Phyllis to one of the parties and sat with

Franklin and the cast from the film. It was fun to take it all in and see all that was going on around them. Phyllis was like a child, glancing this way and that to catch a glimpse of someone "famous".

They stayed at the party a while, but made it an early evening, the excitement was overwhelming, all the attention, but exciting as well. They had a suite with two bedrooms and a common area. After a bit of conversation Phyllis excused herself and went to bed. Andy and Beth sat up for a while, sharing a glass of wine, talking, and admiring that statue.

Finally Andy couldn't take it any longer. He took Beth's hand and led her to their room.

"Just stand there and let me look at you," he said. He wrapped her in his arms and in a quiet voice he said, "I've been wondering something all evening..." he kissed her neck.

Beth smiled. She knew what he was 'wondering'. "About this?" she asked and pushed his shoulders down, so that he was sitting in front of her on the edge of the bed. She slid the zipper down on the side of the dress allowing it to slide to the floor.

Andy's breath caught in his throat, "Bethy," he growled.

"I had to make sure there were no lines showing, anywhere," she purred as she moved closer. "All those gossip rags and photographers, just lurking, waiting..." she continued as Andy held his breath.

"Couldn't have a photo of me with one of *those* captions saying something rude about my choice of attire for the evening," she continued. "The gal at the boutique who helped me with the dress suggested this was a way to avoid that," she flashed a seductive smile his way.

Andy liked what he saw. He rose and grabbed her naked body and pulled her into his arms. Kissing her, they fell to the bed.

The next morning there was a picture of Franklin and Andy on the front of one of the newspapers with a headline that read: "Golden Eye and Oscar's Golden Boy!"

~ ~ ~

June came along and Roddy's work to convince the "powers that be" that a tour wasn't necessary to sell albums worked. The new album was successful. It was already selling great, and Andy's Oscar win enhanced the popularity even more. The song, "Time Goes By" that had already come off the *Billboard Hot 100* by Oscar time was back in the top ten.

In July Andy's house in Galveston sold, and all of his things went to storage in Corpus Christi. Everything was falling into place for the move to a new house. After much searching they found a beautiful waterfront home on eight acres on the bay about a hundred miles south-west of Galveston. It was exactly what they'd been searching for; two stories, nine thousand square feet, with a huge marble entryway, and an elegant circular, open-arm staircase. The back of the house looked out to the bay and was all windows or glass doors; it was entirely open, with a beautiful view. There were seven bedrooms, eight bathrooms, and the biggest kitchen Beth had ever seen.

There was a separate, detached, two-story, four-car garage that would be renovated for use as a recording studio and theatre. The studio was a given, but the theatre would be upstairs and was an added bonus. Everyone missed being able to catch a movie once in a while, so this would give them all an opportunity to enjoy some leisure time. The studio wouldn't be complete for four or five months.

There was a pool and a pool house. The dwelling they called the 'pool house' was so big that they convinced Tom, Needa and their eleven year old son, Drew, to move in. Andy and Beth were looking forward to them being close.

A couple from Sweden had the house built as their retirement home. They lived there only a short time, deciding to retire to the Caribbean instead.

There were some minor interior changes they wanted, paint, tile, new carpet, and then they would move in. It was easier to do all that while the house was empty. Until it was ready they were nomads, even more than was normal for them. They stayed at Phyllis's or the condo in Florida, and lived out of suitcases. They would leave the condo livable so they could stay there when they were in Florida.

CHAPTER FIFTEEN

October 1984, was a busy month for everyone. The guys appeared on *Austin City Limits* for *PBS,* at the beginning of the month. The group made a weekend trip of it. Because Nigel and Christy's baby was due at any time, she was the only one missing. Before fans recognized them and it got wild, they were all tourists for a day seeing the sights in Austin.

Nigel made it home just in time. Christy went into labor early and Mark Andrew Rose joined the world at almost eleven pounds, and not quite two feet long. He was so big Nigel joked that he came out wearing running shoes, with a cocktail in his hand.

Roddy and Andy finally made peace, and it was a blessing. It took a while. First, there was bitterness after their work break-up, then Andy's discomfort with the fact that Roddy was gay. But eventually, their friendship over-rode both and Roddy and Vince became frequent guests. Vince was a chef, and would come to the kitchen and take over. He learned Andy's favorite dishes and made them when he came. That was all it took, Andy warmed up to him quickly. Beth loved them being there. Vince made sure the kitchen had all the things a 'working kitchen' needed.

The house was beautiful and elegant, but it was also homey and comfortable. Andy and Beth loved being there and not on the road someplace. Beth loved nesting and decorating. Of all the rooms, they loved their bedroom the most. Andy left the decorating of the house pretty much up to Beth, but they shopped together for their bedroom, and he ended up being very involved in the choices. The room was huge. One wall was all glass doors, floor to ceiling, wall to wall. They faced the bay, so it was very light. Blinds were installed to retract into a false wall, added so they could be closed if they wanted, but the view was not blocked in any way if they didn't.

After much shopping and looking they decided on white washed pine furniture that went beautifully with the light sage green they had chosen for the walls and the darker shade green bed covers. Andy chose a small round table in deep mahogany with two upholstered chairs in a deep peach color to sit by the glass doors that overlooked the Gulf. Most mornings, he sat there to enjoy his coffee, and he did enjoy his coffee. All of the artwork was from the artist in Eleuthera. She painted bright-colored floral prints for them that Andy had shipped over. A piece of Eleuthera was with them all the time.

> *October 19, 1984 ~ It was cool the first night we slept in our beautiful new room. We opened the doors to hear the sounds. Snuggling in that big king sized bed was the most glorious feeling. Our bed... Our home... Andy got up sometime in the middle of the night and put the Nana quilt over us.*

Andy insisted on security but made sure they were obscure. They were there to patrol the grounds. The band got to a point where it was necessary for safety. There was a big fence around the perimeter of the property, but it was beautiful, not like a prison. Andy suggested that they hire a staff to help keep up what he called, 'the palace.' Beth would only agree to the grounds.

Living in the pool house, Tom and Needa were close if Andy and Beth needed them. They also had their own rooms at the house to stay in when Andy and Beth were away, to make sure everything stayed in order. When they were home Beth didn't want *anyone* there. It seemed to her that they were hardly planted anywhere for very long, so she figured she could manage that. Help could come in when needed, special occasions and such. She just didn't want anyone right there on a full-time basis. Part of it was the *privacy* issue, but the selfish part of her wanted Andy all to herself.

~ ~ ~

In November 1984, everyone went to Corpus Christi for Thanksgiving, and it was a big celebration. Beth decided to cook, but Vince and her mom were right there in the middle of it with her. She knew there was no way they would be able to stay out of that kitchen. She would tell them to go away, but was just as happy to have them there to help. There were eighteen people there, and they all stayed at the house.

They decided to have a large Thanksgiving because Christmas would be quick and busy. Kimmy and Lane would be married on Christmas Eve and Beth was the maid of honor. She'd been going back and forth to Florida to help with the plans for weeks. She'd be going to the condo two weeks before to help Kimmy with last-minute stuff. Andy would meet her there. All the guys, wives, and dates, would be attending.

It would be a beautiful wedding. Andy was singing a song for them that he wrote. No one knew but Kimmy and Lane. They didn't want to take a chance on nosey gawkers ruining the wedding. They'd already made arrangements for security.

The weeks preceding held a bridal shower, shopping for decorations and gifts for Christmas; it was hectic. There wouldn't be a Christmas tree in Corpus Christi because they would be at the condo in Florida. Beth's mom surprised them with a small tree there.

~ ~ ~

Another new year... Christmas was a whirlwind. With the wedding on Christmas Eve the time went quickly. It was beautiful. The church was already decorated with both red and white poinsettias for the holidays. It was an early evening ceremony and Kimmy chose only candlelight to light the chapel. Candles lined the aisle, each attended by the ushers. It was simple, but so full of love. Beth was the only bridesmaid. Lane's dad was his best man and he had four ushers. This was the first wedding Beth had ever been to where there were more groomsmen than bridesmaids, but that was Kimmy, nothing ordinary for her.

Kimmy was a gorgeous bride. Her dress was a faint pink organza with pearl beads adorning the bodice. Being tall and thin she could have worn any style dress. She chose one that was straight and fitted to the bottom where it flared out dramatically. With her blonde hair, she looked like a white mermaid. She wore her hair up with pearls woven into it. Her borrowed item was the pearl necklace that had been Nana's. It was a perfect choice. She carried a small white Bible, from her first communion decorated with a pink satin ribbon with silk Lily of the Valley instead of a bouquet.

Beth's dress was a deep red satin, straight-sheath, almost wine colored. It was very plain, but very elegant. She wore a beautiful ruby necklace and earrings that Andy had given her as an early Christmas present, and carried white roses.

Andy's song, "Love Will Live" – Kimmy and Lane's Song, was a beautiful gift for them. It would be included on the next album.

The reception was a huge party! Vince helped Kimmy with all the catering. There was plenty of food and drink, and they were still at it when Santa arrived, and he did arrive. Kimmy's dad made arrangements for the fat man in the red suit to arrive at midnight. The idea was to help round things up and get everyone headed home, but it backfired. Santa brought gifts for everyone and ended up partying with them until the wee hours of the morning. Andy was in on it, and Santa gave Beth a box to open that contained a ruby ring to match the necklace and earrings he had given her.

After the wedding and Christmas festivities Andy and Beth went to Colorado for a few days. It was fun, but they were never alone there. A few days later they made a special trip to the cottage in Eleuthera to relax. The best of both worlds - get in some skiing and come home with a little tan.

Beth was more in love with Andy than ever.

Life is good… so very good!

~ ~ ~

Music videos had become the big thing. The guys started taping videos for their songs for *MTV*. It was exciting and fun to watch them put a story to their music. Some of the videos were live recordings from their concerts. They liked those best. For some they actually filmed short, mini-movies to depict the story the song told. They hated those, but the times were changing and they had to keep up.

They were ramping up to get in the studio again to start recording. Andy said they all got kinda "itchy" to get started. Nathan called one evening and told Andy he was ready. He said he had a tune in his head that he couldn't shake. So Nathan and Dina came to Corpus Christi. Nathan and Andy got it all rolling again. They must have had enough of a respite. Andy always said when they got music in their heads they needed to let it out.

Beth looked forward to them being there, especially Dina. Nathan was hardly in the door when it started.

'Watching them start the writing process is really beautiful to experience,' Beth thought as she looked on. They were all in the living room; Nathan picked up a guitar and played a melody. He played it once, and then Andy took the guitar and played it back with a little different spin. Nathan got another guitar and they played it together, only differently and a beautiful musical thought was born. They sat at the coffee table with a bottle of wine and kept playing, adding lyrics.

> *January 29, 1985 ~ I swear I could see the wheels turning in their heads. Nathan would hum and mumble, jot something down on paper. Andy would look at it, think a minute then go through the same process, make some changes on the paper, and then they would play through it again together.*

That night, "One for the Road" became the first song they wrote for what would be their next album. That song led to another, and another, and another.

~ ~ ~

By June with the songs written, it began. The studio was complete, and the guys were there sixteen and eighteen hours at a time laying down tracks. It was crazy and exhausting. Beth was happy they were home, and loved the guys being there in the studio. Her mission was to keep them fed, making sandwiches and casseroles for their meals, and baking cookies. She wondered sometimes, if she didn't feed them, if they would remember to eat at all.

Beth loved that she could be a domestic goddess for a while. Dina and Megan came out a couple of weekends to hang out while the recording was taking place. Christy, Little Mark, and Anna came, too. Beth loved her extended family being there. They lounged by the pool for hours. Not only was she a domestic goddess; Beth was turning into a bronze goddess as well.

Andy and Nathan formed their own production company, *Catch the Wind,* and Roddy left the record label to come back to them as manager of the company. Beth knew that Andy was glad to have him back, not that he ever really went away. He still worked with *Traveler* those two years just in a different capacity. He and Vince relocated to the Corpus Christi area, too. Having her good friend so close made Beth happy.

One For The Road would be the title of the album, for all the fans, the people who come to see them. *Jimmy Buffett* had *Parrot Heads,* *The Grateful Dead* had *Dead Heads,* and *Traveler* had *Road Heads.* They traveled in packs all over the country to get to concerts. Sometimes they would see the same fans over and over.

This new stuff was different and the guys were anxious. Beth loved it. She loved to sit in on the recordings, and did a lot. She felt like part of the process being there in the middle of it.

The *Traveler* guys worked so well together, 'like a well-oiled machine', and they were funny, especially when it started to get late. Andy's comfy recording clothes were always wild pajama pants, a sweatshirt and a beanie cap. They kept it very cold in the studio so that it was comfortable for them. The later in the evening it got the more humorous they became, 'punchy' was probably a better word. They loved to play practical jokes on each other. At one point Mark put a headset on and Nigel had smeared peanut butter around the inside of the ear cups. There was always a jar of peanut butter close by. They lived on 'peanut butter spoons' for energy. And they always made it a good time.

If they even made it to the house, they would shower, and then drop wherever there was a place to sleep, exhausted. Most mornings Beth would wake to find Andy sprawled all over their bed, wander around, and find the guys sleeping all over the place, on sofas, in the guest rooms; wherever they ran out of steam. The first one of them awake got everyone else up and got two pots of coffee going. Then they ate whatever was available, so Beth made sure there was always plenty available. Sometimes a bath was a lap in the pool and then they would head right back to the studio.

~ ~ ~

July 13, 1985, was Beth's thirtieth birthday and Andy had a surprise party planned. That morning the guys were in the studio early. Beth brought coffee and cinnamon rolls out for them.

Andy grabbed her in a hug and said, "Guys, I know it's short notice, but we're gonna give it a rest today," he told them. "I just decided that I'm taking my girl out for dinner. Dress fancy, Bethy," he told her, nuzzling her neck.

The idea of an evening alone with Andy excited her, there had been few lately. With all the hours they'd been putting in on the album, she missed their alone time. She chose a short, sassy, red cocktail dress that she'd bought on a recent trip home to Florida to visit her family, and Kimmy.

"Aren't you handsome," she cooed seeing him dressed in a suit, waiting for her.

"And you, my love, are dazzling," he whispered in her ear, leaving a blaze of warm kisses on her neck.

"Where are you taking me?" she asked, pushing him away, or she wouldn't want to leave.

"It's a surprise," he said and pulled her back into his embrace. "Come on," he said taking her hand in his.

Nathan let out a wolf whistle as Beth emerged to tell them all 'bye'. The guys were going crazy with pent-up energy in the pool.

Andy had finally bought the 'rock-star car', a Jaguar convertible that Beth joked about over the years when they would drive his old truck. As they drove away the guys all yelled "Happy Birthday!"

"Top up or down?"

"You *are* referring to the car, right?" she asked and Andy roared with laughter. It was warm, but she told him, "Down, definitely down!"

They drove along quietly, Andy holding her hand in his lap. He finally pulled into the parking lot of Andelini's, a quaint little Italian restaurant about fifteen miles away on the water. Beth knew she had picked well on the dress, and smiled.

The maître d' led them to a romantic, circular booth in the corner, and snuggled in. Andy ordered a bottle of Chianti, and escargot. Andelini's was famous for their Traveling Minstrels and Flower Lady. No one dined there without a serenade and the purchase of a bouquet of flowers. It was one of Beth's favorite places.

Andy poured them each some of the wine, and took Beth's hand as the Flower Lady appeared. She dressed in character, like an old world farm woman, big brimmed straw hat, apron, and a big basket of flowers. There were bouquets of pink roses, red roses, Calla Lilies, and daisies in her basket. Andy chose the Calla Lilies and she presented them to Beth with grand flair. Beth knew that he'd requested them, they were not a flower that was usually present in her baskets, and she smiled at his thoughtfulness.

When she left them Andy brought Beth's hand to his lips; "Have I told you that you are beautiful for an old woman of thirty?"

"Yes, but you can tell me again, I can't hear it enough," she laughed.

He pulled her closer and slid his hand up her back, to whisper in her ear, "You are so beautiful. My Bethy..." He brought her lips to his, and said, "Happy Birthday, my love."

The escargot arrived and they enjoyed it with the wine. One of the minstrels came over and began to play. They roamed throughout the restaurant, playing. As they approached their table, Beth settled back to listen; the music was very pleasant.

They lingered over the meal and shared wonderful conversation. Beth noticed that the dining room was pretty much empty, she didn't think twice about it because it was a Wednesday evening. The waiter came and asked if they would like dessert, explaining that the selections were available on a dessert bar in an adjoining room. Andy took her hand in his as the waiter led them.

"I don't need dessert, but they make the best tiramisu, so maybe a small piece," she told Andy.

When they entered the room everyone yelled, "Surprise!"

Beth looked around; Mom and Pops, Phyllis, Kimmy and Lane were there. Dina and Nathan, Vince and Roddy, all the *Traveler* guys and their families were there, too. There were balloons and gifts, and Vince made her favorite carrot cake. She loved that they were all there, dressed up and enjoying her special day.

Andy worked it out with Vince, who'd become good friends with the Andelini's. He and Roddy made all the arrangements for everyone to come in town, and more of a surprise for Beth, they were all staying at the house.

'*So much for being alone with Andy,*' she thought.

Beth opened gifts from everyone but Andy. He disappeared for a few minutes. When he returned he had a big box, about three feet square, and Beth tore into it. She learned early in their relationship not to be dainty opening gifts when Andy was around. Inside was another wrapped box, and she laughed at the box inside the box. Shooting a look in Andy's direction, he shrugged his shoulders and laughed. Again she ripped paper, only to find another box inside. Now, everyone was laughing. She tore into the third box to find yet another, and started flinging paper everywhere. As she ripped the paper from the last box she found a small gift box. She lifted the lid expecting to find a piece of jewelry, but inside was a key. Puzzled, she looked to Andy.

He walked over to her, took her hand and led her to the door. When he opened it there was a red Mercedes 380SL convertible parked sideways with a big gold bow on top. She was so excited, and she drove them home in her new little car with the top down. When they got back to the house the partying continued until the wee hours of the morning. It was a special evening with all of her favorite people.

CHAPTER SIXTEEN

July 31, 1985 ~ It took seven weeks with a couple of weekend breaks for the guys to go home, but recording was complete, eighteen songs, DONE! Next comes the culling, mixing, sweetening, and engineering to get it just right. After that... my favorite part, choose twelve or thirteen songs for the album.

Things settled down a bit, and Beth and Andy were getting back to normal, whatever that was in their crazy lifestyle. They hoped to release the album in time for Christmas sales. It would be a push, but Roddy was working with marketing to get it in the works. The title track, "One for the Road" would be released in a few weeks.

You are there in the darkness,
Always there,
You are the lights in a sea of black,
This one's for you
For all the nights you were there,
This one's for you

~ ~ ~

By late September, "One for the Road" had made the top ten, where it stayed for several weeks. They released "Love Will Live", Kimmy and Lane's wedding song, as the flip side. Proceeds would go to Kimmy and Lane's favorite charity. Anticipation over the new album was growing.

The guys said this would be the last album for a year or two, they were burned out, and they were firm, no tour. They had been going fast and furious for more than a decade and they just wanted a break.

Nathan was taking Dina and Megan to New York City to work with Susan Marshall on a musical. It was the story of a rock and roll group and their life touring that he'd let simmer on the back burner for some time. He'd worked with Susan to tweak it, and they were just about ready.

Mark and Anna were settling into a new home in Kemah and wanted to enjoy it for a while. Maybe there would be another *Traveler* baby on the way soon.

Both Scott Force and Dane Allen met with the guys and they were discussing a reunion album. Everyone believed it would come together, just not soon. The old and new members were game; the idea just needed time to stew a while. It was good they are talking again, especially Andy and Scott.

~ ~ ~

Beth and Andy were ready to open the doors to their home. They planned an album release party for late October. As preparations began, Beth allowed Vince to take charge.

Following that would be Christmas with a big celebration in Corpus Christi as well. Beth and Vince had their heads together planning and shopping for both for weeks. Together, they were in their glory.

November 9, 1985 ~ The album party was perfect! There were over one hundred and fifty in attendance. There were tents outside for the spillover. Both Dane and Scott were there so maybe that reunion will take place sooner than expected. Guests included record executives, and promoters that the guys have worked with over the years. DJs and local dignitaries from Corpus Christie, Houston and Galveston joined us, and Phyllis came for the weekend, too. The morning host of "Good Morning Houston", Kathy Rose, Andy, Nathan and Dina all went to high school together so we invited her to come and she brought a small crew to tape some stuff for her morning show. It was fun, but I have to admit… Dina being there and having a personal relationship with Kathy helped make it more comfortable.

Almost as soon as the guests were out the door, Vince kicked into gear planning the Christmas celebration. He was a lifesaver, as Beth vowed to never again plan back-to-back gatherings.

Beth was taking a few days to go home to Florida for Thanksgiving while Andy and the guys hit the road for two weeks of TV and radio, to promote the album's release. Kimmy was hosting Thanksgiving dinner and Andy would be flying in just in time to sit down for the bird.

~ ~ ~

The house looked like a picture in a magazine with the Christmas decorating that Beth and Vince had tackled. Vince found a twelve-foot blue spruce and placed it in the center of the foyer with all white lights. Beth decorated it with hand-made ornaments. Some were very special treasures from Nana's collection, ornaments filled with memories that Pappy had given her. Some were ornaments that she found in their travels at craft fairs and festivals when she was able to sneak off, with security close behind.

Many friends and family came in for the festivities. Some were friends from the band's bar days when they were just getting started. Having them there was the guy's way of saying thanks for helping them get started.

Andy gave Beth a beautiful pair of topaz earrings for her gift. They were very different, very unique. *'They look just like Andy's eyes,'* she thought.

~ ~ ~

A new year arrived, once more and their lives continued to move forward on a busy path. In early February, Andy had a business trip planned to go to Los Angeles for few days to work out some appearances that the guys agreed to, and Dina was coming to spend a few days with Beth for some girl-time and shopping.

~ ~ ~

February 12, 1986 ~ Janice Joplin sang, "Take another little piece of my heart…" and once again, I feel like I'm living it. I feel my heart breaking one more time.

Andy left on Thursday for L.A., Dina came on Friday and stayed through Wednesday. They shared a wonderful weekend of shopping and chatter. Beth had a routine doctor's appointment Friday afternoon, and was sitting in the waiting area flipping through the *People* magazine that just came out that day. She leafed through the pages, and as she turned one more page she saw it…

Whoosh… It felt as though it sucked the life from her body. Quickly, she got up and left, feeling like she couldn't catch her breath. She got in her car and drove, not really even knowing what direction she was going. It seemed she drove for hours, and a million miles before she stopped. She pulled into a *Holiday Inn* and stopped the car. She sat there for a while looking around, trying to get her bearings. Finally, she got out of the car and checked in. She went to the room to lie down, and stretched across the bed, knowing that at any moment her head would explode.

She found the magazine in her purse. She must have walked out of the doctor's office with it. She opened it again, and a flood of tears came as she flipped through the first couple of pages. Andy had been in L.A. for a week. He asked Beth to join him, but she had things she wanted to do, and some things she needed to take care of. Mostly, she looked forward to the girl time with Dina.

What the hell? I asked myself that question over and over as I looked at the picture again. It was Claire Ferguson and Andy with a caption that read:

> *"Claire Ferguson and Andy Stevens leaving The Lagoon Bistro in L.A."*

After a while, she picked up the phone and dialed. "Roddy, it's me," she said when he answered.

"Where in the hell are you?" he yelled quick, and frantic, "I've been worried sick!"

It was dark, she glanced at the clock; it read 9:02. "Not sure really, I just drove and when I got tired I stopped," she mumbled.

"Tell me where, I'll be there as quick as I can. The doctor's office called, said you signed in for your appointment, but when they called you back you weren't there and they couldn't reach you! What happened? Why'd you leave?" Roddy was yelling all these things at her.

She didn't reply and he began again; "I've been calling the house all day and there's no answer. Needa told me she hadn't seen or heard from you since this morning. Andy called me when he couldn't reach you, he's worried to death. When I talked to the woman at the doctor's office I thought maybe you'd been kidnapped or something! I didn't know what to do, or think!"

"Had to go, Roddy; had to get out of there, fast, couldn't breathe," she said, and the mumbling continued. "Didn't want to talk," she said in broken sentences.

"What? What happened?"

"Seen the newest *People*? It just came out today, page six, bottom left corner... It's a small picture, but it's there, plain as day," she rambled on.

"No! What is small? What are you talking about?" he asked, panic in his voice.

"The picture of Andy and Claire."

"What picture, Beth?"

"The one taken in L.A. this week of them leaving a restaurant."

"What?"

"There's a picture of them Roddy," she said and the tears came in a mad rush.

"Tell me where you are!" he was shouting.

"No. Not now, I need to rest, I'm tired. I'll call you in the morning. I promise. I just need some sleep. I'm just so tired," she said again and hung up. She already felt worn out, but Roddy's questions wore her down. She knew she didn't have that kind of energy.

She didn't sleep. She tried to watch TV for a while, but kept picking up that damn magazine, staring at the picture.

What? When?' I knew the 'who' and 'where' to that list of questions, but why, why, why?

Finally, she did doze off. When she woke in the morning she went down to the front desk, picked up a toothbrush and toothpaste, grabbed a cup of coffee and went back to the room. She showered and put the same clothes back on. She grabbed her things to go check out; when she opened the door Roddy was standing there.

"Thank God," he said grabbing her.

"Roddy. How'd you find me?" she asked him as he hurried her back into the room.

"I had security trace your credit card." He wrapped her in his arms. "Beth, it's not what you think."

"Oh Roddy, it never is, is it? I'm tired." She sat down on the edge of the bed as he paced. "I live each day waiting to see those pictures, waiting to get those phone calls, waiting to see it on TV and I'm just so damned tired. I thought I was past that, but I'm not. I tried to be, I really did. I want to be, but I'm always waiting and wondering."

"Beth, I talked to Andy last night. I called him after I spoke with you and asked him what in the hell was going on." Roddy sat down beside her, draping a loving arm around her shoulder.

"He met Tedd Marcus at the Bistro, and ran into Claire and Tony. They were having dinner and stopped by to tell Andy they are expecting a baby. What that picture didn't show, didn't tell, was that Tony was there too. The magazine conveniently cropped Tony out of the picture. They've reconciled and Andy saw them at the restaurant and stayed after the meeting to congratulate them."

She sat, quietly staring at him. She heard the words, but somehow it didn't change the way she felt. Still the tabloid crap, lack of privacy, and yes, that insecurity she allowed to keep her from feeling secure. She didn't say anything; she couldn't, so she listened.

"Andy took the first flight he could get this morning. We're picking him up at the airport. Come on." He reached for her hand.

"No, you go on. I need to drive home. I need time. I need to think."

"Come on. I'll get your car back. Go with me."

"No," Beth said firmly.

She got her purse and car keys. "No," she said once more, "I'll see you both at the house. I need to get cleaned up. I didn't have clean clothes to put on when I showered. I want to go home. I'll be there when you get there."

Reluctantly he left her.

She drove with the windows open, no radio on, and allowed her mind to race. It was cool, and the wind whipping through the car invigorated her. She was only about two hours away from home, but it seemed so much further. When she got there she showered again and was ready for Andy and Roddy when they arrived.

Andy rushed through the door and grabbed her. The force of him frightened her, not that he would intentionally hurt her, just that he might break her with the might with which he grabbed her.

"I'm sorry," she said, and tried to back away, "sorry that I worried everyone, sorry that I jumped to conclusions."

Andy didn't say anything, but he didn't let her go, either. He just held her, as if he was afraid to let her go. It was just after two in the afternoon. Roddy left them and headed toward the kitchen. Finally Andy let go and kissed her forehead.

"I'm the one who's sorry," he said. "I should have told you that I ran into them so that if something like this did happen you'd be prepared. I got busy and didn't think a thing about it. I talked to you yesterday morning before your doctor appointment."

"You talked to me the night before you left for Europe with her too, Andy." She reminded him, fighting the tears.

"OK, I deserved that," he said sadly.

"I just..." and the tears came in a flood.

Roddy came back into the room, it was a beautiful day. He opened the glass doors, and a bottle of wine, poured, and handed them both a glass. A light breeze was blowing and it was refreshing. She needed the air.

"I'll go and give you some time," Roddy said. He went to Beth, gently placing his hand on her cheek. It was a comforting gesture. Then he kissed the top of her head and left them.

They sat in silence for a long time, neither knowing what to say. Finally Andy pulled her into his arms. "Bethy, what can I do to make this easier for you?"

"I don't know, Andy, really, I don't know. I always feel like I'm waiting."

"Waiting for what sweetheart?" he asked sadly, hurting for her.

"To wake up and find this was all a dream, for you to not be there anymore, for the bottom to fall out, again," she said, sadly.

He stroked her hair and held her. They finished the wine, walked up the stairs arm in arm to their bedroom, and did what they did best.

Another 'silly misunderstanding' in the end, but I knew it was my insecurity, always my insecurity.

~ ~ ~

Spring arrived and brought a trip to Eleuthera. It was a short trip to celebrate Edwina's life. She passed away peacefully in her sleep at eighty-four years young. They were both very sad to lose her. Over the years she became a good friend to Andy, and then to Beth. She was part of their extended family, and they loved her. The service was a beautiful celebration, not mourning. There was singing and food and laughter.

Beth thought about the service, '*I hope and pray when my time comes it's like that.*'

Eleuthera was alive with spring color. The Bougainvillea was ablaze in shades of pink and fuchsia, a fitting tribute for their loving friend. Her daughter Shirley agreed to assume the care of the cottage, which they both knew meant caring for them as well. It just seemed right to ask her, and she seemed pleased that they did.

They stayed to relax for a few days. Beth pulled a lounge chair into the sun, relaxed and baked — it was warm, not yet hot, and it felt wonderful to her. Andy kept an electric keyboard there and worked on music. Beth loved it there, they were completely alone, and it was nice. It was quiet and she loved those quiet times with Andy the best.

April 21, 1986 ~ Sometimes I wish we could just stay right here on the island forever. The morning walks on the beach are so peaceful, so calming, I never want to leave once we are here.

~ ~ ~

The next months were quiet, calm down-time. There were no albums, no tours, no travel, and no guests. It was just Andy and Beth settling in at home, enjoying the peace and quiet.

August 8, 1986 ~ It's so rare, kind of like Tiramisu, one of my favorite desserts. When I get it, I love it, but I don't have it near enough!

Beth relished every moment, and wished it could just stay that way, but she knew that the life Andy chose would call soon and they would roll back into the crazy chaos that they had lived together for the last eight and a half years.

'Really, has it been that long?' she wondered. There were times it seemed like it was just yesterday, and times it seemed a lifetime had passed; and suddenly, there were times when she wondered if it would always be that way.

~ ~ ~

On Saint Patrick's Day, Beth woke to a room bright with sunlight. The blinds and the glass doors were open, allowing the light in. The smell of fresh coffee and the sweet, salty smell of the bay filled the room as a light breeze blew.

She turned to find Andy stretched out beside her, propped up on his elbow. She stretched lazily, and then sat up and pushed the hair from her face and the sleep from her eyes.

"What'cha doin'? she asked. Looking around, she saw the carafe of coffee on the table beside a vase filled with Calla Lilies. The coffee was usually there if Andy woke first, but the flowers were a surprise.

"Watching you... Do you know how beautiful those eyes are when they first open but are still full of sleep?" He pushed hair back from her face with a soft caress. It was a comforting, familiar gesture, and she curled into him as he wrapped her in his arms. They lay like that just a moment and finally, Andy rose and went to get the coffee. He fixed Beth's exactly the way she liked it; sweet with too much cream, and carried the tray back to the bed. He was wearing a t-shirt that said; 'Wanna get lucky?' Beth laughed, and eyed a gold box on the tray.

"Top'o' the mornin' to ya me lass!" he said with a big grin.

"And to you" she replied looking over the top of the coffee cup as she sipped, and waited.

"I come'a bringin' the blarney stone for ye to kiss!" he said and handed her the box.

"Blarney stone?" she laughed and sat the cup down. When she opened the unwrapped box, she gasped. It was an emerald cut emerald ring with diamond baguettes. It was breath-taking.

"Happy St. Paddy's Day!" he said. "I wanted to do something to celebrate those gorgeous green eyes and I thought today was the perfect time to do it!"

March 17, '87 ~ The ring was gorgeous, the gesture lovely. He took my right hand and put it on the ring finger... not the left. I couldn't take my eyes off it. My mind drifted, thinking about commitment, and as I lay there admiring the ring, I was thinking about the finger he chose to place it on. I find that, suddenly I am longing for that — commitment - missing it.

"Do you ever think about tomorrow," she asked him as he pulled her back to him, wrapping her in the love she knew they shared.

"'Tomorrow' isn't a day of the week, Bethy. I just kinda roll with today."

Chapter Seventeen

In January 1988, the guys hit the road again on a limited travel schedule which seemed to work out fine for all of them. They would head to Miami for a huge festival called *All Star Jam* at *Joe Robbie Stadium*. There would be thirty different big name groups, and three days of non-stop music, throughout the day and night. Some local bands and lesser-known groups would open. The headliners, *Mean Street, Loverboy, Van Halen, Traveler* and a growing list of others would fill in time slots all doing sets throughout the weekend. There were slots left open for surprise appearances. It was a big deal, and they expected more than twenty thousand to attend. Andy and Beth went home to Florida for a few days and he left for Miami from there. Kimmy and Beth headed down on Friday for the event.

Only it wasn't so good. When they arrived Kimmy and Beth checked in with security, as always, for their badges. As their escort took them to the stage area, Beth rounded a corner and saw a young-woman hanging on Andy. Her hands were all over him. She was trying to kiss him, and Beth noticed he wasn't doing anything to push her off. He didn't see Beth watching him, and he was definitely enjoying the attention he was receiving.

Mark spotted Beth, saw the look on her face, and turned to see what she saw. Beth turned quickly and started walking back the way they had just come, with Kimmy hot on her heels, followed closely by Mark. She had no intention of staying.

"Beth!" Mark shouted, "Wait, please wait!"

"No, I'm going home." She said quietly, with a forced calm. She was not going to cause a scene in public, although she was mad enough she could have exploded with one big boom.

"Wait," he shouted again. "Kimmy!" He yelled to her in exasperation.

"Don't look to me for help on this one," she said sarcastically.

Finally he caught up to Beth and breathlessly grabbed her arm.

"Let me go," she said to him, spinning so that they were face to face.

"Wait; let me talk to you," Mark said, his hand still gripping her arm.

"Mark, I said let me go." She turned away, her temper inching closer to the explosion she was desperately trying to suppress.

"Beth…"

"Let go of me!" He did and she took a step, then turned back to face him.

"What?" she shouted, raising her voice more than she had intended. Heads started turning, but she was past caring at that point.

"I just want you to know that whatever that was," he looked back over his shoulder, "it just happened. He has been with us the whole time we've been here. Nothing happened. I just wanted you to know that."

"Well that explains a lot!" She tasted the sarcasm as it spewed from her mouth. "He waited till I got here, is that what you're telling me?" Tears began rolling down her cheeks, only succeeding in making her angrier.

"No, I'm just…"

"Don't 'just' anything! Because it 'just' doesn't matter! He knew we were coming!" She continued stomping away, "Who the hell is she anyway?"

"Who knows?" he said sadly. "Some backstage bimbo."

"I'm going home."

"I'll tell him, talk to him," Mark said.

"Do what you want!" she spat.

It was a long ride home and Kimmy said nothing. She knew Beth well enough to know that if she started to cry she would fall apart. Three hours in the car with silence made for a long trip. Beth dropped her at home to a very puzzled Lane. Kimmy held up her hand letting him know not to ask, yet.

When Beth arrived at the condo there was a message on the machine.

"Hey, baby. I know you aren't there yet. I'm sorry for what happened. It just did. That's all I can say. It was no big deal. Please call me." Then he blew that kiss, as he always did.

She waited until after midnight, knowing their stage times. When he picked up the anger finally released.

"Hey," he said.

"Hey?" she shouted, "Is that how we'll start this conversation? 'Hey!'"

"Bethy, I said I was sorry."

"Sorry? That makes it OK?" She yelled, "Has it happened before?"

"No, I don't do that. Wouldn't do that to you," he said quietly.

"Then why this time, Andy?" When he said nothing she shouted, "Why?" She was angry, but she was more hurt by his nonchalance.

"I don't know sweetheart, it just did." He was playing it off like it was no big deal, which only pissed her off more.

"Will it happen again?"

"No."

"You can't say that Andy!" she yelled as the tears started. "You can't, so don't make promises you can't keep! If it happened now there's a possibility it could happen again, right? I can't live like that!"

"Bethy…"

"No, don't. I can't and I won't." She wasn't shouting any longer. She was shaking, but her voice held a strange calm. She hung up, exhausted, mentally and physically and she went to bed. He called again but she didn't answer.

Around four in the morning she heard the door open and sat up in the bed.

"It's me."

"Get out," she said firm, but calm. He stood planted, feet to the floor, at the foot of the bed. "Get out," she said again. "Leave, I mean it Andy. I don't want you here."

"Bethy…" he pleaded sadly.

"No. I at least need time to think about this."

He sat on the edge of the bed. "I'm tired," he said. "Just let me sleep. It was a three-hour drive and we played all day."

"Fine," she said and took her pillow and went to the sofa and he followed.

"Don't do this," he reached for her.

"Don't touch me!" It came out hateful and bitter.

"Bethy, for God's sake, I didn't sleep with her," he said dragging a tired hand through his hair.

"Would you have if I hadn't come?"

"No."

"How do you know? How can you say 'No'? You said you didn't expect what did happen!"

"I'm sorry."

"Me too Andy, me too, go to bed," she said and turned her back to him.

"Come with me baby," he pleaded.

"No, I don't want you near me right now. I can't. Please just get away from me." It felt like she was pleading and she tried to stifle it and not cry. "You've hurt me so badly that I can't even express it Andy." She felt the sting of tears but she was not going to give him that, no way.

"I'm sorry," he said again.

"Stop it!" she snapped. "Just go to bed."

Instead he picked up the car keys and left. She didn't know where he went, and she didn't really care.

The next morning the phone ringing woke her. It was Phyllis.

"Beth..." she began, and Beth knew she knew.

"Don't," she interrupted her. "Don't defend him, not now."

Phyllis was quiet a minute.

"I'm sorry, I didn't mean to snap at you," Beth said, "but I can't talk to you about this. Not now."

"I won't defend him, Beth. What he did was wrong. I just wanted to tell you that he called and told me everything. He has gone to Eleuthera to the cottage, to think, he said. And pay penance I'm sure."

"I'll call you later," Beth told her. "I can't talk now." She didn't want to talk to her. She didn't want to talk to anyone. She just wanted to lie in bed and hide, bury herself in the covers and never come out.

A few minutes later Roddy called.

"Where in the hell is he?" Roddy asked.

"Phyllis said Eleuthera," she told him.

"Phyllis...? Eleuthera...? What the hell? He's got shows to do!" He babbled, questioningly.

"I don't know Roddy, you should talk to him. You know how to reach him." It was a short, hateful response.

"What's going on? Why aren't you with him?" he asked; his concern obvious.

"Talk to him," she said again and hung up.

A short time later Roddy called back. "Wow," he said when she answered. "What a mess"

"Yeah, I know."

"I've canceled and moved other bands into their time slots all afternoon. The guys are pissed, the promoters are more pissed, but what can we do if I can't get him off the damned island. What a mess," he said again.

Beth said nothing.

"He's sorry Beth."

"Don't do his dirty work for him," she said. "Not this time, Roddy."

"I'm not. He messed up. Once, Beth, once."

"And your point?" It was sarcastic, and hateful, but it wasn't directed at Roddy. She was hurt and angry and he was just on the receiving end.

"Talk to him. Part of this is your insecurity and you know that."

The fact that he was pointing this out only made her angrier. "Don't Roddy. Don't piss me off! I don't want to be mad at you, too!"

"Be pissed if you need to, but think about it. He knew you were coming. There wasn't an opportunity for anything to happen."

"This time," she said, coldly.

"You know him better than that..."

But she cut him off; "One word Roddy, one... Claire." And it tasted bitter and nasty on her tongue as she said it.

"Get over that, Beth. It's past."

"I'm gonna go now!" she snapped back at him.

"Go ahead and when you're done being pissed and feeling sorry for yourself call me back." He hung up leaving her with her mouth open, in a state of disbelief. How could he say that to her, hang up on her?

She crawled back under the covers. An hour later she got up. She was doing exactly what he said she was. She dialed the number and Roddy answered.

"It's me."

"I knew it would be," he said, and she heard the smile in his voice. "Are you done?"

"Done?" She asked, "Done what?"

"Being mad at me?"

"I don't know about *that*. I *am* done moping and feeling sorry for myself. Can you get me to Eleuthera? Tonight? Get me to the cottage without Andy knowing I'm coming. I don't want him to have time to prepare for this. I want it unexpected," she asked.

"That's my girl," he chuckled. "I can."

"Then do," she replied and went to pack.

The flight was longer than usual, or maybe it just seemed so because of her emotions. Roddy arranged for Wilford Minors to pick her up. He had been Andy's friend on the island for many years. When he pulled up in front of the cottage it was dark. The only light came from the kitchen. She asked him to wait, opened the door and went in.

"You here?" she called out. She didn't see him, but the doors to the patio were open. A cool breeze was blowing and the only sound was the ocean.

"Who's there?"

"It's me."

He came in the doors, looking tired. "This is a nice surprise." A smile tickled the corners of his mouth, but it was pensive. "Bethy, come here." He held his arms open, but she didn't budge, she wasn't ready for that.

"No," she said. "Wilford is waiting, I need to get my bags," and turned toward the door.

"I'll do it," he said and walked past her and out the door. He spoke a minute with Wilford, thanked him, went back in and set them down. "I'll move to the small room," he said.

"Why don't we sit down," she suggested. "I think we need to talk."

"Want a drink? Rum and juice or wine," he asked as he headed for the kitchen.

"Wine, thanks." She sat on the sofa, and waited. He got her a glass and returned to sit in the chair.

"Whewww," he said. "I messed up, hunh?"

"Only if you plan on it happening again. Roddy and I talked about this…" She hesitated because this part was very hard for her. "I guess I'm partly to blame." That was a big, nasty chunk to swallow and it hurt going down.

"What do you mean?"

"Oh, Andy, I'm so insecure." She sat the wine down and rose to pace; "I never quite settled into this relationship completely because I worry about this exact situation all the time."

"You don't have to," he said.

"Well, you certainly didn't give me any reason to think differently this weekend," she replied sarcastically and plopped back down on the sofa.

"Bethy," he said and dragged a tired hand through his hair. "I'm tired."

"Too tired to fix this?"

He thought a minute, and then rose from his seat. He went to her pulled her to her feet, wrapped his arms around her, and held her close. He said nothing, and finally, he stepped back and looked at her.

"I'm sorry," he said once again. "I can't say it enough, or differently, or mean it any more, I'm just sorry. I'm not gonna beg. It wouldn't have gone any further. You just have to know that. I love you, Bethy."

She began to cry. "I do know, Andy."

He led her to the bedroom, and they fell into bed, wrapped in each other's arms.

When she awoke it was early. Andy was deep in sleep. It was cool and breezy. She dressed in sweat pants and slipped her sneakers on. She quietly went out the door for a fast-paced walk on the beach. It was a purging. The sun was not quite up yet. She walked and walked. She loved the quiet and solitude. She was alone in her thoughts and prayers, taking in the sights, sounds, and smells of her surroundings.

She'd walked about half an hour when she heard the sound of heavy footsteps, a runner coming up behind her. She turned and saw Andy approaching. As he made his way closer, the sight of him struck her, and she knew at that moment that with him is where she was meant to be, wanted to be, needed to be. She knew that she would forgive him again, and again, and again. He had her heart.

CHAPTER EIGHTEEN

A new decade began and with it came new, exciting changes. In February 1990, Nathan's show, *Life Out There*, opened on Broadway and Beth and Andy were there for Opening Night. It was an exciting time.

Beth loved New York City. She loved the pace of it. She loved it because it was so hectic that people didn't seem to pay attention to those around them. And she loved that they were able to get out and about, lost in a sea of people. They stayed in a suite at the *Plaza*. They'd been there before but it was always for a show so there was no time for sightseeing. This time was different. They were able to enjoy the city as tourists. It was brisk and bright and she loved it all.

After the show they had a late dinner with Nathan, Dina, Megan, and Susan Marshall, Nathan's partner in this new venture. They went to *Forlini's Italian*, a New York City legend described as 'a slice of old New York.' They had Andy's favorite Marsala and after the meal shared Beth's favorite dessert, Tiramisu.

The next day the three girls snuck off for some girl time and retail therapy. Andy went to the theatre with Nathan. Nathan and his family had settled into the New York lifestyle, and loved the city life. Megan had just turned eighteen.

> *February 21, 1990 ~ Where on earth did all those years go? Megan is a beautiful young woman with her sights set on being an actress, working with her dad as a stagehand to get some experience. Nathan was so proud telling us about working with her. He has no plans for a life on the road again anytime soon.*

Nathan missed a lot of Megan growing up because of the travel. Now he wants to watch her career take off... Broadway, not Hollywood for her. She sings and dances, and is auditioning for several parts in off-Broadway productions. She got the best of both parents; Dina's looks, Nathan's musical ability, and a personality all her own.

Seeing Megan, and thinking of Drew and Andy makes me wonder what our children would be like...

~ ~ ~

Everyone was busy with their own projects, but each was getting in the mood, compiling stuff for the reunion album that they had agreed on. Mark and Anna's little one, Amber was born in April and they were happy learning to be a family. Nigel and Christy's 'Little Mark' just started day-school. The guys learned from Nathan that family was important, kids and home were not something to miss out on.

Scott Force, and Dane Allen, two of the original members of *Traveler*, got together with the band. They gathered to talk about a reunion album. The current line-up was doing well, but there were fans who always asked about Scott and Dane, so an idea evolved. Their previous troubles in the group no longer existed, so it was time to move on.

They shared plans and ideas, and things were falling into place for them to start recording. Nathan planned to come to Corpus Christi when they were ready, but all agreed, no touring.

March 29, 1990 ~ I was more than relieved for them not to tour. Andy and I have finally settled into our life together and it's good. Being on the road is the least appealing thing I can imagine.

~ ~ ~

In May 1990, after Tom and Needa's son Drew graduated from high school, he joined the Army. With Tom's family living with them in Corpus Christi, Drew and Andy had become great buddies. Andy tried hard to get him to come to work with him but he wasn't interested, "Yet..." he said many times. He wanted to use the military to get an education in electronics. He told Andy when he completed his time, and school was complete, he'd be back and be his sound engineer. Electronics were his passion.

~ ~ ~

In the fall, after basic training was complete, Drew shipped off to Kuwait in part of the U.S. Gulf War involvement. This was a very hard time for everyone. His letters to Tom and Needa were upbeat, telling them he was fine. But he would write to Andy about being homesick for his family and his girlfriend, Sara.

After reading one of his letters, Andy had an idea that he was very excited about. He dug through the archives and found an old *Jimmy Webb* song that *Glen Campbell* recorded in the late '60s. All the guys, former band members included, gathered together to have a listen to his version of "Galveston" and decided to record it as a single. This was their reunion debut and it got everyone very excited. That excitement, and emotions with the war running high, the song went immediately to number two on *Billboard* where it stayed for many weeks.

Galveston, oh Galveston, I am so afraid of dying
Before I dry the tears I'm crying
Before I watch your sea birds flying in the sun
At Galveston...

~ ~ ~

The guys were ready, set to go into the studio. But it seemed, the closer it came to actually doing it, the more reluctant they became. They had the material and seemed excited, yet there was this looming doom, like all of a sudden they dreaded the whole idea. They just kept finding reasons to delay. Beth suspected they were all holding back because they knew it would mean hitting the road at some point.

Finally, they got together, the 'old' and the 'new' *Traveler*. Everyone was in Corpus Christi, ready to get busy. But in April 1991, the bottom dropped out.

April 23, 1991~ These are bad times. Word came that Drew had been killed in helicopter training maneuvers in Kuwait. Tom and Needa's only child was gone. We were all devastated, but Andy took the news very hard. He and Drew were buddies.

After the funeral, Andy became very reclusive, brooding and miserable. He sank so fast, none of us saw it coming. He didn't sleep, didn't eat, and he neglected everything and everyone, including himself. Nathan went back to New York until Andy got it back together. The guys all agreed they would get together after they got past this awful thing. The loss of Drew affected everyone.

I decided to go to Florida for a few days. Kimmy was due to have a baby any day and I thought maybe the downtime would do Andy some good. Maybe he'd dig out of his funk. I couldn't have been more wrong…

Jenna Beth Parker joined the world the Friday Beth arrived in Florida. She got there just in time. Beth watched Kimmy with Jenna, and knew she would be a wonderful mommy and she could tell Lane would spoil them both rotten.

She'd been in Florida about a week and called Andy every night. His mood was still sour, and seemed to get worse. Conversation hardly took place. She kept thinking, 'one more day' and he'd be better, but that didn't seem the case. Everyone was getting worried so Beth returned to Corpus Christi.

Roddy met her at the airport. She could tell something wasn't right. He hugged her and put her bags in the car, but he was very quiet.

"It's not good, Beth," he said, finally, when they were in the car. "He hasn't shaved since you left. He's lost some weight and he's pretty miserable."

They arrived at the house and when Beth opened the door there were boxes and suitcases in the foyer.

"I'm home, you going somewhere?" she yelled out as she looked around.

Andy came around the corner. She had never seen him so unkempt. He was a total, disheveled mess. His clothes looked like he'd been wearing them since she left. He wouldn't look at her, hands deep in his pockets. She knew that was a bad sign.

"No Beth," he focused on a streak in the marble on the floor. Not 'Bethy' and not even one-step toward her to welcome her home.

Roddy stepped in and Andy looked up. His eyes were black, lack of rest showed in them. Still not looking at Beth, he looked at Roddy. "Take her home, please."

"What?" Beth asked calmly. "I am home. This is my home."

"No, I don't want you here."

She asked, "What do you mean?"

"I mean I don't want you here. I don't want anyone here. You don't belong here," he paused, "not for this…" He still wouldn't look at her. "Please, just go back to Florida." He walked away, back into the piano room. She followed him with Roddy right behind her.

She walked toward him. He stood silent, stiff.

She was in shock. "Oh, and it's you who makes the decisions in my life?" She tried to remain calm, but she was breaking inside. She took a step closer. "Talk to me Andy," she whispered.

"I can't. I don't want to. I just want you to leave, both of you." He took a seat on the piano bench, he looked so sad.

Beth continued to walk toward him; "Tell me sweetheart, what is going on."

"I just want all of you to go away." He looked up with pleading eyes. "Please… just go."

She turned and looked to Roddy. He left the room. She sat beside Andy, her arm around him pulling him close, her hand lightly caressing as she whispered to him; "It'll be OK."

"No, it'll never be OK again… Never."

Roddy returned. "Phyllis is on her way. I have a car picking her up."

"I don't want her here. I don't want you here," he repeated looking at Beth. "I don't want any of you here." He was getting agitated.

"We aren't leaving," Roddy said, and Andy broke. He started to sob.

Again Beth looked to Roddy, still holding Andy as close as he would allow.

Roddy made several calls and as Phyllis arrived so did Andy's personal physician, Dr. David Roth.

They left Andy with Dr. Roth and waited anxiously outside the room.

"He's exhausted, dehydrated, weak... I am going to admit him," he told them. "But not to a hospital. Roddy, I need you to help make some arrangements."

~ ~ ~

The next morning he checked into Glory Ranch, a private secluded, health facility in the Ozarks. They admitted him as Steven Andrews, to help his stay remain as private as possible. Beth, Roddy and Phyllis were here with him. Dr. Roth made the trip as well. After conferring with staff he took the two women and Roddy aside.

"We've confirmed what I suspected, what I think we all already knew," he told them. "Andy is suffering from depression. I want to keep him here for a while, not a day or two," he said, "a while."

Phyllis stood quietly listening. Beth's mind was racing, full of questions she wanted to ask but wasn't sure where to start. It was as if Dr. Roth could read her mind.

"It's a medical condition, Beth. Everything's been building up. Think about it. He's been going ninety to nothing for years. Even the last bit when he was 'relaxing' his mind was still going. Drew's death just brought it to a head. Everything culminated into this thing that was just more than he could handle," he explained.

"It's common, especially with this lifestyle," he continued. "He couldn't just pull it together on his own. You couldn't have done anything different. He needs rest, and treatment that will include some counseling and medication. It's not going to happen overnight. I think you should go home and get some rest yourselves. Let him have a bit of time to warm up to all of this. I've rearranged my schedule to stay for a few days until he gets settled. He's really just very angry right now."

Beth tried to absorb all he was saying, but she couldn't get past going home and him staying there, even knowing he was in good, qualified hands. Again, Dr. Roth knew her mind. "If you stay he'll be concerned about you. If you stay you will want to take care of him and you won't rest. Go home. Be with your family. You too, Phyllis, I'll be in touch."

Phyllis asked, "Can we see him now?"

"I don't think that's good idea. Go, let's just all concentrate on getting him better."

Neither Beth nor Phyllis could begin to fathom the idea of leaving him, but they went. Roddy left with them. They went to Phyllis's home first and stayed a night there. Then Roddy got Beth back to the house in Corpus Christi. He helped get some things situated and packed for her to go home to Florida for a while. Everything was a mess and she didn't want to leave there but Roddy insisted. Needa would take care of things. It would give her something else to think about as well.

Three long months passed and it was the hardest thing Beth had ever been through. Dr. Roth called daily. They were trying several different methods of treatment. Some seemed to help, some did not. It seemed as though it would be an extended course. Andy was in counseling as well.

They would allow visitors only one weekend a month. Beth and Phyllis went every weekend they could. He responded positively to Phyllis, but wasn't receptive to Beth. She felt helpless. She wanted to be there, but she could feel that he didn't want her. She decided not to go for a while. She sent cards and letters every day so that he knew she was thinking about him.

Dr. Roth kept her filled in on how Andy's treatment was going. Beth was still in shock over the whole situation. She went to the house in Corpus Christi to get some more things to take home to Florida. Before she left, she made arrangements to see Dr. Roth. Andy had been under his care for a long time, and he was her doctor as well. She needed to talk to him. She needed to know. She was torn, but she needed to know what was going on.

"I can't divulge everything," he told her, "but I think a huge part of it is guilt, Beth."

"Guilt?" she repeated the word. "Over what?"

"I believe he thinks you want more than he is able to give," he said.

"This is my fault?" Beth asked.

"No fault, it's his perception. I can't say for certain, I can only share what I believe, based on what he's shared with me. I think he feels like you want more, deserve more, but he's not ready to make that step. There's something that's holding him back. He hasn't shared that with me or the therapist, but there is a wall that he isn't ready to break through yet. Give him time."

She sadly responded, "I haven't ever pushed him for anything, I never tried to change him."

"It's his perception," he repeated. "It might take a while, just give him time."

She decided to make the trip to Florida more permanent. She called Roddy and asked for help.

"Are you sure you don't want to give this some more time?" he asked her anxiously.

"I've thought a lot about it, Roddy. After talking with Dr. Roth I think I should go for a while. I think if I go and Andy wants me to come back I will, but it doesn't seem that he wants me right now. I can't stay here and wait, it's tearing me apart."

Roddy helped get what she needed shipped from Corpus Christi. When the moving truck arrived in Florida, Beth used it as therapy for herself. Her mom and Kimmy offered to help, but she needed the time to herself to think and figure out her own plan for healing. With each box she opened, another emotion overwhelmed her. Sometimes it was anger that gave her an adrenaline rush and got her through the next box. Sometimes it was sadness that overcame her and she would quit and cry her eyes out. Sometimes she would just go to bed and continue the next day.

~ ~ ~

November 3, 1991 ~ Three more months have passed, I continue to send notes and cards once a week or so. Roddy tells me that Andy will be going home at the end of the month, and Phyllis will go to Corpus Christi with him. It seems there is no longer a place for me.

Beth re-enrolled in school and would start classes after the holidays. She decided to finish the Communications degree she had begun years ago, with Public Relations as her minor. After Andy was home, Phyllis called every week to tell Beth how much she missed her. Beth wished she wouldn't. Phyllis shared details on Andy's progress. Beth was glad they got him home, but it seemed there was still a long road ahead. He still hadn't called Beth; nothing at all from him. She didn't know what to think, but she knew she had to move on. It took months, but she finally realized that phase of her life was over.

~ ~ ~

In January 1992, Beth began school and it helped her move on. It kept her mind busy. She finally asked Roddy to help get her out of the chalet in Colorado. Financially she needed to move on as well. Roddy told her Andy would pay her bills but she wanted no part of that. They agreed that he would suggest they put the chalet on the market. No one had been there in months. Beth made a list of things for him to ship to her when it sold. He told her Andy was getting better. She couldn't think about that anymore.

~ ~ ~

Sadly, in March, the chalet sold. Roddy sold some of the items so she didn't have to deal with it. Dina made a trip out, alone, to help go through things, and Beth thanked God for her. Some things she would bring into the condo and some memories would be put away to deal with later.

The first day there Dina walked through the chalet and thought about Beth and Andy. Her heart ached terribly. As she wandered around looking for the things that Beth had asked for, she ran her hands over a quilt that she knew Beth's Nana made. She sat down with a cup of coffee and remembered the night Nathan had called to tell her about Beth and Andy. Nathan loved Beth instantly, her laugh, her smile, and her wit, all of it. And Dina did too.

Dina reflected on her past with Andy. He had been part of her life for a very long time; she had seen him through many experiences, Claire Ferguson for one. She saw them together in her mind, at the beginning of their relationship. She knew that it was not a match made in heaven, and she wasn't sorry when it ended. She knew Andy was better without her. Dina prayed he would find a woman to share his life with, because she loved him, and she wanted him to be happy.

Then Beth came along. She was different from any woman Andy had ever even noticed. Dina hoped Andy would see what she saw; a lifelong love. She saw Beth blossom into a woman in the years they spent together, a woman in love. She saw Beth during those few times of Andy's lapse of judgment, and she hurt for her. She saw Beth's strength as she forgave them and moved on, because she loved him so much.

This situation broke her heart. First Andy's illness, she wondered how none of them saw it coming. She hoped he would recover. Dina knew from what she heard that it would be a long process, but she was sadder about Beth. She knew that with most things in their crazy lifestyle when something was good, something usually happened to mess it up. She and Nathan worked hard to make sure that never happened to them. But she was sad for Beth and Andy, sad that these two people who obviously loved each other so much couldn't figure out how to stay a couple.

She continued to pack boxes and reminisce. It was a hard task. She packed the boxes that would go to Beth, slipping in things that would make her happy along with the ones that would hurt her heart. But she also packed some to go to Andy as well, hoping that he would remember the love they shared. And she packed some to send home. Things she knew Beth couldn't handle now, but that she hoped one day she could give back. With each box filled, Dina knew that emotions would overwhelm them all as they unpacked the boxes..

~ ~ ~

The months flew by, and Beth stayed busy with school. She was on a mission, cramming as much as possible into a short time and in December 1992, she graduated with a 4.0 GPA. The Cancer Foundation hired her as their public relations and media representative. She had been volunteering with them for a while. When the position came open they presented it to her. She was very excited to work for a cause she believed in, and get paid for it.

Andy finally called. She didn't talk to him. He left a message congratulating her on her upcoming graduation and new job. It was the first time he had called in over a year. He asked her to call him, but she wasn't sure she could. Phyllis and Roddy told her he was better. Roddy told her he was writing again, but she couldn't let that affect her. She wished the best for him, but she was finally settled. It took a very long painful time. It seemed that her head was back where it needed to be. She had to move on.

It was Jenna's second Christmas, but the first where she would be tearing into packages and having fun. It was also Kimmy and Lane's eighth anniversary. Beth went to stay with Jenna while they went out to dinner. They asked her to spend the night and wake up with them, not wanting her to be alone. Mom, Pops and Pappy were on a cruise and her brothers would all be celebrating the holidays with their families.

~ ~ ~

On Christmas Day, she arrived home about two, after all the Christmas morning festivities and brunch. She was ready to get home, put her feet up, have a glass of wine and relax. They were up so late getting Santa stuff out and ready. Finally, Lane couldn't stand it any longer. As soon as he heard Jenna rustle the first time, he went and got her. She was so excited about it all. It was early and this would now be their tradition – Santa came in the middle of the night so you had to get up and see what he left. It was somewhat exhausting.

When Beth got home there were four messages on the machine. She poured a glass of wine and went to listen. They were all from Andy.

10:02AM – "Hey, are you there?" He sounded good, but cautious. "I wanted to wish you Merry Christmas. I miss you. I miss us. Will you call me?" A longer pause, and then; "Bethy, baby, please just a call."

11:12AM – "Me again… are you there?"

11:49AM – "Bethy, baby I just want to talk. Are you there and just not answering? I tried your folks and there is no answer. Please call me…"

1:53PM – "It's me again. I just talked to Kimmy. She said you'd been there and were headed home. Please call me. I just want to talk."

At 2:20PM the phone rang and she let it go to the machine. "Beth, it's Kimmy."

"Hey," she said when she picked up.

"Did you talk to him? I knew he'd keep calling till someone told him where you were. What'd he want?"

"I haven't called him back," Beth said.

"You will though," she said. "Call him. Tell him to leave you alone if that's what you need to do, but call and get it over with. Get it behind you. You have to close this, and you know it, you gotta do it to really move on. I love you." And with that she was gone.

When she hung up it rang again.

"Hello?" she did pick it up.

"Hey, it's me. Please don't hang up," he sounded tired this time. "I just want to talk." It was a pleading request.

"I won't," she said and settled back on the sofa.

He asked her, "You OK?"

"Yeah, I am." She sounded convincing, but who was she trying to convince him or herself?

He was quiet a moment, then said; "I don't know what happened. I just kinda snapped." He paused. Not just tired, she realized, he was sad. "It's been like this big, black, dark hole."

"I know," she said sadly. "I know what it's felt like for me. I can't imagine what it was like for you."

"Bethy, I know it hurt you. I don't know what happened," he repeated.

She didn't say anything. She didn't know what to say, so she listened.

"Phyllis told me she's talked to you a couple of times, and I know Roddy has," he paused, that sadness in his voice hurt her heart. "She said you were fine," he continued. "I'm glad you have kept in touch with her. She loves you. I won't ask to see you, that'd be pushing my luck, I know. But I wanted to tell you that I am better now, and that I am sorry, so sorry, Bethy. I can only hope that someday, maybe even soon, you can understand."

She still said nothing.

"I'll go now. Merry Christmas, my love."

Before Beth could say another word he said; "I'll always love you," and he blew that familiar kiss and hung up.

He wasn't giving her the option to cut it off. She didn't know what to do, what to think. Fear inhibited her from thinking beyond the moment. She had to leave Andy behind. She didn't cry. It was over, it had to be. And she felt a sadness come over her that she never even believed could exist.

~ ~ ~

Andy didn't know if he could handle her hanging up on him as she had in the past. He had been to a dark place and there were times he didn't even remember. No one really knew how bad it was until it was too late. When he realized that Beth had slipped away, he didn't have the energy to pull her back. He knew how she was, and what she was doing. He made sure to know she was OK. He made Roddy promise to take care of her. But he knew that he couldn't allow her to be part of the nightmare his life had become. He thought keeping her away was protecting her. It took a long time for him to recover. Even when he was on the mend, he kept her away.

Beth sent letters and cards to him, and Andy had seen them all, saved them, along with every message she left on the answering machine. Each was a part of her. She bared her soul to him. He realized that he needed her back in his life. But it was too late.

Part of his healing was writing. He immersed in it. Beth's letters, cards and messages gave him solace as he began to resurface. There was such passion in her words. There was one letter that he read over and over. From her words a song came to his mind. The letter told him that she didn't know what happened, but that her life had to take a different path. She had to move on... 'Had to...' She tried to wait, she tried to be there, she tried to help him mend but she was 'done'.

"That's it," she wrote. "I quit. I'm movin' on."

Her concession became a song. He shared it with Roddy.

That's it
I quit
I'm movin on
Gotta do it for me
This insanity
A life that's been cast way
Seems lost, you and me

"You sure you want to do this one?" Roddy asked as he read the lyrics, but loved the music when he heard it.

"Yeah," Andy told him. "Some girl somewhere will hear those words and thank our Bethy for putting that thought out there so I could write it.

It was then that he realized how badly he needed Beth, but he had to leave it up to her.

Chapter Nineteen

It took a while, but Beth began to date again. It was very uncomfortable in the beginning; she'd been with Andy so long. She met men through Cancer Foundation meetings and functions and would go out for coffee, sometimes dinner. But she kept it very causal, dating no one in particular, just going out occasionally. She just wanted companionship, not romance.

She hated every second of it. She felt like a lot of the interest in her was more an interest in that part of her life than her, personally. She felt they were just nosey, wanting to know about things she didn't want to share. Conversation would somehow always drift to her and Andy. She didn't want to talk about them. There was nothing to talk about anymore. She was trying to move forward and thinking about the past slowed her momentum.

One Friday evening she was out with friends, and they went to a bar where Rick Snyder was playing. His band *Mean Street* toured with *Traveler* on several occasions in the early days. *Mean Street* split up several years earlier and Rick had gone solo. He was doing some big bar shows. There was a group of people going and Beth agreed to go along, secretly hoping that he would see her. He did.

"Well, hello to you," he said happily when she walked up and he gave her a hug.

"Hey!"

"How long has it been?" he asked trying to remember when they had toured together. "Ten years?"

"Thirteen, since the tour ended," she said.

"Where did all those years go?" he laughed. "I'm glad to see you. Listen, I gotta get going here, can you stay and we can talk after the show?"

"I'd like that," Beth said.

"Me too."

Afterward, they went for coffee. They talked way into the wee hours of the morning, about old times, not Andy. It was nice. He was kind and never mentioned Andy's name. When he asked if he could call her, she said yes.

Dating in the beginning stages is hard in any circumstance, getting to know each other, figuring out what to talk about, but she found something in common with Rick that she wasn't finding in the other guys she met. He wasn't curious about her past, he knew about it. They went out often. They got close, the relationship got close, but it never progressed to serious. She wasn't ready to open up to that again, and Rick never pushed. They had fun. She laughed with him, and enjoyed many of the same things. It was a good friendship, and she liked his company. That's what she needed. It seemed to work for him too. There was never more than holding hands or a kiss. Some very good kisses, but never more than a good night kiss, and that was fine with her.

All of the *Traveler* guys were moving on. They began working on their own projects, and families. Beth heard often from Mark. Dina and Nathan called frequently, and occasionally there was a call from Nigel and Stretch. Dane even called once. They all agreed that they could not be *Traveler* without Andy and when he was ready they would be waiting. Nathan found success on Broadway, winning a *Tony Award* for his work on *Life Out There*. It didn't seem the reunion was going to happen.

Andy would call and leave messages for her on the answering machine. He seemed to know when she would be away, because amazingly he never called when she was there. Maybe that was fateful intervention. His messages were kind, eloquent words, telling her this or that, and wishing her well, or luck in something that she knew Roddy had shared with him. They were always long messages, telling her what he'd been doing, but never asking to see her or for her to call him. Just a message, hoping that she was well, that he was thinking of her. She did listen to them but she couldn't give in and call him.

~ ~ ~

In April 1993, Beth's Pappy passed away. It was a sad time. It was one of those things you expect but hurts just the same. It had been fourteen years since they lost Nana. He died, peacefully, in his sleep at eighty-seven years old. He had lived with Mom and Pops since Nana passed away. His health had deteriorated in the last few months, so maybe it was true what they say sometimes; 'it's a blessing'. Pops took it really hard. Pappy had been with him for a long time.

Roddy came to the funeral, Beth knew he would, and she was glad. She also knew that he told Andy because he sent flowers. The card read only; *'Fondly, with many memories, Andy,'* not to draw attention. But of course she knew who it was. He didn't call and Beth was most appreciative.

Pops talked about selling the house and moving to a condo and traveling. He said he didn't want to wait until it was too late to enjoy the woman he loved so dearly.

~ ~ ~

July 28, 1993 ~ "Golden Eye's Journey Back to Life" was the title of the article. I started not to read it, but I did. I had to. This was another of those occasions Norton Edwards contacted me to talk, to take part in the interview for the story. I politely declined, I couldn't do it. So I knew the article was coming.

It was a sad article, with a good ending. Andy was better. It had to be hard for him to talk about what he felt and went through. It was emotional for me to read. It left me drained after reading it. He talked at length about Drew, and how sad he was losing him. His doctor stated, "exhaustion" as the cause for his illness. There had been reports of drugs, and alcohol, but the article indicated what I already knew, that wasn't the case.

The pictures gave my heart such a jolt. He looked so much better than the last time I saw him and that was good. But he also looked beautiful and I wanted to miss him, so badly, but I knew I couldn't. I couldn't allow that pain again. He talked about us in the article but it was brief, a respect for my privacy, and very gracious on his part.

~ ~ ~

The *Traveler* guys together again… it finally happened. Roddy told Beth that after all this time they decided to do a "Reunion Tour" rather than an album. Beth knew that an album would evolve from the tour in the form of live recordings from the shows.

How could they not, so much talent, so many wanting fans.

They were playing only a few of the bigger cities. Orlando was on their schedule in September. She and Rick had been casually seeing each other for seven months.

"Do you want to go to the show?" he asked her after talking to Kimmy about it.

Beth didn't say anything at first; she experienced so many emotions, causing hesitation in her reply.

Rick continued, "Weren't you *Traveler*'s biggest fan for like a zillion years?" He laughed, "Come on, we'll just slip in, enjoy some music, and slip out. It'll be fun to hear them all together."

He convinced her, and promised that they wouldn't visit or anything, they'd "just go". She worried that someone would see her. Not Andy, just someone who recognized her, and then the word would get out, and it would be back to that privacy thing. She had been so lucky, in all the time that had passed no one called and said, "You're on the cover of… with Rick…"

Kimmy and Lane would be going, and Roddy got them the tickets, agreeing not to share that they would be there. Always Beth's 'knight in shining armor'.

~ ~ ~

Beth hadn't been to a real concert in a very long time. She'd been with Rick to many shows he'd done in the time they'd been seeing each other, but nothing big since she came home from Corpus Christi. The seats would be great, not anything special. They would be able to see good, hear great, but there was no chance of them being seen.

The closer it got to going the more apprehensive she felt, questioning whether it was right to go. And then there was Kimmy.

"Don't go if you don't want to Beth, but don't let Andy be the reason." she said, no holds barred, point-blank, from the hip, but, that's Kimmy.

"I just don't know what it will feel like." She knew it sounded like she was whining as soon as she said the words.

"It'll feel like a friggin' *Traveler* concert. Oh for Pete's sake Beth, I'll call Rick and tell him we aren't going if you're gonna be a mess about it. It's supposed to be something fun."

"No." she said, firmly. "No, I'll go."

"That's my girl!"

The day before the concert Kimmy stopped by to see Beth at work.

"Hey there!" Beth said excitedly. "What brings you to my neck of the woods today?"

"A present!" Kimmy replied and dropped a box in Beth's lap and sat on the corner of the desk to wait.

"What's the occasion?" Beth asked as she ripped into the box.

"Just something fun," Kimmy said as Beth peered into the box and let loose a loud laugh.

"Oh my gosh!" She pulled a shoulder length blonde-bob wig from the box and immediately pulled it on.

"Sexy," Kimmy laughed. "I just thought maybe you'd feel more comfortable if you didn't look like Beth Morgan."

"But who will I look like now?" Beth laughed.

"Some hot blonde chick out for a good time!" Kimmy quipped.

"I love you!"

"I know," Kimmy laughed.

When it was time to pick her up, Rick came to the door; they were meeting Kimmy and Lane at their house. He knocked and when she opened the door he stood, his mouth gaping, and then laughed.

"Wow," he said. He pulled her into his arms for a hug, "You make a beautiful blonde. Let's go have some fun!"

'Maybe he likes me better as a blonde!' Beth laughed to herself.

Rick had taken it slow with her for almost eight months. He wanted more from their relationship, but he felt Beth holding on to the past. So he kept things friendly, and waited and hoped, not doing anything to jeopardize what they had.

~ ~ ~

It was a sold-out show; a full house with an excited crowd. *Traveler* opened with a cover of an old *Thin Lizzy* song – "The Boys Are Back in Town" - followed some of their older hits; "Traveler", "Timeless", "Forbidden Place". They played a lot of the older stuff from when Scott and Dane were both still with the band, and then the newest stuff with them all together. What Beth didn't hear was, "In My World", "Makin' Sweet", or "In Your Eyes", songs that Beth was relieved not to hear. It seemed there was a whole block of time missing from their collection. Maybe the thought of that time, the memories, hurt Andy in some way and they decided not to go there, even though some of the songs were big hits.

She knew Mark knew they were there, but he swore he wouldn't say anything. It was a fun night and they left having had a good time. Beth was glad she went.

Chapter Twenty

In October 1993, Beth was preparing for the biggest function in her Cancer Foundation career. She worked with a wonderful committee of people to pull it off. Months of preparation, great ideas and a lot of hard work went into it. They'd planned a tropical theme. She thought of the postcards people sent, she thought about how much she had missed her Nana and came up with "Wish You Were Here". It was a $250 a plate luau of coconut shrimp and grouper. Vince was a huge help. They were on the phone everyday planning menus, lining up caterers who would donate or provide what they needed at a much reduced rate. There were a lot of local dignitaries coming and the program they prepared would be awesome.

Saturday came and it was a great affair. After the meal there were cocktails and a silent auction. This part was open to anyone, and it appeared that everyone had a great time. They worked hard for months getting donations for the auction and calculated that they would end up clearing over $30,000.

To Beth's surprise, Andy was there. He showed up for the auction and cocktails, not the dinner. She knew he was there. She could feel him in the room before she saw him. It amazed her that after all this time that could still happen. She was in the middle of a group of people, talking, laughing, when she felt her skin heat. Her heart jumped, she looked up. He was watching her from across the room. He looked so handsome. He was leaning against the wall with a drink in his hand. She saw the shirt he wore and her heart stopped. *'Did he really still have it?'*

He wore the tropical print shirt she had made for him so many years ago. She let him be alone there for a while, maybe out of selfishness, maybe because she had to. Rick was with a group of people and when she caught his eye he winked. He knew. Finally, Beth made her way to where Andy stood and said hello. It was the first time she had really seen him in two years, and he was more beautiful than ever. She didn't know if she'd be able to breathe or not.

"Hi," she said casually.

"Hey," he said. "Beth, you look amazing." She wore a long lavender and bright yellow tropical floral print, strapless dress. He leaned in to kiss her cheek. "I'm happy to see you."

Not Bethy, Beth. It sounded so different, so formal. She hugged him and his arms around her sent a shiver up her spine, or maybe it was a tingle, or maybe it was that jolt. She could feel eyes on them from every corner of the room.

"It's good to see you too," she pushed back from him. The feel of his arms around her sent alarm up her spine. "You look good. Better," she said.

"I wondered if we'd ever share a pleasant conversation again," he laughed an ironic laugh as he said it.

"Me too," Beth said, giving him a sideways, sly glance.

"You OK?" he asked in almost a whisper.

She waited a few seconds to answer, partly for effect, but mostly because she was unsure what she would say. And then, "Yeah," she laughed, nervously. "I wasn't for a very long time, but it just made me tired. I was tired of being tired. So, I'm over it now." She took a sip of the wine in her glass. Her throat suddenly felt like the Sahara Desert.

A very long time passed, he reached and casually moved a strand of hair from her eyes like it was the most natural thing he'd ever done and then quickly pulled his hand away. For some reason she felt like she had to reach to move it as well, maybe to brush away the touch, the feeling that he left there.

"I'm glad," he said finally. "I hated thinking that you weren't. I hated it, but I felt helpless. Can we sit?"

"I'm here with…" But he cut her off before she finished.

"I know, Rick. How is he?" He looked down at the floor.

"He's well. You should go say 'Hello'. I know he'd like to see you."

"I'll do that." He paused, "It's a great party. I came in after dinner."

Was he trying to make conversation? That seemed so odd after all of those endless conversations, all the nights that they talked for hours on end... now they were struggling with small talk.

"I know," Beth said.

"Can I call you? I won't pressure you; I just want to talk."

"Andy, I just..."

"Beth, just talk; we used to be so good at that." He looked at her. A moment passed, and he looked down again. "Just a phone call." It was a pleading request and it hurt.

"Andy, I don't know if I have that much energy. I said I was OK, I didn't say it didn't still hurt."

That speck on the floor captivated him, or he just couldn't look at her.

"I understand." He looked up, the look lingered, and finally they were eye to eye.

Oh God, that look... those eyes that peer into my soul. I caved.

"I'll be home after eleven, alone. You can call me then." She turned away without another word, and didn't look back. She had to get back to her guests, to her date.

She tried not to watch him, but she did, out of the corner of her eye until he left. He made the rounds, she saw him talk to Rick. She could see the whispering going on among the other guests. She knew it would come when she saw him there. He made a very generous donation in Nana's name before he left.

Rick came to her rescue after he was gone. He put his arm around her shoulder and squeezed but said nothing. Not the touch of a lover, the strength of a good friend. They finished out the evening and headed home. In the car Beth felt the need to say something but couldn't form the words. Rick reached over and patted her leg.

"He was very cordial. I anticipated fifty questions but there were none. He just asked how I was doing. It was a pleasant exchange." He looked over at her as he drove. "You gonna talk to him?"

She looked at him, still seeking the words she wanted, but Rick answered his own question. "You should Beth."

"I am," she said finally. "I don't know why, but I am."

"I know why..."

Rick knew then the friendship he hoped would grow into something more had no chance. He knew where her heart was.

When they got to the condo he walked her to the door, made sure she was in and hugged her; no good night kiss. "You know how to reach me. You call me," he said.

She changed, got ready for bed, and waited. It was almost midnight when the phone rang.

"Hey," he said when she answered. "Thanks."

"For what?"

"Agreeing to do this, I know it wasn't an easy decision."

She wanted to say something, but nothing came out. What happened to that easy conversation they used to share?

"I want to tell you again, the event was great, you did an awesome job. I'm so proud of you. I'm really glad I was there, glad Roddy mentioned it."

Roddy, her good friend, the one constant in her life all those years; *'that life'* she thought. "Roddy told you," she said.

"Yeah, it wasn't like he picked up the phone, called and said, 'Hey Andy, Beth is hosting this Cancer Foundation thing and you should show up' or anything like that. We were talking and he mentioned it. He keeps me posted on stuff like that. He's just so damned proud of you Bethy, how far you've gone with this. He told me you were doing great things with them and I felt like I could help out. For one thing, I know why you do it. I loved Nana too," he said. "And," he said, after a long pause, "I thought, if I could just see you…"

"Andy, don't," she sighed.

"I won't Bethy. I just needed to see you. That's all. Are you happy?"

"I don't know Andy; I was so happy for so long, then so miserable, I don't know if I'm happy or not."

There was a long, awkward silence and then, "Rick?" Andy finally said.

"Don't Andy."

"Is he…?"

"Don't, please. He's a good friend, we go out," she interrupted before he could finish the question. She didn't want to get into that conversation with him. "We get together. I can laugh with him." She hesitated, "I didn't do that for so long. After everything that happened, I hid. And then, I submerged in school and books to keep my brain occupied. I stayed so busy there was no time to laugh. I ran into him a few months ago. He was playing at a bar in town and a group of us went. I stayed to talk to him. We had coffee after the show and we just decided to get together."

"It was good to see you, even if it was just for the few minutes we shared," and then he said; "I miss you, Bethy, so much."

"Andy, please," she pleaded.

"No pressure, just telling you." He paused a moment, and then said; "I want to tell you something, give you a head's up I guess. I have a solo album coming out soon."

"That's great. I heard. How's it going?" she asked and her desire to know was genuine.

"Good, I love the work. I love the music even more. I think it's some of my best work." There was excitement in his voice now, the old Andy. "It's not *Traveler*, Bethy, it's me, very personal, very emotional. A lot of it will strike you, and I thought you should know."

"What do you mean?" It was getting late and she was tired.

"There are some lyrics," he hesitated, "you will know it's you I'm referring to. Some stuff from letters you wrote, messages you left, conversations we've shared. I read every letter you sent, over and over. I listened and re-played the messages. I saved them all. Some of the thoughts came from them. Some came from my heart. I knew there was something there and I just locked myself up and wrote... words and music... It was part of my healing process, the digging out of that hole. I just wanted to let you know."

October 4, 1993 ~ To know that he read my letters, to know he had heard those messages, to know he knew my heart. I felt tears move to the corner of my eyes. All this time...

"Why?" she asked.

"Because it's about you, about us."

"No more 'us', Andy."

"I know, but you'll see what I mean. I'll have Roddy get a demo tape to you for a listen, but I need to ask a favor."

"What Andy, I'm really tired."

"I know, just this one last thing. Listen, really listen, then tell Roddy what you like and what you don't. I won't bother you about it. Go through Roddy if that will be easier for you, but do this for me, will you? Please?"

"Why?" She needed to know.

"Because I realized something not long ago," he paused, and laughed. "All those times when Dane would get so pissed at you, he was mad."

"I know that. Your point now?"

"I figured out why he stayed mad. You had the ear, you listened, you knew what you liked, and said so. What you liked always did well for us. When you didn't like it so much, and we released it anyway, usually because Dane wanted it, it did OK, not great, just OK. That infuriated him. We were together recently, talking about it. He said that it was jealousy. I just want you to listen and tell me what you like and don't. I respect your opinion."

It was quiet for a long time and finally Andy laughed, "Go to sleep on me?"

"No, just thinking. Send it. I'll listen."

"Thanks Bethy."

"I have to go now, really, I have to go."

"It's late, I know. I won't call you again. You know how to reach me, if you want. Take care of you. Good night Bethy." And then he blew that same kiss into the phone that he always ended their calls with, and a flood of memories came rushing back.

On Sunday afternoon, the tape arrived via courier. Roddy told her to "brace" herself. She listened, and listened, and listened again. She was up all night. She listened, she cried, she listened some more, and again she cried. It was good, really good. But it was more emotional than he tried to warn her it would be. No words could have prepared her for what she felt.

Monday morning, when she could, she called Roddy. Andy was right, it was good, and she was raw. She was physically and emotionally drained.

"Hey, it's me," Beth said when he answered. "I know it's early." It came out a whisper that burned her throat.

He laughed, "Never too early for you, my love! You OK?" he asked, knowing that she was calling about the tape. "What'd you think?"

"Oh God Roddy, I was up all night. I think I just died that death all over again." Beth told him, "I'm whipped... drained."

"I know. Good stuff though isn't it?"

"It's so emotional, so soulful. If I had heard it on the radio without any warning I would have lost it, broke down wherever I was. God, Roddy, will it ever stop hurting?"

"I can't answer that, Beth. I know it won't for Andy, probably never. He will never get past this."

"He has to!" she said feeling frustrated, and sad.

"I know honey, but he can't."

"God…" she put her head down on the table, "What am I gonna do?"

"Well, for starters, tell me what you like, what you don't like, and ready yourself. He is anxious and wants to get this out quick. It's still part of that healing process. Andy needs this, Beth."

"I liked it all, not one thing I didn't think was good."

"I know. I believe it's his best work ever. Maybe wearing his heart on his sleeve makes him better, if that is even possible." They were quiet for a minute and then Roddy asked, "Now, what about you?"

"What about me?" she asked, dreading where the conversation was going.

"He wants to see you Beth."

"I know, but, no," she said flatly, no emotion, no excitement, just 'no'. "I can't do it. I could barely breathe when I saw him the other night. It still hurts so much, Roddy. I don't know if I can do it again. Every time something happened it hurt more, and each time it took longer for me to come back. I know what he went through, I went through it, too."

"I know. I've traveled that road with you. I've traveled it with him, too. I'm just telling you what I know." He paused, "Have dinner with him, talk."

"Oh sure and be fodder for the tabloids all over again!" She laughed sarcastically, "I think not, my friend!"

"Neutral turf," he suggested. "Just think about it."

"Oh Roddy, I just…"

"Dinner Beth, you don't have to take him home with you."

"I'll call you tomorrow. For now, release it, all of it! Oh my-gosh, it's just awesome," Beth finally admitted.

"That's my girl," he said. "I love you."

"I love you more."

She hung up and made another call, to Kimmy. "Hang on! Jenna, sweetie put that down," Beth heard her say when she realized who it was.

"If you're busy I can call you later."

"Nope, just gotta get her settled; she's into everything today!" A pause and then; "What's up, you're sounding blue and I know that means something to do with Andy."

Beth laughed, "How'd you know?"

"Uh, hold on, I'm looking at the freckles on the back of my hand, I know you that well! Talk, Jenna is fine now. I have a few minutes, so spill. Tell Dr. Kimmy what's on your mind!" She laughed and Beth knew how blessed she was that Kimmy was her friend.

The tears came easily as Beth told her about his appearance at the auction. Kimmy and Lane had other obligations and were unable to attend. Beth told her about the phone call, the album, about Andy.

"OK, so what do you want to hear from me? I'll say whatever you want, just tell me what you want," Kimmy replied with a flip tone.

Beth barked sarcastically, "What the hell is that supposed to mean?"

"Listen, you already know the answer, right?" Beth heard her take a sip of what she knew was coffee. "There are only two possibilities; you either see him or you don't."

"But..."

"Don't 'but' me, I'm not finished," she said curtly. "It's you. It's your heart. You have to do what you feel in your heart."

"I don't know what the hell to do," Beth shouted. "That's why I called you!"

"No, you knew you'd get it straight from the hip with me," Kimmy said. "You also know what you want and that's why you called me. Reassurance, comfort, all that crap."

"I'm scared!"

"And you should be, but you want to see him, or you'd have just said 'no' and we wouldn't even be having this conversation. You wouldn't have even brought it up with me." Another sip of coffee, "You still love him," she said, knowing it was fact.

"I'll always love him, Kimmy, and you know it." Hearing those words made Beth feel even sadder.

"Right, but you don't know if you can be in love with him because of your past. So go, have dinner, see what happens and move on." She said it with such ease, but Beth knew Kimmy understood the turmoil she felt.

"For crap sake, why doesn't he move on?" Beth wanted to know.

"Because he *knows*, honey, he *knows* he's still in love with you."

"So much past, Kimmy. So much hurt," Beth mumbled.

"Go!" Kimmy interrupted, "Have dinner. Talk, laugh, hell, drink!" She said with easy laughter. "Don't make a big deal of it. It's a meal - you go out to dinner all the time." She was trying to keep it light.

"Yeah, but this is Andy."

"Which brings me to another thought dear friend...?"

"Yeah?"

"Maybe what you need is a good tumble in the sheets; been too long for you..."

"Kimmy!" Beth shrieked.

"Gotta go get Jenna, love you!" And with that she was gone.

Beth waited until Tuesday afternoon to call Roddy. Sleep surely was not part of that time. She knew how to reach Andy. His number had been on speed dial in her phone forever. But she asked where he was, and being the good friend he was Roddy didn't comment, or question. He told her Andy was still in town, told her he loved her, and was gone.

October 6, 1993 ~ I waited a really long time before I dialed. I paced. I wrung my hands. I prayed. I questioned every thought that went through my brain, so unsure of myself. But even more questioning of the whole situation, I was truly terrified. Was I doing the right thing? Was I subjecting my heart to that pain all over again? I wondered what my family would think.... All those thoughts ran rampant...

She dialed many times, but hung up before it rang. "*What am I doing?*" she kept asking herself, sometimes it was a scream. Finally, she dialed and let it go through and it rang.

He answered. "Hey, it's me," she said as soon as she heard the connection.

"I hoped it would be," he said easily. There was pleasure in his voice and it made her smile.

"How long will you be in town?" she asked and thanked God that he couldn't see her hands trembling.

"As long as you want me to," he said. "Do you want me to stay, Bethy?" There was a tease in his question.

"I was thinking we might have dinner, Friday," she mumbled, "if you'll still be here."

"I'll still be here, if you want me to. Do you want to go somewhere?"

"No, not out," she answered quickly. "Just come here, to the condo."

"It'll be OK Bethy, don't be nervous. It'll be fine, nice... I'll bring the wine." And then he blew a kiss into the phone as he hung up. He didn't stay on the line long. Maybe he was afraid she would change her mind.

She tried to work that week. She did so mostly from home, because she was a mess. On Friday, as she prepared for his visit, it felt almost natural, almost, but there was also much apprehension. She looked around. Everything at her home was ready. But she had to stop, remind herself that it was her home, and that he would be a guest. There were things there from their life together. How would he feel? But she really wondered how she would feel.

She was thirty-eight years old. Andy would be forty-four in a few days. It was the nerves of a first date all over again. She had dinner almost ready, and suddenly she began to panic. She felt the urge to call and tell him not to come. Her heart screamed, *just open the door and run like hell!*

She paced, feeling the sting of tears burning her eyes as she did. She could feel her heart pound in her chest so hard that it almost hurt. She felt terrified, but it was dread iced with anxiousness; all those old feelings intertwined with the new. The knock at the door brought reality forefront, and her heart pounded even harder.

"Hey, come on in," she said as she opened the door.

"Smells good." He smiled as he breezed past her, "dinner too," he smiled. He went to the kitchen, opening the drawer he pulled out a corkscrew.

October 10, 1993 ~ My mind raced...Deep breath... regain composure... I closed my eyes and prayed... I didn't want to appear the mess that I felt like. I watched him as he opened the wine, of course he knew where everything was, he'd gotten it so many times before. My heart ached with fear and memories all jumbled into a mess of emotions. It felt like a familiar routine, but it wasn't anymore.

He eased the cork out of the bottle as Beth sat two glasses on the counter. Turning to look at her over his shoulder, Andy said, "Thanks for doing this. We could have gone out." He poured the wine and handed Beth a glass.

"No. No, this is better, really. I really didn't feel like I was up to going out. I'm still a little nervous about this whole thing."

"Don't be nervous, Bethy." As she took the glass he placed a gentle hand on her cheek.

How could something as simple as his touch wreck me so?

"It's just dinner," he paused, looking around. She could read his thoughts before he spoke. "Everything looks great," he said, noticing everything, noticing her home.

"Thanks. Yeah, just dinner," she repeated, and looked around as well.

"It really does smell incredible. What have we got here?" He stood at the stove lifting lids. He sounded so good.

"I just whipped up some Alfredo sauce. I'll cook the pasta and throw in some veggies and shrimp when we are ready to eat. Easy, just something easy," she repeated, the nervousness she tried to hide was more than noticeable.

"Then I picked well on the wine," he said. "It's OK, Bethy, really. Let's sit down."

He sat on the sofa. She sat across from him in Nana's rocker. She couldn't be close to him, she was too afraid. The smell of him was almost more than she could bear; that same soap and musk, that familiar smell of *him*.

"So, Roddy said you liked the new stuff." He had settled back into the sofa and he looked so natural there. He sipped the wine and looked so at ease, so comfortable, with one arm thrown across the back, like that was exactly where he belonged.

"Mmm hmm," she took a sip of the wine.

He leaned forward, elbows on his knees and asked, "What'd ya think, really? Change anything at all, last chance," he laughed.

"Nope... nothing... it's perfect." Another sip...

"Good." He rose, walked to the stereo and put a tape in. "This is a cleaner version. What you heard on the other tape is rough. This will be better, it's had some tweaking."

She knew the process, but she doubted that it could be better. But he was right. It was beautiful. This time that raw feeling wasn't just tears that trickled down her cheeks. It became the body wracking sobs that come from your soul. So much pent-up emotion, another sip of wine and she lost it, completely fell apart.

He went to her and sat on the floor at her feet. He took her hands in his. With so much emotion he expressed his sadness at their situation.

"Bethy, I am so sorry. I had no control, it was beyond me." He cried too, saying those words.

"You are no sorrier than me. Why, Andy?" Beth asked him, "Why?"

"I don't know." He sat there on the floor looking up at her and finally asked, "Can we ever go back, Bethy?"

She waited, a long time to respond. She was thinking, deeply pondering her reply, and then she spoke to him from very deep within her heart.

"Oh Andy," she sighed, "I just don't know. I'm just so scared. I'm afraid that if something happened I couldn't recover the next time."

They sat quiet for a long while, listening to the tape. It was beautiful, and the tears continued to flow. Finally, they went to the kitchen to fix dinner, and again, they fell into an old familiar routine. It was pleasant; they shared good conversation, once more.

After the meal Andy keyed up one of the songs and started it again. He went to Beth and took her in his arms. She backed away, but he pulled her closer.

"Just let me hold you." He held her tight to him, and they fell into step as the song played on.

She could feel the tears running down her cheeks as he held her in his arms. He wiped them away with his thumbs, pulling her closer still, and wrapped her in the place that she loved. That place that she missed. He kissed the top of her head and continued to hold her, humming softly. He cupped her chin and turned her face up toward his and looked into her eyes, and then his lips were on hers, so soft, and so gentle. His hands so light on her back, like a feather as he held her.

He whispered her name, and it took her by surprise. He kissed her neck and she realized how badly she missed him. So gently he kissed her, and then she was kissing him back. It felt so good. Slow and easy, and then it wasn't.

Suddenly it was quick, and heated, and passionate, a frantic removal of clothes as they made their way to the bedroom and made wild love.

When she awoke the next morning with him beside her, she watched him sleep and remembered a million times before when she had done the same thing. She was more frightened of how it would be than how it was. After a while she slipped quietly out of his arms, out of the bed, and went to the kitchen to make coffee. Didn't she know he'd want some?

She rolled the blinds to look out. There was a squirrel working diligently at something in the yard. She watched for a very long time, just standing there at the window with her arms folded across her chest, maybe protecting her heart. And then she felt him behind her. His arms wrapped around her and the embrace was warm, and again it felt natural and right. She turned into him, and he kissed her.

"Good morning beautiful. Oh man, something smells heavenly," he said looking toward the pot of coffee that had just finished brewing.

"What now, Andy?" she asked him.

"Well," he said with that devilish look in his eyes. She laughed and pushed him away. "How about that coffee?"

"I'm serious, Andy? What next?" She poured him a cup of coffee, just like he liked it, strong and black.

"Bacon and eggs?" he said it casually, and they both laughed. He was trying to keep it light.

Beth did fix breakfast, and they spent the day together not discussing anything important. Later in the day, they found themselves in each other's arms again. Maybe Kimmy was right.

As she prepared dinner that evening he sat at the table and they talked, like they had been together forever. It seemed like old times. And then, it was like Beth was hit with a ton of bricks.

"After dinner you have to go," she said.

"I do?" he was clearly surprised. He went to Beth and wrapped his arms around her as she cooked and nuzzled her neck.

"Yes. You have to go. I need to get my head straight and think about this, about us, without you here confusing me even more."

She turned around into his arms. His eyes swallowed her, those beautiful pleading eyes. He reached out and touched her cheek. "Can't we talk it out together, Bethy?"

"No," she said, firmly, "Not now. I need to think Andy. Dinner, and then you go. You really have to go."

It didn't make the meal uncomfortable. She was afraid it would, but she knew she needed time. After they cleaned up, he grabbed his jacket, kissed her on the forehead and headed for the door.

"You know where I'll be," he said easily, "A phone call away."

"I know, now go. Call me in the morning," she said.

He leaned to kiss her. "Don't," she said. "Please don't."

He went out the door and she closed it behind him. With her back against the door, an overwhelming feeling came over her, and she slowly fell apart, and started to cry.

Andy hadn't walked away. He was still there, just standing outside the door. And finally he spoke. "Lock up pretty lady," he said sadly.

"Leave," she said.

She sat in the dark for a long time, playing that tape over and over.

I remember holding you in my arms
Your sweet voice whispering my name
I remember your touch
Can it ever be the same
I need you
You're gone
I want you
I'm holding on
I miss you
You're the one
I let you go
I can't go on

She fell asleep on the sofa listening to the tape. Sunday morning a ringing phone woke her.

"Hello," she said sleepily.

"It's me," Kimmy said. "Did I wake you?"

"What time is it?" she asked as she sat up and wiped sleep from her eyes.

"Nine - you alone?" Kimmy laughed as she asked.

"Yes," Beth said sarcastically. "But if you'd called yesterday morning I wouldn't have been!"

"Ha!" Kimmy laughed out loud, and said, "I knew that's what you needed, a good roll between the sheets! How was it?"

"Like riding a bike," Beth said more sarcastically.

"So now what?" Kimmy asked, knowing that Beth was struggling.

"I don't know; figured it was him when the phone rang." She walked to the kitchen and started coffee while they talked. "It definitely felt good having him here, but how long would it stay like that? I've been there before, I can't hurt like that again, ya know?"

"I do know. I know that this isn't in you, but think about it, go slow, have dinner once in a while, have that roll in the hay. Go back to the way it was in the beginning," she said.

"I don't know if I can, Kimmy. I'm afraid it's all or nothing with him, with me." Beth said as she sat at the table waiting for the brew to complete.

"Just think about it."

"What's my Jenna doing this morning?" Beth asked changing the subject.

"Lane took her for a bike ride; forty minutes of peace and quiet for me! We're going to his folks this evening for their weekly spoil Jenna rotten quota!" She laughed easily.

As soon as she hung up the phone rang again. "Mornin' beautiful! Get ready, we're going out." It was Andy.

"You and the mouse in your pocket?"

"Nope, you and me; come on, say you'll go and I'll be there in twenty."

"I'll be ready when you get here."

She showered, slipped on some jeans, a t-shirt, sneakers and a quick dip through the make-up. She was finishing her hair when she heard the knock at the door.

Opening it Andy greeted her with an armful of Calla Lilies. "They're beautiful, thank you." A quick brush on her cheek and he pounced on the coffee pot.

Beth found a vase as he poured the coffee. "I knew you'd have this!" Rolling his eyes as he drank, he said, "Mmm, the elixir of the gods."

She realized that he was staring at her.

"What?" She ran her fingers through her hair, remembering that she hadn't given it that final brush.

He grinned and took another sip of the coffee.

"What?"

"You're beautiful," another sip of coffee… "You look a lot like Reba McEntire," he said looking over the top of the cup.

"Oh, I do not," she laughed.

"Yeah," he laughed easily, "you really do. Did I tell you I like those highlights in your hair?"

Changing the subject she asked, "What are we doing?"

"Going for a ride, I'm not sure where. Don't fuss too much I rented a convertible. It's a beautiful day, and the top is down, so let's go."

Andy topped his coffee off, Beth grabbed her purse and sunglasses and out the door they went, Andy with the coffee cup still in hand.

It was as beautiful a day as he had indicated, and the top down made it even more enjoyable. As always with Andy the speed was fast and the music loud. Direction told her he was heading toward the beach. They drove south for a while until he found a secluded place and parked. They got out and walked. The sun was shining, not a cloud in the sky. It was warm for November, even in Florida. They walked for a while, and then he took her hand and she didn't pull it away.

After they had walked for a while she turned to Andy and asked; "Now what?"

"I don't know Bethy, you call the shots." He stopped walking and turned to face her, "I know what I want. What I hope. What I pray for, but I won't pressure you." He paused, gazing into her eyes. "You're the one in charge."

They walked again, further, and again in silence. Beth stopped and slipped her hand from his, bent down and picked up a shell to fiddle with. She hoped it would settle her nerves. She looked out at the water, it was exceptionally blue. A light breeze blew as a sea-gull flew over.

"I'm terrified Andy," she said honestly. She stood for a moment basking in the quiet lull of the waves. "Part of me says 'go, but cautiously,' 'go slow,' but I don't think either of us is capable of that." She said without looking at him, she couldn't.

He looked at her and asked, "What's the other part say?"

"The other part says run like hell!"

"Don't listen to that part," Andy laughed.

She turned to him after a while and asked, "Can we go slow Andy? Can you? Because I don't know if I can."

He sat down on the sand and rested his elbows on his knees as he looked out over the water. "I won't push you. I don't want to scare you away. Slow and easy if that's what you want, what you need, Bethy. I'll try," he said.

She sat down with him. They sat there drinking in the beauty of the day, watching the waves breaking before them. They sat quietly for a long time. Every once in a while he would turn slightly and look at her, never making eye contact. Finally he turned and pulled her to him, a hug, just her in his arms. Then he rose and took her hands, and pulled her to her feet. They walked back to the car in silence and drove down the coast for about an hour. There was a breeze whipping through the car, some music playing but no conversation.

Andy found a little English Pub and they went in for fish and chips. The crowd was mostly older folks, so they felt sure they could enjoy the time with little interruption. It was nice, the conversation was pleasant and the company good. The men had a game of darts in progress. When they finished dinner, Andy asked if he could join them for a few rounds. He was having a great time. They were all laughing and the men loved every bit of it. Finally, Andy told them he needed to go. They begged him to stay, he looked toward Beth. They followed his gaze, laughed and told him to "go" but to come again soon.

They drove back to the condo in silence. When they walked up Andy took a key out of his pocket and mindlessly put it into the lock. It seemed a very natural act.

"I guess I didn't remember that you still had that," Beth said as he did.

He looked down at the key. "Been on my key ring for like fifteen years," he pushed the door open. They walked into the living room and he sat down as Beth fixed them something to drink.

"I'll be honest Bethy, there were a million times I thought about just getting here and putting the key in the door and letting myself in. I wanted to, but I didn't. I wanted you so much, but I respect you more. I'm so happy here with you."

Beth just looked at him. He was sitting there on the sofa looking just like he had the first time he'd come there, older, but the same. Fifteen years? Had it really been that long? Part of her couldn't remember a day without him, and another part remembered every single second.

Thinking that she needed to lighten the moment, "It's just as well that you didn't," she laughed. "I bought a gun a while back, Pops suggestion. And I learned how to use it."

"You'd have known it was me," he laughed.

"That's exactly what I meant," she replied, and they both laughed.

He patted the sofa beside him. She hesitated, but he patted again and said "Bethy" and she went. She sat beside him and he pulled her to him. He wrapped her in his embrace, and once again, in his arms is where she belonged.

They went to the bedroom and crawled into the bed and held each other.

Andy stayed in town, and they spent every minute possible together. He would be there for coffee in the morning and lock Beth in at night. He would call later and they shared those late night phone calls like they had done for so many years. Beth continued to work. Andy did too. It was a beautiful time, and slowly they rolled back into their relationship. It was good. Beth loved him so much that she thought she could endure anything.

Maybe it's true the third time and all.

They were happy and it seemed enough. Her family wasn't thrilled, especially Pops, but she knew they loved her and would try to understand any decision she made. She decided with Andy was where she belonged, again.

CHAPTER TWENTY~ONE

November 22, 1993 ~We spent a month together and I resigned my position with the Cancer Foundation to share my time with Andy, once again. It'll be different this time.

They went to Eleuthera the day before Thanksgiving, just the two of them. The cottage was, once again, their haven. It was beautiful; cool nights, warm days. Beth would wake in the morning, start coffee and go to the beach to walk. Quiet, peaceful solitude... She never wanted to leave. In that place there weren't the same challenges as back in the states. There, they were only Andy and Beth. It was just the two of them. They had each other, no one else.

They stayed through the holidays, and the gift they gave each other was only their hearts. No paper or bows to rip into, just themselves, bound together once again. They stayed seven heavenly weeks. But the reality of Andy's life, the real world beckoned. He had obligations.

~ ~ ~

In mid-January, they returned to Florida. Beth packed to go with him to Corpus Christi. She took only a few suitcases, just some of her clothes and a few things. She wanted to be sure. She had been with him again for three months and it was good, maybe the best they had ever been. She thought she could handle anything because she was with Andy again. But being back at the house was difficult. It was as she had left it only without her things. It looked bare. It was a house, no longer a home, and it felt cold and sad.

Andy was busy. He was preparing to release *Memories* in March. "I Miss You" was the first single released, and went quickly to number one. The two of them shared as normal a life as someone in his profession could. He was working with a new band on the final tweaks, and they worked in the studio at home to stay close. Andy worked very hard to make it easy for Beth. He came to the house for dinner every evening. He came in for lunch when he could, or she would take it to the studio. She knew he was trying to keep it as normal as he could, and she appreciated it.

But, as the time drew nearer, and she knew Andy's preparations were in the works to get out on the road to promote the album, it became a laborious struggle. She tried very hard to roll back into the routine of what had been their life together. It wasn't a struggle being with Andy. That part was good, really good. And that made the rest even harder. It was the lack of privacy that she realized she could no longer deal with. Photographers caught their every move, anywhere and everywhere they went, they were there. She was back in pictures with Andy in magazines with headlines like "Together again, again..." "One more time for Golden Eye and Bethy", "How long will it last this time?"

It was maddening to her.

~ ~ ~

April 12, 1994 ~ I stayed at the house alone far more than I wanted because of all the attention. My life had become hell, total utter hell... It was my personal nightmare. Staying at the house made me sad; it didn't feel like home, I felt lost there. It felt more like a prison. We couldn't go anywhere without having to address that we were a couple again. Andy was fine with it, he was just so happy we were together again. But suddenly it was haunting me and I hated it. It was overwhelming and consuming.

Finally it erupted. We were having dinner. Andy had been in meetings all day about the tour. He planned them at the studio to stay close. He was trying so hard, but I had been alone with too much time to think. I walked around the house and remembered, and as the day wore on it all just kind of festered. He was excitedly telling me about all that was going on and suddenly, the walls came crashing in.

"It never stops," she said, in a quiet voice.

"What sweetheart?" He looked up as he asked, and when he did his expression turned to one of alarm.

"The attention," she said. "I stay here, in the house because I don't want to deal with it. I can't go anywhere, can't get gas in the car without someone approaching me."

"It's new, they'll get over it," he said cautiously as he ate. "Soon it'll be old news and they'll move on."

"Will they?" She pushed her plate aside. With her elbows on the table and hands clasped, as in prayer, she rested her head. Several minutes passed.

She got up and began pacing. She looked around. It wasn't her home any more, it was Andy's. The part of her that had once been there was gone. Where? She didn't know. There was no part of her still there. She was a visitor in his home, and suddenly, it felt that way. Realizing that nothing would ever be the same again, it overwhelmed her with emotion.

"I don't know Andy. Soon you'll be touring again and if I go with you, like you want, we'll deal with new crowds, different ones, more stories, more pictures. It won't just be us." Still pacing she said, "I can't stay here and if I go home I'll be a prisoner."

She turned to him and the tears came in a flood. She broke. It was a meltdown. "I can't do it." She sat down in the middle of the floor, sobbing.

"Bethy, you can. You have, and you can again. We can." He got up and went to her, pulling her to her feet, wrapping her in his arms, kissing her forehead.

"No Andy, I can't."

"Don't cry sweetheart, we can deal with this, together." He stroked her hair and pulled her closer.

"Don't baby me. I'm telling you, I can't deal with it anymore, Andy."

She pushed back and looked at him. She looked in his eyes, those eyes that she thought held her future, and she finally knew that what she wanted, what she needed, would never be there; commitment and security.

"I don't want to anymore. I want to go home."

"Your home is with me," he said.

"No Andy, my heart is with you. My home is back in Florida, where my things are. There is a big difference. I need to go home, where my family is, where my work is. I want to go back."

"So we'll go, pack your things, and get them back here. Then everything will be better. We'll get you settled and then we'll leave for the tour. You'll feel better in a day or two."

He had it all worked out, but she didn't. "No! You're not hearing me!" she shouted. "I can't go with you. I don't want to go. I just want to go home!"

She wasn't shouting now, it was a tiny whisper of a voice that said, "I just want to go home."

Clearly hurting, he asked her; "What does that mean for us?"

"I don't know Andy. I just want to go home before I lose myself completely."

And the last headline she saw about herself read;

"Bethy throws in the towel!"

~ ~ ~

May 2, 1994 ~ It's a gypsy lifestyle. Traveling all the time, living in hotels, out of suitcases, eating out every meal, and harder still are the hours that you keep. Sleep all day, work late, play all night. But worse, was the lack of privacy. I just couldn't do it any longer. He wasn't traveling with the Traveler guys this time. There would be no Dina, no Nathan, just Andy and a crew and band he was working with for the tour that I barely knew. They had a brotherhood, with each other, that musician's bond. I would be alone. It was hard and it wasn't what I dreamed of. I missed my family, and friends. Add to that the fact that I was always on edge wondering what came next.

I realized, suddenly, the other things I missed. I never got cards from him on holidays and as silly as that sounds, it was something I realized that I needed. Valentine's Day came and went many times, and I remember one birthday celebration in all those years, and suddenly all the ones that didn't happen began to hurt. I was ready for home and family. Andy never headed that direction. I was ready for marriage and he wasn't talking, and I knew not to try to change him.

So, that last headline was probably right. I was 'throwing in the towel.' I gave up and went home. This time it was my doing, and it hurt far more than I can ever express, but it hurt Andy more. I left him at the airport crying. I saw his tears but I couldn't look back. I had to go. It had to be forward... forward motion. There could be no turning back this time.

~ ~ ~

Beth went back to Florida and into seclusion to let things die down. Andy called daily, she finally asked him to stop. It was more than she could bear. His emotions only made it worse. He begged, he pleaded, he promised, he cried, he postponed the tour. But she needed a normal life, no photographers, no TV, no travel. And if that meant being without him then that's what she had to do. She loved him more than ever, but she knew that she couldn't live that kind of life any more. She was tired, mentally and physically.

For three months she barely left her home. Her family came in, Kimmy came, and slowly she got it back together. Rick called early on to let her know that he was thinking of her. It was a kind gesture and she appreciated it.

~ ~ ~

Andy received a letter from Beth not long after she left and he read it over and over. He could feel her pain, taste her tears and live her sadness.

May 20, 1994
My Dear, Dear Andy,
I'm not sure I know where to begin. I don't know what happened, really. Maybe it was that all of a sudden I had an ah-ha moment, the final straw, my epiphany.

I realized how much I love you, and I always will, but I can't live this life anymore, everything about us being public, no real privacy, every move scrutinized. I just can't do it anymore. I can't.

There is no one else, just me, and only me, if that is what you are wondering. There is, and always will be, only you. My life, my love, my heart, but I had to go, to save myself. I don't know what would have happened if I stayed any longer. I have to plan a course for me, for my future, and sadly, I don't think that includes 'us' anymore. As hard as that is to say, I have to say it.

I keep feeling like I've missed something. It's been fifteen years, Andy, and here we are just like we were in the beginning. I realized what I want, no… it's what I need, and it's more than to just be with you running all over the country, the world with you. As good as that can be, and has been, it's not enough, not anymore. So I had to go, pick up the pieces and move on, rebuild my life.

Please don't call. It's just too hard, too emotional. I need to move on, without you now. I will love you; always love you, forever… But I can't live this life that you chose. I can't ask you to change it because it is who you are, and though you will say that you could, later you would resent it, and in the end you would resent me. I couldn't deal with that.

You have your passion. I know how you feel about your music. I know how it makes me feel. It's your reward, your life. I have to find that in my life. I have to find my passion.

And so, with that, I will leave you with my heart, my soul, my love.
Your Bethy

~ ~ ~

It broke her Pops's heart. He had watched her grow, and learn, and hurt over the years. He tried to step back when he needed to and let her fall, but he was always close enough to pick her up if she needed. He was always there, waiting. She only had to ask, and to assure her strength, he made her ask. Most times she picked herself up and moved past whatever it was, but there were those times when he struggled because he wanted to help her, but she didn't ask. He wanted her to ask this time so she could heal and move on, but she didn't and he felt helpless.

~ ~ ~

Beth had been on an emotional roller coaster for so many years. Kimmy had been on that ride with her. She laughed when Beth laughed, cried when she cried, shared her highs and lows. She had been through all of it with her, because she loved her. That's what friends do.

Kimmy knew that Andy Stevens was absolutely the love of Beth's life, but she watched, yet again, as Beth grieved. And she grieved as in mourning. Beth clung to that life for so long that at times Kimmy wondered if she would recover, but she knew Beth's strength and resolve. Kimmy knew she would bounce back. She prayed that she would find peace without Andy, but wondered, as well, if that was even possible.

Kimmy prayed that all of Beth's insecurities would vanish and that she would flourish as she once had, with the confidence and grace that they had all seen in Beth before. And Beth did recover. She found her place in the world, her world, without Andy Stevens.

~ ~ ~

In June, the Cancer Foundation contacted her. Her job was still open and they wanted her back, so she went. The good thing was the notoriety, the curiosity. That was a plus in getting many things done, fundraisers and such. Everyone knew who she was, but that part of her life was not an option for conversation. Not with anyone, at any time, ever...

Andy finally began the tour and she knew it was successful. She heard small bits about how it was going, but she tried not to get caught up in it. She and Roddy spoke often. There were times he would tell her that Andy asked him to get her in touch with him. Beth continued to say no, she couldn't. She broke once when Roddy called with news that Phyllis had passed away.

Beth thought long and hard, but called Andy because she knew what Phyllis meant to him. She called because she knew what she meant to her.

> *September 9, 1994 ~ When Andy answered, there was a thud. 'Was it his heart or mine?' I wondered. He sounded so sad, so tired. "Bethy... I'm glad to hear from you." And his words made me cry.*
>
> *"It was quick. She didn't suffer." He explained it like he needed to comfort me, and then he was quiet for a minute. "I was in town. That was a blessing, but I wasn't with her. She was alone," and then he cried.*
>
> *I know how hard that was. It's a pain that you can't describe. It brought back the memories of the loss of Nana and him not being there. He asked if I would come, but I couldn't. He pleaded and told me how much Phyllis loved me. And I remembered how much I loved her, but I couldn't go. I just couldn't. There was too much at stake... my heart...*
>
> *"Bethy, please. I need you. I want you..." he cried.*
> *"Andy, please don't. I just can't. I can't come back. Kimmy and Lane will be there, with Roddy. You will have the support you need to get through this. But I can't come. Know that you are in my thoughts and prayers," and I thought, 'my heart.'*
>
> *"Bethy..." he pleaded, and it broke my heart, but I couldn't go there to be strong for him.*
>
> *"I have to go now. Andy, I am so very sorry."*
>
> *"Bethy," but I hung up before he could say any more.*

~ ~ ~

At Christmas time in 1994, a package came via courier, it was a CD. Roddy sent it. He told her it was coming. "Powerful stuff," he told her.

She listened and she hurt. It was so emotional. From his heart, she heard Andy sing; "Love Me Like That Again", a beautiful song about lost love, and she cried.

Love me like that again
Why can't we go back
To the way it was before
I wanna hold you, feel you,
Always be near you

It had been more than six months since she left and this was the first time she had really cried for him in a long time. She almost gave in to give him a call and tell him how beautiful it was. But she knew the consequences and she couldn't.

Chapter Twenty~Two

Beth's life was on a forward path. It had to be that way. No matter how hard it was to leave her past behind, she had to keep forward motion. She kept busy, immersing herself in work. It was an emotional outlet, but it kept her time occupied as well. Her work with the Cancer Foundation saved her.

Soon after she returned to work, she met John Oliver. She had met him many years before at a work function. He was now the Chief Operating Officer for an electronics firm that she worked closely with in the past, and he was on the board of directors for the Cancer Foundation. They worked together on several events and became fast friends.

~ ~ ~

John remembered meeting Beth in 1979. The two of them had spoken on the phone many times over work related items. He loved her wit so much that he would make excuses to call just to engage her. He knew when he met her that he would never forget her, but he knew her story, everyone did. She was 'Andy Steven's girl'. After she left he followed her through the tabloids and was sad for her trials.

John was a man married to his work. He dated through the years but never married. He, too, was passionate for the Cancer Foundation, and when he bumped into her at a board meeting one evening he was happy to see her again. He felt like he'd been waiting for her all these years.

John learned patience with Beth. She was never willing to put herself totally out there, cautious from her earlier relationship, so he waited. Coffee dates filled with conversation turned into dinner dates. They discovered that they had much in common. Friendship turned into a relationship and they were good together.

He learned to deal with 'who she was'. She was often recognized, 'Weren't you…?' 'Andy's girlfriend…' 'I know you, right,' 'Oh yeah, Andy Stevens!' He heard those comments often, and marveled at Beth's grace in response.

John was the total opposite of Andy; there couldn't have been a greater contrast. Quiet and reserved, he was conservative, and handsome in a clean-cut 'suit' way. He was great at conversation, something Beth missed. There was a natural progression as time passed. It was quiet. It was private. It was just the two them. If there was a disagreement, it was private, not headlines in a magazine. It was a normal relationship.

He knew about Andy. He knew there was, and would probably always be, a place in her hear that Andy would never really leave. As their relationship progressed they discussed it many times, at length. They had to, it was necessary. She told John there would always be a place in her heart that belonged to Andy, that she would always love him. John understood, and they moved on. Theirs grew into a beautiful relationship. They loved each other, but she did not 'fall in love' with John. He was a friend, who became her lover, and then her partner. They shared a great deal together, and when he asked her to marry him she said yes.

She called Roddy to share the news. He'd met John, and he was happy for them. And then she called Andy. She wanted him to hear it from her, not Roddy, not anyone else.

"Bethy," he said, when he realized who it was. There was excitement in his voice, but Beth got right to the point.

"I wanted you to hear this from me. Not Roddy, not anyone else. Me." There was a pause. It became long and uncomfortable. And finally she said it; "I'm getting married."

Andy was quiet at first. It felt as though someone sucker-punched him and knocked the wind out of him.

Did he think I would not move on, live my life and all that it meant to live? I'm sure he knew I was seeing someone; sure Roddy had quietly shared that with him.

Finally he took a deep breath; a sigh, and then he said, "I'm happy for you Bethy."

But he didn't sound happy. There was another long pause, and it was Beth who spoke. "I hope so Andy; I want you to be happy for me. I want you to understand that this is what I want in my life, what I need, what I've needed all along."

"You could have had it with me," his voice wavered.

"Andy…" was it hurt or exasperation that she felt, she wasn't sure. "You never asked, never hinted. Fifteen years and you never hinted that it was even a possibility. It's beyond that now."

"You should have told me that was what you wanted, Bethy," he said sadly.

"You should have wanted it enough to know that it's a natural progression when two people love each other!" she told him, trying not to sound hurt. "I would *never* have told you that. You would have felt pushed, trapped. That's not me Andy."

"Do you love him Bethy?" he asked. And then quickly rephrased; "Are you in love with him?"

"I love him enough to want to share my life with him and that is what he wants with me." She thought for a moment, and finally said, "Yes. Yes, I guess I am in love with him."

"Then I wish you the best. Be happy," he said, and hung up. He was gone. They were over, for good this time. That very long chapter in her life closed.

February 1996 ~When I called it wasn't the same as any time in the past. There wasn't the warmth, or that old familiarity. There was only a conversation that seemed necessary between two people. It was sad. I wanted him to understand, but all he felt was hurt. I wanted him to be happy for me, but he was only sad for his own loss.

~ ~ ~

On a beautiful, sunny, cool Saturday in April 1996, Pops walked Beth down the aisle. She was thirty-nine years old and he probably never thought he would get the chance. It couldn't have been a more perfect day. The ceremony was very small and private at an old chapel on the beach. Just John and Beth, their families and a few close friends attended. The list of guests from Beth's previous life was short: Roddy and Vince, Mark and Anna, Dina, Nathan and Megan. She loved them, and wanted them to share this special time. How could she not, for so many years, they were her family.

Kimmy was the Matron of Honor, and Jenna was the Junior Bride and she loved every second. John's dad stood up with him. It was a short and very simple service. Beth wore an off-white, lace, tea-length dress that her mom made. She added Nana's pearls and carried white roses. Her mom was at the sewing machine with Beth, Kimmy and Jenna for days in preparation. She made Jenna and Kimmy's dresses, too. Jenna's dress was a miniature version of Beth's. Kimmy's was peach and very similar. John's favorite white roses decorated the alter, not the Calla Lilies that Beth hid away in her memory because Andy knew they were her favorites. John had always chosen roses for her.

After the ceremony there was a small reception at the home of a friend of John's who had a large place on the beach. The gathering was small, very simple, but very intimate and elegant. Vince took care of all the food, calling caterers and picking a menu, one less thing for Beth to fuss with.

"Beth, you are so beautiful." Roddy took her hands in his, pulling her into his embrace he whispered, "Always beautiful, but today you glow." She was so glad he was there. He had always been there. She couldn't imagine her life without him.

He held her for a moment. She knew his thoughts. For a minute she held her breath, quite afraid to breathe. "Aren't brides supposed to glow?" she asked finally, and kissed his cheek.

John walked to where they stood. Roddy shook his hand and congratulated him. "A true prize," he said.

John pulled her closer, his prize now. "I know. I did come out a winner, didn't I?" he laughed.

~ ~ ~

John and Beth began their life together and they were happy. It was a life built on love and trust, stability and security. It was all Beth ever really needed or wanted. They joined pieces of their lives together, and made a home. She left her past behind, sold the condo sold, and many pieces of her past as well. She packed memories away to make it a clean slate, a whole new path.

It was a quiet simple life and Beth liked it that way just fine. Very seldom did Andy come into her thoughts. Sometimes something would remind her, but it wasn't really sadness that she felt any more. It was usually a beautiful memory. There were times when a hurt would return, but for the most part they were much less painful as time passed.

There were those moments though... Driving home one day listening to the radio, something happened that took her breath away. She had to pull off the road. Roddy had always sent a copy of every song that Andy was working on in advance. He didn't send them for approval; he sent them so that she knew, so that she wasn't caught off guard. It had been a busy time, and one slipped away. Listening to the radio, hearing his voice she cried. The words gave her heart a jolt she hadn't felt in a very long time.

To you I come for comfort
You embrace me, warm me
To you I come for peace
You hold me, calm me
To you I come
Always with you in my heart
In my soul
You are my life

It was so beautiful. The rocker in him had grown into a balladeer and it was beautiful. When she heard the words, her first thought was that he had finally moved on, and it was sad. But as she listened, really listened, longer, and harder, she knew. Later she would hear these words and others speak of them, speculation that he had found someone new. But Beth knew. She knew where the comfort came from. She knew where he found that peace. She knew his heart and soul. It wasn't a woman he sang of. The warmth and the calm were his voice, his music, and his solace.

And she knew then that he would never really be gone from her heart.

That beautiful song earned Andy another Grammy nod, and the statue to go with it.

~ ~ ~

January 1997 brought the first real challenge. It was Roddy's sixtieth birthday and Vince was having a huge bash to celebrate the occasion. Beth felt torn like she couldn't imagine. She knew Andy would be there, but how could she not go? She and Kimmy talked about it, she and Lane were going. Beth would have a good support system, so they went. Vince made all the arrangements. Kimmy and Lane, and John and Beth would stay at the hotel in Corpus Christi where the bash would be held. She hadn't returned there in a very long time.

When she arrived, emotions overwhelmed her like she never imagined, and she had to hide them from John. Just being in the airport rattled her... Once at the hotel, Beth found every reason she could think of to stay in the room. Headache... tired... jet lag... Finally it was time. She couldn't put it off any longer. They dressed for the party and made their way to the ballroom. A quick span of the room told her that Andy was not there, yet. Maybe he had decided not to come, but she doubted that.

Everything was so festive, balloons, music and then suddenly, without even seeing him, she felt the heat on her face as it began to burn crimson red.

How can that still happen?

She knew he was there, someplace, watching her, and she tried to prepare herself. John was on the other side of the room chatting with Nathan, and Kimmy had just left her. For that brief moment, she was alone.

"Hi." She heard that familiar voice coming from the right of her, and she turned. How long could she not breathe she wondered.

"Hey," she said, and tried very hard not to look or sound like she would fall apart at any moment.

I can do this, I repeated over and over in my mind, over and over... over and over... Had it really been almost three years since I've seen him?

"I'm so glad to see you here," he said.

'*Oh that look,*' she thought as he leaned in and placed a kiss on her cheek.

She laughed, "I couldn't pass up the big one!"

"I wondered," he said. He never changed, he was still as beautiful as the very first moment she saw him, all those years ago. "How have you been?"

"Great," she said trying not to sound shaken. "Busy!"

She looked up and Roddy was quickly making his way toward them. Her savior...

"Hey!" he said in a jovial voice, as he grabbed Beth with one of his big hugs "Beth, radiant as ever!"

"Happy Birthday!" It relieved her not to look at Andy for a moment.

"My favorite people in all-the world are all here with me tonight!" Roddy took her trembling hand and held it. "She looks great doesn't she?" he said and looked to Andy.

"Beautiful," he replied.

"There's John," he said scanning the room and he waved. "Have you met John, Andy?"

"No, I've not had the pleasure," he said as his eyes lingered on Beth's.

"John, Andy Stevens," Roddy said, and Andy extended his hand.

"It's a pleasure to meet you," Andy said, and then added, "You are a lucky man. Beth, it was good to see you." He gave a nod in her direction and walked to where Nathan and Dina stood watching the exchange.

Not 'Bethy' any longer. Maybe he had moved on as well.

John leaned to kiss her, as if to mark his territory. Andy stayed across the room the rest of the evening, but always, always, he was watching her, and she knew that because she was watching him.

~ ~ ~

Roddy still sent those tapes to her to have a listen before Andy released something they thought she should know about, and she was always glad when he did. She made sure to listen so there were no surprises after the last one that slipped by. Many of the songs he wrote were still based on their relationship and his 'aloneness' without her. She knew because she knew his heart, his style, and she knew what they had shared. She still played his music. He was still her favorite artist, and she guessed he always would be.

~ ~ ~

In March 1997, John and Beth's life was about to take yet another course, they found out she was pregnant. They were both excited, but John was over the moon. He painted the baby's room pink, and every day came home with something very girlie to add. An early sonogram revealed what John hoped. It was a very exciting time. Carlee Elizabeth Oliver was born on December 1, 1997.

Their lives became busy and full and then the world as Beth knew it changed, yet again.

Chapter Twenty-Three

September 2001 brought great turmoil to their lives. It was a Thursday morning, and John was still in bed. He and Beth were talking, as they did every morning. They discussed the day ahead and what was on their agendas. John had the TV tuned to the morning news and Beth was just out of the shower standing in front of the mirror, naked, starting her usual morning routine, dressing for a meeting. Suddenly John became very quiet.

"Beth, come here." There was a strange tone to his voice, and she thought something horrible had just been reported. The country had just been through the horrors of September eleventh days earlier, and Beth wondered *'what now?'*

She walked over to the bed and bent to kiss him, "What is it, honey?"

"Turn around," he said. And she did. He reached up and touched a place on her bottom, just above the panty line of her left cheek. It wasn't a caress, he was exploring, and she laughed.

"What are you doing?"

"How long has this been there?"

She turned and looked over her shoulder. "What are you talking about?"

He pointed out a mole.

"Oh that, I reckon it's been there longer than I can remember. I think it's a birthmark or something." She started to walk away, but he grabbed her hand and held it to keep her where she was. "What John?"

He had a tone of concern in his voice as he said, "How have we not noticed that before? Beth, it's ugly."

She laughed and said; "Thank you very much!"

"I'm serious, have you ever had it checked?"

"No," she said, his concern scaring her.

"Has it gotten bigger?"

"I don't know. It's just a mole."

But his whole mood had changed in an instant. "Please have that examined as soon as possible."

She told him she would, making mental note to call a doctor. Back in the bathroom, she turned and looked closer in the mirror.

Maybe it is bigger, maybe it does look different. I can't be sure. It's been there for years, it's probably nothing...

Several days went by, and John asked when she was seeing the dermatologist. She admitted that it had completely slipped her mind. The mole had been there so long she just didn't even think about it, couldn't remember when it wasn't there. She told him she would, that she'd just been busy. But John picked up the phone and made the call..

"We go tomorrow," he told her.

The appointment was with a dermatologist, Dr. Fred Wright, and they went together. He examined the mole, and with a very serious tone to his voice, said; "I want to remove it. How long since you noticed it change?"

"I don't know, didn't really realize it had, I guess," she said. "OK, we'll get it taken care of. I'll make the arrangements."

"Now Beth, I want to take it off now. I want to send it off immediately. I don't like the way it looks. Are you familiar with Melanoma?"

Melanoma... I felt panic rise in my throat. I couldn't breathe. I work for the Cancer Foundation; of course I was familiar.

"I want to have this evaluated quickly."

He took it off right there in the office. It didn't seem such a big deal. A shot to numb, four stitches, a little discomfort sitting and a bit of pain and she was on her way.

Carlee was at a 'Mommy's Day Out' at church and Beth was home alone the next day working, making preparations for an upcoming Cancer Foundation event. She'd been on the phone all morning and when she finally hung it up it rang instantly.

"Beth, it's Dr. Wright. I have the results."

"Wow," she said and tried not to sound alarmed, it was the doctor, not an office staffer or nurse, "that was fast."

"I rushed it through," he explained. "I want you and John in my office as soon as you can get here."

"What is it?"

"Come to the office," he said. "We'll talk when you get here."

She called John and told him to meet her there.

"No," he said. "I don't want you driving. I'll be there as quick as I can."

As she waited for him she called Kimmy and asked her to pick up Carlee. "What is it Beth? Something's wrong, I can tell it from the tone of your voice."

Beth told her briefly what was going on. A short time later John came into the house, he held her close and she cried. Fear finally set it.

Suddenly those words "I have the results" kept ringing in her head. "It's something bad isn't it?" John didn't answer her.

They drove in silence. She held John's hand, probably squeezed it to a bruise, but she didn't want to let him go. She wanted to hold on to the strength he provided her, the stability she longed for her whole adult life.

As they drove, Beth looked over at him. He was so tense, his jaw so firmly set. He was always intense, but at that moment it was clearer. His fear mirrored her-own. It was the longest ride she had ever taken. The twenty-minute drive to the doctor's office seemed an eternity. When they arrived they went into the doctor's office, not an exam room. A few moments later Dr. Wright entered.

He cut right to the chase. "Beth, the biopsy results..." "Unclear margins..." "Cancerous cells..." "All those years lying on the beach..." "Sunscreen..." "The sun..." she heard broken sentences as she tried to process everything he was saying, "A form of skin cancer..."

"We need to do some tests, check lymph nodes; do blood work, chest x-rays, CT scan and a PET scan. We need to see where we are with this thing. I think we need go ahead and schedule surgery to get as much of the mole as we can. I'd like to go ahead and admit you tomorrow to do the tests so you'll be right there. I'll be in touch with the surgeon as we get results."

"Tomorrow?" She tried to focus. She tried to listen, tried to grasp every word, but her mind raced. She was making mental lists as she always did, trying to figure everything out, Carlee, work… She knew, as always, John was already two steps ahead of her.

"We'll do whatever we need," he said to the doctor, looking at Beth as he spoke.

The next morning John and Beth were at the hospital at seven, and immediately they started running tests. Later, Beth was lying in bed resting; John was with her. There was a knock on her door. Dr. Wright entered and had another doctor with him.

This can't be good…

"Beth, John; this is Dr. Peter Sampson. He's the surgeon. We've gone through this and he agrees that we need to do surgery."

"The tests show advanced progression," Dr. Sampson told them. "I think we need to move quickly, go in and remove what we can. I'll be honest, it doesn't look good. If you agree, I have scheduled surgery for first thing tomorrow."

It doesn't look good…

"Yes," she said. John took her hand, but her mind was a million other places as the two doctors left the room.

~ ~ ~

At 7:30 the next morning, September twenty-eighth, they took Beth for the surgery. Carlee was with John's parents. John was with Beth, as they wheeled her down the hall to the operating room. He walked with her until they told him he couldn't go any further.

"I'll be there when you wake up," he told her as he bent to kiss her.

When she awoke, she was very sore. It seemed odd that there would be so much pain. She felt some kind of soft wedge behind her to keep her from rolling over. Dr. Sampson and John were standing beside the bed.

"Hey," she whispered to John. He took her hand, and brought it to his cheek and held it there and caressed it. She knew something wasn't good by the look on his face.

"Sweetheart," he paused, and she could feel the lump in his throat.

Dr. Sampson looked at him, as if to give him relief, and he began to speak. "We were in surgery about four hours. You have an aggressive form of melanoma. This was deep, stage IV disease," he explained. "The melanoma has metastasized. The mole's location made access to the liver quick."

"My liver..." she repeated.

"Beth, honey..."

They needn't say another word. I could see it on their faces, so serious, and John looked so sad...

"We couldn't get it all," Dr. Sampson continued.

"Couldn't," she asked, and felt the tears come. "What? When?" She mumbled in broken words and thoughts.

"There is no way to say for certain, but the liver..."

"I know," she said abruptly, cutting him off. Of course she knew. She worked with that kind of information. She knew... She turned away as the tears spilled from her eyes. So many thoughts...

My life, my family, oh God, my Carlee...

John had a hundred questions, Beth had none. He asked about treatment, medication, more tests, he asked about reconstruction.

"We'll get an oncologist in to see you," the doctor said.

"I'll leave the two of you alone now, we'll talk more later." Dr. Sampson reached to squeeze her hand and left them.

They didn't say anything for a really long while. John let her cry, not touching her, not saying a word. "Beth..." he said finally.

"John, not now," she turned to look at him. So many thoughts, more fears, but not now... "Can you just leave me alone for a while, please?"

"I can't honey. I need to be here with you," he said taking her hand in his, holding it, so full of love, and fear.

She turned away, "Where are Kimmy and Mom?"

"Waiting outside; I'll get them if you want."

She waited a while then asked; "What time is it?"

"Just after three; do you want your mom?"

"No, please just leave me alone for a while. For now, you tell them." Her mind was racing; "Someone needs to take Carlee home. She should be home, in her own room, with her things. She is too young to understand being away for very long," again she was mumbling.

"Mom and Dad can do that, honey. I'll call them."

"John," she turned back to him. But he knew before she asked. "Please have Kimmy call Roddy." She could see the hurt on his face, he knew why. "Please..." she repeated.

John left her there alone. He didn't want to, but he finally conceded. The light in the room was very dim. There was a gray hue that shone on everything as her mind raced ninety miles an hour. Gray seemed an appropriate color at that moment. She was sure that the readings on her blood pressure and heart rate must have been going crazy. She tried to gather her thoughts, her courage. She had to try to face that devil called cancer, head on. But everything seemed so jumbled up, so she prayed.

After a while her mom came into the room. She told Beth that Pops was having a hard time and wanted to get settled before he came in. She knew what that meant. Her mind went back to that place in time, she watched him when he lost his mother, and she saw it again when Pappy passed away. He didn't want to cry in front of her. He didn't want to appear weak. He wanted to be strong for his 'baby girl.'

"We'll get through this," her mom whispered.

My mom, so strong... Always there, always strong...

"I know you will," Beth replied.

"*We* will," Liz, corrected her.

"Mom?"

"Beth, don't. There are so many things."

Beth interrupted her, "I need to, Mom. John and I talked with Dr. Sampson briefly, seems it's pretty far along. He wants me to see an oncologist, but he doesn't think any of those things will help, I can tell. It must be pretty bad. I've seen that in what I do. If the Dr. gave any kind of indication that it would help I'd consider any of it, but he didn't, so I know, and I don't think I'm ready or willing to go through all that. I need to be me, to be whole for Carlee as long as I can. I don't want to be sick and tired from chemo. I don't want my hair to fall out. I don't want her to remember me that way. I just want to be there for her as long as I can."

She got quiet, trying to gather her thoughts, "I want to tell you something."

"I already know, honey," Liz stopped her, placing two fingers to her lips to do so.

Beth took her hand, so soft, so comforting and all those times she had held it in the past came back in a flash. "Do you Mom?" she asked. "Do you really?"

Such a wise woman, my mom...

"Yes sweetheart, I know." She paused, a long, thoughtful moment. "I know you and I know your heart. I know you are going to tell me you want Andy here."

"I do." They sat quietly a while and Beth finally asked, "Is it wrong, Mom?" Liz caressed her daughter's hand, but she didn't say anything. It wasn't necessary.

"Mom, I am so torn. John has to be OK with it. He is my life, but I can't go through this without seeing Andy again." She looked away, maybe ashamed, "So long," she continued, still not facing her. "We were 'us' for so long."

Liz held her, and together they cried.

~ ~ ~

Liz Morgan struggled with the news of Beth's cancer. Any parent would. She couldn't imagine losing a child. *'A parent should not outlive their children'* she thought.

They were more than mother and daughter. They were friends. When Beth was young they did everything together, with Kimmy. And now Liz wondered if her own love of the beach was to blame for this.

She watched now as Beth struggled with her feelings. She loved John, Liz knew that, but she never quit loving Andy. Liz knew that, too. She said many prayers over the years that she and Andy would be OK. And every time he hurt her she prayed that Beth would recover. She never blamed Andy. She blamed that lifestyle. Beth needed and wanted; instead, she gave and gave.

~ ~ ~

When Pops came in the room, he had a wan look, but he wasn't crying any more. "Hello baby girl," he leaned and kissed her. "How ya doin'?"

Beth took his hand, squeezed it. "Not too bad. My back hurts the most, I think, lying on my side." He walked around the bed, sat on the edge and began to rub her back, with a soft, loving caress. It made him feel like he was doing something important, and it was easier for him to be where he didn't have to face her. This way he could hide his own fears. When he wasn't rubbing her back, he gently stroked her hair, such a tender gesture from those strong hands.

"Pops, I need you to go be with Carlee. The two of you," she said looking at Liz. "Give Tom and Evelyn a break, I'm sure they will want to come here for a while. It'll be good for you to get away, and good for Carlee to be with you for a while. I'm sure she is wondering about all of this. She needs as much 'normal' right now as we can give her."

"John asked if they could bring her in to see me, but I said no. I think the hospital would allow it, but I don't want her to see all of this," Beth said motioning to the pumps and IVs. "It might scare her. Hopefully I'll be home soon and she can adjust there."

"Pops…"

"Yeah?"

"I love you."

"I love you, too, baby girl." He exited the room quickly. She knew he was crying.

"The boys want to come see you," her mom said finally, referring to her brothers.

"I want to see them. Tell them to come."

"We'll get through this," her mom said again. She left a few minutes later. Shortly after that Kimmy came in. She was quiet. Beth knew she'd been crying.

"Kimmy, please!" Beth said, "Not from you! I need your strength, your vitality! I'm OK. Really, I am. I'm not giving up, but I know what's going on and I am OK."

Kimmy bent and kissed Beth's cheek. And the tears came.

"Stop, I need you, listen to me," Beth pleaded. Kimmy took her hand and sat in the chair so that they were facing each other. "I have something important to ask you." She listened intently, like what Beth was about to say was more important than anything she had ever heard. "This is a really big deal, my friend."

"Anything Beth, you know that, anything."

"I'm kinda hungry, go get me a diet Coke and a bag of chips, will ya? Real chips, not any of that diet crap, the yellow bag chips, but a diet Coke, OK?"

She laughed at the request, and it was exactly what they both needed.

"OK, now that I have the Kimmy I love here and not the one who was sweeping the floor with her bottom lip I have to tell you, you're gonna be awful popular around here for the next little while and probably past that. You'll be needed like you never dreamed. Are you up for the challenge?"

One word, "Anything," she said again.

"Have you called Roddy?"

"It's taken care of," she replied.

"Thank you." Beth looked away to blink back her own tears.

"John will need you and Jenna to help with Carlee. Jenna is old enough to understand this, Carlee won't."

"You know she'll be taken care of. She's like my own," Kimmy assured her.

"That's what I needed to hear. Mom and Pops..." Beth had to pause a minute. "Kimmy, Pops is having a really hard time. Stay around; they are your family too."

"I know."

"Now, go to the house, please; take Mom and Pops and keep them busy. Get them out of here. They need the distraction. Get things situated there, I'm gonna beg to bust outta this place as soon as they will entertain the idea. If I have to lie around I can do that at home."

"Whatever you need."

"Thank you, now go." Kimmy rose and Beth squeezed her hand. Kimmy started to well up again. "Hey, wait. There's one more thing," Beth blurted.

She turned back to see what it was that Beth would ask of her. Had she asked her to move mountains, she would have tried, so Beth knew she had to make it light. She walked back toward the bed and Beth pulled her close,

"Bring tweezers when you come back. My eyebrows are in bad shape," she whispered. Another laugh and Kimmy was out the door.

Beth lay back for a while, tried to get comfortable. Suddenly she was very tired, and she dozed.

CHAPTER TWENTY~FOUR

It was early morning when she awoke, and it was Andy who was at her bedside. She truly believed she was dreaming. John was across the room in a chair and Andy was at her bedside.

Seeing her eyes flutter he took her hand and a flood of memories washed over her. She could remember the feel of the first time he held it. She could taste that first kiss a million lifetimes ago. With time and age Andy had developed fullness about him, his face and his stature, that made him only more beautiful to her. It felt like that first glimpse of him all over again.

"Hey beautiful," he leaned and kissed her forehead.

"Yeah, right," she laughed. "When did you get here?" She wiped sleep from her eyes and rustled through her hair with her fingertips.

"I left as soon as I got the call."

She looked to John as he rose from the chair, her wonderful friend and partner, "I'll let the two of you have some time," he said and turned to go.

"John..." he turned back toward her when she said it. "I love you."

"I know sweetheart, I love you, too." He went to the bedside, squeezed her hand and kissed her cheek. "I'll be back in a while. Make her behave Andy."

"I'll do it."

~ ~ ~

Andy flew through the night to get there. He'd been in L.A. on business and Roddy had already started making arrangements as soon as he had spoken with John, before Andy even called him.

"She'll need the people she loves around her. We need to help her through this." Andy heard John's words again in his mind and he struggled for many reasons.

As the plane made its way east he tried to rest, but his mind wouldn't allow it. He thought about all those trips to Eleuthera and her baking in the sun. He thought about the days by the pool in Corpus Christi and wondered if all that had anything to do with what she was going through.

He thought about what was ahead of him and knew he would be losing her all over again and he didn't know if he could deal with it. He would see her with her family and he didn't know how he could handle that knowing the feelings he still had for her.

But he went because he knew nothing could keep him away. He would do whatever he could to help as long as her family allowed.

~ ~ ~

When he arrived, John met him at the hospital. He had the driver deliver Andy's things to their home. His parents were there with Carlee. Beth was asleep so they went for coffee and John shared more about Beth's condition, the results and prognosis.

As John talked, Andy wondered if he could be that kind of man. Could he share the woman he loved with someone from her past? John's offer overwhelmed him.

They went to her room and she was still sleeping. She looked so tiny and frail, lying there swallowed by the pillows they used to prop her up, to keep her from rolling on the wound.

After John left, Andy scooted the chair closer. He took Beth's hand and brought it to his cheek. He just held it there. He couldn't let go. Finally, he put his head down on the bed. It seemed a lifetime had passed, and in a way, it had.

His fear was unmistakable. In spite of all the thoughts and fears Beth was dealing with, it was Andy who needed comforting. She gently stroked his head.

After a while she felt the need to say something, "I need some coffee, would you please?" He rose to get it. John had a carafe of coffee waiting; he knew she'd want some. Beth needed that moment to catch her breath.

"Half of the left cheek of my butt is missing," she began, when he turned away, and she laughed. "I always said it was too big anyway. Good thing it was this cheek," she joked. "If I had to lay any other way to sleep it'd be miserable. I wouldn't be able to do it, and you know it."

"Beth, don't." He said it so softly; it was almost a whisper.

"Oh hell, Andy, if I don't laugh I'll fall apart. There are so many thoughts, so many fears, so many plans that I don't even know where to begin. They'll do more tests to see," she mumbled. "John asked about reconstructive surgery, but I could tell the doctor didn't think it was something to even consider. It's bad. I know it is."

"I know, Bethy. John told me everything. He was most gracious to let me come. He was very kind when he called."

"John called you," she said, her surprise was clear.

"Yeah, you didn't know?" He looked back over his shoulder at her. "Roddy got him through, but it was important to him that he be the one to tell me. I called Roddy and he had already talked to John and kicked into adjusting my schedule and stuff. I flew out immediately, met John here early this morning. You were out of it so we went and had coffee. He's a good man Beth." He paused, as if to swallow back tears. "I've also talked to Kimmy and your mom. Roddy will be here later."

"John called you," she said again. It was a near inaudible mumble, but the thought that it was John and not Kimmy or Roddy that called Andy made him all the more dear to her. "I didn't know."

"Mmm hmm," he came back with the coffee and she tried to sit up. He sat the cup down and tried to help her find a comfortable position. "Dina and Nathan want to come."

"Tell them to come on," she said. She took a sip of the coffee that he had fixed exactly the way she liked it, too much cream and sweet.

I'm a mess! Even that cup of coffee made me want to cry!

"Andy?" And finally she did begin to cry.

"Don't," he reached and stroked her hair.

"I have to tell you…"

"Bethy, don't," he said again. "Not now. It can wait."

"No, I have to, I need to." He handed her a tissue and she wiped her eyes. "I need to tell you, you broke me. You tore my heart out, more than once, you know, and I still loved you. Still do, never stopped." She told him as the tears flowed.

He started to speak but she held up a hand to stop him. She had more to say.

"Let me finish, I have to finish. There's this place in what little bit of my heart you left behind that belongs to you, just to you, always has from the time I first met you, always will, my first love. There was always room for my family, for Kimmy, for John when he came along, and Carlee, but you took over the biggest part. I tried to move you out of there, but nothing I did worked."

"I broke me, too, Bethy." He brought her hand to his lips and she remembered that feeling. Then he turned it and kissed the palm, bringing it then to his cheek and holding it there.

"Don't misunderstand what I am saying. I love John and Carlee more than I can put into words. But I fell in love with you and never fell out. I tried. God knows I tried."

He looked at her and she saw those tears in his eyes, too.

"Kimmy knows, my family knows, hell I think even Carlee knows. She goes to sleep at night listening to *Traveler*," Beth laughed. "John knows. It's no secret. He's known all along. He accepts it and loves me anyway, in spite of it. 'The future…' That's what he always says, 'He was your past. I'll have the future.' So much for that," she mumbled.

"Stop," he said and looked away; she knew it was to dry his eyes. She squeezed his hand.

"Andy, look at me." He turned back to face her, "I'm OK with this. It's certainly not the path I would have chosen, but it's the hand I've been dealt. It seems inevitable. They have told me there isn't much they can do. It's pretty much just a matter of time."

She laid her head back and mumbled "I don't know if I was dreaming or what but last night I kept hearing "Timeless" over and over and over in my head, she softly sang the words that were in her head.

We're timeless, we're unaffected by change, we're eternal…

"I heard it over and over." The pain meds were making her sleepy. "All the time, in my thoughts in my dreams, you just never go away." She continued to mumble.

He no longer tried to hide it. He was still holding her hand and he put his head down on the bed beside her again and he cried. She stroked his head, to comfort him, to comfort her, too. The feel of his hair in her fingers made her cry as well.

John looked in. He saw the exchange between the two of them. He saw that love and it hurt him to the point that it was almost unbearable. He loved her more than life. To see her with Andy and know that she still felt that way for him was a pain he'd never felt before. He walked away to think.

Andy and Beth stayed like that for some time. Beth dozed, and later a nurse came in to check her blood pressure, replace the IV bags and such. Andy moved the chair so the nurse could get to Beth. Beth saw the look, the recognition; she saw the question on the nurse's face, sure that she wondered why he was with her and not her husband, but Beth didn't care. He was there and that was all that mattered.

"I'm not going to leave," he said finally.

"I knew you wouldn't."

"I'm going to ask Kimmy to help me find a place to stay. Everything else is on hold."

"No," she stopped to think a minute.

"Oh yes, I'm staying right here. 'No' is not an option."

Beth knew he wouldn't go, and worried about it, but really didn't know if she cared. She wanted him there.

"I need you to go for a while," she said. She needed to think things through. She needed to gather all her thoughts and try to figure out what to do about them.

"Go?" he asked, "everything OK?"

"I think so. I'll see you later. Go."

A short time later John came back in the room, sat down beside her, and took her hand.

"You really should get some rest," he said. "Stop that brain churning and close your eyes and rest a while."

"Too much going on in there," she said with a heavy sigh.

"I know Beth." He looked so sad. "I know," he said again. "We have so much to talk about and take care of."

"I know. Who'da thunk it, hunh?"

"Don't joke."

"Oh, John, I have to or I'll die." He brought her hand to his cheek and held it there and the irony of those words made them both cry.

~ ~ ~

It was almost midnight when the hospital staff told John and Andy they had to leave, Beth needed to rest. John took Andy home with him and settled him into the guest room. It took little thought. He knew it was the right thing.

They sat up for a while. Sharing a bottle of wine, they talked about what was ahead.

"You are welcome here," John said. "Make yourself at home, please."

"John," Andy began.

John continued, "Here are the keys to the SL; it's in the small garage. Use it to get back and forth."

"I don't know what to say," Andy said.

"You don't need to say anything, it's not necessary. It's what Beth needs, that is what I have to do."

"I can't tell you how grateful I am."

The next morning when she awoke John was there with Dr. Sampson and Dr. Davin Reilly, the oncologist. Dr. Reilly was transferring Beth's care to his practice. John had met with him, and Beth could tell by the look on his face that it wasn't favorable.

"Beth," He extended his hand. "It's nice to meet you. Your husband tells me that you are not into formalities, so not to call you Elizabeth."

Friendly, warm smile, so far so good on the bedside manner...

"Nice to meet you, too, I'm not going to beat around the bush here," Beth said.

"John and Dr. Sampson both said you would be frank," he laughed easily.

"I'm not willing to go through any extended treatments that will keep me away from my home, from my child, any longer than I have to. I know the deal and it's OK. It's quality, not quantity the way I see it. I want the rest to be the best, ya know?"

"I agree. We'll do another CT and liver scan to see exactly what we are dealing with. We will do that today."

"Well then, that just about says it all doesn't it," she said.

"I'll see you again before I leave the hospital this evening," Dr. Reilly said as he turned to go.

He and Dr. Sampson left and the room was very quiet. John sat down beside her with a heavy heart. It showed on his face.

"It's the way it needs to be John. It's what is right, for Carlee, for you, but mostly for me."

"I know," he said sadly, the reality really sinking in.

They took her for the tests a short time later. When she returned to the room, Roddy was there. He just sat there beside her for the longest time. He would look up as if to speak, but the words wouldn't come.

"It's OK," she told him after a while. "You can talk about it."

He took her hand. "I have something to tell you. Andy and I have already talked to John, but now I need to tell you."

"What is it?"

"Beth…" One word was all he could muster at that moment. He was visibly shaking.

"What Roddy? What is it?"

"Beth, I need to tell you about something that happened a few years back."

"OK," she listened intently, cautiously.

"When Andy was in the doldrums, the pits of hell… When we sold the chalet…" He was struggling and she squeezed his hand.

"It's OK Roddy. Talk to me."

"When all that was going on…"

"Yes?"

"Andy, he had me do something and swore me to secrecy at the time. And as I've helped you with this kind of stuff all these years I've kept something very important from you. The time to tell you just never seemed right, so I kept putting it off. I know you and I…"

"What?" What secret had he kept from her?

"When I invested the chalet money for you, Andy had me transfer some other things into your name. It hasn't needed to come up before now, it was secure, taken care of."

She looked at him waiting, and asked; "What things?"

"Song royalties."

"What does that mean?" Beth asked.

He paused for a long moment. "You are a rich woman Beth."

She laughed, "What do you mean?"

"Any song Andy wrote for you, about you; that he noted so in the song notes or sheet music, he had me transfer a percentage of the royalties to you, a large percentage."

He paused and took a deep breath in order to continue. "I knew at that time that you wouldn't take it. You'd be stubborn because you were hurting. You wouldn't have taken it because of your pride. So it's all in trust now. The lawyer who handled the sale of the chalet took care of it all. It was set up to be taxable when dispersed, so there really wasn't an urgent need to tell you before now."

"I don't understand."

"You need to talk to the lawyer Beth. You need to decide what to do with the money and make arrangements. I was going to tell you when you and John married, and then after Carlee was born and then, well, I just didn't. It was all taken care of legally. I should have told you, I just never did. It was in a safe place. You need to take care of this, Beth, before..." He grasped for what to say next, "Before something happens," he said. "Right now the Cancer Foundation and your folks are the beneficiaries. You need to change that. I should have had it taken care of when Carlee was born," he was mumbling now.

"Well," she blew out a big breath and looked at him. "How much are we talking about?" she asked after a while.

"Beth," he looked at her. "Every song we are talking about was a hit, a big money-maker, you know that. Andy felt like he had enough. He wanted to take care of you, forever."

"How much Roddy?"

"Couple million by now."

"Millions?" She repeated the word, clearly in shock.

"Yes sweetheart, millions. Carlee will never need for anything financial."

"I see." She needed a minute to process what he had just said. "I have a Will," she said finally.

"This is in a trust, it's excluded. You need to take care of this, Beth."

"I need Andy," Beth whispered. Not John, Andy.

Roddy rose to leave the room. "Wait," she said. "Please sit back down. There's something I need your help with."

"What is it?" He sat back down. "You know I'll do anything, Beth. Anything."

She thought for a minute. "This isn't an easy request, for many reasons, but it needs to be done. I need you to, please, contact Norton Edwards. You know who he is, the *Rolling Stone* articles, I need to talk to him. It's important. It's time."

He just sat there, drinking in what Beth had just asked him to do. He knew why she asked, and it was hurting him.

"I'll do it." He rose and started for the door.

"Come back," she said.

He walked back to the bed and she took his hand, pulling him to her. "I love you," she whispered in his ear and kissed his cheek. "Send Andy in please."

"Mmm hmm, I love you more," he said back and turned away.

"I love you mostest," she laughed. "Look at me." He looked back. "I'm OK. I'm better now. My child will never want for anything because of this."

"She'll want, Beth. She'll want for something that none of this will take care of," he said sadly, and he left.

Andy came in a few minutes later. It was getting late in the day and the light in the room was low. He was wearing light-colored jeans and a black pull over shirt, that ponytail still hanging down his back. Most men at his age couldn't pull that off any more, but Andy could. He looked so beautiful, sad, but so beautiful.

"Hey," he said.

"Andy," she reached for his hand. "Thank you."

"Don't..."

"I need to. I find peace knowing that Carlee will be OK. It's a little overwhelming, I have to admit."

"After all we went through," he slipped his hand from hers to pace. "I needed to know that you would be taken care of if something happened to me. I would always take care of you, no matter what, but if I wasn't there, I wanted to make sure you were OK, even if we weren't together." He paused, "Half of who I am is because of you."

He reached into his shirt and pulled out that gold chain with his half of the Mizpah.

"Oh, I can't believe..."

"I haven't taken if off since I put it on Bethy." He finished her thought.

I don't think I even know where my half is...

"Even after John," she was thinking out loud, "I am sure you could have done something to change the royalty thing..."

He stopped her. "Beth, I wouldn't have. What if something happened to him? I needed to know that you would always be OK. I should have been the one to tell you. It should have been me, a long time ago, but I was a coward. I was afraid of your pride, afraid that you would turn me away, afraid I couldn't handle that, so I just gave it to Roddy to handle, like almost every important thing in my life."

"Thank you."

There was silence in the room for a long time. He stood at the window, hands in his pockets and peered out, not really looking *at* anything, just not looking at Beth.

The light got lower, and finally he began to pace again. "Bethy, Bethy, Bethy," he said. "All the things I should have done," wringing his hands as he did.

She reached out and he came to her, and she squeezed his hand. "Shoulda, coulda, woulda," she said. "Fate, Andy, everything happens for a reason. I believe it's all part of God's plan." Then she added; "He must have something else in store for me..."

Still holding her hand, "Oh, Bethy" he said, "Look what we missed. We could have been, we could have had, we could have done..."

"It wasn't meant to be."

He asked, sadly, "Why?"

"I've thought about that a lot over the years. You weren't the marrying type. You couldn't settle down Andy."

"I could have, with you."

"No, or you would have," she said.

They sat quietly for a while. Twilight fell over the room. Beth dozed and when she woke it was John who was sitting there.

"Hi," he said.

"Hey darlin'," Beth answered. He rose from the chair, went to her bedside, and leaned to kiss her. "Thank you," she added.

"For?" he asked her.

"Andy..."

"It's what needs to be. I know that." They were quiet for a while, and he finally scooted the chair close to sit and took her hand. They stayed just that way until they came in with her dinner. John got up and fussed with the tray. It gave him something to do with his hands, his nerves.

"You should eat," he said.

Beth looked over the plate, "Maybe later. I'm really not hungry."

"Andy offered his cottage in Eleuthera for you to recuperate. If you want that we can make it happen." He returned to the chair beside the bed.

"No, I really just want to go home."

In reality she couldn't even begin to imagine being there with anyone but Andy. It wouldn't feel right, wouldn't be right.

"When can I bust out of here?" Beth asked after a while.

"When do you want to?"

"Yesterday," she said, and laughed.

"We'll talk to Dr. Reilly in the morning, see what he says."

"John?"

"Yeah baby?"

"I love you."

He squeezed her hand. "I know honey. I love you too, so very much."

Again Beth said, "Thank you."

He laughed, and asked again, "For?"

"Loving me."

"I always will."

The next morning they met with Dr. Reilly. He explained what the tests revealed, information that, in her heart, Beth already knew. John cried. She explained to them both that knowing this just made her decision to not endure any kind of treatment other than pain management all the more right.

John, not Dr. Reilly, asked several times; "Are you sure?" Beth knew she was, she had thought and prayed, and thought and prayed some more. Dr. Reilly didn't do or say anything to try to change her mind, an affirmation of sorts. This would be what was best.

~ ~ ~

Three days later Beth went home. Mom and Pops, her brothers and their wives, and Kimmy had all worked hard to prepare the house for her arrival. They worked hard making it just right for her and all that was going on. Her brothers, Ethan and Michael, got a big comfy day bed and put it in the sunroom. That was the closest she would get to outside for a while. Her time would be divided between there and the bed in her room.

Andy settled into the guest room. Kimmy and Beth's sister in-laws, Angie, Rachel, Ashley and Stephanie, had cooked and baked for days, and the freezer was full. They would surely never go hungry.

Beth was so happy to see Carlee. She just couldn't get enough of her. She didn't understand the 'boo-boo' she just knew that Beth had one.

A Hospice nurse came daily to change the dressing, check the area's progress, bathe her, and keep her pain medications up to date. She was an older Jamaican woman named Angel. Beth thought about how appropriate that was. Her accent reminded her of Edwina. She was a kind, caring, warm, and wonderful woman in her early sixties. Each day as she prepared to leave she would hold Beth's hand silently, in prayer.

That moves me beyond words.

~ ~ ~

Carlee took to Andy in a big way. She followed him everywhere, made him hold her hand and kept him a captive audience. At three and a half she was very talkative and very inquisitive. She wanted to be with Andy all the time, asked him a million questions. She would love on him continually, wrapping her little arms around his neck. It was so precious. One evening Andy was sitting in the floor Indian style, legs crossed, and Carlee was sitting in the opening of his lap, her legs lazily draped over his, leaned back against his chest. He was reading to her and she was 'reading' back to him.

Watching them Beth ached, terribly. Seeing Carlee with Andy made her think about them. What would their children have looked like? Carlee was John head to toe. She had John's darker skin tone, her curly hair was auburn. But she shared Beth's passion.

Beth knew it made Andy think too. He would watch her playing, looking at books, sitting with him, and he wondered as well.

She had been home a little over a week, but movement was minimal. There was still a lot of pain and since she was still on bed rest that is pretty much all she did. It had been thirteen days since the surgery and she was waiting for Angel to come help her bathe. She needed to stretch her legs. The bathroom was right there and she knew Angel would be there any moment, so she went in to get the towels ready. She hadn't been in there alone since she had been home.

There before her was a big mirror, actually it was two mirrors that came together in a corner so you could see forward as well as behind if you turned at the right angle. 'Behind' was calling her. There had been no opportunity before now to look. She needed to know. She raised the gown and closed her eyes. She hesitated, scared, but still curious. She had no idea what to expect, but there it was. She became weak in the knees and thought she was going to faint, when she saw Angel in the mirror. She took Beth into her arms and held her as she cried.

Amazingly to everyone there had been no press of any kind outside or calling. Andy had pulled off the 'great escape'. He was content to stay right there. He wanted to lay low, knowing that being out and going back and forth might cause unneeded chaos.

John went back to work quickly and Andy spent a great deal of time with Beth. Between Kimmy and Andy, and her Mom and Pops, Beth didn't need anything. John was able to get back to that part of his life. It was important that he did. For a couple of weeks Beth stayed in bed until her bottom healed. Someone would help her from the bed to the day bed, but she was pretty much confined to one bed or the other.

Andy would go to Beth after John left for work and stay until he returned home. John and Kimmy made arrangements for Carlee to start a day school and Kimmy would take her and pick her up. When John was home Andy spent his time in the sunroom. Roddy sent his portable keyboard and a guitar, and Beth knew he was writing.

"Honey, that money," Beth said to John one evening after dinner.

"I know, I'll call the attorney and get him over here as soon as you're ready."

"Call him tomorrow, please. I want to tell you what I'd like to do. Roddy says keeping it where it is it will continue to grow. We haven't had a need not knowing it was there, so let's proceed that way. Don't you agree?" John nodded in reply.

"I would like to donate some of it to the Cancer Foundation. I think that it's right to do that. There's so much."

"I think that's good. I've talked with Roddy and Andy, and it is a lot."

"I know." Quietly, for a moment she thought. "Make sure Carlee goes to school, honey. Help her find who she wants and needs to be. She is so like you. Kimmy and Mom will help you. Get her in dance. We can do that now. She needs a diversion."

"Yes, I know."

"Make her eat broccoli, brussels sprouts and peas," she laughed, needing to lighten the moment.

"Beets? What about beets, Beth?" he asked, smiling.

216

"Thank you. John?"

"Yeah?" he smiled at her.

"I know that you will move on. You are so handsome, so successful." She reached and caressed his cheek. "Some woman will come along and be so blessed to find you, just like I was."

"Beth, don't."

"Oh, honey, I have to, and you will, and I want that. Carlee will need female influences in her life."

"She'll have Kimmy, and your mom, my mom…"

"But not all the time," Beth added. "You don't want to think about it now, with me here, with all that is going on, with all this emotion, but I want that for you, for her. Don't be alone. You will both need someone."

"Beth…"

"And something else, John, please be friends with Andy. I know you can. He's a good man, honey." She rested a moment, thinking. "Keep him in Carlee's life. She adores him."

"I know." John paused a moment, his brain racing, Beth could tell, and then he added; "I didn't know how it would feel, Beth, you know, him being here and all. I just knew it was what we needed to do."

"I know it's not a normal situation, but I am glad you can accept abnormal," she laughed.

He needed to leave her for a while, thinking about Andy, thinking about Beth, thinking about the two of them… he didn't want her to see what he was feeling. He rose and kissed her. "You need to rest. I'll get Carlee ready and bring her to say good night in a little while."

~ ~ ~

During one of John's business trips that kept him away overnight, Kimmy took Carlee home with her for a sleepover. Andy had been playing with a tune in the sunroom late into the evening. He went to look in on Beth. She was sleeping, and with all that was going on she looked so peaceful, beautiful. She looked so tiny in that big king-sized bed on her stomach, hugging the pillow, as was so familiar to him. Always with that one leg drawn up, fist at her mouth.

And for the umpteenth time as he watched her sleep the moon shone upon her face, and he cried. He realized at that moment what was really going on, and that he was going to lose her again, forever this time. He felt sad, for everyone, but the selfish part of him was only sorry for himself. He stood there for some time watching her sleep, and she stirred, finally, and rolled to her side and saw him.

"Hey," she said in that sleepy voice he loved, "What'cha doin'?"

"Just enjoying the view."

She laughed and started to sit up. "Don't," he said, "I'm sorry I woke you."

"You didn't. I just woke up. I'm really thirsty." She sat up and pushed a hand through her hair. "What time is it?"

"Just after two."

"Why are you still up?"

He went to her and poured a glass of water from a carafe that was kept beside her bed. "I was working on a tune that popped in my head. You know me. Once it starts I can't let it go; gotta get it while it's there."

"Let me hear it," she said, reaching to switch on the light beside the bed.

"Later, go back to sleep, I'll play it for you later. Now you need to rest."

"No, now, we're both up so humor me."

"OK, wait and I'll go get the guitar."

"No, stay Andy." She patted the bed beside her. "Don't leave me. You can hum it, I'll get it," and he knew that she would.

She slid back down, lying on her side as he started to hum the tune, then sing the words.

> *Captivated*
> *Anticipated*
> *That's what you've done to me*
> *That's how you've made me feel*
> *Hypnotized*
> *Mesmerized*
> *That's what you've done to me*
> *I know this love is real*

Then he stopped. "Just playing with it," he told her.

"Play more, finish it. It sounds good," she murmured. She turned more on her stomach, toward him. "Andy?"

"Yeah?"

"I hurt really bad. Would you rub my back?"

"Anything you need, you know that," he said, and she rolled to her stomach.

He put his hand on her back and began to rub lightly. To him it was a loving caress. Just to touch her was heaven. To her it was helping ease her pain. He started to hum the tune again, no words, just melody, as he rubbed. After a while her breathing changed and he knew she was asleep again. He turned the light out and rubbed and hummed some more as tears rolled silently down his cheeks.

Chapter Twenty~Five

October 31, 2001 ~ Norton and Beth's journey begins

Today I arrived to set in motion the process of gathering, collecting, and assembling the memories that Beth wants to share with others through her story.

I spoke with Andy for a while and then he led me to the sunroom where Beth was waiting. Kimmy was there getting Beth situated on the day bed. It was almost five weeks after her surgery and she was up and able to get around some, but still could not sit because of the wound. She could only lie on her stomach or side.

"Hello Beth," I said and leaned to kiss her cheek.

"Thanks for coming. It's nice to see you again." Andy and Kimmy left us there, alone.

"It's really my pleasure. Thank you for choosing me to work with you on this. Roddy and Andy explained the circumstances."

She told me that the first thought through her head was; *'Thank God he didn't say he was sorry.'* It was *very important* to her that no one felt sorry or pitied her in any way. That would have made it 'unbearable'.

She thought a moment, quietly, choking back emotion and replied; "When I knew what I needed to do, I knew I wanted to work with you."

Suddenly, her tears came in a flood. I looked around and found a tissue for her.

"Sorry, I've become a bit of a gusher lately," she said. "Anyway, I finally got a hold of a copy of that first article you did on Andy so long ago. Gosh that was twenty years ago wasn't it? It was great. I had seen the pictures, have copies of some of them but I didn't read it until recently. It was too difficult before, too many memories of that time. But as I read it I really liked the way you told the story. Kimmy knew that one day I'd want to see it so she saved it and brought it to me recently. The second article was sad, all of it such a lifetime ago," she said sadly.

The realization began to sink in. She knew what was happening, what she was doing, but it hit home really hard when I arrived. She told me that she was sad, really sad, for the first time. Up to that point she had been in more of a scramble mode getting things in place in her head. Getting things lined up to do what needed to be done.

"I tried to be ready for your arrival. I thought I was, but nothing could have prepared me for what I felt when you walked in that door," Beth said with a heavy sigh.

We were preparing her 'legacy,' what she would leave behind for others to know about her.

"I apologize that I have to lay here like this, can't sit, you know," she said waving a hand in a nervous gesture. "We'll just pretend I'm a goddess and maybe someone will come and fan me and bring us grapes," she laughed trying to lighten the mood.

"I have kept a journal, a diary, all these years, actually since I was a young girl. The first was a gift from my Pops and it turned into a ritual. It's something I do, keeping my thoughts, my memories, and my special conversations. They are all treasures to me. I didn't want to forget, ya know? There are many of them. Take whatever you need. I have the 'Andy Volumes' stored. I will have Kimmy get them for you. Use whatever you think."

"And Norton, can I call you Nort? Norton sounds so formal," she said with a giggle.

"Call me anything, just don't call me…"

"Late for dinner!" Beth finished the joke. "Thanks, I really needed to laugh…"

"OK, Nort, so here's the thing, I want to talk. I want you to talk to Andy. I want you to talk to John, Kimmy, and my folks, just everyone. It's important to me that you do. Carlee will need this."

"And when the time comes," she had to stop a minute. That lump in her throat so big, she could hardly swallow. "Later," she said, "give the journals to Andy. And between now and then if either of those men in my life says something wonderful about me, share it with me, deal?"

"You got it. When do you want to start?"

"Whenever you are ready, I'm somewhat of a captive audience for a while yet."

"Would you object to me recording our conversations? I like to go back and listen, later."

"Not at all."

And so the process began.

~ ~ ~

November 10, 2001~ Kimmy gathered up all the journals and brought them to me first. They'd been boxed up in the attic. I was glad to get them early. I read through some of them before I handed them over to Nort. So many memories, most good, but a few, well…

Talking was much easier than she thought it would be. I tried to keep it comfortable and she made it easy to do that. Our conversations were like chatting with an old friend. We talked a few days and then I took the journals and left for a while. As I left I told her that I needed to do some research and would return in a few days.

"That just means you are going off to read the journals," she laughed, then added "No one else has ever seen them."

"I will treat them as the treasures they are."

~ ~ ~

I was gone about a week. I read every word, and as I did, each revealed the emotions she felt when she wrote the entries. I called several times to ask questions but not many. She was very detailed sharing her thoughts, and the pictures in my mind were so clear I felt as though I was there. Her words bore passion that, as a writer, I could appreciate. Some of the entries made me laugh and some were so descriptive that I could feel her emotions. When I returned we sat and I asked more questions, and as I did she cried.

"Tears come so easily these days," she said in apology.

"Don't apologize. I felt tears sting my own eyes a few times as I read."

"I worried about what this would feel like, but it just feels like old friends talking about life, not like fifty questions or an invasion of any kind. After all this time avoiding the media, spilling my guts seems odd."

But she knew why she needed to, for Carlee. She might hear things as she grew up and Beth wanted the real stories available to her. Not the tabloid stuff that she had lived with most of her adult life. Maybe the stories would answer questions that she would not be there to answer for her. Kimmy could, but these would be Beth's words, her gift to Carlee.

~ ~ ~

Friday after Thanksgiving - November 23, 2001 ~ Ten weeks post-surgery, and it has been a special, busy time. The house is full all the time. It seems that every day people are coming in to visit and I love every second of the chaos!

There was a huge dinner party for Thanksgiving. Roddy and Vince were there. Liz and Vince were in the kitchen and cooked all the traditional favorites. As they banged pots and pans in preparation, a great friendship grew. They included me in the celebration along with every one of Beth's family, her brothers and their families, Kimmy and her family, Dina, Nathan and Megan.

The feast of Thanksgiving was everything that you could dream. Everyone shared stories, laughed, and ate, and ate, and ate. It was a wonderful celebration. Beth relished in all the people, the attention and the love. She looked around at the room she never dreamed could hold so many people. It was a day that she was happy.

November 26, 2001 ~ I will always think of that as a room full of love! I worried at first that it would be somewhat melancholy, 'what if this is the last one,' but it didn't seem sad, or reserved in any way. It was truly a celebration and everyone had fun. Fun has been short around here lately. The kids all played, and Megan got on the floor right in the middle of them. The guys watched football and everyone had a great time.

Liz, Kimmy and Dina tried to get Beth to go Black Friday shopping. Even though she was getting around pretty good, and the wound was healing well, she still had a really hard time sitting for any length of time. An inflatable donut was a part of life these days. And the Thanksgiving festivities had worn her out. They offered a wheelchair ride but she just wasn't interested. She finally told them, that she just didn't feel like it, didn't want to shop; didn't want to deal with the crowds. She just wanted to stay home. That whole day after Thanksgiving shopping thing was not appealing in any way. John took Carlee out for a while to see Santa.

With them all gone, I was alone with Andy, and I liked that. We were able to share great conversations again. He'd gotten past being so blue, and that helped a lot.

~ ~ ~

Andy and Beth were in the sunroom. He loved any time he could be alone with her. They shared great conversation again and it both warmed and broke his heart. They'd been talking, sharing memories for the book.

Andy was quiet a moment, reflective; "I need to tell you something," he said finally. "I've been trying to figure out how for a while, but I need to explain. It's been 'in there' too long," he said pointing to his head, and then his heart.

Cautiously Beth asked, "What is it?"

"You may have to bear with me," he told her. "I've only talked about it once in my life before, and that was a bad time."

"I'm not going anywhere," she said.

"I want to start by telling you that it doesn't justify anything, but maybe it will help you understand," he was trying not to ramble, but emotions were bubbling to the surface. He rose from the chair and paced trying to keep them in check.

Watching him Beth knew this was something major, something from that 'dark time' in his life.

"Not long after *Traveler*'s name got out there, after people started knowing who we were, recognizing us," he began, "I had a call from this woman who said she needed to talk to me about my dad. I blew it off at first, but she was saying things that held my attention so I agreed to meet with her. Thinking about it, I knew I really didn't want to. I realized that I kind of knew what she wanted to talk about. As you grow older you start to recall things from your youth that maybe didn't seem such a big deal at the time.

"My dad was gone a lot, he worked long hours. Phyllis and I had a good life, but he wasn't around so much. When he was home he was a good father, and it appeared he was a good husband. I never heard them fight, but as I got older I realized that I never really heard them talk much either. I was just so happy when he was home that I focused only on his being there. I loved him so much.

"I met this woman for coffee, Rebecca," he said remembering. "She told me I looked like my dad and as she said the words the realization really set in. *'She knew him.'* She looked familiar, but I didn't remember her from family things or friends of my mom and dad, and then it hit me. She had been at his funeral. And I remembered Phyllis being uncomfortable when she came in. But you know she wasn't the type to cause any kind of scene, nothing to draw any attention to her.

"Rebecca told me right up front that she didn't want anything from me and that she had no intention of going to anyone else with what she was going to share with me. And then I knew for sure.

"'Your dad and I were lovers,' she told me. She didn't beat around the bush with 'we were friends,' 'we worked together,' just came right out with it. All I could think about was Phyllis. And as I listened, my mind raced and I knew that she knew, all those years, she knew it..."

Beth wanted to say something, but she could tell it wasn't the right time, he wasn't done unloading.

"She told me that they 'shared a bed' for fifteen years.

"Shared a bed..." he repeated, "my dad, Bethy, he was a cheater and a liar. All those nights 'working late'... he was with this woman and Phyllis knew it, and she stood by him and loved him anyway.

"After I was home from rehab I talked to her about it. I had to, and she told me she knew. She told me she forgave him. *'How?'* I wondered at the time, and then I thought of you and every time you forgave me, but it was too late for us by then. When I knew that I could commit to you, when I knew that I could go forward and be true and honest to you, it was too late. I loved you, love you now more than I can say, but I was afraid to commit to you, afraid of hurting you."

Beth didn't know what to say, so she listened. She knew how hard it was for him to share this with her. She wanted to comfort him, but she knew that wasn't what he wanted. It wasn't why he was telling her. He wanted her to know why he held back all those years. It made her sad for him, as well as her. But she knew; if fate had led them down a different path all those years ago she wouldn't have Carlee, wouldn't have had the Cancer Foundation.

'Everything is part of a greater plan. We can only move forward and learn from the past,' Beth thought.

~ ~ ~

Carlee's Birthday - December 1, 2001 ~ Today is Carlee's fourth birthday. We woke her early and everyone sang to her, and she loved it. Then John took her out to lunch while Andy, Vince and Kimmy got a little party together, just family, but there seemed to be a lot of that lately. Carlee loved the Little Mermaid. Kimmy ordered a cake. Andy, Vince and Mom put aqua tulle all around to make it look like water. When she and John returned everyone was there and the party began. Keeping in the theme of things Andy had Roddy get her a pearl necklace. I'm afraid she is going to be spoiled, but my girl was so happy!

~ ~ ~

December 3, 2001 ~ I'm feeling so much better and I'm up, out of bed more. I love sharing in all the activities that lead up to the holidays. I still can't sit. Soon, I hope... Andy, John and Carlee put up the Christmas tree last night and made it fun! I just sprawled out on the sofa on my stomach and said things like; 'more on the left, add some tinsel over there...' I think Andy enjoyed it. Carlee just adores him. I think the feeling is mutual, and John is jealous. But I think it's OK.

This was a repeat performance for Carlee and John, but a new thing for Andy. All those years and Beth couldn't remember him ever even hanging an ornament on the tree.

Beth and Carlee sat at the kitchen table and wrote her Santa letter. Andy looked on and smiled at the picture he saw. Beth folded the letter when they finished and they put it in an envelope and addressed it.

"Daddy will mail it in the morning."

John took the list to go out Santa shopping. Kimmy had taken Carlee to her house for a while, so once again, Andy and Beth were alone. She tried to get him to get out for a while, not shopping, just go for a ride or something, but he wouldn't hear of it.

December 4, 2001 ~ I know, first of all, he doesn't want to chance being recognized so he is laying-low to avoid any chaos here. I also know that none of them want to leave me alone for a second. But I know, too, that Andy wants to squeeze in every second that he can as long as John is OK with it. I like it, too.

~ ~ ~

There had been so much going on that no one paid much attention to things going on outside the house. Roddy called daily, but it wasn't much about business, he called to check in. This day was different, though. Andy had released a greatest hits album in March. There was new material on it and Roddy called with some wonderful, exciting news of accolades for Andy.

"*Yesterday, Today and Forever*" had been nominated for a Grammy for Song of the Year. It was very exciting news. Andy was being stubborn about it, and said he wasn't going to go to the awards ceremony. Beth knew it was because he was afraid he'd miss something there with her. The ceremonies were still weeks away. Beth made it her mission to wear him down telling him he needed to go, needed to be there; needed to celebrate.

He really needs to go, this is a big deal!

~ ~ ~

Christmas 2001

Beth didn't want any Christmas celebration for herself. She wanted to make it all about Carlee. There wasn't a gift greater than the love of family that anyone could have given her. The best gift for her little girl would be to have the most fun holiday ever. They did make a big deal celebration of the day. Her family was there, her brothers and families visited all day, all of them together, so it was a special time for Beth. Dina and Nathan came in, and of course Roddy and Vince were there. It wasn't the big sit down meal like at Thanksgiving, but Vince and Liz put together a spread of party foods that everyone nibbled on and enjoyed all day long. Her family always said if Beth could live on chips and dip, cheese and crackers, and a birthday cake, the corner with the border and a rose, that she'd be the happiest girl on earth.

~ ~ ~

Beth talked and talked to Andy about the importance of him going to the Grammys but he wasn't budging. He had no desire to leave her. He stayed with her every second John was away and he couldn't imagine loosing those precious moments.

And then, suddenly, he had something on his mind. He thought long and hard, and struggled, but he had to proceed. One evening after Beth was asleep he opened a bottle of wine and invited John to join him in the sunroom.

"I have an idea that I'd like to talk to you about," Andy said to him after a while. "I have already talked to Dr. Reilly, because I wanted to make sure she was able before I even brought it up to you."

"What is it?"

"I would like to ask Beth to go with Roddy and me to the Grammys. I haven't mentioned it to her. I wanted to talk to you first."

John sat for a while looking across the table and wondered how he would respond. *What was best for Beth? What would it mean for them?'*

"I know this is a difficult request, John. It isn't easy for me to ask. Roddy will be there the whole trip." Andy felt he needed to clarify. "We will charter a plane so the flight will be comfortable for her. We would leave on Monday, the ceremonies are Tuesday evening, and we would return Wednesday. I think Roddy can pace it out to give her plenty of time to rest. He will make arrangements for private arrival and departure from the event. We would have a suite for her to assure her comfort."

'He isn't begging,' John thought, *'he's giving me a proposal for consideration.'*

John still said nothing, though. He was going through the facts in his head just as he would any proposal presented to him. He sipped the wine, and gave each consideration the full thought process.

Andy watched him and could see the wheels in his head turning. He knew it wasn't an easy request.

"I have to do what is best for Beth," John finally said.

Andy nodded. He understood how important that was.

John paused a moment longer and asked, "And Dr. Reilly knows this and gives his approval?"

Andy nodded again.

"It might be good for her to get out." And he knew that was so. But his decision caused turmoil for him. The bottom line was that if he agreed he would be allowing her to return to her past, and he feared that outcome.

Feeling like he could read John's mind, Andy wondered how he would answer such a request, but he didn't think he would have been OK with 'her past' staying in the same house. Andy realized how different from himself John really was.

Finally, John responded, "It will be good for her. Yes, you should ask her." And he worried what that decision would come to mean in the end.

Andy did ask her to go and she was very excited. She'd been feeling pretty good, physically, and the thought of the trip gave her a mental boost as well. She talked to John, a lot, about going to the Grammys with Andy. She was torn with mixed emotions. He told her over and over again that it was fine, it was the right thing to do; it would be a good diversion.

It terrifies me a little...

~ ~ ~

January 1, 2002 ~ Another year passes and it all goes far too quickly. I am trying to absorb every precious moment that I can.

Norton comes and goes, working on the book, but he has also become part of this family, these people who I love. He spends hours with me, but he visits with everyone, I know he is gathering info, but I see friendships forming...

As the time drew closer to the Grammys Beth was suddenly concerned about being out, worried about her appearance. Kimmy came over one evening with a gift to help ease her mind. She had gone to *Frederick's of Hollywood* and presented Beth with panties with built-in buns. She had gotten several pairs and had them altered so that only the left side was padded. Everyone got a big kick out of those.

January 16, 2002 ~ I have this big, huge dent where the cheek of my butt used to be. Those panties sure helped! Kimmy wants to take me shopping. I don't think I feel up to that. I'm sure I have something, or maybe she can just go and find something, I'm not that excited about it, the shopping I mean.

Beth was alone in the bedroom, a somewhat cherished moment because alone time was very minimal any more. She went in the closet and dug until she found it. Wondering if it might still fit she found the black dress from the first trip to the Grammys. She still had it. She took it from the garment bag and pulled a pair of the padded panties on and slipped the dress over her head. She'd lost some weight the last couple months so it was kind of loose, not clingy at all. She stood in front of the mirrors in the bathroom, turning this way and that to see it from every angle. It looked good.

She called Kimmy, and shared her thoughts about the dress. Kimmy loved the idea. She went to Beth's and Beth put the dress on and modeled it for her.

"Perfect!" Kimmy said.

"I think I like that word!"

She told John about it but he kept encouraging her to go find something new. She didn't see the point. She decided not to tell Andy.

I'll just wear it and see if he even notices.

Andy and Roddy had all the arrangements made for their trip. They chartered the plane, booked the hotel room, and as promised, planned private entrance to and from the ceremonies. They wanted as little press exposure as possible.

CHAPTER TWENTY~SIX

February 2002 ~ The Grammys

They flew out early Monday morning and arrived in Los Angeles around noon. Andy and Roddy wanted to make sure Beth had plenty of time to rest. The plane had lounge seats so she was able to spend a lot of time lying down, but the flight was still long, and she ended up sitting a lot of the time, and she felt it.

Settled in her room, she turned on the TV and stretched out across the bed on her stomach and dozed. Roddy's room was on one side and Andy's on the other. One of them had a door that came into hers, she suspected, but she wasn't sure which. After a while there was a knock at that door and it opened and both stuck their heads in.

"You decent?" Roddy asked, and Beth laughed.

"Come in," she said, and started to roll over to sit up as they did.

"No, no, just stay right there for now. Relax." Roddy told her. He carried a bottle of wine and some glasses.

Andy carried a beautiful vase filled with Calla Lilies, placed them on the table beside the bed, and sat down beside her.

"Well, this is nice, thank you both," she said.

Roddy went to the little kitchen to open the bottle.

"None for me," she said.

"It's OK, we checked with Dr. Reilly, unless you just don't want any," Andy told her. "You doin' OK?" He rubbed her back in a loving caress as he asked.

"Yeah, I'm good, just a bit tired, as for the wine I'll have a glass, maybe two!" she laughed as Roddy poured. It was the Chenin Blanc that Andy liked, chilled and it tasted good. She rolled on her side and they chatted and enjoyed the wine for a while and then there was a knock at the outside door to her room.

Andy rose, went to allow a young man pushing a cart into the room, followed by another, and another. The room was a suite with a table and chairs, they set three places and left. Andy blew up the donut cushion that he brought for her to sit on and pulled a chair out. Beth joined them at the table. Andy sat down and Roddy started lifting lids. There was salad, Chicken Parmesan and pasta. It was heaven. Beth didn't realize how hungry she was until she began eating. They brought another bottle of wine with the meal. Andy opened it and poured Chianti into their glasses.

Done with the meal, Beth sat back, satiated and happy. "Thank you, this was very nice. Good food, great company," she said. Thoughtful for a moment, she added, "Thanks for not wanting to go out. It's still a little weird, all of this, but mostly, you know, my bottom."

"Looks fine to me," Andy said, with that devilish grin, and she laughed, remembering Chicago.

"Beth, I'm gonna head out. I have some calls to make. Vince sends his love." Roddy rose, leaned to kiss her, and headed for the door, always the diplomat.

"Roddy?"

"Yeah?" He turned back to look her direction.

She held her breath a moment, trying to maintain composure. "Thank you again, for all of this. It's very special."

She looked down, feeling that all too familiar lump in her throat. It didn't take much to feel it there anymore. Looking up again, she said, "I love you."

"I love you mostest," he said. But he left, quickly.

Andy went to the phone and made a call and a few moments later the wait staff came and took away the remains of their meal. Returning to the table he finished pouring what was left in the bottle into their glasses. It was then that she realized they were alone, there were none of the distractions of home or family, it was just the two of them. They were truly alone for the very first time in many, many years. He reached across the table and took her hand and brought it to his lips.

"Bethy," he said. That familiar gesture, that familiar feeling, both physical and emotional, "I guess you have figured out by now, that's my room," he said looking toward the opened door that connected the two rooms. "I'm just a whisper away."

Still holding her hand he went to her and led her to the sofa. Her heart pounded to the point that she knew, without a doubt, with the next beat it would slam right out of her chest. They sat there in the quiet for a while. Finally, he put his arm around her and pulled her into him, just holding her there for the longest time. There was no conversation, just Beth there in his arms, and finally he let go. They sat quietly, and finished the wine.

"I know you're tired," he said finally. "I'm gonna go now and let you get some rest. When you're ready to crawl in, stick your head around the corner so that I know you're OK. If you need anything, just call my name." He slid to the edge of the sofa.

"Andy?"

"Yeah?" he said and reached to push a hank of hair back from her face. It was such a familiar gesture. He'd done it a million times before.

"Thank you. I wasn't sure what to expect. Thank you," she said again.

For a moment he said nothing. He just sat there looking at her and finally said; "Bethy, I love you so much. Thank you for allowing me to be here with you."

He cupped her face in his hands and brought her lips to his. Gently, tenderly, and softly, he pressed a kiss to them, and then to her eyelids and rose to leave.

"Rest, tomorrow is a big day," he said as he left.

Beth showered and got into her PJs. She peeked around the door, into his room. Andy was on the phone, and he blew her a kiss. She went to her bed and crawled in. Sleep came fast and easily for her.

~ ~ ~

The next morning was a lazy one. Beth had forgotten what jet lag felt like. She got up and as she wandered around, she found a note on the table from Andy.

Good morning beautiful,
Pray that you rested... I peeked in and you looked so peaceful.
I'm off to the theatre to rehearse for the show tonight. Roddy is

*running errands and taking care of business, he'll check on you
when he gets in. Call for room service. Coffee's good...
XO's
Andy*

She called for the coffee and kicked back to relax. Andy offered a
trip to the spa for the day but she said no. She would just pamper
herself.

*I don't know how I would feel with someone else seeing my
bottom. It's not the prettiest thing I have ever seen.*

Around one, she started to think about calling room service for a
bite to eat when there was a knock at the door. She opened the door to
find an older woman dressed in a white sweat suit.

"Can I help you?" she asked.

"Carolyn Neff" she said with a lovely French accent, extending her
hand. Beth took it and instead of the handshake the woman grasped
Beth's hand with both of hers and patted. It was a warm gesture.

"I'm here to help with anything you need. Mr. Beamer asked me to
assist you." She had a small duffel bag on her shoulder.

"Come in," Beth said, "I'm sorry. I didn't mean to be rude and
leave you standing in the hallway, I just didn't expect anyone."

She entered and set the bag down. A young man was there to help
her in with a folded table. "I'm a retired nurse and I do physical
therapy and massage. I'm on staff here at the hotel. Mr. Beamer
explained your situation to me. He said you might want a bubble bath
instead of a shower. He verified with your doctor that it was OK for
you to sit in the tub."

"I can *sit* in the tub, bubbles and all?" The woman nodded and
smiled. "Isn't he just the most wonderful man?" Beth was so excited.
"I haven't had a bath in months! How he spoils me!"

*The suite had a large garden tub Jacuzzi and I have to admit
that I longed to get in.*

"Oh! Yes!" Beth said, "Yes! Let's do it!"

From her bag she took salts and perfumed oils. She helped Beth
ease into the tub. There was a knock at the door that adjoined the
rooms. Once situated, she made sure Beth was comfortable, and

Carolyn slipped out, pulling the door to. Beth heard Andy's voice, and then she heard music, *Bach in Woodwind*, his favorite chill music.

'*Hmm…*' She eased down into the hot water and turned the jets on. It felt so good. She lingered there for a while, then turned the jets off, let the warm water out and replaced it again with hot and lounged there even longer.

When Carolyn returned she helped Beth up and into a warmed robe. She felt warm, pink and wrinkly from the water, but it was heavenly. She led Beth to the outer room where she had set up a massage table. There was also a platter of cheeses and fruit and some orange juice.

"Oh my!" Beth said with excitement. She had a snack and then Carolyn helped her on the table, covered her with a blush colored satin sheet and started her magic. So relaxed, Beth dozed off, awakened by a knock at the door. Carolyn went to answer it.

"Hello," Roddy said to Carolyn. "Hey beautiful," he said to Beth as he entered the room. He'd taken her dress to be pressed for the evening's event.

"Have I said how much I love you?" Beth laughed.

"Yes, but you can tell me again." He bent to kiss her cheek. "Mmm, you smell wonderful."

"Thank you! What a wonderful surprise this was!"

"I can only take credit for part of it. You can thank Andy, too."

"I will!"

"Need anything?" he asked as he caressed her neck. It was a tender, loving gesture.

"I can't imagine for the life of me what it would be," she said as Carolyn started on her back again. It felt wonderful.

Life is good…

"OK then, I just wanted to check. See you around 3:30PM."

The two women shared wonderful conversation as Carolyn worked. After the massage Carolyn helped Beth to a cool shower. When Beth stepped out she'd brought a chair into the bathroom with the donut, and Beth sat at the counter and did her hair and make-up, and then Carolyn helped her into her dress.

"Thank you so much, for everything."

"You look beautiful," she smiled. "It was my pleasure to help you this afternoon," she said as she packed up her things and started for the door.

"Wait," Beth said. She hugged the woman long and hard. "Thank you again for making this so special for me."

"You will remain in my thoughts and prayers," she said and kissed Beth's cheeks and left her there to finish up. All that was left were accessories.

John wanted very much to buy her jewelry to wear, but Beth didn't see the point in it. She had so much and while she appreciated the thought, she decided to wear the necklace and earrings Andy had given her so long ago when she wore this same dress. She rarely had occasions for something so extravagant and *'this is perfect,'* she thought. Dressed and ready, she called home to check in.

"Hello princess," John said.

"Queen," Beth corrected him with a laugh, "The princess is there with you."

"How's it going?" he asked.

"Good."

"I miss you. Everything OK?"

"Yeah, I guess I could use a vote of confidence on my hair and stuff," Beth laughed.

"I'm sure you look wonderful," he said. "How was your day?"

"Roddy and Andy treated me to a bath and a massage and I had help dressing for this whole shindig," she laughed.

"I know. I was in on the secret, Dr. Reilly, too. We all agreed that it'd be a nice surprise. Did you enjoy it?"

"Oh my goodness! Yes! All of it! It was heavenly!"

"Have you eaten?" She knew he worried about her.

"Had some bar mix, you know peanuts and stuff, before I came back to the room. I was hanging out downstairs in the bar for a while, watching a basketball game with some college boys."

Silence on the other end, "Hello? I was kidding!"

"I knew that," he laughed.

"Actually, Andy and Roddy are feeding me after the show. Roddy had some fruit and cheese sent to my room. I haven't seen Andy yet today."

"Well, I'll buzz off. We love you. Beth…"

"Yeah?"

"Have fun."

"I will! Kiss Carlee for me, and Kimmy. See you tomorrow evening."

"Bye sweetheart. I love you."

Finished, she was ready. She looked in the mirror. *'This is as good as it's gonna get...'* she thought.

There was a knock at the door and she went to open it. Roddy was there.

"Wow!" he said. "You look incredible!" He took her hand and twirled her to see all of her.

"Flatterer... 'Incredible,' hmm? I think I like that word!"

"Andy will be ready in just a minute. He called and asked me to let you know. I'll see you in the limo."

"Well, a good-looking man for each arm. How lucky can a girl get?" He kissed her cheek and left. She walked to the sitting area and sat on the edge of the sofa.

Suddenly she was very nervous. *'Was this right?'* She felt good enough, but now the prospect of it all made her very nervous. A light knock on the door between the two rooms, and it opened. Andy peered around the edge of the door.

"You ready?"

She rose from the sofa and made her way toward him. He was wearing a very non-traditional tux, longer jacket, string tie rather than a bow tie and that hair down his back in a ponytail. He looked like heaven and again, she felt that huge lump in her throat.

He walked into the room. Saying nothing he put his hands on her shoulders and held her at arm's length, taking it all in. It seemed like forever. Then slowly he rubbed his hands down her bare arms, and took her hands. He pulled her into his arms and held her against him.

"Stop, I'm gonna cry," Beth whispered.

"No, you can't. You'll wreck your make up." He laughed lightly. "You smell delectable," he said, leaning to sniff her neck as she pushed him away.

"I will cry, I feel it coming, it happens way too easily these days, so stop, please."

"Then let me just tell you that you are gorgeous." He paused and the look lingered, still. "It's like a dream, Bethy."

"A dream?" she repeated.

"Yeah, like I've seen you here before," he smiled. "Like Yogi Berra said, 'It's kind of like a déjà vu all over again'." And again he pulled her into him.

"You have seen me here before," she whispered and looked up at him.

"I have?" He stepped back for another look. Deep in thought for a moment, and then, "The Grammys, before..." he said, remembering.

"Yes, think anyone will write that I wore the same dress?" she laughed.

"Everyone will be so captivated by your beauty that no one will remember. Bethy..." He took a deep breath.

That look...

"Andy, don't," she said, "We have to go." She pulled away from him and turned around to regain her composure.

Deep breaths, in and out... in and out... in and out...' She was trying to calm herself.

"Sit down a minute. Please," he said and went to the phone and made a call. "Yes, Andy Stevens. Please let Mr. Beamer know that we'll be just a minute longer. Thank you."

He sat beside her and took her hand and held it. "I have to get my head right before we walk out that door."

"What do you mean?"

"Bethy," he said her name, and she heard him take a big deep breath. "I'm having a really hard time right now. Give me just a minute."

She said nothing. She just sat with him holding her hand in his lap. It seemed a very long time passed before either of them moved.

Finally he let go of her hand, "OK," he said, rising. "We better go." And before Beth knew it was coming, he pulled her into his arms. It wasn't rough, but it was startling. He kissed her, and it was that kind of kiss, that breath-taking kind of kiss.

Oh God, I prayed, please don't let me lose it. Give me the strength I need to get through this night...

"Let's go." He took another big breath, grabbed her hand and hurried them out of the room.

When they arrived, the limo took them to a back entrance. Roddy made arrangements so they didn't have to make the big entrance' no red carpet, no press. Beth was more than relieved.

As they entered the theatre she was like a giddy, young girl all over again. It reminded Andy of the first time they shared that experience and how happy she was. And then, it reminded him of the one time that he came that they didn't share, and how badly he missed her then.

They went to their seats. Andy had the end seat, Beth was in the second and Roddy to her other side. She looked around and saw many familiar faces, but also a good many new faces that she didn't recognize. It had been a very long time since she had been in this environment.

Once Beth was in her seat she saw Andy turn and wave hello to someone and then heard a familiar voice.

Rick Snyder, how many years has it been?

"Beth, hey!" He yelled, "Oh my gosh, what a surprise this is. It's been a long time!"

Beth started to rise to hug him. "Don't," he said. "Please sit." He took her hands and leaned to kiss her cheeks, then turned and shook hands with Andy.

"You look great Beth!" There was a pause, followed by that *'What do I say now?'* look.

"I heard about everything. I've wanted to call, but I didn't know how it was so I talked to Roddy a couple of times instead. He has kept me up to date. You look great, really great; beautiful!"

"Roddy told me," Beth answered. "Thanks. I have more good days than bad. This is a good one," she smiled. "It's so good to see you again."

"You, too, Andy. Good luck. You deserve it, man, no competition in my mind. That song is stirring." He looked at Beth again, winked, and then said; "You guys take care." He took Beth's hands again, kissed them, and said, "Beth, my prayers are with you and yours."

'That wasn't so bad,' Beth thought. He didn't poke or pry about why she was there, and he didn't say he was 'sorry.' Andy spoke with several other people and then took his seat.

He leaned and whispered in Beth's ear, "A rose between two thorns," and laughed. He took her hand and held it in his lap.

The awards began. Several times she saw the camera. She tried not to look, but she thought about Pops and Carlee and she smiled.

Andy was performing during the ceremonies and after a while he left them to go to the stage area. There was a grand piano in the middle of the stage and Andy walked out to roaring applause. He sat down and when he began to play Roddy took Beth's hand to hold it. It was a sweet gesture from her good friend.

As Andy sang "Yesterday, Today and Forever", Beth listened. She really listened this time. She'd heard it before. She thought it was a beautiful song. It struck her that he had mellowed and with the years his voice only got richer, smoother. It felt like velvet when you listened. Sure, still his 'Rock Star' ponytail but his singing style had mellowed. As she listened to the words she closed her eyes. Andy was playing the piano and behind him in tuxedos were a group of violinists accompanying him. It was so beautiful. He was singing about a love that would "outlast time."

> *Yesterday you were mine*
> *We shared a love*
> *That would outlast time.*
> *You loved me*
> *You shared your heart,*
> *Our love was meant to be.*
> *You shared your life, your love with me.*

She suddenly felt tears rush to her eyes. It hit her all of a sudden that he was singing to her, about them. She hadn't paid attention to that fact with all that had been going on. She squeezed Roddy's hand thinking the gesture might keep the tears from coming. She couldn't cry.

"Roddy, pinch me," she said softly.

He squeezed her hand instead.

"Harder," she whispered.

And he tightened the grip; "I know," was all he said.

She leaned toward him and put her head on his shoulder. "Oh my-gosh, I didn't know until now," she whispered. "I never heard it like this before. Didn't realize..."

He took her hand in his left, put his right arm lovingly around her shoulders and pulled her closer.

Andy finished and received a standing ovation.

The Song of the Year was the next award, and as they recapped the nominations, Andy waited back stage. Amy Grant and Vince Gill were reading the list.

That Grammy nomination meant far more to Beth than Andy. But she was so proud of him that he wanted to win it because of her, happy that she was there with him to share the whole experience.

"And the winner for Song of the Year..." Amy tore into the envelope. "Andy Stevens!" She shouted, "Yesterday, Today and Forever!"

He walked back out on the stage, Amy hugged him and Vince shook his hand. He walked to the podium and looked out over the audience. Beth told herself he was looking at Roddy, but she knew who he was looking at. He took a minute to begin as the crowd applauded.

"Thank you." He looked down and took a breath, "Thank you from my heart for liking what I love to do. They all come from my head, but that one came from deep, very deep in my heart. This one's for you." He raised the statue and blew that familiar kiss.

That's all he said, all he needed to. She knew what he meant. Her family would know what he meant.

He didn't come back to his seat for a while. Roddy explained that he was getting some press obligations over with so that they could make a quick escape when the ceremonies were over. He didn't say anything when he returned. He took Beth's hand and held it in his, the rest of the evening.

When it was over the three of them exited through the same back way they had entered, to a waiting limo. Once in, Andy took out his phone and dialed.

"Hello," he said casually. "Hang on," he handed it to Beth.

"Hello?"

"Mama, I saw you!"

"Hello sweet girl! Why aren't you in bed, it's so late!"

"Daddy and Aunt Kimmy let me stay up so I could see you! I miss you."

"Oh Carlee, I miss you, too," and all the emotions of the evening and the sound of her sweet child's voice brought the tears to her eyes. "Tell Aunt Kimmy to get you in bed and I'll be there tomorrow to tuck you in. I love you so much sweet girl. Let Daddy have the phone, OK?"

"Hey," he said. "We saw you. Carlee had a nap after supper. She wanted to see you on TV so bad. I thought it'd be OK. You looked pretty Beth. Are you feeling alright?"

It struck me at that moment the difference between these two men; 'Pretty' to John, 'Beautiful and delectable' to Andy.

"Thank you. Yeah, pretty much. Tired, but I'm OK, don't worry." She knew he would anyway. "I'll see you tomorrow. Good night, honey. Wait, OK?" Andy was reaching for the phone.

"Thanks John, Roddy and I had the best looking date in the place. She's fine. We'll get her home safe."

~ ~ ~

John had seen them on TV. He had seen their faces and it was an image he couldn't get out of his mind. He knew they had all seen it. He heard the emotion in Andy's voice as he sang; it was so strong. John listened this time and he had heard the words differently as well. He heard the love in Andy's voice during his acceptance speech, and he had seen that vision of him back in his seat, holding Beth's hand in his lap. It wasn't just a friendly gesture. He saw the look on Andy's face. He was a man sharing a moment with the woman he loved. The woman *he* loved. He knew Beth's heart and he hurt.

~ ~ ~

In the limo, Beth leaned back into the seat. Roddy was across from her. He picked her feet up and put them in his lap. He slipped her shoes off and started to gently rub, and Beth fell asleep. It was about a twenty-minute ride to the hotel. When they arrived, she woke, her feet still in Roddy's lap, her head on Andy's shoulder. It was around 9:30 West coast time.

As they rode up in the elevator Roddy said; "I had dinner sent to your room Beth. I'll see you in the morning." He kissed her cheek and left them in the hallway as he entered his room.

Andy put the key card in his door, Beth hadn't taken a purse. They entered through the door to his room.

"Something smells good," she said. "I didn't realize how hungry I was! I'm gonna go change, I'll be right back."

"No, Beth," he said. "Wait, please wait."

She turned to look at him; "Don't change. Not yet, I want to look at you. Let's just have dinner."

He turned the TV on to one of the music channels and found classical music. No words, just soft, lulling music. It had been a long evening, and she sat the whole time, so he put the inflatable donut on the chair and Beth sat down. They shared a wonderful meal, and a glass of wine. They chatted like old friends about the evening.

"Andy," she said finally. "Thank you." It came out awkward, and she added, "For the song…"

He leaned back in the chair, but said nothing. He took a sip of the wine, holding the glass by the stem, he lightly swirled it. Looking at her, he was taking it all in. "Be still a minute, I want this picture engrained in my memory." After a minute he said, "No, my love, thank you."

When they'd finished the meal, he came to her chair, reached for her hand and she rose. He was so quiet, so in thought. They headed to the sitting area. She went toward the sofa but he stopped her, pulling her gently into his arms.

"Bethy," it was a breathy whisper. He pulled her closer and she moved into him. He took her hand and their fingers twined together. She felt the warmth, inhaled the smell of him, melted into his arms, and let the cares of the world, her world, her illness, everything… drift away like butterflies in the spring.

He hummed the tune in her ear as they began to move slowly to the music. He kissed the top of her head, a gesture that brought her to tears.

"Don't," he said. "Please don't cry. Just let me be here. Let me hold you for a while, no pressure, no tears." He held her back to look at her. "OK?" But she still she cried.

When the music was over he took her hand and they went to the sofa. She sat, pulling her feet up under her. What did she care if that dress wrinkled? Andy put his feet on the coffee table and pulled her closer.

This is wrong, but how could it be when it feels so right. How could it?

Sometime later, Andy rose and went to his room. He carried the phone from his room to Beth's. He pushed the carts with the remains of their dinner into the hall and turned lights off as he returned to the sofa. He left a dim lamp on a table close to the door lit, casting a soft golden glow over everything in the room.

"Bethy…"

She prayed once more, *'Oh God, give me strength…'*

She looked at him, but could not speak. He sat down beside her again, reached toward her and framed her face with a light touch.

'God, please give me strength,' she prayed again.

He pulled her into his arms, on his lap, and kissed her. She returned the kiss.

Such passion I have never felt. Not from Andy or anyone else.

"Just let me lie with you," he said, softly. "Sleep, Bethy, just let me hold you. I won't ask for more."

She remembered all those years ago when he had said those same words to her and the tears continued.

'God please…' she kept praying.

She couldn't speak, but as if in another body, she saw herself rise from the sofa; holding his hand, she walked with him to the bed. She sat as Andy removed his shirt and shoes. Leaving his pants on, he pulled her to her feet. He unzipped her dress and she stepped out of it letting it drop to the floor as he held the shirt for her to slip into.

It doesn't feel wrong.

They lay there in the dark for some time, Beth in Andy's arms. His hand, so light on her back, finally made its way to her bottom. He lightly, lovingly, touched, explored, and caressed the place where the mole had been. It was so sweet, so tender. He wanted to know. In all this time, John had hardly even looked at it, but John had never explored her body the way Andy had. She felt tears on her skin that were not her own. Then he wrapped her tighter in his embrace and once again, she spent a night wrapped in his arms. They both cried for the past, and maybe for the future.

~ ~ ~

In the dim light of morning she slipped out of his arms and rose. She stood by the bed for a very long time looking at the sleeping man that she loved more than life. She smelled him on the shirt, remembered the night before, and it took her breath away. It felt so good, and it hurt more than anything she had ever felt before.

She quietly went to Andy's room with the phone and called for room service to bring a carafe of coffee. All those years, didn't she know that he would want it when he woke? She told them to bring it to his door so that the knock would not wake him. A short time later she put the tray of coffee on the bedside table. She sat in the middle of the king sized bed she shared with him the night before, and scooted beside him. Her hands went to his back, lightly rubbing, and then she lay down and wrapped her arm around him and kissed his back. He rolled over and pulled her to him.

"Hey," he said kissing her.

"Hey back to you. How 'bout some java, Joe?"

"How well you know me."

She sat up, poured two cups, and sat Indian style, beside him. Andy slid up against the headboard. "What time is it?" he asked pushing the hair back out of his face, sipping the coffee.

"Just after eight." Beth wrapped her hands around the cup as if the warmth was necessary. She held it tightly to steady her nerves.

"Been awake long?" He rubbed sleep from his eyes and sipped what he always called the 'elixir of the Gods'.

"Just long enough to get a really good look at you before we go home."

"Bethy..." and he reached for her. She sat the coffee aside and slid down and into his arms, her head on his chest.

He stroked her hair and kissed the top of her head. "Bethy," he said again.

Lying in his arms, her mind was racing. She had obligations at home. She loved John, she loved Carlee, but at that moment all she could think of was that life was too short, this life. She thought about Pops. She thought about her mom and Kimmy.

What would they think?

She thought about all those years before and the ones since. Her heart and her mind were in different places. She felt guilty because she didn't feel guilty. The feel of Andy's arms around her made her forget all the pain, physical and mental, and she didn't know what she was going to do. Her heart was breaking. Her love for him was overpowering every rational thought she had.

"Bethy," he said once more. She pushed back to get a better look at him, but said nothing. "We don't have to leave." He pulled her back into his arms, and there was a long, awkward silence.

"Thank you," she said caressing his cheek. "Thank you for all of this. I feel happy for the first time in months."

"No, thank you. Thank you for letting me be here with you, and for being here with me. When I think of all the time we've spent apart." He hesitated, "God, what did I do to us?"

"It doesn't matter now," she said, sadly.

"It does, Bethy. It matters."

"We were so good for so long, and then we weren't. And then we were and then we weren't," she said and laughed.

"And now we are," he said. "We are really good, Bethy."

There was a long gap of speechless time, and finally Beth said, "I love you Andy, and for whatever length of time 'always' is, I always will."

"Bethy, I love you so much" he said wrapping her tightly in his embrace.

"But there's more to it now. It's not just me. It's not just us anymore."

"So what do we do?" he asked pleadingly.

~ ~ ~

John lay awake all night. In the morning he made some calls for work, called Liz, and went into Carlee's room. She was sound asleep. He watched her chest rise and fall with each breath she took. "I love you sweet girl," he whispered and placed a kiss on her forehead and left the room.

He put his bags in the trunk of his car and waited for Liz to arrive. He was off to Atlanta for a business trip the he had quickly set up in order to be away when Beth came home. He wasn't ready to face his own fears.

~ ~ ~

It was after eight that evening when Beth arrived home, Andy at her side. They found Beth's mom there and Liz explained John's absence. But Beth knew. She suspected that Liz did, too. She went and looked in on her sleeping angel. Liz had bathed and tucked her in. Beth sat on the edge of the bed and rubbed her back, kissed her forehead, and breathed in the scent of her, then dimmed the light.

Andy had gone into the sunroom to give them a moment. "Mom?" Beth said as she sat down at the table. Liz handed her a cup of the coffee she had just made.

"Beth, his heart is broken. He thought he could do this, share you with Andy. He thought it was what you needed and he did it for you. But he knows that you still love Andy." Liz stood behind Beth's chair and wrapped her arms around her daughter. She paused and added. "We all know that sweetheart."

"Mom," Beth began again, "The hard part is that I love John."

"He knows that, too, Beth and that is why this is so hard. When I saw that vision of you on the TV last night you were absolutely radiant. You looked so beautiful, so happy. You glowed like you haven't in a very long time. Andy did, too. Pops saw you and said aloud, before he thought, that you looked better than you had in months. And then I saw John out of the corner of my eye. I saw him break. When we got home Pops and I talked, we knew. Kimmy called me this morning and she knew."

Beth was sad, but she still didn't feel the guilt that she thought she should. She loved Andy. She had never stopped.

As though Liz could read her mind, she told Beth, "Sometimes circumstances change things. I'm not going to judge you, I understand. I understand when you love someone so much. Beth, you should call John."

Without saying a word she went to the bedroom.

Andy waited a moment and went to the kitchen when he saw that Beth was gone. He braced himself but he knew he needed to go.

"Liz…"

She looked up at him and saw the emotion on his face. She saw the look in his eyes. She had known this man for so long that she knew his heart, too.

"The coffee is fresh, and leaded," she added. "I thought it might be a long night."

He poured a cup and sat down at the table. Liz reached across and patted his arm. "Talk to me," she said.

"I'm sorry," he said first. Liz looked at him over the rim of her cup. "Nothing happened that Beth should be ashamed of," he continued.

"She's my daughter Andy, I knew that much," she smiled at him.

"We shared a bed, nothing more. We held each other." He looked away.

"But you did," she replied. Andy looked up and started to protest, but Liz held up a hand to stop him. "Your hearts," she said. "You shared your hearts Andy, and we all saw it."

He took a big gulp of the coffee. "I have loved her since the first moment I laid eyes on her. Through every up and down we've had, I have never stopped. I thought years ago that I had lost her forever and then this," he struggled, "this… this horrible, horrible thing happened. And she was returned to me. John gave me a gift, but I took something away from him in order to get it."

"I love her so much Liz," he paused and sipped the coffee, "I can't imagine another day without her." And the reality of that hit them both.

"I know," she replied, sadly. "I know, and now you have to figure out what to do about it."

Beth was standing in the hallway at the corner of the kitchen. Her intention was to call John but she hadn't. She'd thought about it, but she wasn't sure what she would say. She washed her face, then went to look in on Carlee again, and was headed back to the kitchen when she heard the exchange between these two people she loved so much. Her eyes filled, and spilled at their conversation.

She returned to the bedroom and sat on the edge of the bed. She reached for the phone and dialed, knowing nothing would ever be the same once he answered.

"Hey," he said sadly when he answered, knowing it was her. "I'm sorry I left without talking to you first. I knew I couldn't be there when you came back; I couldn't face you. I needed to clear my head," he rambled.

"John," Beth started to speak but he cut her off.

"Beth, I'm hurt. I'm not angry," he explained. "Really, I know you, and I know that you are struggling with this more than I am. My not being there will make this easier for both of us. I'm not coming back for a while. I made arrangements to take care of some things here. I'll be in Atlanta for a few weeks. I'll call Carlee every morning and every night," his voice wavered.

"John, I love you," Beth said.

"I know, but it's not enough anymore, is it?"

She thought a long moment before she answered, "No," she said, finally.

In the matter of a few days, once again, Beth's life changed.

~ ~ ~

Beth was feeling good. She hadn't had any medical issues in a while. Angel wasn't coming daily, just once a week to take blood pressure, samples, and such. Things were going smoothly. Everyone was settling into the changes. Nothing was moving too quickly and she liked it that way just fine. John returned two weeks after he left and packed up some more things. Beth anticipated a bad encounter upon his return, but there was none.

John asked to talk privately. "I filed for legal separation," he told her when they were alone. "We can proceed however you see best, whatever you want. I won't contest anything. I don't want to fight, it will only hurt Carlee."

"John, I'm sorry," she said with tears in her eyes.

"Beth, don't, it's OK. I thought with time you would get over him, but it wasn't meant to be was it? I know what it feels like to love someone that much."

He leaned and kissed her cheek. "All I ever wanted was for you to be happy. If this is what it takes then that's the way it has to be."

"I want you to know, I don't regret a moment of our time together. We wouldn't have that beautiful child if you hadn't loved me." She smiled thinking of Carlee.

"We have that," he said.

"Where will you be?"

"Not too far, you know I can't be away from her for very long," he smiled. He hugged her and turned to leave and as he walked to the door Beth realized that it would be OK.

Chapter Twenty~Seven

April 2002

John let her go. It all happened quickly. She asked for nothing. Another chapter in her life closed and a new one was beginning.

'Beginning...' she let out a heavy sigh whenever she thought about that. *'For how long?'* She wondered continually, only not over Andy this time. She tried not to dwell on it, but it was always there, just below the surface.

She and Andy were renewing their relationship, learning each other again and it was good. He was making himself part of her life and learning what that was in those years they were apart. They found daily rituals that his lifestyle kept from them in the past, coffee and the paper in the mornings, dinner together, with Carlee at night. All of that kept his mind racing.

They made only one change to the living arrangements. Andy had Roddy ship their bed from Corpus Christie, and he moved into her bedroom, unable to think of another night without her in his arms. The first night they slept there Beth cried, remembering the first time, a lifetime ago. She stayed awake all night; unable to believe he was there with her.

~ ~ ~

"Spring in Eleuthera, what do you think?" Andy asked over coffee one morning, thinking the cottage for a few days would be good for her.

Carlee was in day school, and dance. Beth was working on the book and just wanted to stay home.

"Maybe later," she told him and prayed that there was a 'later'.

Beth was happy. Andy was happy. John was around enough that Carlee adjusted, and she loved 'Papa' being there. It was OK and Beth was happy about that. She still wasn't comfortable being out, so people came in. And the change in their lives didn't seem to surprise anyone.

In the daytime Andy didn't wanted to stay as close to Beth as possible, so he wrote; music and his thoughts for the book. He put anything to do with his career on hold. Time was far too precious, and it had taken him a lifetime to learn that. He spent a lot of time wandering around the house. He wanted to know about the part of her life that he'd missed. He would flip through photo albums and his heart would break with each photo of Carlee, for many reasons. He would pick up a framed photo of her from a table and wonder what it was about that particular one that it Beth chose to display it. What occasion, what memory... Beth loved remembering whatever was going on at the time and sharing it with him. Andy fell in love with Carlee, love like he never dreamed possible.

~ ~ ~

There came a couple of bad days. Beth was emotional and very weepy. She just kept saying, "I'm really not up to snuff."

I feel tired and weak, not moving too quick, and I'm taking too many naps.

When Andy expressed concern, Dr. Reilly explained that it was normal for her to have bad days and reminded him that there had been very few. He put her on an anti-depressant and it helped.

His new family life, and Beth's bad days seemingly in control again, Andy kicked into high gear. He was on a mission. He knew what he wanted but first he needed Roddy's help. Andy called him, and Roddy was ready. He gave him the details, and Roddy got busy with what Andy needed. A few days later Andy was in Beth's office, at the house, to receive Roddy's fax.

He called him. "That's it Roddy, thank you. Take care of it, please."

On Mother's Day, 'Papa' and Carlee got up early and made French toast to serve Beth breakfast in bed. Beth watched, from the hallway, peeking around the corner at the activity, and couldn't have been happier. She snuck back to bed when they were almost ready and the three of them backed up against the headboard and ate and giggled. Andy relished every moment and Carlee was ecstatic over the whole affair.

The next day a courier arrived with the package.

Andy called Kimmy for the other help he required. The following day she called Beth.

"Hey! Jenna wants Carlee to spend the night Saturday, is that OK with you?" Kimmy asked. "It'll give you a bit of respite."

"I think she would love that!"

"We'll do pizza, and movies. Jenna got a new sleeping bag and she's so excited to use it! Carlee can sleep in the old one. I'll dig Lane's out and we'll all sleep in the floor. It'll be so much fun for them!"

With that settled, Kimmy made the other plans Andy needed.

~ ~ ~

On Saturday, May 18, with Carlee at Kimmy's, Beth and Andy were alone. They snuggled on the sofa watching a DVD of a Robert Redford, Brad Pitt movie. "I'm getting hungry. How about some popcorn" Beth suggested.

"Let's wait just a few, this is too good."

"We can pause it," she said.

"In a minute," he looked at his watch. It was getting close...

His phone rang and he checked the caller ID; "It's Roddy. I gotta take this." He walked into the kitchen as the doorbell rang.

"I got this," Beth shouted.

She looked out the window beside the door. There was a caterer's van in the driveway. The peephole showed two women in white uniforms.

"Hello," she said sweetly. "I think you must have the wrong house."

They looked at the paperwork, then the house number. "No, we're right where we're supposed to be. Are you Beth?"

"I am," she replied, puzzled.

"We are Gina and Marie and we have your dinner," one girl said.

"My dinner?"

"Yes ma'am! Can we come in and set up?"

She turned and Andy was behind her. "Hello ladies! Come in!" he said. With a sweep of his hand he directed them to the dining room and the kitchen and led Beth back to the movie. The two women carried in several large totes.

"What's going on?"

"Shh, it's a surprise. Watch the movie."

About half an hour passed. Beth had no clue what was happening in the movie. She was too busy wondering what was going on in the kitchen. She smelled wonderful smells and heard lots of activity.

Gina came around the corner. "All set!"

Andy finally paused the movie and reached for Beth's hand. "Shall we?"

They went into the dining room where the light was soft, and there were candles of all types all over the center of the table, various heights, colors and styles. There were rose petals scattered around. There were two places set, one at the end of the table, one to the side. There were beautiful china plates and crystal that was not Beth's at each setting. One plate had a Calla Lily lying on it, a bud vase filled with water to the side.

Beth looked at Andy, "What is going on?"

"Have a seat," he pulled a chair out for her, and she sat.

Gina took the flower and placed it in the vase as Marie brought the salad and filled their glasses with wine.

"Andy?"

He took her hand, kissed it; "Please, eat."

She took a bite of the salad and tasted pear and Gorgonzola cheese along with the greens, walnuts and a tangy dressing. She sipped the wine that she knew was Andy's favorite Chenin Blanc. She enjoyed, but she was curious.

Gina came and took the plates away as Marie brought them a lovely Chicken Marsala and pasta. Gina returned and filled their glasses with Chianti and said, "Enjoy, we'll be back in the morning to clean up. Dessert is in the fridge!"

They shared a wonderful evening, great conversation which Beth did enjoy, but she continued to wonder.

Done with the meal, they finished their wine and Andy rose to go get the dessert.

He returned with two slices of Tiramisu and more of the Chenin Blanc.

"OK. What. Is. Going. On?" she asked emphasizing each word.

Andy looked at her over the rim of his glass as he took a sip. "You want to know right now?"

"Yes, I can't stand it any longer! What is going on?"

"Are you sure?" he asked teasingly.

"Yes!"

He said a silent prayer, reached in his pocket and rose from his seat. Taking Beth's left hand in his, he dropped to one knee.

"No," she whispered.

"No? But I haven't asked yet..."

"I mean, No! I can't believe it," she laughed a nervous laugh.

"Elizabeth Ellen Morgan Oliver..." he said nervously as he took the ring from the box. "Bethy, I've waited far too long to do this, so 'No' is not an option."

He leaned to her and placed a kiss on her lips. "You were wrong about me," he whispered.

"I was?" she replied with tears spilling from her eyes.

"I *am* the marrying type," he said with tears in his own eyes. "Will you be my wife? Mrs. Andrew Stevens," he said and slipped the ring on her finger.

Beth threw her arms around his neck. "Yes!" she said. "Yes, yes, yes!"

Lying in bed, later, admiring the ring she rolled to him. "Are you sure about this?" she asked. "I mean, who knows what tomorrow will bring."

"Are you changing your mind? 'Cuz I think we made a deal." He kissed the tip of her nose.

"No, I just want to make sure you know what's ahead of you, ahead of us."

"No one ever knows what tomorrow holds, and I have never been more sure of anything in my life," he said wrapping her in a loving embrace.

"OK then, me, too. When?"

"You tell me," he said pushing her back to look into her eyes.

"Is tomorrow too soon?"

"Not for me, I already told you, I waited far too long..."

~ ~ ~

After a busy week of preparation, on Saturday, May 25, with their friends and family present, Andy and Beth became husband and wife. The ceremony was in the gazebo by the pool in Kimmy and Lane's back yard. Beth wore a beautiful pale pink dress that Kimmy and Liz picked out. She carried a bouquet of plum and white Calla Lilies that Andy ordered for her. He wore the tux he had worn to the Grammys with a white Calla Lily on his lapel. And instead of Pops giving her away, she and Andy walked together hand in hand. Roddy was his best man and Kimmy and Carlee stood up with her. All the *Traveler* guys were there with their families, and Angel was as well.

It was a beautiful ceremony. Beth's only request; that 'till death do us part' be removed from the vows they exchanged. Andy's request; that the minister who performed the ceremony call her 'Bethy'.

There was only one dance. Andy took her in his arms as Etta James sang "At Last..." He held her close and kissed the top of her head as she cried.

Gina and Marie prepared a lovely reception. Everyone ate, drank, and celebrated something that none of them believed would ever happen. John came to take Carlee home with him. He made a big fuss over her dress and she informed him; "Papa belongs to us now, Daddy."

"Yes, he does, sweet girl. Yes, he does."

That night, after everyone was gone, Beth was tired. That was a lot of excitement and activity for her in one day. Even though she was feeling good she still tired easily. She changed and went to the big bed they shared, to rest. Andy set candles all over the room, turned on soft music, and went to where Beth waited.

"Bethy," he said in a soft whisper; and they made love. It was full of joy and tears. It was bitter-sweet and beautiful.

~ ~ ~

She was feeling good. Carlee stayed with John while Andy took Beth to Eleuthera for a few days. The doctor OK'd a short trip. Beth wondered if she would ever see that beautiful place again. It was a relaxing time filled with nothing but 'them'. They made love, they talked and they enjoyed. She wasn't able to make those long walks that she used to, but she found that she didn't need that now. She did it before for the respite, for the solitude, to clear her head. Now, all she wanted was to be with Andy.

Many media outlets requesting information on their marriage had contacted Roddy. *People* offered a large sum of money and Roddy released an exclusive photo and statement in exchange for a donation to the Cancer Foundation. The cover of the magazine showed a beautiful photograph of them together in the gazebo with the words, "At Last..." It was the first time Beth knew she was going to see herself in print. It was a good article, no trash talk or untruths. They published pictures that Andy and Beth released, and an article that I wrote. The end result was beautiful.

CHAPTER TWENTY~EIGHT

June 2002

Summer was in full heat. It seemed the longer the days were, and the more that passed, the bad days became more frequent. Beth didn't want to go outside for anything. Kimmy, John and Beth's parents all took turns and saw to it that Carlee was kept busy. She got in plenty of summer activity. When she was at home, Beth wanted Carlee as close to her as she could. Beth, Andy and Carlee would watch movies and play games, read and cuddle. Andy was getting very good at *UNO ATTACK*. Beth loved lying on the sofa listening to the giggles, from her two loves, as they played.

Beth would bathe Carlee and get her ready at night, but it was Papa that Carlee wanted to read those bedtime stories, or sing to her. Beth would stand in the doorway most nights and watch, drinking in the sweet scene. Carlee would lie there, intently listening, hanging on every word Andy read. Her little eyes would fight to stay open and as Andy would finish, she had just enough energy to reach up and pull his face to hers with those chubby little girl fingers and kiss him goodnight. That vision gave Beth such peace.

~ ~ ~

A high fever meant a night at the hospital because of temperature spikes. They had to call rescue, and that meant a ride in the ambulance. The high fever had her disoriented and she got a little wacky on them.

John came to stay with Carlee. He took the guest room and the irony that came with it.

For Beth, IV fluids and a cool bath brought her temperature down to one hundred and she went home the next morning. Angel came daily now. Once they were home, Andy babied her. He soothed, pampered and protected, and she loved it.

~ ~ ~

June 18, 2002 ~Today is my worst day so far. I've had a low-grade fever and a nasty headache all morning. It's making me feel light-headed, queasy and nauseous. Just the light in the room when I open my easy makes me feel sick and my back hurts something awful.

Andy kept her in bed all day. When Angel came she told Andy to call Dr. Reilly. He told them he would meet them at the emergency room. Andy called and Kimmy came to take Carlee home with her.

At the hospital, Dr. Reilly told them he wanted to keep her overnight for observation. She begged and cried. Andy was a mess. He wanted to do what was best but it seemed to him that if she was so upset about it, taking her home had to be a better option. He told Dr. Reilly that he'd make sure she rested if they'd just let her go home.

"Overnight," he told them, "I'm not giving in on this. Before you go home I want a portacath installed. It will make all of this easier for you. It's a port that we'll put just beneath the skin near your collarbone to administer medicine by IV when needed." He explained, "This will keep us from having to stick you with needles over and over."

He explained that they needed to bump up to two nurse visits a day. Andy made a call to Angel and she said she was available for anything they needed. Dr. Reilly said they should get someone else to come for the second visit, but Angel wouldn't hear of it. They set her up in the guest room. She wasn't leaving Beth.

I can't complain because, really, I haven't had too many bad days since my butt healed. It's pretty much been smooth going until this last week or so.

They scheduled the procedure for five the next morning. After that, Beth could go home. The goal was to assure her comfort. Andy stayed in the hospital room with her that night. She was given something for the nausea, something for pain, and she slept through the night.

After the procedure Andy took her home. He got her situated and comfortable on the day bed in the sunroom. Angel brought lunch for them but Beth had no appetite. Kimmy brought Carlee home around two. She went to sit with Beth for a while, as Andy entertained Carlee. He was playing her a song on the keyboard he traveled with. He would sing, and then she would repeat.

"She is such a little mocking-bird, it's a very pleasant sound," she told Kimmy as she listened to Andy and Carlee.

Kimmy wanted to know that Beth was OK. Andy and Angel had to push her out the door with a promise to call if they needed her, but she didn't want to leave.

The next morning, Beth woke with a temperature spike that left her feeling disoriented. Andy called for Angel. They got her into a cool shower. Angel put a shower stool in for Beth to sit on. Andy helped her sit and was standing there in the shower's spray to hold her. It seemed to help. Angel helped her into the bed while Andy changed into dry clothes.

Andy called Kimmy to come get Carlee, Beth needed to rest. John was out-of-town so Kimmy would keep her overnight. After Angel got Beth settled, all Andy wanted to do was lie there with her. He didn't want to leave her for anything.

The following morning her fever spiked again. Angel called the doctor who demanded they meet him at the hospital.

"No ambulance!" Beth told them, so Andy drove her, and Angel went along.

Dr. Reilly said an overnight stay in the hospital was mandatory.

"Please, no!" Beth begged.

"I want to run some tests," he explained.

"Please," she cried. "Let me go home."

Andy felt helpless, and as Beth continued the tearful conversation with Dr. Reilly, he felt more so than at any time in his life.

"I know what's going on." Beth said in a tired, weak voice, "You want to run tests to confirm what we all already know. It's getting worse. *I know that!* I can feel it in every bone in my body. Angel has talked to Andy and me, at length. I know what to expect. Being here won't make it better, or easier, so please, please," she pleaded, "Let me go home. I will be so much more comfortable there, so much happier…" The conversation was wearing her out and she laid back into the pillows, tears streaming down her cheeks. "Please," she said softly, once more.

Dr. Reilly took Angel out of the room and they were gone about ten minutes. Andy was holding Beth's hand, afraid to ever let it go.

The doctor and Angel returned to the room and he pulled a chair beside Beth's bed. "OK, here's the deal," he said. "Angel is in charge. She knows what to do, when, and how to do it, so you are going home. Andy, Angel is in charge," he repeated with a smile. "Do not let this strong-willed woman overpower you. Angel is the boss."

"I hear ya," Andy said.

At eleven that evening, Andy checked her out and took Beth home, Kimmy and Liz were there waiting. They took her straight to the bed. Angel went with Kimmy and Liz to fix a bite to eat and Andy crawled into the bed beside Beth. She pulled him close and he wrapped his body gently around hers.

"I'm not ready Bethy, I'm not ready to lose you," he said wearily.

"I'm not ready either, but I'm resigned to it. So let's make the best of a bad thing." She took his hand and held it to her cheek. She had waited so long for these moments with him and they were going by way too fast.

CHAPTER TWENTY~NINE

In Beth's Words

As time passed and Beth's illness progressed, her journal entries became more detailed. She shared more stories, memories, and pain through the tape recordings we shared. The memories her family and friends shared are what became the story of 'her'.

July brought a lot of talk to the recorder. Anytime she was alone she was talking. She was tying up loose ends. She left this especially poignant message for Andy.

Andy, the holder of my heart,
I didn't know where I would begin, quite unsure what I would say. I'm still not, as I start. There is so much... so many feelings, so many memories, and so many emotions. I want you to have all the journals when Nort is done with them. They are yours, all the many volumes I have kept over the years. I would like for you to share them with Carlee someday. I will say, 'when you read them', because I know you, and it may not be right away, but I know you will. Just read and know that my heart and soul went into every page, every entry, every word.

That first evening when you walked into the room you became a part of every part of me. It seems so long ago... And even as I moved on and made a life and a family without you, you were still there in those pages. You'll see...

Kimmy dug all the journals out, and in the days before Nort took them, there were times I would wake up in the middle of the night, pull one out and read. Maybe it was a good time we shared, there were so many. Maybe it was a sad time, the ones I tried so hard to forget, seemed important again. Maybe it was just a time I needed to remember. They've been hidden away, for so long.

Did you ever read the book Bridges of Madison County, or see the movie with Meryl Streep and Clint Eastwood? It was on TV in the middle of the night not long ago. It was a night that I couldn't get comfortable or turn my brain off so I turned the TV on. Such a moving love story... My journals remind me of the love the woman had for the character that Clint Eastwood played. She met him when he came to town to do photographs of the covered bridges for National Geographic. They had a weekend together, and all those years she kept the letters, pictures, and journals of their time together hidden. Hidden, too, was her love for him. She stayed in her marriage because it was the right thing to do, but she never stopped loving him. She died with that love still hidden.

The difference, I guess is that my love for you was never hidden, even when we parted. I tried to move on in my life, and I made a life with John, and later, with my beautiful little girl. But I still loved you.

And then you returned... and I am so glad you are back in my life.

The Grammys... Andy, thank you for that last gift. I do not regret, nor do I have any feelings of guilt. I didn't do anything I'm ashamed of, I slept in the arms of the man I love, the one I have loved for half my life. Thank you for that. Thank you for making it easy for me not to feel guilty. I know it changed everything, but it seems that we were meant to be together.

I think back on all the things we've shared and I love you all the more. I hope you know that you made my life better these last months. What you gave up to be with me... I can't imagine if it hadn't been this way. I don't know if I would have had the will to go one if you hadn't been there, being able to share one more day with you.

I will leave this world still madly, deeply in love with you. I love the sound of Beth Stevens... Mrs. Andy Stevens... Always, all ways, I am your Bethy...

~ ~ ~

July 13 2002 ~ It's my birthday; I keep thinking of the irony of that. So much, so many, so little, so few... My gifts, my desires, my dreams... All of that keeps running through my mind, with so many memories attached. I know that will sound like a ramble and it probably is, but if you think about it, you'll get it.

I saw 'Rent' on Broadway a while back. Megan had a small part. Recently, the lyrics from one of the songs keep going through my mind over and over... "525,600 minutes... how do you measure a year in the life...?"

Oh, the numbers of minutes I keep re-living, keep remembering, keep wishing for... They have been like flashes of light the last few days, some overwhelm me and some make me so happy that I believe I can make it a little longer."

Someone gave me a pamphlet a while back that described cancer as a gift. I thought at that time, that 'a gift' was the farthest from the real deal as anything I could imagine, but it is, I guess. It's a gift to appreciate what is, what was, and what precious time is yet to come. But I like to think of my gift more like one of Nana and Mom's quilts...

When I was growing up, Nana and Mom both sewed. It 'pieced' them together. Mom's parents passed away when she was young, and Nana, with only a son, loved teaching Mom to sew. The quilts were a bond that brought them together. They saved every scrap of fabric from everything they ever made. Each pattern has a meaning. I love the one I have on my bed now. I run my hands over it, see the colors, and each piece of fabric reminds me of something. They are filled with memories and stories. All of that is on my mind now.

I want my life to be remembered as a quilt. Wrap it around you. Let it warm you. Each of you is a piece of my quilt of life. Each of you put there for a different reason. Maybe your block of time was a small one, maybe you were the center block of color in a particular pattern in the quilt of my life, but each of you, are an integral piece. Some blocks in that quilt are the cornerstones, maybe of the whole quilt. Maybe it was a cornerstone of a part of the pattern. Security. Honesty. Integrity. Love. Some blocks were the strength I needed at a certain time. Some blocks are the compassion I needed at an especially difficult time. But each block represents love. My quilt would not be complete without your part in the pattern. I want to leave pieces of my quilt for each of you.

~ ~ ~

Everyone tried to make Beth's birthday special. She was feeling pretty good, but Andy suspected that was because everyone was there, surrounding her, and she loved those times. All of her family was there. Kimmy and Lane were there. Even Angel joined in the celebration. Dina and Nathan came in. Roddy and Vince were there and they were all staying at the house. She was in her glory. Vince made two of her favorite things, macaroni and cheese and carrot cake, and she actually ate. She made everyone swear not to bring gifts.

Later, she said good night, and Andy excused himself to go with her to help her to bed. After she was settled, he pulled a gold box from the bedside table.

"No gifts! We talked about this," she scolded.

"Please, just open it," he laughed. He was lying on his side beside her, elbow bent, holding his head up with his hand watching her.

She looked over, her heart so full of love. He leaned in, kissing her.

She lifted the lid off the unwrapped box. Inside, there was a ticket stub and a small plastic bag. She looked at him again.

"Go on," he encouraged.

First she took the folded ticket, wondering what on earth it was for. It looked worn and tattered. Unfolding it her heart skipped a beat.

June 24, 1978
Orlando Civic Center
Mean Street
Traveler
The Bend
Doors open 6:00PM

"Oh my goodness! Where did you get this?"

"Open the bag," he told her.

She did, and tears rolled down her cheeks. It was her half of the Mizpah.

"Kimmy found your treasure box. I asked her if she might help me find the charm, the ticket stub was a bonus."

She reached for him and he leaned to kiss her.

"This is the best gift I've gotten in a long time!" She laughed, and said, "Open that middle drawer in my dresser please. There's a white box with a gold chain. Will you please put the charm on it and put it on me? I want to wear it. Forever," she added.

"I know why the charm, but why the ticket," she asked. She thought she knew but she wanted to hear Andy's words.

"Because it's the night I got the best gift I've ever received." He lay back down beside her.

She rolled to him. "Hold me please." She felt good that evening. Angel made sure she was comfortable. In his arms she felt so much love. She caressed his cheek. He kissed her neck, and she rolled on top of him. "Make love to me," she said, looking down at him.

"Are you sure?" he asked, thinking of the others, but not really caring.

She slipped out of her gown. "It's my birthday," she smiled at him. "I'm sure." He was so gentle with her, so tender. She cried sweet tears the whole time. She couldn't remember a moment in her life without him… didn't want to.

~ ~ ~

That night left everyone in Beth's family circle smiling. She looked so good, so happy. Liz and Pops were lying in their bed talking about it. "The gathering was bitter-sweet." Connor said.

"Yes it was." Liz replied. "Beth was happy." She was thoughtful a moment and looked to her husband.

With a heavy heart he asked her, "It won't be much longer will it, love?"

"I don't think so, she gets weaker every day. She is so tired, and she doesn't eat enough. I don't think so," she said again.

"I was sitting with her the other day. She talks a lot, not as much to you, because she is afraid she will make you cry," she looked at him tenderly and continued. "She records a lot of that, for Norton, for the book, but this was just us. She thanked me, and I want to share that conversation with you."

"She thanked us for allowing her to 'become all that I am.' She told me in her words, 'The lessons you shared were what helped me, be me. I became who I am because of those lessons of love.'"

Liz looked, and Connor was indeed crying. She smiled at him, knowing he had already started to grieve.

Liz continued, "She told me that she had the very best childhood a girl could ever have. She said, 'The older boys paved the way. With them you set the guidelines, the boundaries of how far we could push, but not how far we could go. Then I came along and Pops eased up, that tender heart of his... When the younger boys came along you both allowed me to help start their paths. It helped me in the decisions I've made with Carlee. Lessons learned are easily shared.'"

"She thanked us for loving and supporting her, even when we didn't think she made the right choices. She told me, 'I know you struggled when you didn't think I did. I know you wanted to pick me up each time I fell, but made me get up on my own, instead. You allowed me to learn and grow and I am a better person for it.'"

"She went on to tell me, 'Thank you, for being so understanding of Andy and me, then. Thank you for welcoming him, always, but especially now, it means so much to me that you did. I'm sorry about John, I loved him; I love him now, but I don't know if I could have had the peace that I find now, without Andy.'"

"And she told me, 'I remember when Andy won the Oscar. In his acceptance speech he told Phyllis, "You are the one who gave me the wings and believed in my flight." I could never, in the entire world, have put it better. Thank you for my own wings...'"

Liz was crying now, too, as she shared Beth's conversation. "And she told me that she could never put into words, what that first journal you gave her meant to her. She told me it was the best gift she ever received."

"Now," Liz said in a tearful voice, "that and all the journals that she kept over the years will be a gift to all of us."

~ ~ ~

Nathan and Dina put Carlee to bed that night so that Andy could get Beth settled. They joined Roddy and Vince in the sunroom, and they were reminiscing with a glass of wine when Andy returned sometime later.

"She's asleep. It was a good day for her," he said as Roddy poured him a glass.

Dina looked at this man that she had known most of her life, and so many emotions ran through her mind. He was finally settled, finally at peace, finally with the woman he loved. And she remembered, so many times over the years when she hoped he would find that. She was happy that he did, but sad it was so late and that it wasn't going to take him, take them, him and Beth, into their older years. She sipped the wine, listened, observed and reminisced.

She remembered Nathan telling her about the night Andy and Beth met. He had used the term 'melted'. That didn't seem like such big news to her. She had sure seen a number of young girls over the years that had 'melted' in Andy's presence. But then Nathan told her that Andy melted, too. That was the surprise.

Dina loved when she and Beth had opportunities to be together. They were fewer than she liked, but they were always good. She wished now, there had been more. When she left the last time, Dina knew they would be part of each other's lives. But she was so sad, because she had never before seen love like that.

When she received the call from Roddy about Beth's condition, she hurt, and knew they all would. She and Nathan went as often as possible. When Dina saw her the first time after the surgery, she was in bed. She was small anyway, but she looked so tiny. *'I remember her taking my hand, and thinking I never wanted to let her go, if I could just keep her with me.'*

She wanted to talk and Dina was more than willing to listen.

'I remember every word of that conversation because it meant so much to me, but it meant more to Beth,' Dina thought.

"I know it probably seems weird to everyone." It was a whisper, a tiny, quiet voice that spoke. "Andy being here…"

"No honey, not weird at all."

"I hope not, it had to be this way, Dina." Her eyes filled with tears. "I can't imagine my life, the end of my life, without Andy here." Dina held on tighter as she cried.

"Oh, Beth, I still can't imagine how you and Andy stayed apart." She sighed, "I just mean that you ever got to the place where it wasn't you and Andy anymore, ya know?"

"I do, I guess *it* just wasn't meant to be."

But it turned out that it was, only it was too late, they would have precious little time together. And it broke Dina's heart.

~ ~ ~

Andy turned to Kimmy, "Thanks for finding the charm, she loved it. She loved the ticket stub, too," and he explained to the others what he meant.

Looking at him, Kimmy saw the love in his eyes, and she thought about Beth.

There had been days recently, when she thought back over their years together. She could remember the day they met, like it was yesterday. She could feel Beth's hand in hers as they walked into the classroom that first day, and so many times after that. Each memory played back like a movie.

Kimmy thought about all those years on that roller coaster life, the ups and downs with Andy. One evening before John left, when he was away on a business trip, Kimmy and Andy were together and she told him how he had broken Beth. It was a no-holds barred conversation. It saddened him, because he was broken, too. Kimmy realized then that none of them ever really thought about what he must have felt. They focused only on Beth and her hurt.

Kimmy wished that she could will her back to health, but it was too far along when they found the cancer. She would hear people say things like "it's a blessing they discovered it so late. It spares everyone the ordeal of the treatment." But all she could think was, *'If we had only found it sooner.'*

She watched Andy now and was glad for the bond they shared. They spent many days sharing memories and stories, for the book. She was glad he and Beth were finally in that place they belonged, together.

~ ~ ~

Roddy, too, was remembering as they chatted about Beth. She was unlike anyone he had ever met.

'Truly unique in my mind and in my heart,' he thought.

He found it intriguing, in the beginning, to find what it was about her that got a hold of Andy. She didn't fit the mold; turns out that was why it worked.

He thought about her laughter and wit. It was always refreshing because it was never expected. She was so quiet, and then she would pop out with something so funny that everyone would burst into hysterical laughter.

'Joy… always sheer, utter joy!'

Over the years, Roddy worked hard to help make that lifestyle easier for her. He tried to comfort when there was hurt and see to it that she was surrounded with love and anything she needed. Time and again Andy hurt her. Roddy didn't believe it was ever intentional. He just didn't know what he needed himself, and when he figured it out, sadly it was too late. But fate saw differently and brought them back together.

Her sickness was a devastating blow to everyone, but she reacted with nothing short of 'grace under fire'.

He was remembering a few weeks ago, cleaning a drawer in his office he found an old answering machine tape. He searched and found a cassette player and popped it in, not knowing what he would find. It was God's way of saying that life would go on. It was a message from better times. Beth was leaving him a message and got tickled about something and burst into a giggle. He had the tape reproduced so that they could all hear that infectious sound again.

That evening of remembering went way into the night. They all comforted each other, shared tears and laughter, many smiles and good times remembered.

CHAPTER THIRTY

August 2002

Sadly to everyone with each day that came Beth weakened a little more. They could all feel her slipping further away. She began to experience headaches and tremendous pain in her body. But the weakness was the hardest on her. She wanted to be up and able to enjoy her friends and family, but she couldn't do it any longer. It was hard on everyone. They had all come to rely on her strength throughout the ordeal of her illness and when it was no longer there, they all hurt.

In those final days, her home was as she loved it, full. Everyone came. Andy and Roddy saw to it that those who had stayed away for fear of tiring her or being in the way, came. John came often, sometimes to just get Carlee away from it all. Beth wanted her there all the time, but they both agreed that she needed to get away from the situation every once in a while. John would always look in on her. Vince and Liz channeled their emotions into food to keep everyone fed.

The room she shared with Andy now, everything peach in color, was dimly lit at all times. He kept candles lit rather than lamps. It made a soft glow about the place, and Beth. She looked angelic and beautiful. A florist came daily so that Andy could keep vases filled with fresh Calla Lilies. Music played softly, usually his favorite collection, *Bach in Woodwind*. It was soothing and peaceful. He had pictures all over the room so she could see them. Carlee, her family, pictures of her with

Kimmy, pictures of her through the years with the *Traveler* guys, pictures of her and Andy from all through the years… He made sure all her favorite things were around her.

She slept a lot, but Andy never left her side. They moved a chair and ottoman beside her bed and when he wasn't lying beside her, he was stretched out in the chair. Angel would try to get him to go and rest, but he wouldn't budge. After all those years, he wanted to make sure she knew he was there every time she opened her eyes.

Angel cared for Beth so lovingly. She kept her pain medicine so that she was comfortable. Angel had grown to love her so much over the months she had been with them. And they were all in love with her, so grateful for her tenderness. Beth appeared peaceful and that made it a little easier for everyone.

The last conversation she shared with Andy was especially moving. Her words were so powerful; "I begin each day with a prayer, a prayer that I can get through the day without so much medication that I don't know my surroundings, a prayer that this situation is not a burden to those I love, a prayer that the day will hold something to give me peace and hope, and a prayer for strength, not so much for me, but for all of you. And ya know what Andy? I end each day praying that same prayer all over again."

In the latter days she no longer woke, but Andy was certain that she knew they were all there with her and that she was loved.

~ ~ ~

She left us on September 24, 2002, peacefully, in her sleep. She was kept medicated and seemingly pain-free those last days. Andy was beside her, holding her hand. Angel knew, and she called them all together. Her entire extended family surrounded the bed. There was so much love in that room as her eyes fluttered, a slight smile upon her face as she took that last breath, so much like a sigh of relief.

Angel asked everyone to leave the room after a few minutes. After a little while she called for Andy to return. They all left him alone there for a while. He took her hand and held it in his one last time. It was still warm and he held it to his cheek to feel that warmth. He prayed for a long while and then cried for his loss.

"Those first tears were selfish ones. They were for me, for what I had lost and would have to endure. I thought I had cried them all out long ago. Then, I cried for the others who had lost her and what their lives would be like without her. I cried for Carlee, now without a mom to teach her the things a mom should," he told me.

~ ~ ~

The days after were even sadder. As they began to plan a memorial for her, calls began coming in from everywhere. The tabloids now had the news and shared it graciously. People were calling, wanting to attend. Finally it grew into such an affair that the memorial was held at the local civic arena. All the *Traveler* guys, past and present, along with their families came. Andy's friends from the business, music people whom she had met and connected with during that phase of her life, attended. Many more were from her time with the Cancer Foundation. Her work there touched many.

Calla Lilies filled the front of the auditorium. It was breath-taking. Everyone gathered pictures and a friend of Roddy's made a running slide show that flashed on a jumbotron they arranged to be in there. Andy chose many pictures of Beth from the Chicago trip, so many years ago. The outside photos on the windy beach were his favorites. There was one, a black and white, of Beth lying in the sand on her stomach laughing, the wind blowing her hair in her face, but the sparkle in her eyes was beautiful. There were pictures from their wedding. Liz had all stages of her life represented and lots of pictures of Beth and Carlee. Kimmy added her favorites as well; one of Beth and Carlee in a garden of daisies laughing... It was incredibly beautiful.

There were many curious fans. The *Road Heads*, who had followed *Traveler*'s career over the years, were there. They felt such a bond to this woman they really didn't know. They were welcomed with open arms. It felt they belonged there.

Andy sang "In My World". It was very emotional and he struggled. It was not the same strong voice that sang it so many times before. It was a voice that wavered with emotion.

You're there with me
In my world
The future I see
You've shared a beauty never known...

During the song, there was suddenly flickering light from the back of the room and everyone began to turn, realizing what it was. Andy stopped singing and became very quiet as the *Road Heads* continued to light lighters, in the same way they do at concerts. Someone dimmed the lights in the auditorium. It wasn't odd. It wasn't out of place. It wasn't disrespectful. It was a symbol of love, and anyone else in the place that had a lighter followed along. It was a beautiful, beautiful tribute. And again Andy began. Tears flowed freely at this gesture.

Andy and Beth's family received thousands of cards and letters telling how Beth touched their life in some way. Some didn't even know her, but the stories of her passing and the dignity she showed during the last months of her illness touched them. Some were *Traveler* fans that just wanted to express their feeling of loss.

She made the headlines one last time. After all the years of stalking her, there was finally a beautiful tribute headline. The cover of *People* magazine the week after she passed away read; "A Life Well Lived." Andy chose that beautiful picture he loved so much of Beth lying on the beach in Chicago, and there was an excerpt from the book. It was a promise made to keep them all away when Beth was so sick. It was a beautiful article with pictures of her life.

Beth's circle of friends and family all grieved in their own way. It was a treasure to see, to talk with them as they shared their thoughts and see the love and loss.

Chapter Thirty~One

Remembering ~ Kimmy

While I was assembling my notes and thoughts, I shared some of the journals with Kimmy. There were things that I thought she would want to know before I put it all together, those pieces of Beth that maybe she knew about but not in Beth's own words.

She loved looking through them, telling me that she always wondered what was in those books that Beth couldn't leave behind if they traveled or she would run to when something special happened. I watched her hands caress the pages as she spoke to me about those that I had marked.

"So much that I knew, so much that I shared in, and yet so many things I didn't realize. I love that she used the analogy of the quilts. I know what quilts meant to her, they were pieces of love. When I think about Beth's quilt, I was one of the pieces just off the center of the quilt. She was part of my life for so long," Kimmy said.

"My best friend, the one I shared everything with, is gone. I show strength, for Carlee, for Andy, for Liz and Connor. I grieve privately. Liz gave me the treasure boxes of pictures, scrapbooks, tickets, trinkets and such that we shared together, cards and letters we wrote to each other where we expressed our dreams. When time allows I go through them to reminisce. I miss her so much. My life is better because she shared hers with me."

Memories ~ Andy

I think about what life brings, and gives, then takes away. My life is forever altered. Unlike Beth, my thoughts on all these years are not written on paper. But the memories are so vivid that I can replay every moment like a movie in my mind. The title that pops in my head is *The Good, The Bad, and The Ugly*, but I guess there was some *Love Story* there as well.

That summer in 1978 is where my life with Beth began. I loved reading her journals, her thoughts on that beginning. Her laughter grabbed my heart that night, and never let go. Something about her made me see her soul, even in that first glance.

Unlike any other woman I've ever met, she was a contradiction. She was quiet and shy, but fun, witty and charming once you broke the shell. Pleasing to the eye, comfortable and casual, nothing flashy, yet I noticed. Every inch of her took my breath. The top of her head barely reached my shoulders when I stood beside her. Everything about her, except her personality, was tiny. I noticed it all.

It seemed there was always a sparkle in her eyes. They were the greenest green I have ever seen, like fresh new leaves in spring. I found myself unable to leave her side that first night. I enjoyed every moment I spent with her. When it finally came time for her and Kimmy to leave, it was morning and I hated the thought that I might never see her again.

I asked if I could call her, she agreed and our journey began. I wanted to spend every moment possible with her, flying her here or there to squeeze in time with her. We learned more about each other. We loved each other. She became mine. My Bethy...

Eleuthera was our refuge. The quiet calm there seemed to put her at ease. So many mornings we spent there I'd wake and she'd be gone and I would find her walking on the beach. She said she could think when she walked and the sounds of the ocean gave her peace. I was there not long ago and opened a closet and found her walking shoes. She left them the last time she was there. I can't bring myself to do anything with them, so they sit in the closet to remind me of the peace she seemed to find on the island.

This business isn't easy. Life on the road, travel, no privacy, wild hours, female fans; it was hard on her. I never knew how important that solitude was to her, until it was too late. I loved having her with me. I saw the difficulty and turmoil it caused her, but she seemed OK to be wherever we were, so I just rolled with it. I realize now, how arrogant that was. I didn't really know how hard it was for her until I read the emotions in her journal from that time. It saddened me greatly that I played a part in that havoc.

With all the good, there were also trying times in our life together. I made mistakes over the years. We saw our way through each storm and back into each other's arms. The year 1991, took me to a dark place; parts of that time I don't even remember. It was a horrible time and the beginning of our undoing. The one constant in my life, the one good thing, and I pushed her away. I hurt so bad that I pushed everyone away. It was a time of deep despair and I reached a low that I never dreamed possible.

During that time, through Roddy, I followed what Beth was doing the best I could. I tried to help care for her in any way possible, but I could barely take care of me. I couldn't allow her to be part of the nightmare my life became during that time. I had to protect her from what I was going through. At least I thought that was what I was doing.

Once on the mend I needed her back so badly. She'd become such a part of me that I couldn't begin to imagine my life without her. I tried to keep my efforts subtle, because I didn't want to push her further away. But she wasn't receptive. I took a chance that night, showing up at that Cancer Foundation event. I had to see her, and when I did, I realized only then, exactly what I let get away. I kept at her until she gave in, came back to me, and once again we were 'us'. It was the happiest time in my life, in the life I shared with her. It was the time when I started to really think about a lifetime with her.

Only suddenly it wasn't good anymore. I tried, but that overwhelming feeling of the life I led finally beat her down and she left. I didn't screw up that time. I didn't send her away. She walked away. Actually, I think she ran. Once she said that maybe she should, "run like hell…" I think it was then that she did. I gave her time. I continued to hope and pray that she would see her way back to me, but she moved past me. My music became my life. The years passed. And Beth moved on… to John and little Carlee.

Then I received that call. It was harder than I could ever imagine. It was John telling me of her illness. The life crawled from my body as he spoke. I was numb. He invited me, allowed me, to come and share this time with them, as a member of their family.

"She needs the people she loves around her," he told me. "We need to help her through this time in her life." I struggled with John's news for many reasons. I would be losing her all over again and I didn't know if I would be able to deal with it. But I also wondered if I held some of the blame. I had a lot of time to think on the flight east. I thought about the beach in Eleuthera, the days she relaxed at home in Corpus Christi by the pool. Was all that part of the problem – the cancer? No one could be sure... I had seen that mole and never gave it a second glance, a 'beauty mark' I thought when I noticed it the first time.

She was asleep when I arrived at the hospital. I pulled a chair beside the bed, waited, and I prayed. I know it wasn't as long as it seemed before she awoke. And when she opened her eyes, to see them again, moved me beyond words... She spoke and it was a weak, whisper of a voice, but that sound was heaven to me. We talked, and we talked, and we talked.

I put everything on hold. No touring, no promotional jaunts, Roddy handled everything about the business side of my life. I was going to be with Beth. John made arrangements for me to stay with them. I began to understand what drew Beth to him. He knew her needs, sometimes even before she knew them herself.

In the beginning stages she insisted that daily functions remain as normal as possible. She wanted that for Carlee. That beautiful child, a part of Beth, stole my heart. John went back to work and that meant travel. When he did he left Beth in my care. It was so good of him to understand that I needed to be there in whatever way he would allow. Those times with her, those alone times were so special. Sometimes she would sleep and I would wait. Sometimes it was back to the conversations that we had been so good at and that I so desperately missed those last years.

One day, early on, when we were talking, she asked why I hadn't moved on. "I had that one love, and I blew it," I told her. "I've dated but what I find is that I compare everyone to you. She looked at me, as if deep in thought, as I continued. "That's not fair to anyone. Not to you. Not to me, and surely not to the other person. So I just keep it causal."

She was the one in my life that I could never replace. I found, with each passing day that I really didn't want or need to. But there was another 'woman' in my life. Her name is Carlee Elizabeth. I'm her 'Papa', and I absolutely adore her. Nothing about her reminded me of Beth, except that she was Beth's child. Seeing her with Beth, I saw us, saw the children we could have had. I would bring this up to her when we were alone talking. She always said the same thing, "shoulda, coulda woulda, if it was meant to be it would have been." And I told her how stupid I was, how foolish to let her get away. I could have been going through this with her. And with her grace and style, she would remind me, that I was.

When John was working, we filled our days with talk. We worked on the thoughts for the book. We laughed and cried over memories. I would think to myself that her life in print would be a wonderful legacy for Carlee, for all of us. All that was coming together nicely, she was pleased and Norton Edwards became a good friend to all of us. Another member of Beth's extended family.

Then came L.A., that trip to the Grammys, that new beginning for us. I think John knew what he was risking, but he always put Beth first. When I went to her room, when she was ready to go to the ceremonies, emotions, that I never anticipated, hit me. I could barely breathe. She was absolutely stunning. So beautiful, glowing and gorgeous, that it left me unable to speak.

The ceremonies were such a treat for her. Being out and dressing up, she was an angel that night. It was exciting for her, seeing people she hadn't seen in several years, people from 'her past.' And I wanted her there with me more than I can say.

Winning the award for that song and her being there was greater than any gift I could imagine. Despite all that was going on, our hearts and souls were finally at a calm place where she was comfortable. Finally, after twenty-some years, she was at ease with us. Roddy left us to dine alone after the award ceremonies. We enjoyed conversation; a good meal and I held her, for as long as I could. We spent that last night, wrapped in each other's arms and we slept.

When we returned she became mine once again. Going home to her life in Florida was hard. I didn't know what we would encounter. Beth was married, she had a child, a family life; what would that mean. But when we arrived, John was gone. His keen insight... he knew. And I wondered what that would bring, but in the short time I knew him I learned that he put Beth first. He left without incident, and Beth and I made a life together.

As the changes and adjustments were taking place in our relationship, my life finally revolved around hers. It was a beautiful routine and I cherished every moment with her, and that beautiful little girl. We were a family. In any quiet time, I wrote. I found peace putting my thoughts into words, feelings poured from me like wine from a jug.

Standing in the darkness,
I watch her sleep,
It brings me peace.
When there is happiness
I watch her laugh,
It gives me joy.
Even in silence
I watch her dance,
It gives me freedom I've never known before
She is my life, my world and so much more
My one true love

~ ~ ~

The very best time of my life was far too long coming. Walking to the gazebo with Bethy on my arm, knowing that we were finally going to spend the rest of our lives together was bitter-sweet. I couldn't imagine a happier day. Yet in the back of my mind I wondered what the 'rest of our lives' really meant. And I was sorry it didn't happen earlier, but always she would remind me; "Shoulda, coulda, woulda…"

"At Last" couldn't have been a more appropriate song. All those years, all those memories, at last we were where we should have been all along; together, really together.

We had some good days, Eleuthera, learning her all over again. Back home, learning Carlee's routine. They were the best times in my life and I rejoiced.

But the weeks went by, and with each, Beth deteriorated a little more. She stayed tired. That vibrancy was diminishing and it was sad to experience. She slept longer and when she was awake she wanted Carlee with her as much as possible to get in every squeeze, giggle, and cuddle possible. I couldn't leave her side, because I wanted the very same thing; every squeeze, giggle, and cuddle possible…

Those last days went by much too quickly. We were all there together, by the bed when she took that last breath. And then in the last moments I was there with her she gave me one last gift.

You are with me always
The things I shoulda done
It's all a dream away
A piece of me
A part of me
My heart a part of yours
The dreams we coulda shared
It's all a dream away
A thought
A plan
To be your man
It's what I woulda done
It's all a dream away.

~ ~ ~

I will treasure the feel of her, the smell of her forever. It's been almost two years and we've all moved on, but we've done so together. Beth's extended family, because of Carlee. John shared her with me, and I am forever grateful. I love that little girl so much.

Recently *Traveler* was given a star on the *Hollywood Walk of Fame*. It was to celebrate the band's thirtieth anniversary. Even though we have moved on, we still get together every so often and do a song. Most times, they are for a charity that one of us holds dear.

We were all there for the "Star" ceremonies, Carlee, Beth's mom and dad. Kimmy and her family, Roddy and Vince, Norton and of course all the *Traveler* guys and their families were there. It was a grand celebration.

When they unveiled the star it was magical. It was Dina's gasp I heard first. The star was, as usual, but this one had a tiny sparkle in the top point of the star. The designers did it to represent Beth who was so much a part of who we were. Of course, there were tears, by all of us. Carlee and I sprawled out on the pavement beside the star, and Kimmy took a picture. That beautiful little girl is my 'star' now. That picture, along with the one of Beth from the beach in Chicago and our wedding picture are on my desk.

As I read her journals, the chronicles of us, I experienced such emotion. I read with pain the holidays and birthdays that I didn't acknowledge. I said it's hard, this lifestyle. I missed a lot of things that Beth longed for. Thinking back, now, it wouldn't have been so hard to be what she needed. It wouldn't have taken much more than a card to please her, something as simple as decorating a Christmas tree meant something to her. I didn't realize it until too late.

She was a simple woman. I didn't make the time she needed, and reading her words tore me apart. Yet at the same time, they breathed life into me. She was so willing to give, happy to do whatever I needed. She always put her own needs on hold and I was selfish enough that as long as she appeared happy, and we were together, life was good.

I think now, on a phrase that she often used; "Shoulda, coulda, woulda." And I know the things I should have done. Wish for time to go back, to do the things I could have done. And dream about the way it would have been. But that is past now, and as she said; "fate saw differently for us."

Norton gave me copies of the tapes as well, and the sound of her voice was heaven. I listened over and over. Sometimes I play a portion of a tape where I know I will hear her laugh. There are copies that I've put away for Carlee, too. She will need to remember that laugh as well. And she'll be able to read the gift of love that Norton compiled from all the notes, tapes and journals. But hearing her mom tell those stories will give her one more gift.

When I think of that quilt she referred to, I have so many thoughts. I remember snuggling under the Nana quilt. I also think about combing antique stores when we bought the chalet. We went into one store and hanging there, on an old wooden rack was a quilt. To me it looked old and worn, but Beth saw the beauty of it.

"Look at this!" She ran her fingers over the fabric, of course she knew what the pattern was. "Oh Andy! This is a treasure!" she yelled excitedly. We took it home and she had a frame made for it and it hung on the wall at the chalet. When the chalet sold Roddy didn't know what to do with the quilt. Knowing what it meant to Beth, he had it put in storage. But time passed and it was forgotten, until I read the journals. I pulled it out and hung it in my office to remind me of the treasure Beth was.

I still wear that Mizpah; only I have both halves now. It keeps her close to my heart. All of this reminds me how special Beth was; how we are all better because of her, because she loved us, because she was Beth. I will go on, we all will, but I know now that I will grieve for what we could have had for the rest of my life…

CHAPTER THIRTY~TWO

The Gift

It's time to put a ribbon on this and call it the gift that it feels like. I read and reread her journals, listened and listened again to the tapes. I met with her friends and family; they shared with me what they thought, what they felt, and what they remembered, about their time in her life. Beth's story, the legacy that she left us is now complete. I can't say for certain, but I think we were all changed, I know I was.

She taught all of us about dignity. She taught me that friendship and loyalty are first and foremost. And she taught me that you never forget your first love.

I gave Andy the many journals Beth wanted him to have when I was through. I wondered how he would react. She hadn't told him of this gift and he cried; only I realized that they were tears of joy. He had her back. He left for a short time to go back into the recording studio and *A Dream Away – Bethy's Song* became one of his biggest solo hits.

This is the end of what I hope is a wonderful tribute to a beautiful woman. I hope that I have told her tale well, given her the gift that she wanted for her family and friends to share. The gift of that quilt she wanted to leave them with; the gift of her heart.

Coming Soon
When I Look to the Sky
Book Two in the Rock and Roll Trilogy

Moving On – June 2003

Andy sat on the stool behind the glass watching for Marco to give him the thumbs up. When he did, Andy slipped the headset on and listened for a moment. The music began, first a piano intro, followed by violins; finally he leaned toward the microphone, closed his eyes, and sang the words, fighting the emotions that bubbled to the surface every time he sang them.

> *You are with me always*
> *The things I shoulda have done*
> *It's all a dream away*
> *A piece of me*
> *A part of me*
> *My heart a part of yours*
> *The dreams we coulda shared*
> *It's all a dream away*
> *A thought*
> *A plan*
> *To be your man*
> *It's what I woulda done*
> *It's all a dream away.*

Marco DiMario, Andy's sound engineer, watched from behind the glass. Andy's friend, Nathan Perry, was beside him at the sound board as Andy sang. When Andy pulled the headset off, he looked up and saw Nathan with a big grin as Marco rose from the chair and gave him another, enthusiastic, thumbs up. Nathan opened the microphone to the studio up and yelled, "It was awesome! You want to hear play-back?"

"I'm coming over there," Andy replied. He was anxious. This song was the last one of the tracks they were recording. He knew he shouldn't have saved it for last. It was the one that was most important to him; it should have been the first, but he couldn't do it, so he recorded tracks for every other song until this was all that was left. The studio musicians finished their portion of the recordings and left yesterday. He had no more excuses, and now he was done - he hoped. Exhaustion had finally set in. They'd been in the studio for a couple of weeks, and he had a lot going on outside the studio, as well. He only had a few days left to get ready for his trip, and he was eager to get things done. He pushed the door open and headed to the sound board where Marco and Nathan were waiting.

"Well," he said with a chuckle, "by the stupid grins on your faces I guess it was OK."

"OK?" Nathan said and thumped him on the back. "Way better than OK…"

"Are you ready?" Marco asked, but before he started the play-back added, "And remember, this is raw, no tweaks, no nothin'…raw!"

Andy sat down, leaned back in the chair, put his feet up on the console, and closed his eyes as he listened.

"Yeah," he felt the corners of his mouth turning up into a smile. "I guess we did it, saved the best for last. What time is it?" he asked abruptly.

"4:10," Marco told him.

"She'll be home now. I gotta call her." He went to the console where he'd dropped his things when he got there. He picked up the phone and dialed, leaned back in the chair again, and a big smile crept across his face when she answered.

"Hello, beautiful," Andy said.

Nathan watched. No one ever saw this side of Andy anymore, unless it involved her, and he smiled. It had been almost nine months since Beth passed away. Nathan worried for his friend in the beginning, for many reasons. Her death had been hard on him, but he'd had other struggles in the past and Nathan worried about that. He watched as he heard Andy ask how her day was, told her how much he missed her, and that he couldn't wait to see her.

"Three more days," he said. "I love you, too, bye sweetheart."

He looked up and both men were watching him. "She just got in and she can't wait to see me," he chuckled. "Can't help it, dang, I love that girl!"

Nathan was glad Andy had her in his life.

~ ~ ~

They stayed at the studio until after midnight. Marco left them, and Andy and Nathan went to the house. Andy hated even walking in the door, but it was almost a done deal. The movers would finish boxing up tomorrow. Everything but the studio was ready for the truck to take east. He worked out a deal with the new owners to convert the studio back into a garage if they would give him three months to break the studio down and ship the equipment. That gave them time to finish the album. Marco would still be going there to oversee things once the tweaking was complete.

"Want a glass of wine?" he asked Nathan.

"Sure," he replied and kicked back in one of the reclining ends of the sofa.

Andy returned with a bottle and two glasses, poured, and then sat in the other recliner.

"You nailed that song. I know it wasn't easy, but damn!"

"After Marco does his magic I want to release that one as the first single."

"I hear ya. It's good, man. Better than good... incredible," he said, then added, "big hit, my friend, I know these things! So, where are you taking her this trip?" Nathan asked.

"I talked her out of Eleuthera..."

ABOVT THE AVTHOR

    Barbara Stewart (1959 -) was born in Baltimore, MD, and grew up in Pennsylvania, and the central east coast of Florida. She resides in the Jacksonville, FL area with her husband Gene and their fat cat, Kooky. She has worked in the electronics industry, and most recently in health-care. Barbara is a volunteer for the American Cancer Society, winning the Hope Award for volunteerism in 2009.

    Her favorite musicians and songs brought on the "rock and roll fantasies" in her work. Sprinkled through her stories are humor and sadness based on experiences she has shared with family and friends. Those who have read her stories, and know her, tell her they 'see and feel' her experiences with them in the words on the pages.

    Sweet Surrender (February 2012) was her first published book, and came from a challenge for National Novel Writing Month (NaNoWriMo ~ November 2011). *Rock and Roll Never Forgets* is her next/first book, she refers to it as 'her heart'. The story came to life in 2003 when Andy woke her in the middle of the night and said "Hey! I've got a story you need to write!" The second book in the Rock and Roll Trilogy – *When I Look to the Sky-* will be ready for release in 2013.

    To share your thoughts, and receive updates, visit Barbara at:

www.barbarastewartwrites.com
bsswrites@yahoo.com

https://www.facebook.com/pages/Barbara-Stewart-Author/352239824808537

Twitter: @bsswrites